MW00476654

Alphas LIKE US

KRISTA & BECCA RITCHIE

Alphas Like Us   Copyright © 2018 by K.B. Ritchie
2022 Special Edition
"Hell's Kitchen - Moving In" Bonus Scene Copyright © 2018 by K.B. Ritchie

All rights reserved.
This book may not be reproduced or transmitted in any capacity without
written permission by the publisher, except by a reviewer who may quote
brief passages for review purposes.

This book is a work of fiction. Names, characters, places, and
incidents either are products of the authors' imagination or are used
fictitiously. Any resemblance to actual persons, living or dead, events, or
locales is entirely coincidental.

Cover Illustration by © Haley Secen

Paperback ISBN: 978-1-950165-49-0
Hardcover ISBN: 978-1-950165-50-6

CHARACTER LIST

Not all characters in this list will make an appearance in the book,
but most will be mentioned.

Ages represent the age of the character at the beginning of the book.
Some characters will be older when they're introduced,
depending on their birthday.

The Hales

Loren Hale & Lily Calloway
Maximoff - 22
Luna — 18
Xander — 15
Kinney — 13

The Cobalts

Richard Connor Cobalt & Rose Calloway
Jane - 22
Charlie — 20
Beckett — 20
Eliot — 18
Tom — 18
Ben — 16
Audrey — 13

The Meadows

Ryke Meadows & Daisy Calloway

Sullivan - 20

Winona – 14

The Security Team

These are the bodyguards that protect the Hales, Cobalts, and Meadows.

SECURITY FORCE OMEGA

Akara Kitsuwon - 26

Thatcher Moretti - 27

Farrow Keene – 28

Quinn Oliveira– 21

Oscar Oliveira - 31

Paul Donnelly – 26

SECURITY FORCE EPSILON

Banks Moretti – 27

…and more

SECURITY FORCE ALPHA

Price Kepler – 48

Bruno Bandoni - 52

…and more

Prologue

FARROW KEENE

*I head to the hospital's break room in blood-*splattered scrubs. As I pass the ER beds, a few patients side-eye me, but not because of the red stains. They scrutinize my dyed white hair and my visible tattoos: the inked symmetric wings on my neck, the writing on my fingers, and more. Basically, I'm far from looking like a poster boy for *Doctor of the Year*.

But I'm not about to slow down or glance back at these patients unless they're coding or I'm called to help.

I know better.

At Philadelphia General Hospital, I'm used to the constant gawking, and that shit bugs me about as much as water would a shark.

I just do my job. I save lives and watch some end. I go home, and unsurprisingly, it starts all over again.

See, being a doctor shouldn't feel mundane. It shouldn't feel anything close to ordinary, but it's all I've ever fucking known, and it's getting to me.

Really getting to me.

I push through a door. 11:54 a.m.—medical interns and residents jam-pack the break room. Standing and sitting, talking loudly and eating. Pizza boxes overflow the few tables and counters where a pot works overtime to brew coffee.

I don't ask about the spontaneous pizza party. It's always someone's birthday in the hospital, and there's always cake.

As hungry as I am, I need to change out of these scrubs. I'm about to reach the door to the men's locker room but a voice stops me.

"Keene, what'd you get?" Tristan asks from across the crowded break room.

I comb a hand through my bleach-white hair. Some of the residents quiet down, listening for the answer.

Short and stocky Tristan MacNair leans on the windowsill, pepperoni pizza in hand. His sideburns touch his jaw as though he's stuck in the 1970s, and his curious eyes flit to the bloodstains on my scrubs.

I wouldn't say we're close friends or even enemies, but he's a Med-Peds intern like me.

"Thirty-year-old male," I tell him, "stab wound to the neck with a key and to the upper abdomen with a knife. Couldn't intubate or ventilate, so he needed a cric. Morris did the chest tube." Apparently this fucker attacked a female runner this morning, and she keyed his throat. He fell on his own knife.

Karma is a beautiful bitch.

"Who did the cric?" Tristan asks.

My brows rise. "Me."

Dr. Leah Young, a second-year resident, almost drops her pizza. "Morris let you do an emergency cricothyrotomy?"

"Yeah." I made an incision between the cricoid and thyroid cartilage in the patient's neck to obtain an airway. Normally my lips would upturn, but my excitement towards medicine has waned this whole month of August.

I grab the doorknob, about to leave.

"Your shift ending?" Tristan asks, quickly straightening up and balling his napkin.

I nod. "Done for today. You?"

"Just starting." He stuffs his mouth hurriedly with pizza. He wants in on that patient.

Too bad for him. "The guy was tachycardic and hypotensive," I tell Tristan. "We just sent him to the OR for surgery."

"Dammit," he groans, then slumps and swallows his food. "I always miss the good ones."

I wouldn't have minded trading places with Tristan, and that—*that's* a fucking problem. For most of my life, I've wanted in on the action. Excited to learn new things, to do new things with medicine.

To help people.

Now I'm willing to just hand over an emergency cric and tube thoracostomy.

I want to blame it on my 28-hour shift, but I've had much longer shifts and been more tired than this.

When I enter the locker room, I shut the door, drowning out the commotion. Cedar lockers line every inch of wall; most cubbies house white coats, extra clothes, toiletries, some books and snacks.

I find mine in a corner.

It takes me a couple minutes to change out of my scrubs and into a *Smashing Pumpkins* V-neck and black pants. My mind tries to reel, but I've done a great job most of my life not overthinking shit.

I'm not starting now.

By the time I pocket my keys and grab my motorcycle helmet, my phone rings. I check the Caller ID and then put the cell to my ear. "What do you need?"

My father rarely calls to shoot the shit, and I'd rather cut to the chase.

I hear him rustling through papers. "What rotation do you have this week?" he asks, his tone warm and relaxed. One of the many reasons why the three famous families (Hales, Meadows, Cobalts)—his patients—essentially love him.

He even has a small ponytail and drinks fucking mint juleps and mojitos on the weekend, but simply put, he's not a laidback, soon-to-be-retired physician. He's constantly working, and I can hardly picture my father hanging up the white coat.

I sling my backpack strap over my shoulder. "ED."

He knows that stands for *emergency department*. "Does your shift end soon?" He must be typing on a laptop, keys *click click click*.

"Just ended." I shut my locker.

"I'm in Spain for the week—"

"I heard," I cut him off. "Ryke Meadows is climbing a five-hundred-foot cliff." He's a skilled professional climber, but the Hales, Meadows, and Cobalts like to ensure if the worst happens, their concierge doctor is present.

"Right," my father says a little bit distantly, his attention split. "I got a call, and you're in distance."

Finally, we've reached the point. "Call" means "medical emergency." And I know exactly where this conversation is going.

I lean my shoulder casually on my locker. "I just got off a twenty-eight hour shift. Ask Uncle Trip to take your calls."

"He's here with me in Spain."

I roll my eyes. *Shit.* "I'm not a concierge doctor."

"You will be after you're board-certified," he says more clearly, loudly—assertively. "You've joined me on enough calls. Think of this as a test-run for when you take over as their primary physician."

I shake my head on instinct.

I know what I want to say.

I quit.

Two words.

Two words that I should be able to spit out. I can tell the old man *fuck you* fine, but I can't say *I quit.*

It has more to do with me than my father. Once I tell him that I want to quit my residency and change career fields, I have to be sure that I'm ready. I have to be able to burn the white coat and be completely satisfied.

I can't vacillate between *maybe* and *I don't know.* I have to fucking know. Or else my father will try to convince me to stay, and I need to confidently shut that shit down.

He's the gateway to my freedom from medicine. From a generational legacy that has consumed me for an entire lifetime.

Once I open that gate, I need to walk through and never turn back around.

Right now, in this moment…I'm not a hundred-percent sure yet, and I'd rather speak to my father face-to-face than say those permanent words over the phone.

I tuck my helmet beneath my arm. "Let me call you back when I get to my apartment—"

"Farrow," he says quickly, concern tensing his voice.

I push into the break room and snatch a piece of pizza on my way out. Using my shoulder to prop my phone against my ear, I tell my father, "I'll call you back—"

"Wait." He stops me from hanging up.

"Hold on," I say and wait to speak again until I'm outside, sun beating down on the pavement. Sirens blare as an ambulance speeds towards the emergency entrance, and a couple women in teal scrubs smoke on a wooden bench.

I put the phone on speaker to free my hands. "Okay." I bite into my pizza, the first thing I've eaten in over twelve hours. The food sits like lead in my empty stomach.

"Listen to me, Farrow. I've been where you are."

No shit. I check traffic before I cross the street to the parking lot.

"I know being a med intern is hard," my father continues. "You work long, excruciating hours, and you leave a shift exhausted. But whatever you saw and did today, don't bring it home with you. Don't let it torture you."

He assumes that I'm emotionally unavailable to handle his call. I may've had a fifteen-year-old girl code seven times in the past five hours, but I've never let any of that affect my job.

The problem: if I plan to quit medicine someday soon, then I shouldn't be setting myself up to be a concierge doctor.

It's that simple.

I approach my black Yamaha motorcycle in the parking lot. "I'm not that spent," I tell my father. "I'm just not exactly excited to take house calls and check a little kid's flu symptoms."

"The call isn't about one of the little kids, and it's not an illness."

My brows arch, and I find myself frozen in place. *Not an illness.*

I can't ignore this call. No part of me wants to sit on the sidelines when I have the ability to help. But it's making walking away from medicine that much harder.

I kick up the Yamaha's stand. "Who's hurt?" I ask for details, subtly agreeing to what my father wants.

He knows it too. "We'll talk more when you're at your apartment. Call me back." He hangs up first, but only after he dangled a giant carrot in my face.

I pocket my phone and put on my helmet, flipping down the visor.

And like a stupid ass, I hunger towards the temptation.

When I graduated medical school, I decided to save on rent and room with other doctors from Philadelphia General. I live a little north of Center City in an old gothic school that was converted into lofts. I don't really give a shit about the "original chalkboards" or the dark walnut paneling or a city view.

Basically, it's cheap with three roommates and close to the hospital. Good enough for me.

Inside my apartment, I set my motorcycle helmet on the kitchen counter next to a Post-it note and then dial my father's number.

The note is for me, the same one I see every other day. I barely skim the scribbled words:

Farrow. tell your friend that he needs to leave.

~ Cory

Leaning on the cupboards, I bite off the cap to a pen and then push my phone to my ear with my other hand. I fill up the Post-it with two large letters.

no

I'm rarely at my apartment. Someone else staying here in my place shouldn't be a problem, and to be honest, I doubt I'll even be living in this apartment long anyway.

The phone line clicks.

"I'll email you the patient's medical history over a secure server," my father starts right where we left off, "and then—"

"Back up," I interject, not wanting to read anyone's medical files if I don't have to. Because I'm quitting on them soon. Flipping through their med history is invasive. "Who and what am I treating?" I tear open a packet of oatmeal and grab a paper bowl in case I need to leave in a hurry.

My father must be moving around, his loafers *click clap* on the floor. "Excuse me," he says faraway to someone else. "Thank you…okay, perfect. I'll be out at the cliff site in fifteen minutes."

I pour oatmeal powder in the bowl and turn on the faucet.

More loudly, my father says, "Farrow?"

"Still here." I hold the bowl beneath the faucet.

"The patient is Maximoff Hale."

My brows furrow, and my face scrunches in motherfucking *confusion*. "Moffy really called you for help?" I ask.

It would take two seconds around Maximoff to understand how much the guy dislikes needing to be saved. For any reason. Even if he were in cardiac arrest, I can't see him phoning my father.

But say Moffy did, then it'd have to be serious.

"Yes, he really called—"

"*Shit*," I curse as water overflows my bowl of oatmeal. Quickly, I shut off the faucet, and I overturn the watered oatmeal mess into the drain and wash my hands. Rarely does anything distract me like this.

"He was asking for instances where he should go to an emergency room," my father explains.

I dry my hands on a dishtowel. "I don't know Moffy that well, but he seems like the kind of person who'd make *lists* to prepare for things that haven't happened yet."

"You do know him," my father refutes. "You know all of the Hales, the Meadows, and the Cobalts. We both do. Getting to know your patients is why we're able to provide the best care."

I roll my eyes.

I'm used to the daily medical lectures, but I don't need or want one right now. My father never removes the white coat. Metaphorically and literally. It's who he is, and shit, I don't want it to be who I am anymore.

I can't only exist as another name in the Keene dynasty. It means that my life isn't mine, and that scares the fuck out of me. Life is finite; we all die, and when you're dead, you're dead.

I couldn't wish my mom back. I have a single memory of her and a handful of pictures. I know that I have only one life, and I need to live for what I love.

Not what my father loves.

Not what the Keenes need me to be.

I have to live for me.

I quit medicine.

I quit.

But I picture Maximoff Hale hurt, alone. In need of someone.

And I know I'm not quitting today.

Still, my father hasn't convinced me that this isn't just wolf scout earning a "preparedness" merit badge. I pass the phone to my other hand and say, "Okay, but this could still be Moffy over-preparing like he always does."

"If you heard his voice over the phone," my father says, "you'd know he wasn't calm. He was tense. And you know Maximoff. So now what do you think?"

There's a reason for concern.

I rub my jaw, my pulse hiking a fraction. No more delay, I leave the kitchen for the hall closet. "Did you narrow down the problem or am I going to have to pack a bag with everything?" I gather my black canvas trauma bag and check supplies: gauze, sutures—shit, if he needs an IV...

"It could be a fracture, maybe possible head trauma."

I hurry. "Did he sound disoriented?"

"He sounded worried and distracted."

I remember the last time I saw Maximoff. I can still smell the salt water and feel the heat from the torches. July, just last month. His family threw a summer party on a yacht, and I talked to Moffy for a minute.

I remember how he stared off into space. How it took me thirty seconds just to catch his attention.

My lips upturn at the memory. "That guy is always distracted."

"More distracted than usual," my father notes.

My smile fades fast, and I stuff a blood pressure cuff in the bag. I search for my missing stethoscope, unzipping sections.

Maximoff fought with his cousin on that yacht. Both threw punches. And he's been caught in more than a few brawls before, mostly with hecklers. "Do you think he was in a fistfight?" I ask my father, just as I find my stethoscope in a front pocket.

"No," he says. "He never calls me after any fight."

I zip up the bag, stand and grab my keys off the counter. Then I remember... "He's at Harvard."

A six-hour drive from Philly.

If he's badly hurt...I shake my head. Six hours feels too long. Before I think of alternatives, my father speaks again.

"I already booked the private jet," he says. "I'll email you the details. You should be arriving at Cambridge in a little over two hours."

I nod. "Good." And I can sleep on the plane.

"Before you board, I need you to stop by the house and get more supplies." He means my childhood house in Philly, where he still lives and keeps medicine for emergencies. "Moffy's blood type is B-positive, and if he has a serious fracture, give him lidocaine intravenously and assess. He'll refuse an opioid."

"I know." His parents are recovering addicts for alcohol and sex, and he's cautious around addictive painkillers.

My father lists all the supplies, and I mentally file the information. When he's finished, he says, "After you treat him, make sure to write a report and email me."

"Sure."

"And if you have any questions, I won't have cell service. You can always call your grandfather or Rowin—"

"I'm not calling Rowin," I cut him off. "We broke up last week." I sling my bag on my shoulder and check the plane schedule on my phone. Calculating how much time I have. *Not much.*

The phone line is silent.

I head down the narrow hall towards my bedroom, phone back to my ear and say, "If that's it—"

"You shouldn't let work affect your relationship. If you need help balancing the two, you can talk to me."

"Not everything is about medicine," I say more coldly than I meant. My jaw muscle tics. "I know you liked him, but it's over. If there's nothing else I need for Moffy, then I'll let you go."

"That should be it," he says, his tone still warm. "Take care."

I hang up and slip into my small bedroom that I share with Cory. A six-foot metal bookshelf separates his side from mine, medical texts stacked on each shelf.

The friend that Cory hates is currently passed out in my single bed, tangled in my black sheets. And he's not alone. A mystery blonde girl sleeps beneath his tattooed arm. Her bra and red dress litter the floorboards.

I don't care. At this point, the bed is more Donnelly's than mine.

But I'm in a fucking hurry. I chuck my motorcycle keys at him, and they land with a thud on his chest. "Donnelly."

He squints and pats at the keys while glancing at the nightstand clock. It's past noon, and the potent scent of Lucky Strikes and bourbon lingers.

"Fuck," Donnelly groans and runs a hand through his tousled chestnut hair.

The blonde girl underneath his bicep starts waking. Rubbing her eyes, her mascara and lipstick are smudged. I spot the Zeta Beta Zeta keychain attached to her leather purse.

This isn't the first sorority girl Donnelly has brought to my apartment to fuck.

She eyes me skeptically while stretching off the bed and grabbing her dress and bra. "Who are you?"

"I'm about to leave," I say more to Donnelly, but he's not looking at me.

"He lives here," Donnelly tells her with a yawn. He sits up against the headboard and watches her collect her shit.

She tugs on her dress, checks her phone and stands, not paying that much attention to him. "Okay...thanks, Daniel."

"Donnelly." He mouths to me, *great lay.*

My brows spike and lips rise. I mouth, *didn't ask.*

He grins and unscrews a nearly empty water bottle. Downing the last drop, he swallows and motions to the girl, then me, with the bottle. "He's a resident at Philly General."

She surveys me head-to-toe while tying her tangled hair in a pony. "You're seriously a doctor?"

I lean my shoulder on the doorframe, loosely crossing my arms. I may be constantly relaxed, but I'm keeping track of the very last second that I can waste before I need to leave. "I'm *seriously* a doctor, but I'm just a first-year resident." I look to Donnelly. "Which is technically called an intern."

He tosses the empty water in an arch, and the bottle clatters in a trash bin. "Same thing." His South Philly accent is thick.

"Sort of," I say. "I haven't taken my Step 3 exam to become licensed yet."

I'm twenty-four-years-old and I've already graduated medical school and I have that MD. But I won't become a licensed physician until I complete the USMLE exam.

Donnelly shakes his head. "Unnecessarily complicated."

The girl frowns. "What?" She can't understand what he just said with his Philly lilt.

He tries to enunciate. "*Unnecessarily*—"

"Forget it," she cuts him off and checks her phone.

I'd like this girl to make a quick exit about as much as she wants to make one. I cock my head. "Need me to call you an Uber?" I ask.

She texts quickly. "My friend is picking me up. Can I have the address?"

I tell her the address of the apartment complex, and then Donnelly swings his legs off the bed and reaches for his jeans. "Hey," he says to the girl, "if you wanna come along, I'm going to Wawa for lunch—"

"Wawa?" she cringes. "Ew."

I almost laugh. Fuck, she hates Wawa. My smile stretches, decently entertained because Donnelly is going to lose his shit.

"Ew?" he repeats. "Girl, Wawa is a great wonder of Philly—"

"It's just a convenience store. God, I don't understand people's obsession with it."

Donnelly cringes. "Didn't you see my tattoo?" He rotates slightly and flashes her the inked Wawa logo on his shoulder blade.

She tucks a flyaway piece of hair behind her ear. "*Boy,* it was just sex. I don't care if a one-night stand is creepily obsessed with a gas station or not—and don't act like this was anything more for you. You don't know my name either."

"You've gotta be a Betty," he says. "Betty sounds like the name of someone who'd trash Wawa."

She struts past the bed with her high heels in hand. "My name is Sylvia."

I turn a fraction of an inch to let her pass through the door. She eyes my trauma bag and then disappears to the kitchen. *Three minutes left.*

I unpocket a stick of Winterfresh and peel the foil.

"See ya never, Betty!" Donnelly calls, and the front door slams shut. He jumps into his ripped jeans. "Can't believe I stuck my dick in a Wawa hater."

I pop my gum in my mouth. "You've stuck your dick in worse." I straighten off the doorframe.

Donnelly buttons his jeans. "Nothin' worse than a girl who hates Wawa."

I whistle. "And your fucked-up standards persist."

He grins and tugs his ragged shirt from last night over his head. He notices my trauma bag, and his mouth downturns.

I don't unearth this thing from the closet every day.

Two minutes.

"Bike keys are on the bed," I explain, chewing my gum. "I'll be out for a while. You can use it if you need to."

Donnelly doesn't own a vehicle of any kind, and if he's not borrowing my Yamaha, then he's stuck on foot or with public transportation.

I veer into the kitchen, not loitering around any longer.

Donnelly follows close behind. "You tell your old man about being a bodyguard yet?"

I steal Cory's apple out of a fruit bowl, and I glance back at Donnelly. "Not yet."

A while back, Akara Kitsuwon suggested I try security training. He owns the Studio 9 Boxing & MMA gym, which became a hub for the famous families' security team.

Donnelly and I were sparring on the mats, like we sometimes do, and in a break, I offhandedly mentioned being burnt-out from medicine to Akara.

Next thing I know, I'm in security training and Donnelly joins the ride. Now we're both in the final course of training, and I'm one foot in medicine, one foot out.

Donnelly takes a jug of milk out of the fridge. "Been thinking about when you'll tell him?"

I bite into the apple and hold Donnelly's gaze for a short beat.

Once I tell my father that I'm quitting medicine to become a 24/7 bodyguard, I'll lose him, and Donnelly knows this.

My relationship with my father is built on the notion that I'd become a doctor. That's my worth. My life's purpose. Remove it, and nothing is left.

Let's put it this way: I was his student first, son last. Small talk was typical; anything deeper almost never happened, and sure, he was always busy like most fathers are. But I didn't have a mother, and he didn't hire a nanny or babysitter to look after me.

Instead, he put me in dozens of extracurricular activities. Made me fend for myself more than half the time.

And one of those activities was martial arts. I started at five-years-old and never stopped. It's ironic that my love of MMA is what eventually led me to the Studio 9 gym, and ultimately, what opened the door to security training.

I can't even be upset that I'll lose my father with this career change. Because I don't feel like I ever had a good one to begin with.

When will I finally tell the old man that I quit? I don't make regimented plans like that.

I spit out my gum into a trash bin. "It'll happen when it happens," I tell Donnelly and eye the oven clock. *One minute left.*

He unscrews the milk cap, but his attention stays on my bag. "What's with that?"

"My father got a call. I'm helping out one last time." I take a large bite of apple.

He chugs milk from the jug. "Tell whatever Hale needs you that I say *what's up.*"

"No," I say easily and head for the door, "and man, stop assuming the worst about the Hales." The parents are addicts, but they're in recovery and sober. And they're better than most mothers and fathers that Donnelly and I grew up around.

"Can't help it." He wipes his mouth on his bicep. "They're the Bad Luck Crew."

I roll my eyes and clutch the doorknob. "You may be assigned to one of them."

"Nah, I already requested the Good Luck Crew." He means the Cobalt family.

I smile into another bite of apple. "Have fun with that." I kick open the door, en route to Maximoff Hale.

When I'm in the elevator, I pull out my phone and contemplate calling or texting Moffy for more information, to ensure he's okay, but I don't even have his number.

Fucking hell.

I pocket my phone. Not long after, I take a cab to my father's house in Northwest Philly, pack the supplies and medicine in my bag, and I reach the airport in plenty of time to board the private jet. Moderate turbulence and decent shut-eye later, I'm on the ground.

An unknown source has already granted me access to Moffy's dorm hall. If I made an educated guess, I'd say Security Force Omega is on top of this clandestine emergency. But Maximoff isn't aware that any doctor is coming, as far as I know.

His dorm room is on the fourth floor next to the communal bathroom. I knock on the scratched wood. Waiting. No noise.

Answer, wolf scout.

I knock again. Complete silence, even inside the hall. Most students must be on campus, the old dorm quiet in the afternoon.

After another knock and more silence, my jaw hardens. In the email my father sent, he left an instruction: *if Moffy doesn't answer the door, call his bodyguard to open it.*

He could be unconscious on the floor. I'm not wasting time or handing over that easy task to someone else. I turn the knob. Locked.

No hesitation, I pound my boot in the wood. The door *bangs*, but it needs a couple more kicks to bust in.

I don't even prepare for the second kick before the sound of footsteps echoes on the other side. He's moving.

Good.

I expel a heavier breath through my nose.

The door opens to a nineteen-year-old, six-foot-two celebrity with a jawline cut like marble.

Instantly, his forest-greens catch my brown, and I meet his questioning gaze. I run my tongue over my silver lip piercing and break eye contact.

Quickly, I sweep his swimmer's build for visible signs of a wound. His jeans are loose on his legs, his green tee tight on his chest. I don't see an injury, and an earbud cord dangles over his shoulder.

He must've been listening to music, unable to hear me knock.

"What are you doing here?" Moffy asks, voice firm. He even peeks over my shoulder.

"It's only me, wolf scout." I push further into the cramped dorm room before he can shut me out. I whistle at the unmade bed to the left, a Harvard crimson comforter rumpled and sheets balled. "Bad roommate?" I ask and drop my bag to the floorboards.

Maximoff crosses his arms, his biceps bulging. "That could be my bed." He nods to the messy area.

"No," I say matter-of-factly. "That's your bed." I point to the orange comforter tucked into the wooden frame. "And that's your desk." His oak desk is wedged nearby, a philosophy textbook cracked open and a highlighter uncapped like I caught him in the middle of studying.

"Great." He rakes a hand through his thick, dark brown hair. "Now that you've Sherlock Holmes'ed my dorm, you can leave happy. Mission accomplished."

"I'm not leaving," I say seriously.

Maximoff isn't an idiot. He sees my trauma bag. He knows I'm here because of the phone call he made to my father. I don't need to spoon-feed him this information.

But we're at a slight standstill because he's not forthcoming about his injury. I examine him from about four feet away. He usually has a tan complexion, but he's lost color in his face. And he's sweating.

"You look pale," I tell him.

He blinks slowly. "Thanks."

I tilt my head. "That wasn't a compliment."

"I was being sarcastic."

My brows rise, a smile at my lips. "I know."

Maximoff grimaces and rests his hands on his head like communicating with me is brutal. The times we talk, I like irritating the shit out of him, but today's different. He's my patient.

"Jesus Christ," he growls under his breath.

"Moffy—"

"I'm fine," he says strongly, his hands dropping to his sides. "If I thought I wasn't, I would've gone to the ER. Alright, you can go do whatever the fuck you do on a Wednesday afternoon. I'm sorry you had to come up to Cambridge." His apology sounds extremely sincere.

"Don't be," I say. "I'm supposed to be here."

Right here.

Right now.

This was my choice. I could've told my father no, but I said *yes* to this call. To Maximoff, and I'm not leaving until I'm sure he's safe.

He cracks a knuckle and stares off, lost in thought.

I wait and comb a hand through my dyed hair. A few pictures line his desk, most of siblings or with his best friend Jane. I recognize one group photo from St. Thomas with all the families squished together, a summer vacation. The picture leaked on the internet a few years back.

"So you're not leaving then?"

I look back at him, his attention focused on me again. "Not until you tell me what's wrong, and man, you don't need to describe *why* anything happened. I can work with a bare-bones story." Not having the full picture will irritate me a little bit—shit, normally it wouldn't. But I'm already craving to know more about him.

I skim Moffy in a short once-over and look away.

He's Maximoff Hale.

I almost laugh to myself. Fuck, he's too pure. Too wholesome. And I just got out of a long-term relationship—there are reasons I wouldn't. So many more reasons that he wouldn't.

Not now.

Possibly not ever.

"I cut my leg," he suddenly says, but the words come out slowly like thick tar on his tongue.

I eye his jeans while his rigid stance hardly shifts. "Where?"

"My thigh."

"That's a problem," I say easily. "Your femoral artery—"

"I would've bled out hours ago if I cut my femoral artery. I'm okay."

I try not to smile because it'll just agitate him. "Web M.D. says you're okay, but I haven't yet." I squat and unzip my trauma bag. "I still need to see the wound. What'd you cut yourself on?"

Maximoff stops protesting, and he unbuttons his jeans. "I don't know."

I frown and open the packaging on a pair of gloves. "What do you mean, you don't know?"

"I was off-campus last night with some guys on the swim team. It was dark." He steps out of his jeans. Bandage is wrapped around his muscular thigh, gauze thick beneath. He dressed his wound perfectly.

Maximoff notices me staring, and he starts smiling. "Better than you would've done, huh?"

I snap on one medical glove. "I'm still better than you at everything, wolf scout. Don't get excited."

"Excited around you? Yeah, I'm never even close."

I didn't mean it sexually, but here we are.

I look up, just as he looks down, and he swallows, his Adam's apple bobbing. Shit, our banter hasn't exactly taken this route before.

Since I'm older and wiser, I decide to eliminate the strange tension with "professionalism" and I ask, "Did you clean the wound?"

"Yeah."

"Take a seat on your desk chair." I stand and slide my trauma bag closer with my foot, just as he sits like a fucking board. His gaze plasters to my movements. I lean over his chest, the smell of chlorine rushing towards me, and with my ungloved hand, I grab his *Fundamentals of Philosophy* textbook.

"What are you doing?" he asks, hating to be in the dark. Clearly.

I put the textbook in his palms. "Read, take notes, study. Don't watch me."

"Farrow—"

"Trust me, wolf scout." I crouch, snap on my other glove, and start undressing his bandage that edges close to his gray boxer-briefs. I pause not even one-fifth through when I catch him staring and *overthinking*.

"You don't need to overanalyze what I'm doing, Moffy. Just focus on your own shit."

He glares. "My leg is my own shit, thanks for asking."

I roll my eyes into a smile. "You're welcome." I continue unwrapping the bandage while his gaze is attached to mine. *Trust me, trust me,* I try to emote until he finally gives in and reads his text with a frustrated breath.

I concentrate on his wound, blood seeps through—*fuck*. I unwrap faster. "You bandaged your thigh without stopping the bleeding first?"

He glances down. "It was stopped."

I reach for my suture kit. "When'd you cut it?"

He shuts his book and thinks. "Uh…" Maximoff pinches his eyes. "Three, four in the morning. I was out—"

"With your swim teammates, I heard that part." I kneel on one knee for a better angle. Blood completely soaks the gauze, and I try to gently pull it off the cut.

He winces and grips the edge of the desk. "Fuck."

"Sorry." I discard the gauze in a plastic bag and squeeze his cut closed with my fingers. A couple inches higher and that would've sliced through his artery. "You were lucky."

"I know." He rubs sweat off his forehead with his arm. "I wasn't drunk last night, if that's what you think."

"That's not what I'm thinking." I pull out more supplies. "You've been bleeding out consistently since early this—what's your pain level from one to ten?" I cut myself off and ask since he's sweating and gritting his teeth.

His nose flares, wincing. "It doesn't matter. I can't take a painkiller."

"It does matter." I planned to disinfect the wound first, then administer a shot of lidocaine, then suture, but I change the order and hurriedly unpackage a syringe and needle.

He white-knuckles the desk, the room deadens while I work and he concentrates on breathing. I give him a shot of lidocaine to numb the wound. Then I wipe the area with an antiseptic and irrigate with saline.

In less than two minutes, I'm done with both, and I start suturing the deep cut. I break the quiet first. "When was your last tetanus shot?"

"I was eight." Too long ago.

I look up. "You sure?" I really don't want to open his medical records, and I need him to be sure.

"Pretty positive."

I trust him enough. "I'll give you a tetanus shot before I leave." I pierce his skin with the needle and weave the stitch.

Maximoff clears a ball in his throat. After I finish the sutures, I redress the wound with clean gauze and bandage. He slides forward on the chair.

"I can do that," he says and reaches for the gauze.

I put a hand to his chest, my gloves new. "Just relax."

He lets out a short laugh. "Right." He cracks a crick in his neck and stares faraway again. *Where'd you go, Moffy?*

I watch him for a second, then wrap the bandage. "No swimming until the stitches are out—"

"What?" His voice spikes, eyes snapped towards me.

That woke him up. "You can't swim in a chlorine pool with this kind of cut."

Maximoff breathes out a weighted breath, and he keeps shaking his head. His eyes strangely carry a mountain of emotion and then no emotion at all. Like he's fighting to show me something and then nothing. "I'm on the Harvard swim team."

I expect him to say *I need to swim*, but he stops there.

He opens his mouth, then shuts it, conflicted.

I raise my brows. "Sad?" I ask.

"No." He shakes his head repeatedly. "You know..." He licks his lips. "Last night, one of my new teammates shoved me in a pile of trash. There was metal and..." *He was cut.* He looks away, then his tough eyes meet mine head-on. "They don't want me here."

"Do you want to be here?" I ask.

He doesn't answer. His face is blank.

I crave to hold his gaze longer, but I force myself to look down. And I tape his bandage. "You should've gone to Yale. Everything is better there: the people, the dorms, the alumni."

He feigns confusion. "Really? I heard they churn out white-haired know-it-alls with pretentious lineages and asshole tendencies."

"Asshole tendencies," I repeat with a laugh. "I think you mean heroic tendencies."

"I tell you I got pushed into fucking metal, and you take that moment to tell me Yale is better than Harvard."

Yeah, I'm an asshole. My smile stretches as I stand up, snapping off my gloves. "It's still accurate."

His gaze lingers on me for a long beat. "Maybe," Maximoff admits. It's hard not to stare at him.

I clean up, and I don't let him help, even when he asks. He's still a little weak.

"Why are you here anyway?" he asks after I give him a tetanus shot in the deltoid. "I know your father is with my Uncle Ryke, but I thought Trip would be here instead." I'm known to tag along to calls, not pick them up on my own like I'm in-line to be a concierge doctor.

I pack up the suture kit, and I toss him a bandage for the small spot of blood. He's been dying to do something himself, and he can at least stick a Band-Aid on his shoulder. "My uncle is with my father," I tell him. "They needed extra hands. This is a one-time thing."

Maximoff thinks hard.

I'm going to be a bodyguard, wolf scout.

The truth weighs inside of me, and as I get ready to leave, I recognize how much is about to be left unsaid.

1

FARROW KEENE

"He's going to throw a punch," Oscar Oliveira says, observing my hot-blooded, twenty-two-year-old boyfriend.

I watch the same scene from the same vantage point as Oscar.

All six of us in Security Force Omega "guard" the double-door entrance of the Philadelphia Orchestra Hall. Two thousand of the richest fuckers I've ever seen fill scarlet velveteen seats. The main level and balcony tiers are packed tight, and a string quartet plays a classical piece on stage, ruby curtains drawn open.

Tucked up against the left-side emergency exit, my boyfriend looks ready to combust.

Maximoff speaks hushed, but his brows furrow and he gesticulates madly. Inching closer and closer to the uppity suit-and-tie organizer of tonight's "unprecedented" event.

I slowly chew my gum, arms loosely crossed. But I hardly blink. I watch.

And the forty-something organizer with Gucci shoes and glaringly white teeth visibly steps towards Maximoff.

In an affront.

My arms drop, instinct about to propel me down the left aisle—

"Farrow." My name is spoken in a warning.

Out of the corner of my eye, I spot Akara Kitsuwon, the Omega lead.

"Farrow," he repeats, his friendly expression now strict. Reminding me not to leave my position. His tailor-fit black Hugo Boss suit is identical to all of security.

Not exactly my style. I shrugged off the required suit jacket an hour ago. What remains: a black button-down tucked in black slacks. I run my thumb over my silver lip piercing and eye my boyfriend.

I can't fall back in line yet.

Maximoff grows more incensed, his eyes flamed and body bowed forward with fervor. Like if he tries hard enough, he can mold the lopsided world upright.

I want to be beside him. To ease him back, to hold him. Cool him off. Even if his fuse has been justifiably cut short tonight.

Never did I think we'd end up here, just two weeks after I detained Maximoff's stalker, who turned out to be Jane's friends-with-benefits. I comb a hand through my dyed black hair, and I restrain myself from rushing to him.

See, I'm still the 24/7 bodyguard to Maximoff Hale, but I'm not supposed to protect him at this specific event.

Security rules.

And we all know how I feel about rules.

Behind me, the double door cracks open, and six heads turn. Mine included.

Oscar grasps the handle, widening the door for…a server in a tux. He balances a tray of champagne and descends the aisle.

Oscar lets his annoyance cross his face as he lets go of the handle, the heavy door closing itself. "It's official," he says.

I pop a bubble and tilt my head to the oldest Omega bodyguard, and also, one of my longest friends. "You've been demoted to a doorman," I finish his thought.

"Not just me, Redford."

"Technically, you're the only one holding the door," I say, half-interested because in my peripheral, I watch Maximoff shake his head repeatedly at the organizer and force out the word *no*.

Adrenaline pours through my veins, goading me to go to him.

"No one's a doorman," Akara says as he texts on his phone. "We're guarding the entrance." He pockets his cell, subtly reminding us of the stipulation we all agreed to.

Security Force Omega gained a decent amount of public fame after the Hot Santa video leak back in January. Tumblr pages are dedicated to Oscar's little brother alone, and some fans will ask for our autographs when we're on-duty with our clients.

To keep our jobs in security, we all agreed to a big change: *no working large scale events*.

Now it's the middle of May, and Alpha is attached to our respective clients tonight. Protecting them. And we're here doing a job that temp security could easily do.

I lean back casually on my heels and spit my gum in a trash bin.

Akara glances down the line of us, from Thatcher to Quinn to Donnelly, me, and Oscar. "Any of you want off-duty? Because you're all free to leave at any time."

No one moves a muscle.

The fee inside this event costs two grand. Out of our price range, and we all want inside to keep an eye on our clients from afar. Even if it means being regulated to securing the entrance.

By the way, that entry fee is one that Maximoff would never set. This is an event that Maximoff isn't even running. One that he'd never construct in a lifetime.

One that has been unequivocally contentious from the start.

I study the escalating argument between Maximoff and the organizer. The middle-aged man seethes, his face beet-red, and he sneers a response through gritted teeth, slicing the air with his arm at Maximoff.

As though to say *no*.

And then he clutches Maximoff's shoulder—*that's enough*. I leave my position and head down the red-carpeted left aisle.

Several rows of wealthy pricks had been snapping photographs of Maximoff instead of the string quartet, and their lenses start to swerve towards me.

"Price to Farrow." The Alpha lead's voice blares through my earpiece. "Return to your position at the entrance."

Maximoff's muscles flex. He places a palm on the organizer's chest to keep the man at arm's length, but they're both speaking over each other. Violinists drown out their verbal fight.

I never reach for my mic to reply.

"Price to Farrow," Price repeats. "Maximoff has a bodyguard on his detail tonight and it's not you. Return to your position."

I've seen the SFA bodyguard hovering ten feet from Maximoff.

I even know that bodyguard. Bruno Bandoni is a fifty-two-year-old silent type with the stature of a heavyweight champion. Bald and bearded. I used to work alongside him in Alpha, only because he's the 24/7 bodyguard to Loren Hale.

I don't hate Bruno, but he's one of the more regimented men and he's not fond of me. Tonight, that's definitely not changing.

"Akara to Price." Akara speaks through comms. I'm too far away now to hear the Omega lead without my radio. "Let Farrow check on Maximoff. He'll only take a minute."

The event organizer hoists a threatening finger at Maximoff, one angered motion from grabbing his face.

Motherfucker.

"Omega isn't making these calls at *this* event," Price says through comms while my stride lengthens. "Alpha is in charge, and Farrow, if you reach Maximoff, then you're officially off-duty tonight. You can stay here as security or as the boyfriend to Maximoff Hale. *Choose*—"

The forty-year-old's freckled hand clutches Maximoff's sharpened jaw, and I'm close enough to hear the man spit, "*Listen.*"

Instinct rams me, and I sprint the last two feet, wedging my body between them—just as Maximoff tears the unwanted hand off his face and then swings. I catch his fist in my palm and walk him backwards.

Come on, wolf scout.

Bruno yanks the organizer back by the collar, every movement a snap-second. Shorter than a breath.

Maximoff fumes, chest rising and falling heavily, and his red-hot fury still drills into the organizer behind me.

I open his fist that I caught and clutch his hand with my hand. Squeezing.

Maximoff blinks, his attention almost, *almost* mine.

Our chests press together, his gray *Camp Calloway* shirt, green jeans, and Timberland boots unlike the suits and tuxes in the orchestra hall. It's his way of gaining a modicum of control during an event that's completely out of his hands.

With my other grip on his shoulder, I walk forward, forcing him to keep walking backwards down the aisle. Nearing the stage. "Look at me," I say, my voice husky. "Wolf scout."

His chest falls, muscles still flexed.

My pulse thumps.

I skim his striking but also tensed face, and my hand slides across his broad shoulder and rises slowly up his neck. I hold his jaw; I tighten his hand in my hand, and my lips veer to his ear. "Maximoff Hale, will you marry me?"

He flinches, eyes widening and brows knotting with a thousand questions, and even more philosophical queries.

MAXIMOFF HALE

I overthink.

About every fucking thing. You know that. But in this second, I let out the first thing in my head. "What?" I ask, too edged.

Farrow stands an inch taller, black hair pushed back, his know-it-all smile stretching to gorgeous drop-to-your-damn-knees levels. "Take a breath, wolf scout."

Am I holding my breath like I've just plunged into the deep-end of a freezing pool?

Maybe.

Probably.

Alright, definitely. I can't even think about the *idea* of marriage, not here; it's something I haven't discussed with anyone but Jane—wait...

Farrow raises his brows at me, near laughter.

I start nodding, knowing before Farrow says, "Man, I'm fucking with you." He needed to catch my attention. I won't admit out loud that it worked, but it fucking worked.

I try to force a grimace. "Thanks for that, asshole."

Farrow whistles. His grin has to be hurting his face. "He calls it like he sees it." He holds my jaw, his tattooed hand warm but silver rings cold.

The moment quiets.

Our eyes roam one another, and I breathe and breathe, the pent-up rage trying to deplete with his relaxed presence pushed up against my rigid body.

He hangs his arm over my shoulder, all cool confidence, his fingers skimming the back of my neck before disappearing in my hair.

I inhale a deeper breath. I've let another captain inside my ship, and everyone—the security team, *We Are Calloway* production crew, my family, the world, *you*—knows it.

Right now I'm aware that we're in an orchestra hall, so close to the stage that the classical music overpowers our voices from eavesdroppers.

But Farrow and I are standing in direct view of two-thousand sets of curious eyes.

Our relationship has been public for about two weeks, and this— touching my twenty-eight-year-old boyfriend with a crowd in sight— still gets to me. Most of the time in a good way, other times...I find myself watching the people watch me, something I almost never do. Cameras have always been scenery to my colossally strange life.

But I notice them more now, and I worry a bit that they're bothering Farrow. He just lost his fucking privacy, and this is only the beginning.

He said he'd tell me if the press or fans piss him off, and so far, he hasn't said anything about it. I trust him, so I'm not going to overanalyze.

My muscles try to unbind, blood still set to simmer from Douglas Cherrie, the patronizing event organizer that I almost punched.

I'm not proud of it.

I shake my head, jaw aching from clenching. "I thought I could reason with him," I tell Farrow. "Remind him that Luna is only eighteen and she doesn't want this..." I lift my gaze to meet Farrow's understanding. "I asked to switch places with her. He said *no*. I offered to buy Luna back—and Jesus Christ." I cringe at those words.

Buy Luna.

Like my little sister is property.

"Hey," Farrow says, drawing me closer, his hand shifting to the back of my head. Camera flashes spotlight us, and we both rotate our backs to block the harsh glare.

Farrow lowers his voice, and I strain my ears to hear him over the music. "Price is on Luna's detail for the charity auction," he says. "It's a little bit disturbing that a sixty-year-old fucker won the bid for her, but you don't need to be paranoid. Your dad and mom have been breathing down security's neck all night, and almost everyone in SFA is watching her."

My shoulders just won't loosen, my neck strained. I've been in DEFCON 1, damage control mode for the past hour and a half.

And by *hour and a half*, I mean *millennium*.

Farrow studies my features. "Shit, you're so moral."

I stretch my arm over my back. "You're so damn cool. How do I become just like you?" I ask, sarcasm thick.

He rolls his eyes. "Okay, smartass, it's a charity auction. Not a prostitution ring."

I frown, my jaw locked for a long pause. Until I ask, "How sure are we that it's not?"

"Maximoff," he starts like this is paranoia, but he pauses. Because I'm not in control of this H.M.C. Philanthropies charity auction. I have no details.

We have no details.

I signed on because *this*—right here—was the stipulation Ernest Mangold made, the one task the entire H.M.C. board said I had to complete in order to be reinstated as CEO: a charity auction that they orchestrate. I'm supposed to be told where to go, what to do.

A follower. Which I've never fucking been.

I finally understood why the H.M.C. Philanthropies board chose this—why they even agreed to vote me out of the company I built and let Ernest take my spot. I've always rejected the board's *charity auction* proposals where my cousins and siblings were the ones up for bid.

I would never in a million light-years agree to this unless they had kicked me out and held it over my head like bait.

Which they did.

Farrow lets go of my hand, just to clutch my waist. His fingers glide beneath my tee, and my skin electrifies at the touch.

More confidently, he says, "This is nothing but an innocent, aristo-cratic, stuck-up gala"—our eyes dive deeper in each other, our mouths closer—"because if it were anything that threatens your body, your life, I'd break the neck of the motherfucker who bids on you."

"Pretty sure I'd break a neck first," I joke.

Farrow shakes his head, but he looks like he wants to kiss me. I probably, most definitely, look like I want to kiss him.

But his tattooed fingers suddenly touch his earpiece, his gaze drifting.

While security speaks to him through comms, I can't stop thinking about everyone else's fate at this auction.

I'm thinking about my sister.

About Jane my best friend, and then my cousin Beckett and even Charlie. The four who signed-up for this insanity. Sullivan bowed out when she heard the title of the event, too uncomfortable, and Beckett planned to join her—but Charlie, of all people, convinced his twin brother to do the auction.

I don't know why.

No one really does. Charlie wouldn't say, and we're still not friends. I have a couple texts from him that aren't insults, and we haven't thrown a punch since the FanCon. So there's that progress. Really, though, I'm glad I know why he hates being around me. Even if it's painful knowing that who I am hurts Charlie.

I glance back at the entrance where Omega stands in a row. Through those double doors, Jane is consoling Luna in the lobby. My sister went eerily quiet after an old man won her, which led me on a tirade towards the event organizer.

I couldn't fix it. I couldn't change it or make it better for her.

And I'm trying to be okay with that.

It's so damn hard.

I rub the back of my strained neck, muscles taut.

Farrow swivels a knob on his radio before he returns his hand to my neck. "Here. Let me." But he doesn't massage my muscle.

Because Bruno approaches.

Our arms fall off each other. Almost out of habit. We even add a couple inches of distance between us, side-by-side.

But the Alpha bodyguard can't be here to reprimand us for touching. We're allowed to touch publicly now.

"Farrow," Bruno says curtly, not acknowledging me as he comes to a stop. He extends a hand to Farrow, but not in a shake. His palm is out flat like he wants something.

"What's going on?" I ask Bruno.

He looks at Farrow as he answers, "Farrow is off-duty tonight. I need his radio and gun."

Farrow doesn't flinch, and he's already unclipping his radio from his belt. Before I advocate on his behalf, he tells me, "I chose this. It's okay."

My frown darkens. "You chose to go off-duty? In what universe?"

He winds his earpiece cord around the radio. "The universe where my boyfriend was grabbed."

"I don't know what the fuck you're talking about," I lie. "I didn't get grabbed." Contesting Farrow is like word vomit at this point.

He gives me a pointed look while he takes his holstered gun out of his waistband. Discreet. None of the seated guests have a view of his hands.

Farrow tells me, "That's cute that you keep pretending I can't see." His gaze descends my six-foot-two build in slow, agonizing desire.

Christ.

Without tearing his gaze off me, he passes the gun and radio to Bruno. As the Alpha bodyguard steps back, giving me a wide space, Farrow whispers with a teasing smile, "Excited?"

"Opposite." I swallow hard.

"You sound a little choked."

I'm dying to be alone with him now, and I dig for the last of my bearings and say, "Fuck you."

"I think you mean *fuck me*," he says matter-of-factly.

A growl scratches my lungs, and I eye his lips—the music falls silent. My head turns to the podium on stage beside the string quartet that has stopped performing.

An auctioneer in an Armani tux adjusts the microphone. "Hello." His even-tempered voice booms. "And we're back. I hope you all enjoyed that intermission and the excellent performance from Harmonious Strings." Soft clapping. "Next up for *Win a Night with a Celebrity*…"

All humor dies in my chest as I hear the name of this event again.

It's not sexual, the board has told me. As though my brain is hooked on sex—because my mom is a sex addict, maybe. I don't know. I'm not fucking sure. But I can't be the only one who thinks a night with someone means a hookup.

I have a boyfriend.

I'm the only one up for bid that's committed to another person. Guilt already gnaws at my insides. But with Ernest as CEO, my family's wealth inside the philanthropy is at risk.

I'm caught in a moral web between family and love, and I'm wondering how those two missed an intersection and when they started running in opposite directions.

"What are you thinking?" Farrow whispers while the auctioneer repeats a few technical details about bidding.

I stare faraway in thought. "I think this is the part where I'm supposed to choose between my company and the guy I love." I look right at him. "Real or rumor?" SFO say that a lot, especially when we were on tour.

Real or rumor.

His eyes caress mine. "Rumor. This auction is a pseudo-fake thing, wolf scout, and what you and I have is real. Whoever bids on you isn't a threat to me." His brows arch. "Bluntly, you're *not* cheating on me by going up there, and you can't walk away from this. It'll kill you not to try."

Yeah.

But what if trying kills me too?

"Maximoff Hale," the auctioneer with slicked hair and spectacles calls me up to the podium, and two-thousand eyes fix on me.

3

FARROW KEENE

As I retrace my path up the aisle, headed towards Omega, Maximoff climbs the few stairs to the stage.

Stoic, unbending, and undeniably striking, he stands beside the podium like a 15th century sculpture, body and jaw carved from marble. And the affluent crowd is about to bid on the modern, real-life version of Michelangelo's David.

He's mine.

I don't love him because he's a coveted piece of art to the thousands here and the millions outside. I love him because he's so pure it hurts, so moral it aches, and so strong-willed it kills me not to speak to him, not to be near him, not to look at him or to protect him.

Velveteen seats squeak, bodies shifting to open purses and reach in pockets for a remote device called a *clicker*. The auction is electronic, no hand raising or numbers hoisted.

My boots feel heavier.

Each step is cumbersome and barbed as I put more distance between me and the stage. Instinct says *turn around, don't leave him.*

Don't leave him.

I fight the urge to rotate, race towards the stage, climb up and kiss the fuck out of Maximoff. My jaw tics, and I stuff my hands in the pockets of my slacks.

I'm not losing him.

I'm not really leaving him. What I said was true: this isn't real, but shit, the desertion is a kind of torment I've never experienced. It bites at my heels as I walk away and let him do this alone.

Since I'm not his personal bodyguard at this event, I can't be a part of the "night" portion of a *night with a celebrity*. The "night" is planned one week from now. At a location Ernest hasn't disclosed yet. And I have to trust Bruno to protect Maximoff there.

Unless I can win him myself.

I pull a clicker out of my pocket. I already registered my information and bank account, and this is my attempt to prevent bad shit from happening.

I reach SFO, and no one seems surprised that I went "rogue" and chose my boyfriend over door-duty. It's not just me being a maverick. If that'd been their own client, they'd be hard-pressed to say they wouldn't do the same.

Akara spins his phone in his hand; he'd be tenser if Sulli, his client, were participating in the auction. "I can't vouch for you anymore with Alpha," he tells me. "It's not sticking, and we're in a spot where Omega has less leeway."

I nod. "Okay." I can't say I'll change my actions, but I'd rather Akara not put his neck on the line for me. I can take all the heat.

Oscar motions me forward, about the same time I slip between Donnelly and him. I face the stage, and my stomach overturns.

Maximoff is staring off in the distance. Lost in his head. Almost like he's not here.

I'm not close enough to wake him up.

"...the grandson of *two* Fortune 500 moguls with the billion-dollar companies Fizzle and Hale Co..." The auctioneer pushes up his silver-rimmed glasses and reads a bio to the audience.

I partially tune him out and whisper to Oscar, "How much do you think he'll go for?"

"More than you have, Redford."

I roll my eyes, but I would've said the same thing. This is a fucking pipe dream, but Luna only went for twelve grand. Jane was forty.

Oscar bats his eyelashes. "It's the thought that counts."

"Did you come up with that one all on your own, Oliveira?" My curt voice draws his lips down. This shit is actually serious to me, and he notices.

"How much do you have to spend?" Oscar asks, his strict tone matching mine.

"Twelve grand."

Donnelly smacks a pack of cigarettes on his palm, but he won't smoke in this venue. "You really sold it?"

"I had to." With all the fines I incurred on tour for breaking security rules, my bank account sat idle at three hundred bucks.

I don't need to be an Ivy League grad to know Maximoff's price tag will be much higher than that.

"Sold what?" Quinn Oliveira asks. The youngest bodyguard sidles over to us, distancing himself from Thatcher Moretti: the six-foot-seven immobile bodyguard who hasn't budged verbally or physically since we've been here.

A silent Thatcher is my favorite Thatcher. Because when he's speaking, nine-times-out-of-ten it's to reprimand me. Since he accepted his demotion, no longer a lead of any force, he scolds me *eight*-times-out-of-ten now. But he has no real power over me anymore.

"Farrow sold his bike," Donnelly answers, sliding an unlit cigarette behind his ear.

Quinn gestures to me. "Bro, I would've bought it. I've been looking for one."

I keep watch of the stage, Maximoff, the auctioneer, and Omega all at once. "What would you've offered for a five-year-old FZ-09?"

"It's a Yamaha," Oscar says to his little brother.

"I know," Quinn snaps and rubs his unshaven jaw, frustrated.

Oscar raises his hands. "Just trying to help."

Quinn ignores him and nods to me. "Four grand."

"And that's why I didn't sell it to you," I say easily, and then I catch some of the auctioneer's words.

"…at nineteen, Maximoff Hale attended Harvard University and swam for their team…"

I heat, the clicker damp in my palm. I rub my hand on my shirt, then I glance at Oscar, feeling his gaze on me. He's perceptive and clever, a lethal combination for those who don't want to be analyzed. But I don't mind.

"You can say it," I tell him.

He puts a hand on my shoulder. "I've never seen you like this."

I've never cared about someone like this.

"What'd you sell it for then?" Quinn asks me about my bike.

"Twelve grand," I say distantly, hearing voices escalate in the lobby behind the double doors.

Quinn frowns. "No way it's worth that much."

"It's not," I say. "The guy was an idiot."

Truthfully, I put the ad on Craigslist and mentioned how the motorcycle belonged to "Maximoff Hale's boyfriend" and a middle-aged man bit the bait. He said he had no plans to ride it, and after he made an offhanded joke about a CVS deal on *lotion*, I wasn't going to ask.

Oscar watches the stage, then me. "Should've just sold the boyfriend's motorcycle. He's more popular than you." Oscar knows that fame is why I got more for less.

"I'm not selling my boyfriend's Kawasaki to win him," I say. "Also, his bike is a piece of shit." The brand is great, but he's had his Z1000 since he was sixteen and crashed multiple times, as aggressive on a bike as he is in a car. I tried riding the motorcycle, and it had almost no torque.

Oscar opens a snack-sized bag of Lays. "Fans don't care if his bike is a piece of shit or a plastic vehicle in Barbie's dream house."

Donnelly digs in the chips. "You know Akara's bike would've sold for more."

Oscar slaps Donnelly's hand away. "This is *snack-sized*. For one person. Me. Get your own."

Donnelly gives him a middle finger.

Akara hears his name, vaguely listening to our conversation. "I'm never selling my bike, guys." He has a CBR1000RR sportbike that he wrecked, but he cashed in a favor with Banks, the most skilled mechanic on the team. Thatcher's twin brother worked on the Honda, removed the fairings, fixed the engine, and turned the bike into a street fighter.

It's beautiful and worth more than what Akara paid for it.

"...at twenty-one, Maximoff Hale was honored with the *World's Philanthropy of the Year Award* for founding one of the most profitable charities..."

The noise behind the door grows louder, footsteps pounding, and we all shift before the door creaks open and a head pops out. I see a tight bun, Botoxed forehead, and an ankle-length dress, no...I don't recognize this woman.

But her beady gray eyes land on me.

"Mr. Keene," she whispers. "Come here, please." She gestures towards the lobby.

I'm not leaving. "What is it?" I ask.

She glances nervously at the few heads we turn from the audience. Whispering, she says, "I've been informed that you are no longer serving as security tonight. I can't let you in the orchestra hall without paying the entrance fee. I'm sorry."

I run my hand over my strong jaw. Someone on the security team had to have "informed" the event staff. My narrowed eyes drift to Thatcher, but he's still staring unflinchingly ahead.

Focus.

I act quickly and whisper to the woman, "I can pay afterwards."

"You can't. I'm sorry. If you'd step into the lobby, we can get your entrance fee squared away and you'll be able to return."

I may not make the start of the bidding, and I make a split-second decision. I raise the clicker between Donnelly and Oscar. "Which one of you fuckers wants it?" I'm trusting them to bid for me if I'm not back in time.

Oscar licks his salty thumb from his chips. "Can't choose between us, Redford?"

I'd like to make that choice, but I met them both nearly at the same time in my life. I was just eighteen, and ten years later, we're all still here.

I can't say who needs each other more or less. We've all just been there in rough terrain, and that's why I can't choose right away.

Oscar sees and takes the clicker. "Donnelly isn't good with numbers. Go."

On my way out, I warn, "You bet over ten grand, Oliveira, and you'll be paying for my bar tabs for the next decade."

Oscar crumples the chip bag. "Love you too, bro."

I slip through the doorway, and the auctioneer's voice fades.

With the heavy door opened for a half a second, Thatcher turns to peek into the lobby. He's clearly looking for his client, and I don't let him see Jane.

I kick the door closed, his glare meeting mine before it shuts.

"This way." The woman directs me past a fancy concession bar that sells wine, caramel popcorn, and cocktails.

I follow and survey my surroundings. The carpeted lobby is quiet, even as a throng of security hovers near Luna Hale and Beckett Cobalt.

Maximoff's little sister sits on the staircase that leads to the balcony levels, and she's showing Beckett something on her phone. Could be a fanfic story that she wrote. She looks better than earlier. More talkative.

Near the restrooms, the woman stops at the registration table, laptops opened and papers stacked in neat piles.

"Farrow?" Jane exits the girl's bathroom, a blue tulle skirt over leggings, and cat-eye sunglasses perched on frizzy brown hair. "Isn't Moffy on stage? He needs one of us out there in support—"

"I'm dealing with some shit." I gesture to the table, and the woman stiffens at my language. "Sorry," I apologize to her and open my wallet. "You can go, Cobalt."

Jane frowns.

"You're right," I tell her. "He needs you." I want his best friend to be in sight if I can't be, but it's not easy to swallow the fact that *money* is what's obstructing me.

Jane studies the table, the woman, my wallet, putting two-and-two together. Especially as the woman tells me, "We don't take cards for the entry fee. Only check."

Shit.

My fingers freeze on my wallet. "Who carries around a checkbook?" I ask, my gaze drifting as soon as Jane unzips her yellow-sequined, banana-shaped purse.

I blink once and Jane already has the checkbook open, bending over the table to write the amount. "Two thousand, correct?" she asks me.

I appreciate the gesture, but I prefer buying my own way. "Jane—"

"You'll pay me back." Her blue eyes flit up to me as she scrawls her name. "You don't have time to argue, and if you have another plan, please let me know."

I don't. "Okay." I nod.

I'm not sure if she's doing this more for Maximoff or for me. I almost roll my eyes. Of course this is for Maximoff, but I'm lucky that he has Jane unflinchingly on his side.

"Thanks, Cobalt," I say as she rips the pink check out of the book.

Jane offers a small smile, and then passes the check to the woman.

I don't waste another second that Jane's given me. And she's right in tow as I reenter the orchestra hall.

Thatcher reaches a hand above Jane's head behind me. Just to hold the door open for her, but she follows my lengthy stride. Catching up quickly.

The auctioneer is already spewing numbers at rapid speed. "2k, would I get a 3k? 3k, would I get a 4k? Somebody bid now, make it 5k."

I can spend twelve grand again since I didn't need to use two.

When I near Oscar, he clicks the clicker, but the device lights up red. Meaning he was too slow, and someone else whose device lit up green locked in for that bid.

"Boyfriend is popular," Oscar says and passes the clicker to me. "I only got the 1k bid, which is null and void now that it's at…"

We all listen to the numbers…*7k.*

I click at *8k.* Flashes red.

"Merde," Jane mutters.

Fuck, there are too many bidders.

"Somebody bid now, make it 9k."

Finally, the device lights green.

"9k, would I get—10k, we got 11k—,"

Fuckfuckfuck.

I click and click.

Red. Red.

"We got 12k—"

Green. I hold my breath, and we all wait to see if a rich prick bids on him.

"Somebody bid, make it 13k," the auctioneer chants. *Don't.*

I want him.

"13k!" he shouts and bangs a hand on the podium. He pushes up his slipping glasses. "Would I get a 14k?!"

My stomach drops.

I can't let this eat at me; I saw this happening from the start, but an acidic taste runs in the back of my throat.

Jane has her knuckles to her lips, worried.

That's not good. I look down at her and ask, "What's the chance that one of your family friend's bids on him like they bid on you?" Jane has already gone through this process tonight. After Maximoff is finished, Beckett and Charlie are the only two left.

14k. I hear the number grow.

"Terribly small," she whispers, and me and the rest of SFO listen closely as she explains what most never hear. "The old woman who bought the night with me—she was the friend of my socialite grandmother, and my grandmother has never doted over Moffy the way she does me. She buys me thousand-dollar tea pots when she knows that I dislike tea, and she only gifts Moffy store-bought cards with no signature."

I catch myself grinding my teeth.

Donnelly tightens his loose cartilage earring. "Grandma Calloway sounds like a b…" His voice trails at Akara and Thatcher's reprimanding looks. "…itch. *Bitch.* I meant *bitch.*"

15k.

"Paul," Thatcher snaps.

Donnelly lets it go without care.

I'm stuck watching Maximoff stare off in space, green lights flashing in the hands of the audience, and my muscles tighten. That acidic taste in my throat keeps rising.

Jane shifts her weight, nervous.

17k.

"Redford," Oscar says my middle name with a flat tone. It's serious, and I instantly follow his vigilant gaze to a boxed seat, up in the third tier across the orchestra hall.

Where Charlie Cobalt sits.

His bowtie is undone, white button-down sticking out from his slacks, sandy-brown hair ruffled.

Oscar has been keeping an eye on his client, and something's not right. Charlie is bent forward, hands on the railing, unblinking.

Watching. Too carefully.

He's usually slouching or slumping in disinterest. But Charlie zeroes in on the audience while clickers blink green and red. Too interested in this outcome.

All of a sudden, Charlie bolts to his feet and disappears through the upper-tier door.

Oscar whispers, "He knows something."

"And he's not going to tell us shit," I say softly. "This is Charlie."

"He'll tell his older sister." Oscar's dark curls fall over his forehead as he nods towards Jane.

Jane looks uncertain.

I tilt my head. "You're his *sister.*"

"He can be abnormally private," she says as though being left out doesn't hurt. "We should find Beckett—though, Beckett will only spill Charlie's secrets if it's life-threatening."

I don't pretend to understand the Cobalt family hierarchy of secret-keeping and secret-spilling. None if it has any ounce of order or sense to me.

"Boss, I'll get my client," Donnelly says about Beckett. He already pushes the doors to the lobby before Akara says, "I'll go with you."

They leave.

25k.

Oscar brushes his earpiece, someone's speaking, and I never thought I'd miss my radio or Alpha in my fucking ear.

While I wait for him to fill me in, I concentrate on Maximoff. He stares at the wall, his trance broken, but he's listening carefully to the number.

28k.

Oscar touches my shoulder. "Charlie is coming here to speak to you. It can't be good."

"No shit." My voice dies as the double doors blow open. The pop of noise causes a wave of mutterings and heads to turn.

Charlie couldn't care less, his attention plastered to me.

"What is it?" I ask. That acid in my throat is bile. I taste it. My gut— my intuition that I rely on—sickens with dread.

He nears quickly, his shoulder brushing mine at the same height, and he says hushed but fast, "You have to win him."

I shelter the urge to ask why. "I don't have thirty grand—"

"I'll wire you the money," Charlie cuts me off, not removing his intense yellow-green eyes from my face. "*Farrow.*" Urgency is on my name, but I can't tell if fear, worry, or something else accompanies it.

He reaches for the clicker in my hand.

I pull back, and not wasting time, I press the button. The device blinks green and I enter the 30k bid. Someone else bids 31k, but I manage to get to 32k before anyone else can.

"Charlie," Jane whispers, "the H.M.C. board said we're not allowed to pool our money into any bids. It was a stipulation—"

"Fuck the board," Charlie says beneath his breath, and to me, he says, "Continue."

I comb a hand through my hair. "If this is serious, Charlie, security has the ability to shut down the entire auction—"

"Maximoff wouldn't want to end an event early," Charlie cuts me off.

A short laugh sticks to my throat. "When have you ever cared what Maximoff wants?" *37k.*

"It's fine," Charlie says, glare on my glare. "It's fine. You're going to win him. The solution is right here."

I should grab Maximoff off the stage. I should leave with him, but I can't tell if that instinct is just me being hyper-vigilant of the guy I love, combined with the after-effects of a stalker.

I'd like to say that Nate, *that sick motherfucker*, didn't affect me, but I'm standing here questioning my natural instincts.

My memory makes years feel like yesterdays and weeks feel like minutes ago.

Great for sex. Better for love. Shit for what Maximoff calls *doomsdays*.

I can still feel the animal blood pouring down my head. I can feel Nate's limbs slipping out of my grip and how my adrenaline thrashed my pulse...

I almost shut my eyes. But the image will still be there. And I have to live with this forever, but I wish it didn't have to fuck with my reflexes.

Normally I wouldn't hesitate this long. *Fuck it*. I make an abrupt choice and put trust in Charlie. I stay here to bid on Maximoff.

There's no going back.

"Who else is bidding on your cousin?" Oscar asks Charlie.

Charlie is quiet. He had the best vantage point in the boxed seat, and he could tell whose clicker kept lighting green. I stare at backs of chairs and heads. Unable to distinguish the person I'm electronically contending.

"Charlie," Jane snaps angrily and speaks in rapid French. He replies back just as swiftly in the same language.

The auctioneer spouts off, "45k, got 46k…" My clicker lights green, locking in the bid, but the auctioneer's voice suddenly fades, and the orchestra hall goes strangely quiet.

The auctioneer frowns and lifts a tablet he's been using. "It looks like a bidder has put in a high offer."

"Oh no," Jane breathes.

I run my tongue over my lip piercing, watching concern pass through Charlie's features.

He brushes a hand through his disheveled hair. "It's fine." But I can't tell if he really means it.

I grit down. *Fuck this.* I look at Oscar. "I'm getting him." I'm getting my boyfriend off the motherfucking stage.

Oscar nods.

"Wait a second," Charlie says with more confidence, holding out a hand.

The auctioneer sets down the tablet. "We'll start the auction at the highest offer." He clears his throat. "Two million, would I get a two-point-one mil?" *No chance.* I don't even know if Charlie has access to that amount of money, and he could lie and say he does.

I pocket the device, and Charlie stares ahead, not stopping me.

"Going once," the auctioneer calls.

My stomach somersaults. "Charlie, who's bidding on him?" I ask.

"Going twice."

Charlie's eyes are locked on the stage like he's in a daze. "No one good."

"Sold!"

Violins screech as the quartet plays again, calling for an intermission, and hundreds rise, congesting the stage and aisles.

Get him.

I head down the right aisle, and I'm surprised when Charlie Cobalt follows me, step for step.

4

MAXIMOFF HALE

When I was seventeen, I told my dad, "I don't think I'll ever fall in love."

I couldn't imagine a person fitting into my unconventional life. I couldn't imagine a companion at my side.

Not like that.

In my head, there'd be no one for me. No man. No woman. No person. I'd be alone, and it was supposed to be okay. It'd be okay that it would always be just me, only me.

My dad, with amber eyes that can cut the soul into jagged pieces, stared right…*right* into me. Where most would fear him, I bathed in warmth—those sharp-edged eyes, with their bitter history and raw truths, comforted me.

And he said, "Before I had you and your siblings, your mom was the *one* good thing in my life. And I know I'm supposed to tell you how love conquers all. How we could move mountains together. But the love we had almost destroyed us both. Love is like having a mortal wound and you're bleeding out and no matter how hard you look, you can never find the goddamn cut." He never broke eye contact.

I kept looking. Listening, feeling his words.

"It's its own special brand of pain," he told me. "Because no matter how much you love, you're still a passenger to their life. You have to watch all their bad decisions. You can't think for them or change them. Just be there for them. And sometimes, it's not going to be good enough.

Sometimes things happen out of your control." He paused. "Love is pain, and you know what...I feel sorry for anyone who hasn't met it yet."

I think about that.

As my boots cement and the stage lights overpower my vision, rows and rows of blurred faces staring back, I think about love.

How I thought I'd never feel it.

The pain.

The kind my dad scorned but also ached for.

I don't want Farrow to be a passenger to my bad choices, watching my fucked-up decision to be sold for a night.

But I keep picturing Farrow Redford Keene...I keep imagining him running down the aisle. Coming towards me. Because if our positions were reversed, I'd want to pull him off this damn stage. And I'd know I can't, he can't.

I'd feel like screaming and screaming and *screaming* just to reach him. Until my veins burst in my neck and my lungs set on fire.

Until my last breath was used to call his name.

I imagine him climbing on stage in one swift motion. His intense focus meeting my tough gaze, his hand catching my hand, his inked arm sweeping around my shoulders. Pulled together, not letting go, *never letting go*—but I don't see him, or even hear him.

He's just the agonized love inside my head.

"Sold!" the auctioneer yells.

I blink out of my thoughts and near the stage stairs.

A delicate hand touches my shoulder—and I swing my head, meeting the kind eyes of a twenty-something girl.

Probably an event coordinator.

Probably. Christ. My face twists in a bitter expression that I almost never fucking wear.

Because I'm not even a tiny bit sure who she is or her job description or why she's on stage. I've been told next to nothing. At this event, I'm just a celebrity guest.

The one up for bid.

At the events I organize, I know everything. Down to the names and faces of the clean up crew.

Ernest didn't think I'd cooperate if I had knowledge, so he's blindfolded me. Worse, I have no idea where the auction money is going. The board muttered something about *humanitarian projects*. Which is vague and nondescript.

And the company should be clear and upfront with all the guests tonight. So I'm not thrilled about the money raised at the auction. Being reinstated as CEO of H.M.C. Philanthropies is the only good thing that'll come out of this.

"Sorry," I apologize to the girl before I ask, "who are you?!" I have to shout as the classical music blasts next to me, a violin in my ear.

"An event coordinator!" She flashes a *Night with a Celebrity* event badge with her name: Tami. "We're taking a fifteen-minute intermission!"

"Who's up next?! Beckett or Charlie?!"

She shrugs and forces a smile as an answer.

Great.

I descend the few stairs. Guests mingle in the aisles and around the stage. Bruno grants me about fifteen feet of space, enough that I forget he's even here.

I'm closer to the right aisle, and that's when I see him.

Farrow slips through the chatty masses with a determined stride. His shoulder bumps into a woman, and champagne almost spills on her emerald necklace—wait, why is Charlie behind him?

I move faster, squeezing past guests as Farrow weaves between other bodies. Both of us in pursuit of the other.

"Maximoff," a few people call for me. Wanting to talk.

I don't stop.

Not until no one and nothing barricades Farrow from me and me from Farrow. His arm instantly curves around my shoulders, and with his other tattooed hand, he holds my jaw, his lips against my ear as he whispers quickly, "Charlie knows who won the two-million dollar bid on you."

My heartbeat pounds against Farrow's hard chest.

Two-million dollars.

I nod stiffly. I had no idea I was won for *two-million*. I must've tuned out that part, and I can't conjure the kind of person who'd spend that life-changing amount on me.

We both turn towards my cousin who nears. Charlie plucks a champagne flute off a server's tray and downs the drink in two gulps. He sets the glass on an armrest of an empty seat.

Not giving a fuck.

Typical. But his indifference doesn't grate on me right now. Because I'm majorly confused.

"Who won me?" I ask Charlie, and I keep my arm around Farrow's waist while his arm hangs over my shoulder.

Charlie steps closer so we're in a huddle, no one overhearing, and he loosens his already loose bowtie. "Ace Steel."

My brows knit. "Who?" I look to Farrow.

He stares hard at Charlie. "Never heard of him."

Charlie runs his hand through his hair and pulls at the strands. Not anxiously. He does it when he's bored, too, and it always makes his hair stick up in odd places—and Jesus, I don't know why I'm fixating on this.

Yeah I do. Because I've been sold for two-million dollars. Because Ernest has invaded my wheelhouse, steering my ship towards someone with maybe-possibly-fucked-up intentions.

Charlie takes a pair of black sunglasses out of his pocket. Prolonging the answer, and he slips them on. It's nighttime. We're indoors. Cameras aren't even flashing at us. There's no sense in most of what he does, and sometimes I think that's why he does it.

I let out an agitated breath. "Charlie—"

"Ace Steel is a porn star."

What.

The.

Fuck.

My brows scrunch more. "You're fucking with us," I state.

Charlie shakes his head once. "Not this time. And I know what pornography companies do to our families, so I warned your boyfriend.

He failed at winning you, and that's not on me."

Farrow rolls his eyes, but I'm super-glued to the fact that Farrow tried to win me and rescue me off that stage. I'd say I don't need rescuing, but I'd be willing to let Farrow rescue me.

I just wouldn't outright tell him that.

My chest rises in a deeper breath. I have no idea how he would've paid for me, but I guess it doesn't matter since he lost me.

Metaphorically.

And a porn star *literally* won me. Awesome.

"You sure it's a porn star?" I ask Charlie.

He gives me a look like I'm being senseless. "Of course I know. You can Google him if you don't believe me."

I get why I don't recognize the name Ace Steel. I don't watch porn, but Farrow does...or did—or maybe he still does. *Stop thinking.*

"Straight porn," Farrow says matter-of-factly. That's why the name didn't ring a bell for him. Farrow only watches gay porn.

A straight porn actor just purchased me.

I tilt my head backwards and stare upwards.

Dear World, is this a joke? Sincerely, a wide-eyed, severely bewildered human.

I crack my stiff neck. "Let me conceptualize this," I say to Charlie and motion to my head. "Ace Steel is a guy who only does straight porn with girls?"

Charlie overturns his champagne flute, the lip of the glass to the armrest. "Correct."

This makes no sense.

Farrow is eyeing the center section of seats. I can't tell what he thinks or how he feels about this.

I rake a hand through my thick hair. "Why would he want to buy me?"

Charlie arches a mocking brow. "He could want to do a scene with you."

Huh? "A what?" I have no clue what *scene* means in this context.

Farrow peels his gaze off the audience, just to glance at me, the corners of his mouth rising.

My neck almost heats, his amused expression practically broadcasts that I'm now six years younger, six years less experienced, and he's older, wiser.

Stronger.

I am younger, but he's definitely not *that* much wiser. At least not in everything.

Farrow lifts his hand to hold the back of my head as he says, "A scene is just the term used for pornography shoots. Actors are paid per scene filmed, et cetera, and there could be multiple actors in one scene." He barely pauses before asking Charlie, "Is that him?" Farrow points someone out in the center section, on the row nearest us.

"That's him," Charlie confirms.

I don't stare long, my focus on Farrow. "I'm not interested in whatever this porn star has to offer. So if that's why he bought me, he can save his money." My tone is firm like this could be just an ordinary business deal.

You know, *normal*.

Weirdly, it kind of is.

Porn producers used to call me all the time, especially when I hit eighteen. And I get it. I'm the son of a sex addict. People are curious, and curiosity sells as much as sex. But I always had zero desire to upload me fucking *anyone* for you to see.

Now that I have a boyfriend, my desire has plummeted to negative-infinity, and my stomach is in fucking knots.

Farrow rubs a thumb against the back of my neck. "Loud and clear," he tells me. "We'll let him know." He gestures for Ace Steel to come over, and the man who stands up looks like a Spartan warrior with gunmetal eyes, a quarterback build, and stubble along a hard jaw. He's older than me, probably around Farrow's age.

And he wears a tux like he has millions of dollars to spare.

My phone starts ringing.

Farrow looks at me, and I dig my hand in the pocket of my green jeans.

I clutch my phone and check the caller ID: *Winona Meadows*.

Sulli's little sister.

"It's Winona," I tell Farrow, since Charlie has disappeared into an empty row ahead, slouching on top of a seat, sunglasses still on.

It's family. I don't want to ignore her, but there's a porn star currently squeezing his way out of a row to meet me. And…I don't want to leave him with Farrow. My boyfriend sees my confliction, and says, "Go," he nods towards the door. "I can deal with this guy."

I hesitate.

"Maximoff," he urges. "*Go.*" Farrow sends me a single look that says, *I'll catch up with you later, wolf scout.*

"I'll be back," I tell him and quickly put my phone to my ear. Walking up the aisle, I glance backward just to see Ace approach Farrow and extend a hand.

Farrow doesn't shake it and instead starts talking, lips moving rapidly but casually. Always at ease during tornadic activity.

My lips lift, settled with this decision. But then Winona's voice fills my ear in a mad rush, and I stop in the middle of the aisle. My smile falls, and I start mentally gathering battalions.

"Moffy, it'll be past my curfew soon, so hey, let's skip the whole *you shouldn't be here, Nona* bit and tackle the important parts," she says in one breath.

Before I can reply, she's going on, "We need to talk to you. I think it might be bad, really bad. You don't need to say anything yet. I'm about to text you all the details." She hangs up.

So you know Winona Briar Meadows as the fourteen-year-old fearless animal lover with a spirit as wild as the Meadows family. You follow her Instagram account that's littered with nature photography and rock climbing excursions. If she's not advocating for animal rights with Ben Cobalt, then she's hanging with her girl squad and keeping to herself. You beg her to post more selfies, and you criticize her when she doesn't.

I know her as Nona, my cousin who could practically be my little sister. Who I used to carry on my shoulders through the Costa Rican forest while she snapped photos of every damn thing: the leaves, the dirt, the ants and the trees. She would bloody her hands, run off a cliff, and split open her heart for any living thing, and it's terrifying.

Fair Warning: I will decapitate you with a rusted blade if you fuck with this one, and she'll probably try to stop me.

My head is spinning on Nona's words *we shouldn't be here* and *bad* and the "we" in *we need to talk to you.* Who's with her? Where are they? And what the fuck happened?

Near the double door entrance, I spot Jane.

She's stuck chatting with the old woman who bought her. I flag down Janie, and she pries herself away from our grandmother's friend. Strutting down the aisle, her banana purse thwacks her hip.

I haven't talked to my best friend all night, and she's one of the people I'd want on my side during a shit storm.

I catch Jane's hand. "Bonsoir, ma moitié," I say, kissing her cheeks.

"It's just you and me, old chap," she replies. "And the older crew, security, and about two-thousand dreadfully stuffy socialites."

Cameras flash as we greet one another, and her blue eyes dart to the left, but not for long. She pushes her wavy hair off her shoulder. "Now that you're public with Farrow, one would think they'd care less about analyzing our friendship."

"That's too predictable, huh? I guess our friendship is just *that* good."

She smiles brightly, but her lips downturn as my phone vibrates in my fist. "I know that look. Who's in trouble?"

"Winona. We may need to leave early." I slip next to Jane so she can skim the text with me. The message has a ton of random nature and animal emojis.

Ben drove us to the Philly Orchestra Hall. We ditched paparazzi, and we're parked in this dead-end alley thing on the side. We're waiting here for you. Please come to talk. It's very very important. — Winona

"Their personal bodyguards are here for the event, aren't they?" I ask Jane.

She ties her hair back, cheeks flushed hot. "They were given temp bodyguards tonight. It's likely Ben and Nona ditched them, and it's even more possible they're here to protest the auction."

"I don't know." I stare off, thinking. "Winona and Ben are passionate about these things, but they'd both rush in and not just wait in Ben's car. It seems weird..." I trail off and notice Charlie alone, still slumped on a seat.

He tosses his bowtie to the floor.

I've stopped bringing him into the fold. Because he kept ignoring me every time I did. And maybe he still will, maybe he'll hate that Winona called me first, but I don't want to chisel him out of my world anymore.

I look to Jane. "Should I ask your brother to come with me?" Jane has always played neutral in my feud with Charlie, but I can tell it's strained her relationship with him.

She smiles. "Oui, oui." *Yes, yes.* "Vous deux, allez-y. Je vais rester avec Beckett au cas où il serait bientôt appelé. Je ne veux pas qu'il soit seul." *You two go. I'm going to stay here with Beckett in case he's called soon. I don't want him to be alone.*

I wave Charlie over, and he surprisingly drops to his feet and saunters to me. I explain what's happening and finish with, "Want to help?"

Charlie stares at the ground, processing everything. And when his yellow-green eyes lift up to me, he answers, "You're in luck. I'm available."

I was prepared for a fight, but this is better. So much better. And I turn on instinct, looking for someone else.

Farrow.

He's still chatting with Ace Steel down the aisle, but Akara and Oscar flank him like they're two-seconds from pulling him backwards.

I cup my hands around my mouth. "Farrow!" I call out, and nearly every head swerves in my direction.

Farrow locks eyes with me, and I know, in this second, that I want him with me.

So I text Winona: me, Charlie, and Farrow are coming in a sec. Don't drive away.

She's fast to reply.

Isn't Farrow like 6'5"? Ben's eco car is too small for all 3 of u — Winona

I type quickly as a six-foot-*three* Farrow approaches, and I send: not if you sit in the middle seat in the back.

K. Hurry. — Winona

I plan on it.

5

MAXIMOFF HALE

Heavy rain beats the sleek, blue electric car in a deserted alleyway. Car windows are fogged.

An overhang on the side-exit keeps us dry, and Farrow catches my arm before we run into the midnight storm with Charlie.

My cousin already disappears into the front passenger side.

"Half of Omega is waiting in security's Range Rover in case Ben drives off," Farrow explains as he quickly fits in his earpiece and hooks a radio to his belt.

"They really let you back on duty?" I ask, and we step into the rain together, our boots meeting the slick road.

Farrow jogs around to the other door. "I'm the best at what I do, wolf scout. Everyone needs me. Case in point." He puts a hand on the car's wet roof.

I clutch the door handle. He's right, but there's a difference between security and me. "I don't just need you though."

I want you.

I want you.

God, I want you.

I express the carnal words in my eyes, and his chest elevates, seeing every loving *want* written on me.

"Damn," he mutters, rain dripping down his temples and off his jaw.

Damn.

I inhale strongly. Yeah, that's about right.

It's a good start to a doomsday. Because I'm not always that smooth, and something needs to go right before everything goes fucking wrong.

We both slip into the rear doors at nearly the same time. Shutting out the rain. I brush water out of my soaked hair.

Winona rotates to me in the middle seat, her face delicate and feminine compared to her older sister's strong squared jaw. Her hair, lightened to dishwater-blonde from the sun, falls on a man's button-down that's knotted at the waistband of her cargo pants.

Her hazel-flecked eyes bore into me with so much emotion that it tries to knock me backwards.

"Are you okay?" I ask.

"No, I'm not okay," she says powerfully, her eyes glassing and chin threatening to tremble.

"We're going to help, alright?" I hug Nona, and she grips my shoulders.

I rub her back, and I flip a figurative switch. Trying not to feel the hurt that she feels. My eyes rise to Farrow.

He studies my stone face, and he mouths, *I'm here for you.*

I nod. I know, but I'm not sure how to be everything they need without shutting off emotion. What Farrow called a survival instinct.

When my family breaks down, I fortify.

"Nona, don't cry," Ben says in a whisper, turning around from the driver's seat. "Because then I'll start crying again and we're not going to move past the waterworks stage of this crisis."

You know Ben Pirrip Cobalt as the sixteen-year-old savvy environmentalist who makes friends easier than all of my family combined. He'll even be your friend. He's probably already followed you back on Twitter or Instagram, and he's liked your pictures ten or twenty times. You think he's one of the coolest Cobalt boys—with his accessibility, his windswept brown hair, baby blue eyes, and pretty boy charm—and you wouldn't be wrong.

I know him as Ben, sometimes *Pippy*, the youngest and most free-spirited Cobalt boy and my little cousin. A guy who wears his heart on his sleeve, who hurts over sad, broken things, and I know he wishes more people paid attention to important causes than the beauty mark on his cheek.

Fair Warning: I will hold you beneath a frozen lake and drown you if you fuck with him.

"You smell foul," Charlie says to his brother. Ben does stink like locker room B.O., but Winona has to be used to the stench. If it bothers Farrow, he doesn't let on.

Ben scratches his hair. String-braided bracelets (made by Winona) fall down his wrist. "I'm doing a water-only wash period. I'm on week four."

"It's not working," Charlie tells him and scoots his seat back on me—

"Charlie," I growl, the seat crushing my knees. Nona sits back up and rubs her cheek with the heel of her palm. She opens a box of salted crackers.

Charlie is ignoring me. In case you were all wondering.

"Are you cool?" Ben is asking Farrow, and at the same time, Winona crosses her legs on the seat. Giving me room to shift mine in her space.

"Thanks," I tell my cousin.

She offers me a cracker, and I pass since they taste like salted tree bark. And she offers Farrow one, which he accepts.

"I won't nark if that's what you're asking," Farrow says and pops the cracker in his mouth. He chews slowly, his face scrunching, and I almost start laughing.

"Cool," Ben nods.

Farrow coughs in his fist, then unpockets a pack of gum. "Your cousin already likes me better than he likes you, wolf scout."

I give him a middle finger, and his mouth curves upward. I tell Farrow, "Ben likes everyone. It's not that big of an accomplishment."

Ben flips on his windshield wipers. "I definitely do *not* like someone."

"Who?" Farrow and I say while Charlie mutters, "This is new."

Ben checks his rearview mirror. "I also don't like idling in a dead-end…you all mind if I drive out?"

I think he's worried about being trapped in an alleyway if paparazzi find us. But like Farrow said, Omega is in a Range Rover nearby, probably watching for incoming vehicles. They'd alert Farrow before we'd get blocked in.

"Vas-y," Charlie says. *Go ahead.*

Ben reverses his car.

I extend my arm across the back of the backseat in a death-clutch. Jesus, I *hate* riding backseat. In any car, with any driver. I wish being a passenger on a tour bus could've cured me of this, but I'm just not that lucky.

Farrow clicks his mic on his collar. "Omega to Farrow, we're heading out." He rests his elbow near my hand, then lays his arm on top of mine, his thumb stroking my bicep.

It takes me back to my car, that moment when we decided to be a couple, in a relationship. Where we had our first kiss.

I wonder if he's thinking about that too, or if I'm just sentimental because this is my first relationship, first love, and that was the most meaningful first kiss I've ever had in my life.

Ben switches the automatic gear to *drive* once he reaches the main road, and then he aims for an on-ramp to the highway.

"The Range Rover behind you is Omega," Farrow tells him.

"Thanks," Ben says and fixes his side mirrors with a button. Rain pours harder and pings on the roof.

I really want to know why they're both upset. "Who do you not like?" I ask. "Did they do something?"

Winona munches on a handful of crackers.

I give her a look.

"I'm a nervous eater," she mumbles, crumbs everywhere. "And you're not going to like what we have to tell you."

Ben merges onto the highway. "It's your brother."

Xander.

"What?" Charlie and I say in unison. My face contorts in confusion, and my pulse thumps in my ears.

"I did something," Ben mutters, guilt in his voice. My muscles bind. He's the kind of person who'd blame himself for accidentally stepping on an anthill. So it's hard to gauge the seriousness.

Ben flicks his blinker but struggles to switch lanes and concentrate on this conversation.

I look out the rear windshield. "You can go, Ben."

He tentatively scoots the car to the left lane and then accelerates to about seventy-five, the traffic sparse at midnight. His finger keeps tapping the wheel.

"I don't understand," I say to Ben. "I know you and my brother had a falling out, but I thought you still liked him."

"Something's changed," Ben replies. "But it's my fault. It's really all my fault." I don't know what to take from that.

Suddenly, Farrow drops his arm from me to press his earpiece, trying to listen. The rain slams down, and I check over my shoulder. A few incoming cars surround us when they have the whole highway.

Farrow almost rolls his eyes before swiveling the knob on his radio.

I whisper, "What's happening?"

"Three SUVs," he whispers back, Winona between us who can probably hear. "Akara is yelling at Quinn to relax. He's getting amped."

Winona shakes cracker crumbs into her palm. "I still like Xander."

Alright... "Someone explain this, please," I say.

Ben takes a tight breath. "You all remember how I used to bring Xander to the school's hockey games, sometimes soccer?"

That seems like forever ago. Ben Cobalt is a social butterfly the exact *opposite* of my brother, but they somehow got along. To be in Xander's life, you have to wedge yourself in there, and Ben always snuck in.

Up until about a year ago.

Their "falling out" happened.

"You said you two grew apart," I remember. It made sense. They were getting older, but Ben was one of the only people who could get Xander out of the house. And my brother has been more recluse since he lost Ben as a friend, but I never thought Ben actually disliked Xander. They just don't talk that much anymore.

"That's not really why," Ben says. "I mean, we did grow apart, but..." He tries to increase his windshield wiper speed. "I stopped bringing Xander to school events after something happened."

Something happened.

And my brother didn't tell me. And I wasn't there for him. Guilt tries to roil inside me, because if he was hurt or in some kind of worse pain…

Charlie hooks his sunglasses on his shirt. "That's not vague at all."

Ben side-eyes him before switching lanes to bypass an SUV. "Sorry I'm not using excessive adjectives and nouns to your liking." He looks back at Farrow through the rearview mirror. "If you don't know by now, Charlie thinks I'm *dangerously naïve* to the point of stupidity, and he wastes no opportunity to remind me."

Farrow pops another bubble in his mouth. "Cobalts are something else."

Ben glances quickly at Charlie. "Now *that's* vague."

Charlie pulls at his hair. "I wouldn't expect anything more from someone who believes Maximoff is boyfriend material."

Ouch.

Gotta give it to Charlie, he knows my insecurities.

"Jealous that he's in a relationship?" Farrow asks easily while lifting his boot to the seat and balancing his arm on his knee. His confidence is radiating.

Charlie glares back at Farrow with a look that says *you're wrong.*

Farrow combats him with a harder stare that says *I'm right.*

I wish Janie were here to help us stay on track. "What happened?" I ask Ben and Winona. "Did Xander get hurt?"

"Not exactly," Winona says, brushing crumbs off her lap.

"I was friends with these guys at school," Ben clarifies as he accelerates.

"Ben is friends with everyone," Winona rephrases.

"Yeah, but when I brought Xander along, I always introduced him to these people that I thought he'd like…Is that a pap?"

"On your right," Farrow confirms as three SUVs line up to obstruct Ben from taking an exit.

"Speed up," I suggest. Since that's the only way he can pass the cars and get off the highway.

Ben scoots forward, his visibility terrible as rain pelts the windshield. "It's basically hailing. I can't speed up."

"It's not hailing," Farrow says matter-of-factly. "You're fine. Stay in this lane until you feel comfortable."

Farrow backseat driving is infuriatingly sexy.

Anyway, we have no destination, but my phone keeps vibrating in my pocket. Uncle Ryke and Aunt Daisy, Winona's parents, are concerned since she's past her curfew. When it hits 1:00 a.m., I expect the same onslaught of messages from Uncle Connor and Aunt Rose about Ben.

Once Ben leans back slightly, less edged, I ask, "So Xander met some guys through you at these soccer and hockey games?"

"Yeah," Ben nods. "And I thought it'd be good for him. I didn't think...I mean, I couldn't have known..."

Winona drops her head, upset.

Ben scratches at his hair. "People at school knew that Xander is on antidepressants—rumors about that are all over the internet."

I tense.

"Why is security's car changing lanes?" Ben asks, almost panicked.

"Security is playing defense with the other vehicles," Farrow explains. "SFO is stopping some cars from reaching yours. Don't worry about them. Oscar is a good driver."

"Okay..." Ben adjusts his grip on the wheel. "At the games, students asked Xander if they could have some pills, and Xander actually started giving them his meds—and I should've looked out for your brother, Moffy. It's *my* fault." Ben talks fast, the words rushing out of him all of a sudden. "He's susceptible to peer pressure, and he didn't ask for money or anything in return. He just wanted to be *liked* by these dudes."

My heart is in my throat. He was only fourteen. "That's why you had a falling out?" I realize.

"Yeah." Ben flicks his blinker but decides not to switch lanes. He tries to ease back. "I figured if I stopped inviting Xander out with me, he couldn't give anyone his pills. Since he's homeschooled, it made it easier..." He wafts his *Save the Planet* shirt from his chest. "After a while, we stopped talking, and he just..."

Retreated.

My brother retreated and barely leaves the house.

I rub my jaw, my muscles searing. "Who knows about the pills?" I ask and eye Farrow who touches his earpiece. He checks over his shoulder, on the lookout for paparazzi traffic that steadily amasses.

Ben lowers the volume of his stereo as Charlie turns the radio on. "Some kids at school, me, Xander, and Nona know," Ben says. "And now you three."

Winona twists her otter pendant necklace. "Moffy," she says to me. "We thought he stopped."

My stomach caves.

"A kid in the neighborhood started texting me about it," Ben finishes. "This morning." He extends his arm backwards to pass me his phone, and the one gesture causes Charlie to stare out the window. He must feel like Ben just chose me over him.

My ribs shrink my lungs.

I could hand the phone back to Charlie, but with my little brother at the centerfold of this, I have an aching need to be in control.

So I do the shitty thing and keep the phone. I already know Ben's passcode: the date his pet bird Pip-Squeak died. And then I open the most recent message from the neighborhood kid—

Farrow drops his foot to the floor. His nonchalance suddenly depletes.

When that happens, I feel like someone needs to hoist the Bat Signal in the air and call for the Avengers to Assemble.

"Farrow?" I whisper, catching his gaze. I lean back while Winona bends towards the middle console to speak to Ben in Spanish.

Farrow leans back with me, and he whispers, "Eight more cars, four are SUVs, and they most likely have cameras. Oscar can't block them all. Ben's about to get bombarded unless he can speed up and make an exit."

I move into damage control mode. I pull Winona back so she's not bent forward. "Buckle, Nona."

"I already am."

But it's too loosened, and I don't need to ask. Farrow already pulls the strap to her belt, tightening her in.

I snap my belt off and slide to the seat's edge. Just so I can speak more directly to Ben. Farrow is glaring at me for unbuckling, but I'll be quick.

"Go faster," I tell Ben.

His eyes flit to me. "Did you read the text?"

"Not yet. Accelerate, Ben. You can pass the Kia on your right."

Ben presses the gas, but lets off as rain slams harder. "I can't, Moffy."

Charlie rubs the fog off his window. "You should pull over. I'll drive."

I can't even offer since I still don't have my license back. Not that they'd feel that safe since I have a speeding problem, but I've never wrecked.

"Pull over where?" Ben shifts forward, his chest rising and falling quickly.

"The emergency lane," Charlie says.

"I can't see it."

"*Maximoff*," Farrow says through clenched teeth. Winona fists my shirt to pull me back. I end up sliding backwards on my own, and I pull my seatbelt across my chest and snap in.

I glance at Farrow.

He looks like he wants to kiss me and kill me. "Don't do that again."

"Bodyguard orders?" I ask.

"Boyfriend *rules* since you love following them so much…" he trails off, checking the traffic through the rear windshield. "*Shit.*"

I see what he sees. "Ben," I say, "switch to the left lane." We're in a middle lane, and a truck on the driver's side is gaining speed.

Ben flicks on his blinker. His car sensors start beeping, alerting us about an approaching vehicle. "I can't get over."

He's sixteen and *just* got his license in March. All I want is to take the fucking wheel.

Ben tries to accelerate again. "Moffy, you should read the text out loud."

I hesitate.

Not sure if this is a good distraction from paparazzi or a bad one. But I end up looking down at the phone in my hand.

And I read, "Colin texted, *heads up, dude, Easton Mulligan is getting pills from your cuz. Thought that shit stopped, but Easton's been bragging about it. Even saw the bottle.*"

I don't know how I read that without a single inflection.

I don't know how my heart is still beating.

My muscles burn, shoulders locked, and my impassive face carries nothing. Xander needs his meds, and he's just giving them away so that he can make friends. Hurt claws at me, wanting to just grab him and hug him and tell him this isn't right. Somewhere inside, I almost can't fucking believe this. Somewhere inside, I think I'm screaming at the top of my lungs for this to reverse.

But that emotion is lost with a switch, too deep to reach.

The car is so quiet I can hear Ben's heavy breath.

"I'll talk to him," I say. He can't deal drugs. Or is it even considered dealing if he's giving them away freely? Jesus.

"Be gentle, okay," Ben breathes. "I can't…I mean, Xander just…he lost his door again, right? He's not in a good place."

"Yeah," I say, nothing in my voice.

Farrow studies me for a long beat, and then his tattooed fingers touch his earpiece again, his gum chewing slows down.

I pass the phone to Charlie since Ben is still concentrating on the road. "Just let me handle this," I say and add to Winona. "Don't tell the girl squad what's happened." Last thing I need is for the entire family to be in on this before I even talk to Xander.

"My babes won't know," Winona confirms, and by *babes*, she means my sister Kinney, then Audrey Cobalt and Vada Abbey. Her shoulders loosen, and she exhales in relief.

Ben gains speed but falters as the storm brews. He decelerates. "Thanks, Moffy—" A camera flashes at the driver's window in pitch black night, jarring Ben.

He swerves right.

"Ben!" Winona yells.

"I can't see!"

Charlie instantly grabs the wheel and straightens the car.

"Relax," Farrow tells the teenagers, slightly turned as he watches security's car behind us.

We're wedged between a truck and an SUV, both windows rolled down. Cameras wrapped in plastic point at our car.

"I can't see," Ben mutters again. He grips the steering wheel harder.

Flashes blast in quick succession. Imagine a strobe light in your face on a freeway at seventy-five miles per hour in pouring down rain, and you just got your license three months ago.

"Slow down," I suggest. "Just ride here. They'll get bored and leave."

Now Ben is pressing down on the gas. "I can try to pass one—"

We spin out the second he pushes eighty-five, no traction to the wheels on the wet road—my arm extends over Winona's chest to protect my cousin, and I feel Farrow doing the exact same for her.

As the car revolves, there's no time to glance left or right. No time to course correct or overthink or call out to Farrow.

There is just human life and love and pain.

My world blinks past me and the right side, my side, *slams* into the concrete median with a violent *bang*. My body wrenches forward against my seatbelt. A *crack* steals my breath away. Hot tears slip out of the corners of my eyes—I can't breathe.

And then, the car flips.

6

FARROW KEENE

Everything is eerily motionless except for the ping ping ping of rain hitting the underside of the car. The smell of rain on metal overpowers my senses, and slowly, I gather my bearings.

I'm upside down.

We all are, but I'm the first to barrel through disorientation. My earpiece dangles on a cord down my chest, my radio cracked. Every airbag blew, every window shattered, and the greatest impact was on...*no*.

"Maximoff," I call out, my voice hoarse.

His car door is crushed against the concrete median. Charlie's door is also smashed but not as badly.

I cough a few times, my pulse spiking. I can't see Maximoff that well. Winona's hair cascades down and shields him from view.

He's fine.

I try to pretend.

He's fine.

Winona blinks a few times, then inhales a sharp breath. In shock.

"Winona, you're okay. Just breathe," I say, drawing her attention while I also feel for my seatbelt buckle. I know her sister Sulli better than I know her, but within the security team, the Meadows girls are known for being tough.

Wide-eyed, Winona nods slowly to me. A gash runs down the corner of her lips. She needs stitches.

"Does anything hurt?" I ask. "Your neck, back, legs?" I unbuckle myself and gradually lower to the bottom of the car. Really, the roof. My boots crunch the glass, and I try to open my door.

It's jammed.

"No," Winona answers in a short breath. "No, I think…I think I'm okay."

I crouch and I look up at an upside-down Maximoff. He blinks like his world is still spinning. I sweep him rapidly. What I can see: a clavicle fracture, blood trickling from his nose, shallow breathing.

He's not okay.

I need to lift up his shirt, but I hear my boyfriend in the back of my fucking head. Screaming at me to check on his cousins first.

"Maximoff? Talk to me," I say, but he's still coming to.

It takes the greatest amount of effort and force to tear away from him and focus and triage. I open my mouth to call his name again, but I stop myself. My heart is being shred to fucking pieces.

Winona's eyes dart to the front. "Ben?" Fear pitches her voice.

He groans from the driver's seat.

"Ben, Charlie, how do you feel?" I ask, moving closer. I examine both in a long glance.

Blood drips down a small laceration at Ben's hairline. Tiny cuts prick his face from the glass shards.

"Huh…" he says groggily.

"Help my brother," Charlie winces while he clutches his extremely fractured leg.

I'd like a backboard and a neck brace for Ben, but the longer we stay inside a demolished car, the more dangerous and potentially life-threatening.

Get them out.

"Ben," I call while I shift back to my door. "What's your birthday?" I peek beneath the deflated side airbag. The window is punched out and large enough that a body could crawl through.

Winona all of a sudden unbuckles herself, and I catch her shoulders so she won't fall on her neck. She squats like me.

"Ben, what's your birthday?" I repeat.

"Uh…" he groans. "Huh…?"

I start unbuttoning my black shirt. "Maximoff?" I call out, but my boyfriend is still disoriented. Unresponsive.

Come on, wolf scout.

I breathe hot breath through my nose and pass my shirt to Winona. "Put this against your lip."

She presses the fabric to the corner of her mouth.

"Ben," I call loudly, "what day is it?"

"Huh…?" he mumbles.

"REDFORD!"

I've never been happier to hear my middle name. I flip up the deflated side airbag. Rain soaks Oscar as he crouches, curly pieces of his hair stuck to his forehead.

He's assessing me.

"I'm fine! Take Winona!" I call through the roaring storm. "Charlie has a fractured leg in the passenger seat! Ben may have a concussion!"

"Ambulance won't be here for a while!" Oscar shouts back while I help Winona near the window. "Maybe thirty minutes! Most are in use because of the storm!"

I carry the weight of this shit situation in my eyes.

Oscar nods back and tries to rub water off his face. "I know! You're it, Redford!"

Meaning, no one else on site has this level of medical training. Oscar has some experience from studying sports therapy at Yale, but it's not exactly the same.

Oscar yells over a crack of lightning, "We should get them out fast!"

I nod, agreeing. Oscar grips Winona by the armpits and pulls her out through the window. She's still in a slight fog or else she'd most likely want to stay with Ben.

Once Oscar has her, I call out, "Maximoff!"

He's more coherent and currently trying to unbuckle himself. But he can't move his right arm.

"Farrow," he says, frustrated and raspy. "Are you…okay? Oscar has

Winona?" It's like he's ensuring he didn't just hallucinate that.

"I'm fine. She's okay," I confirm. "Don't move—"

"Charlie and Ben?" he asks and grits down, pain wrenching his face.

"*Don't move yet*," I say deeply with an outstretched hand. "Just wait." It's hard for him, but he physically has no choice, and I shift carefully and quickly towards the front.

Both Cobalts hang upside down.

"Charlie," I call.

Charlie winces, and he keeps looking at his brother in concern.

"Talk to me," I tell Charlie while I take Ben's vitals, my fingers to his carotid pulse. I listen to his chest with my ear.

Normal breath sounds.

"My leg is broken," Charlie states through his teeth, and he wraps his arm around the seatbelt before unbuckling—I reach out and help him slide to the bottom of the car.

"Ben, do you know where you are?" I ask, and I snap the seatbelt. Careful with his head and neck, I hold all his weight. Shit, the youngest guy in this car is the tallest at six-foot-five.

He blinks, still dazed. I check his eyes, and then I lean him against his intact door, the window already shattered.

At this point, I understand clearly who's critical and who isn't.

One person is critical.

Just one.

I return to the back at the same time Maximoff drops down too easily, like he's done this before with a broken collarbone.

He hasn't, by the way.

His Timberlands hit the shattered bottom, and he clutches his forearm to his chest.

I can't even surface a glare as I say, "You stubborn idiot."

He crouches, his breath shortened. "I'm feeling great. Thanks for... asking."

"I didn't ask," I say, my fingers to his neck. I mentally file his fast heart rate. "Anything else hurt?"

"No. Yeah, I don't know. We need to get my cousins out of here."

Before either of us move, Oscar returns and lifts the flap of the airbag. "Redford?!"

"Ben has a concussion!" I call out. "Eyes are dilated, but he's not critical!" I explain how he's accessible through the driver's window, and Oscar has Ben out in a minute flat. He doubles back for Charlie and helps his client out the same side.

I turn to Maximoff. "I'm going out first so I can help you."

He doesn't argue or combat me, and that just about kills me. Because it means he's in severe pain.

I slide out the window backwards. Rain instantly pours on me, soaking my inked chest. Drenching my hair and dripping off my lashes.

Now it's his turn.

I kneel and clutch his waist, not his arm or shoulder, and I pull Maximoff out the window. He uses the strength in his legs, and he almost screams through his teeth.

I have him out of the overturned car, and he tries to pick himself up to stand. He wheezes.

"Stay down." I can't touch his collar without hurting him more. He just has to listen.

And he does with no pushback. It fucking guts me.

Maximoff lies on his back, tilting his head to try and make sense of the dark, stormy surroundings. I kneel closer to his side, concentrating on his injuries, but I still see the cameras flashing.

Akara, Quinn, and some of Epsilon security restrain the paparazzi who've jumped out of their vehicles on the highway. They try to snap photos of the wreckage. Right where Maximoff lies on the pavement littered with metal and plastic car parts.

I can't move him yet.

Security yells and pushes paparazzi backwards.

"Can we help?!" a pedestrian asks, other cars parked in the emergency lane. Epsilon creates a barrier to keep them back from us.

Quickly, I rip open his soaked shirt at the collar until it tears in two. Welts bloom around his ribcage, and he has trouble catching his breath.

"Where's…Nona?" he asks, worried. It's all killing me. Every word he says, every gasp of breath he takes is eviscerating me.

"Range Rover with Ben and Charlie," I answer. Near the wreck, Oscar leans into the Range Rover, doors open, and I assume that Ben and Winona are inside. Waiting for the ambulance.

Charlie has a suit jacket over his head, and he rests against the hood of the Range Rover, putting all his weight on his left leg.

Maximoff winces, his palm floating above his abs. Rain continues to beat down on us, and I hover over my boyfriend to protect him from the storm.

"Chest pain?" I ask, already knowing by sight.

"Yeah…" He wheezes again.

I put my ear to his chest. Absence of breath sounds on the right, and no visible movement. I take his vitals again. *Tachy.*

I've never treated a loved one before.

Fuck, I've never loved someone the way I *love* him. With a father married to medicine and no mother, I didn't grow up seeing love, but I sought that in every relationship, and I thought I met it.

But I realize that I never even came close.

Then I fell for him.

It's a love that pummels me every time I wake and crave to near him. Every time I see his morality and think, *how good you are, and fuck, I'm lucky.* It's a love that beckons me towards him when he's gone. One that reaches into my core and wraps itself around me. It's that persistent, unforgettable undetachable love.

He's in critical condition, and he can't know what I know. I've never lied to him, but I can't tell him this. Right now, I'm the first and last defense against fatality.

"Oliveira!" I shout, the night sky rumbling as sheets of water pound the pavement and us.

Oscar leaves security's car and sprints to me. "What do you need?" He crouches so neither of us has to yell.

"The trauma bag." We keep one in security vehicles in case the concierge doctor needs supplies. "You'll find a needle decompression kit, and get me an umbrella." I almost have to shout since he takes off running. Realizing the enormity.

"Farrow..." Maximoff inhales a ragged breath, forearm tucked to his chest. He tries to gesture me closer, but his fingers only twitch.

I hover over my boyfriend, my palm on gravel above his head. Rain thumps against my back but helps keep his chest and face dry.

"You're bleeding..." He tries to reach out again, to help *me*. He grimaces, his arm immobile.

"Don't," I say. "Just relax, wolf scout."

His eyes drift to my temple. "You're bleeding, you know..."

I touch my temple, the cut small. "It's nothing. Tell me how you feel."

He licks his lips. "I feel...great." His Adam's apple bobs. "Like I could fly to the moon, pick us up some lunch, take my Audi out for a spin." His eyes melt against mine before flooding with pain. His face twists.

I stroke his dark, wet hair out of his face. "It's not lunch time and you don't have a license."

He almost grimace-laughs, and then he coughs roughly. Really roughly, and suddenly, Maximoff solidifies to marble. He notices blood splashed on pavement.

He's coughing up blood.

My head swerves to the car. "Oliveira!" He has to be struggling to find the kit. I check the time on Maximoff's wristwatch.

"Farrow..." Maximoff says, swallowing, his teeth stained with blood as he winces. "Just...tell me."

He wants to know what's wrong with him. *It's killing me. It's killing me.* "Maximoff—"

"You've never...held anything back before..." He takes a shorter breath.

My eyes sear and well, but rain washes my agonized face. I'm dying... with him. I take a deep, punctured breath and get my shit together.

Breathe. Give him what he wants.

Like always.

Gravel digs in my palm as I shift closer. "You have a flail chest; ribs four through seven are fractured," I say. "Hemoptysis, coughing up blood, indicates a pulmonary contusion." Off his confusion, I say, "Your left lung is bruised." That's not the serious injury. This is... "You're in severe respiratory distress on the affected right lung. Neck vein distension, no breath sounds, tracheal deviation. It's a tension pneumothorax. Your broken rib collapsed your lung, and now air is filling in the pleural cavity."

I don't explain how at this stage the pneumothorax can cause obstructive shock. Lack of blood flow to the heart, and the heart will stop pumping blood to his body.

Maximoff nods slowly, listening. Understanding. He's good at that, and he knows. I know he knows that this could be fatal, so I say, "I'm not going to let you die. You hear me?"

He grimaces, blood still filling his mouth. "You're...smarter than me."

"Stop." I need him to say how I'm the know-it-all asshole. How he could've regurgitated all this shit just as easily as me, even if we both know that's not true.

I help lift his head as he coughs.

His forest-greens stay on me, screaming *love me*.

Love me.

And he says, "You've always been smarter than me."

"Don't." I shake my head repeatedly. I can't listen to him admit that I'm wiser, older and stronger. "*Don't.*" My head whips. "OLIVEIRA!" I yell at Oscar to hurry the fuck up, and cameramen scream questions at me about whether Maximoff is alive.

I tune out the chorus of *alive* and *dead*.

Maximoff stares right into me and chokes out, "I love you, you know that?"

We're both crying. "Stop." I clutch his sharp jaw. I'm a stubborn idiot too. Because I refuse to say *I love you* back in a goodbye.

Maximoff takes a shorter breath. "Tell Jane I love her..." He swallows a knot in his throat. "Tell my parents they're the greatest..."

"Maximoff—"

"I love you," he repeats.

"*Stop. Stop.*" I can't do an ending with the one person I've loved enough to want to last forever. I can't. I haven't even told him that I can see forever. I haven't said all that needs to be said yet.

"Take care of my sisters...my brother—"

"Look at me." I hold his face as his breath shortens. "You'll be here tomorrow and the next day. *This* isn't it, wolf scout. You're not ending here. And I'm *confident*..." I nod over and over, his eyes flooding. "You will see your sisters grow up to be old women and you'll see your brother become an old man—and I'll be right by your side."

He blinks and tears fall down his sharp cheekbone. "You will?"

"Yeah," I nod. "You're stuck with me, wolf scout. I'll annoy the shit out of you every single morning for decades. Longer, and our kids will take your side because you're *good* and lovable."

He breathes deeper. "We have kids?" His iron-willed eyes drift to imagine this future, *our future*. "How many?"

A rock lodges. "As many as you want," I say, never lying to him. "And when I agitate you and I really hit a nerve, you'll joke about how you wish you died in this car crash."

His lip wants to lift. "Romantic." He coughs, then grits through pain. "*Fuck.*"

His skin is starting to discolor, and as I look out in the rain, Oscar is running towards me with an umbrella and the kit.

"...Farrow," Maximoff chokes.

"Shh," I whisper.

"...I don't want to die..." His neck strains.

My chest is on fire. "That's good, wolf scout." I nod. "Because I'm not writing down your will right now."

Maximoff stares upward. "Thanks...like you write anything down..."

I grab all the medical supplies Oscar collected. He snaps open the umbrella and shields rain from us while I work.

I tear open antiseptic and cleanse the site. Then I take out the needle catheter from the kit. Quickly, I run my finger over the top of the third rib and the second intercostal space, midclavicular line on the right side.

My hands are shaking.

In all my life, my hands have never shook.

"Take a second, Redford," Oscar tells me.

I breathe out. *Relax, Farrow.*

My hands steady.

No more hesitating, I insert the needle catheter, and a rush of air expels like the burst of a balloon.

Maximoff inhales deeper, and his right lung finally has movement. I keep the catheter in place and remove the needle. He's more stable. And now, all I can do is wait for the ambulance.

I hover over him again. "Better?"

He nods once, taking another breath. He's still in a lot pain from multiple fractures. Our eyes latch for a heady moment as a flash strikes the air.

As the night sky rumbles above us.

Maximoff stares out in a short second before he looks back at me and says, "That's us."

I don't follow. "Plato talking to you again?"

He groans, then coughs.

"Relax," I tell him, ambulance sirens blaring in the distance. And it's only when lightning cracks the sky and thunder roars again do I realize what he meant by *that's us.*

Thunder.

Lightning.

My brows rise. "I'm lightning then, and you're thunder. You always follow me every time I appear."

His lips lift in a choked laugh. "You're right…you will annoy me to death."

My chest swells, and I can't hold back. I lean down and kiss Maximoff, gently, on the lips, and he tries to kiss back and even sit up. But I don't let him.

Later.

There will be a later. There has to be one.

7

MAXIMOFF HALE

A heart rate monitor lets out quiet beep beeps.
An IV is hooked in my vein, connected to bags of fluid, and I ended up asking Farrow what the nurse clipped to my finger: a pulse oximeter.

I've been dazed for a while.

Maybe since I was put on a stretcher and wheeled into an ambulance and brought to Philadelphia General.

I think about how I've been stalked, threatened bodily harm and death. How I've crashed my motorcycle dozens of times, back-flipped into ravines, skydived, wiped out on a snowboard, eaten pavement after skateboard tricks, swam in strong ocean currents, and after all these things, all this damn time, I've never been afraid to die. And then tonight.

I was afraid.

I was fucking terrified.

My mortality, my fragile life, just crashed against me, and I remember that I'm only twenty-two. I remember that I can't control the direction of anything, and I'm a passenger to the universe—but *God*, this ride can't end for me. Not here, not now.

I wasn't ready.

I'm not ready.

I begged and pleaded to receive one more minute with Farrow. I'd been surrounded by the love of family for twenty-two years, but I didn't even get a full year with the love of another man, a companion, a soul mate—and maybe I was being selfish.

Asking for more when I'd been given so much already.

But then I thought about how he never had a family that really loved him for him. And I thought, if not for me, don't do this to him. Don't gut him.

So I'm not returning this second chance, this extra time. Maybe it's why I can't stop staring at him now.

Then again, my brain has always been obsessed. I'm pretty sure he knows that too.

"Aren't you supposed to be reading to me?" I ask Farrow as he clutches a paperback in one hand, *my* paperback, and flips a page. "You know, *out loud.*" I sit up as best I can on the firm hospital bed.

Farrow has claimed a seat at the end of my bed.

My bare legs stretch over his lap. One of his inked hands moves up and down my leg, settling on my kneecap for a few seconds before moving again.

"I'm saving you from a dull read, wolf scout." He flips another page.

He'd say everything on this planet is a dull read because he rarely reads, and he already folded the cover and dog-eared the pages just to irritate me.

"I've read that philosophy book before," I tell him.

His eyes flit to me, a spark of amusement in them. "I know. You have a hard-on for Cicero. There are little highlight marks and scribbles on basically every line."

I almost smile, and I lick my dry lips. "Not *every* fucking line."

He flashes the page he's on. It's annotated to hell and back.

"Fine," I concede. "I like Cicero." I lie on top of the hospital sheets, my throbbing right arm secured in a loose sling. A thin blue hospital gown reaches my thighs and hides the reddish-bluish bruises that mar my abs and chest.

My sore body thuds in a harsh rhythm like I've been run over a billion-and-one times, but I have the best distraction in front of me.

"He loves Cicero," Farrow repeats as he skims the book.

"*Likes,*" I correct.

His biceps look ripped in a Yale T-shirt, but the crew-neck conceals the symmetrical pirate ships on his collarbones and inked skull on his sternum. He said he gave Winona his black button-down for her busted lip, so he ended up borrowing the shirt from Oscar's gym bag.

Farrow flips another page. His speed-reading is fucking annoying.

Another page turns.

More seriously, he asks me, "Why do you like him?"

"You jealous?" I try my hand at teasing my boyfriend.

His brows slowly lift at me like I'm the geekiest fucking geek that ever did geek. "Of a dead Roman philosopher?"

"Yeah."

"No," he says like I've lost my mind. "There's no competition living or dead." He skims the next page.

I try to shift my arm, but pain shoots up my shoulder. I bite down and stay still, and if Farrow can tell I'm hurting, he doesn't nag me.

Thank God.

I already have two enormously worried parents who stopped by about fifteen minutes ago. My mom brought a towering stack of my favorite comics and philosophy texts. To help distract me from the pain while I wait for news about surgery on my collarbone.

She also gave Farrow a tight hug and had to "air hug" me. And my dad—he was choked up, glassy-eyed. They're just grateful I'm alive. The paramedics told them that if Farrow didn't release air from my lungs, I probably would've died before they arrived.

But if you know my dad at all, he's a hard sell. Saving my life is like half-a-brownie point. For my mom, Farrow earned every brownie that ever existed in every universe.

I watch my boyfriend flip another page. "Cicero is timeless," I tell him, trying to explain what's always hard for me: *why do I like x, y, z?* I have too many reasons, and they all jumble together at once. "...a lot of thinkers and theorists derive from his ideas and philosophy." I pause. "He wasn't perfect, but he fought against a Roman dictatorship...and I think he would've been Plato's ideal philosopher."

Farrow raises the book somewhat, just to read, "'*However short your life may be, it will still be long enough to live honestly and decently.*'" He looks at me. "Sounds like you."

"Maybe," I say, thinking hard, "but what if I want to live longer at the risk of being less decent?"

Farrow sucks in a breath, his hand stopping on my knee again. "You're posing that philosophical question to the wrong man."

"Why?" I try to sit up more.

"Because nine-times-out-of-ten, I'm going to tell you to take any risk, and if it means you'll live longer, then there's actually no debate." Farrow flips a page, his eyes drifting between me and the book. Until he's just looking at me. "Tonight shook you up a little bit." It's not a question.

He can see.

I nod. "All I know is that I know nothing, and I'm alright with that as long as you're in my life—and that's fucking hard for me to admit. That I'm clueless about where I go from here and what the fuck I'm doing, but it doesn't matter as much as you matter to me. And I'm rambling..."

His lips curve upward, and he waves me on. "Keep going."

"You," I retort dryly.

He rolls his eyes and stares at the ceiling before his gaze falls on me. "In medicine, I've met a lot of death, and it's made me appreciate the present and not regret or fixate on the *could've beens*. But if something happened to you tonight and you became a *could've been*, it would've crushed me for the rest of my life." His chest rises in a bigger breath, and he finishes with, "And all I know is that I know *everything*."

I blink slowly. "Give me my book so I can throw it at you."

Farrow smiles. "Let me think about that." He doesn't think about it and he keeps my paperback right in his hand. But his other hand leaves my knee and crawls up my thigh.

I like that. Too damn much.

My phone rings near my side. Every person in my family has texted about a dozen times. I have plenty of new ones, especially from my siblings.

You're not cool enough to be a ghost, so you're not allowed to die. — Kinney

My dad said she tried to sneak into the car. Just so he'd *have* to bring her to the hospital. He caught her, so she's grumpy and still at home. None of the parents want any of the kids on the road. At least not until the morning when the storm is supposed to die down.

FaceTime me when it's not like 3 a.m. Going to bed. Glad you're ok. Love u. — Xander

My brother's texts remind me about what I learned tonight. He's been giving away his pills to the neighborhood kid. A truth that I clutch but can't confront just yet. Not while I'm stuck in this hospital. This is something I need to talk to him about face-to-face. Everyone just assumed Winona and Ben drove to the orchestra hall to protest the auction, so no one knows about Xander.

On my wayyy!! — Luna

I smile at Luna's text. But the call isn't from my siblings. It's from my best friend.

I click *speakerphone* so Farrow can hear. "You all close yet?" I ask Janie. "We're still in terribly slow traffic," she says.

I picture Jane packed in a car with Beckett, Luna, Thatcher, Quinn and Donnelly. All six are headed here from the orchestra hall.

"Be careful," I tell her and shut my eyes for a second, pain radiating down my ribs.

"Updates?" she asks.

I open my eyes and stare at the closed door. "Sulli just got here with all the parents, about a half hour ago. She's with Winona." *In the room across the hall.* I try to squash the guilt because it's my job to protect those girls. Uncle Ryke...has to hate me.

I hate myself for putting her in that much danger. For putting Ben in danger.

"She's fine," Farrow says and reaches for a tin of chocolates on a nearby tray table.

"Her lip is being stitched up," I correct. "She's not fine."

"She'll survive," Farrow says easily.

Jane interjects, "I've already spoken to Sulli."

I try to sit up again, my muscles screaming. So I stop. "Ben is in another room. My dad said his concussion is mild, and I think Charlie is getting surgery on his leg soon—"

"I meant updates about you," Jane says. "I've talked to my brothers and my parents already, too."

I frown, a little hurt. "Tu m'as appelé en dernier?" *You called me last?*

Jane takes an audible breath, upset that I think that. "Not because I wanted to. Your mom said I should give you some time alone with your *one true pairing* before I call."

Farrow is laughing at my mom's wordage.

My neck heats.

Jesus. My mom loving us together plays too damn well into Farrow's hand, and I lose every round when we go head-to-head.

"My mom needs to take it easy," I tell Jane.

". Aunt Lily loves love."

"She can *love* my love ten billion times less in front of my boyfriend. That'd be perfect." I can almost feel Jane smiling on the other end. And I can also feel it fade in the quiet.

"Moffy, please tell me how you are," she whispers and when I don't answer right away, she adds, "I hate that I'm not there yet." In the background, I catch Thatcher saying that he'll take a back route. He must be driving.

I rake my hair with my left hand, which tugs the IV tubes. "I'm still waiting for the surgeon to check the X-Rays."

"You need surgery?"

"I'm not sure—"

"He needs surgery," Farrow cuts in with that matter-of-fact voice, husky but soothing. Gravel tied in silk.

I watch him open the lid to the tin and inspect a chocolate.

I tell him, "There's a *zero* percent chance you know that just by looking."

He unwraps a truffle, and I hone in on how his fingers peel the red foil. Christ. I need to stop being in love with how he moves.

Farrow is smiling a self-satisfied smile. *Beyond* human comprehension. "There's a hundred percent chance I know you fractured your clavicle, wolf scout." He pops the chocolate in his mouth.

I make a face. "Why do you have to call it a *clavicle*?"

He chews slowly, brows rising. "Because that's what it's called."

"It's called a fucking collarbone."

"Man, it's the same exact thing, but only one pisses you off, so I chose that one." His smile stretches as irritation scrunches my face.

Concern encases Jane's voice as she asks, "Is he in pain, Farrow?"

"So much," I answer sarcastically. "Save me, Janie."

"I wasn't asking you," Jane says, very serious. "Farrow? How is he?" She's really worried about me, and I feel badly for teasing.

Farrow unwraps another truffle and instead of sweeping my body for signs of pain, he just holds my gaze. "Maximoff is stubborn. Not a new malady."

I give him a look. "If *stubbornness* is a sickness, then you suffer from it too."

His brows spike. "Never said I didn't, and that's cute that you want me to share your sickness."

Don't smile. "I didn't say that."

"Sure." Keeping his mouth closed, his lips rise as he chews another chocolate.

I am in pain, but he's making me forget what hurts. A perk to having a brain that pretty much cums over his mere presence.

I raise my phone to my mouth. "Jane," I say. "I didn't put you on speakerphone so you'd be more worried. I'm alright."

I can't imagine what crossed her mind when she heard we'd been in a car crash. Two of her brothers, her best friend and her best friend's boyfriend, *and* her little cousin. I can't imagine what any of our family was thinking.

"Have you looked at any news articles about the accident?" she asks.

"Not yet." I've been prolonging that, but I'm sure the crash made headlines. I've actually tried not to check social media too much lately. Not since I've been public with Farrow.

Muffled voices grow louder on Jane's end. "Sorry…hold on, we're solving a mini-directional crisis. Too many people in this car believe they know Philly roads the best."

I keep her on the line, but I let her deal with the directions. And I catch Farrow peeling a third chocolate.

"Are you really going to eat all my chocolate?" I wonder. Aunt Daisy brought the heart-shaped tin as a *get well soon* thing. She says chocolate candy is second best to chocolate cake.

"You can't eat anything before surgery," he reminds me. "I'm doing you a favor. Less temptation, wolf scout." He pops the third one in his mouth.

"It's working. You're making them look disgusting."

"Must be why you keep watching me eat them," he says, one-upping me with absolute ease.

Goddammit. "I wasn't," I lie.

"And there goes your honesty merit badge."

I watch him put aside the tin, and he uncaps a permanent marker with his teeth. His brown eyes flit to the machines next to the bed. Numbers scroll over the screen, lines bounce up and down, and I can barely make sense of it.

But he can.

As quickly as Farrow looked, he's back on course. His large hand runs from my knee down to my ankle, the touch full of hot affection, and he holds my ankle with strength but tenderness that pools warmth inside of me.

Farrow starts scribbling something on top of my left foot.

"That better not say *fuck me*," I tell him.

Farrow stops writing, and his gaze lifts to mine, all humor in his eyes. He blows out the cap from his mouth. "If I were going to write *fuck me*, it wouldn't be on your foot." With another thought, his smile widens in near laughter. "Unless…you want me to fuck your foot."

"Fuck off," I say, about to reclaim my leg, but his grip tightens. That, I like even more.

I crane my neck and catch sight of the scrawled letters.

not this foot

My brows pull together as I stare at him like he's flown to the garbage planet Sakaar. "If I'm even having surgery, you do realize it's nowhere near my foot?"

"Can't be too careful," he says casually and moves onto my calf. "That's rule number one in the Wolf Scout Handbook. In case you've forgotten your own rules." He pulls back to view his handiwork.

not this leg is even bigger.

Dear World, why am I smiling? Best Regards, a smiling human.

"I'm back," Jane says with a giant breath. "So, we have a lot to discuss when I arrive. Like how you were bought by a porn star."

Just as the words *porn star* boom in the air, the door opens to my hospital room—and I'm pretty positive the doctor just heard that.

I'm repping the Hale Curse hard tonight.

I lift the phone to my mouth again. "Jane, the doctor just got here."

"Good luck, old chap."

"À tout à l'heure, ma moitié." *See you soon, my other half.*

I hang up, and I realize Farrow has stopped writing on my leg. His focus drills into the young doctor, and before I can speak, Farrow tells him, "You're in the wrong room."

Farrow knows this doctor.

It's my first thought. The doctor actively disregards Farrow, his attention only on me.

He must be in his late twenties, exceptionally tall with swept-back auburn hair that curls beneath his ears. He looks like he could audition to play Bill Weasley in *Harry Potter*.

You know, the oldest, hottest Weasley.

He's not in scrubs like the ER doctors and nurses I've met tonight. All of which had to sign NDAs. Underneath his white coat, a navy geometric-printed shirt is tucked in charcoal slacks.

I strain my eyes to read the stitching on his coat, but I can only make out the *MD*.

The doctor starts approaching the bed. "I'm Dr..." His voice dies out as Farrow slides my legs off his lap and stands up.

My boyfriend steals the chart out of Bill Weasley's grip. Then he sits on the bed's edge and flips through the clipboard papers like nothing just happened.

Bill Weasley casts a cutting glare at Farrow.

"Maximoff," Farrow says, at ease as he skims my chart, "meet Rowin Hart." He looks directly at me, and he adds, "My ex."

What.

The...

MAXIMOFF HALE

Fuck...?

Farrow's ex is right in front of me. Something that I thought could only happen in an alternate universe. One that I honestly didn't want to visit.

The pain in my collarbone makes way for a foreign feeling. A kind of strange discomfort that wants to twist my face.

"*Dr.* Rowin Hart," Rowin emphasizes to me.

I'm staring at him in a whole new light. He has a hoop cartilage piercing, and as he nears the heart monitor, I spot a tattoo of a star below his earlobe.

This guy just looks *cool.* Cooler than me. Someone that Farrow could and probably would get along with—Christ, I don't even know how long they dated. Do I want to?

My jaw clenches.

Why am I doing this to myself? I'm more than confident and secure in my relationship with Farrow. My mind just won't stop overanalyzing meaningless fucking things that don't matter, that *shouldn't* matter.

Like how *win* is literally in the name *Rowin.*

I know, I know—it's disconcerting. You don't have to tell me twice.

While Rowin reads the machines and Farrow reads the chart, I sit up a lot more, using my good hand to pull my body up against the inclined bed.

Rowin steals the chart back. "I'm genuinely shocked that you didn't tell your celebrity boyfriend about me."

The truth is that I asked Farrow not to give me details. I didn't want them.

Maybe that was a mistake.

I don't know. How can anyone know?

Farrow twirls the marker between his fingers. "I'm not doing this with you, Rowin. You don't get to fish for info about my relationship."

Rowin's dark blue eyes stab Farrow. "You're the one who broke up with me. After a two-year relationship, after I *proposed* to you." *What.* "I can wonder and question why you wouldn't tell your current boyfriend any of that."

Because I asked him not to, I think again, not fast enough to say it out loud. Farrow is already speaking.

"Go ahead and question, wonder," Farrow says, glaring at his ex. "But you're being masochistic as fuck by resurfacing shit from four years ago."

Rowin looks goddamn murderous at this point. "You know it's my thirtieth birthday today?"

Farrow almost rolls his eyes. "Fucking hell—"

"You're the same asshole who can't even fucking regret or apologize—"

"I'm *sorry*," Farrow says as he stands; this argument is giving me whiplash. "I've told you *I'm sorry* seventeen times for hurting you, but you never want to hear it. I will never understand why you want me to rehash that night over and over again and keep rubbing salt in your wounds. To remind me that I'm an asshole? Man, I easily admit I'm one. And I don't regret rejecting your proposal when I would've regretted marrying a guy I didn't love. It's that fucking simple."

Heavy silence blankets the hospital room while Rowin stares fixatedly at the chart in his hands. Trying to squash the emotion that tenses his face.

Farrow slowly sits back down on my bed, grinding his teeth.

I'm suddenly glad that I've never had to deal with an ex. But I can't cheer about being the winner here for never experiencing this massive migraine. Not when someone looks raw and cut open in front of me, like Rowin currently does.

Rowin clicks his pen to jot down stats or something on the chart.

"Happy Birthday, man," I tell Rowin sincerely.

He freezes.

Farrow has his hand over his mouth. I'm not really able to distinguish his expression. It puts me on edge.

I just made things really fucking awkward.

Awesome.

I recover with more confidence and ask, "You two met in med school?"

"Yeah," Farrow answers, his hand dropping to my knee. "But we were put in different residency programs."

Rowin glances briefly at Farrow's hand on me, then he scribbles on the chart. His eyes land on me for a short second. "You're too sweet to be with someone like Farrow."

Farrow rubs my leg. "You'd be surprised how much of a dick Maximoff is."

I laugh, which hurts like hell, pain flaring in my chest. I cough, and both guys hawk-eye the machines that beep a bit louder.

A few more seconds pass.

"You're not doing the surgery," Farrow states plainly to his ex.

"I never planned to. I'm not in a surgical residency anymore." Rowin tucks the chart under his arm.

Farrow frowns. "Your coat says *Orthopedic Surgery*." He motions to the embroidered name and department on the coat pocket.

"I'm getting a new one made." To me, he says, "Dr. Rhee will be in soon to explain the surgery, but in short, he'll attach a metal plate and screws to hold the bones together."

Farrow combs both his hands through his hair. "Wait," he says, "if you're not here for the surgery, then why the hell did you stop by?"

To fuck with Farrow, probably.

Maybe to fuck with me, Farrow's boyfriend, too. But it seems kind of callous. Especially after a car accident.

Rowin faces me, not Farrow, and he tells me, "Dr. Edward Keene has requested that I be your physician after post-op. I wanted to introduce myself before you went into surgery. Any medical or rehab needs, you'll defer to me—"

"What?" My mouth parts, and I almost go to stand up but cords tug. *Dammit.*

I always thought Dr. Keene would eventually refer me to a new physician since he refused to be mine. But Farrow's *ex?* It's underhanded and fucking wrong.

Farrow shakes his head repeatedly, his nose flaring. "My father put you up to this?" he asks Rowin.

"This isn't some sort of conspiracy," Rowin says. "I'm in training to join the Hales, Meadows, and Cobalts' med team."

"*Med team?*" Farrow repeats. "It's never been called that."

"It's what your father called it. Maybe because he's looking to hire beyond the Keene dynasty. He told me that his brother Trip has been on sabbatical for over a year, and Trip's wife, who I believe is a family doctor, wants to take leave to have another child."

I remember Trip's two sons are under seven, and Farrow told me that his uncle is already grooming them for medical school.

Rowin continues, "Your grandfather is retired, so that just leaves your father. And he's understaffed as the famous families grow older. He needs more concierge doctors."

A long pause strains the room.

Farrow rises to his feet. "I hope you know that my father chose you as retaliation against me. You're not his special physician that he picked out of the pack."

"I really don't care why he offered me the job," Rowin says. "The pay is unbelievably high and the hours are better than surgery. Hell, all of the Med-Peds residents and three-quarters of Surgical would've died for this position. It's too rare to pass."

"No," I suddenly say aloud, wincing as I crunch upward. Both guys tell me to stop moving. I glower at Rowin. "*No.*" My voice is firm. "You can't be my concierge doctor. You can be anyone else's in my family, but not mine."

Farrow's ex is not prying into my medical history.

And if he already has, I don't want to know.

"That's fine," Rowin agrees. "I'm not sure who you want to replace me, but hopefully you'll find someone because you need PT after surgery." He inches backwards, barely glances at Farrow, and he tells me, "If you'll excuse me, I need to go check on your cousins."

Rowin leaves.

The door clicks shut, and Farrow remains standing but turns to face me. His eyes carry more apologies than usual.

I bend my knees so he can sit down. "I can remove Rowin from whatever med team there is if you want."

"Don't worry about that. I don't care enough about Rowin to get him fired." Farrow doesn't take a seat yet, but he rests a knee on the firm mattress. His gaze never drifts off mine. "I'm sorry that I didn't tell you about him—"

"I asked you not to, Farrow." I gesture to his chest with my good hand. "It's not a big fucking deal."

"Okay, but if I had known you'd ever meet Rowin, I would've told you about him and how he proposed. I didn't want to blindside you, ever."

I inhale, trying not to smile. "Maybe I can try to accept your apology."

"*Maybe,*" he repeats like I'm full of shit and I've already scribbled hearts around M + F in my diary. Just so you know, I don't have a diary. And if I did…Farrow would be all over it.

He places the chocolate tin on the tray table, and I watch him pick my philosophy paperback off the bed.

I try to open and close the hand that sticks out of my sling, and my brain must short-circuit because I say without thinking, "Your ship name with Rowin is literally *FarRow.*"

Farrow goes still, the paperback rolled in his hand. His brows slowly rise at me. "Wolf scout, there is no 'ship name' between me and Dr. Fart."

I laugh once, a pain stabbing my ribs. I shut my eyes, and when I open them, Farrow is closer, checking an IV tube.

He glances down at me. "How long have you been obsessing?"

I hate that I'm confined to this bed and I can't stand at eye level with him. "Since you uttered the word *ex*," I say, not denying the truth. "He has a tattoo—"

"Stop."

"And a cartilage piercing—"

"Maximoff."

"He's not unattractive—"

"Trust me, wolf scout. You're much *much* hotter."

"Thank you, I know," I say confidently.

The corner of his lip pulls upward. "I love when Cocky Maximoff comes out for me."

I'm about to say it's not for him, but another annoying thought hits me. "He's a doctor."

Farrow whistles. "Your perception is something."

I lean my head back on the hard pillow, staring up at the ceiling, then the wall. "You two fucked in the hospital a lot, like they do on TV?" The worst mental image of Farrow and Rowin pops into my head. "In the…what do they call it?"

That room thing.

With the bed. Where all the doctors crash between shifts. I picture that. My overactive imagination puts my boyfriend's mouth passionately up against another guy's mouth; and maybe it'd be a turn-on for some people, but it just knots my stomach—

"*Maximoff.*"

I blink awake to his fingers snapping at my eyes, his hand on the pillow next to my jaw. Leaning over me, his knee on the bed.

Fuck. I rake my hair back.

Farrow stares at me strongly. "Stop torturing yourself, man."

"The on-call room," I mutter as the answer suddenly reaches me.

His hand encases the sharp lines of my cheekbone and jaw. Fully. Securely. His gaze dives deep and touches every damn part of who I am. "I love you, Maximoff," he says. "And I know you overthink because that's what you do, and this is new for you. But I love *you*. And I know it fucking hurts to see someone from my past because it fucking hurt when I went through your NDAs. So if you need me to tell you five-thousand times, a million, that I'm so fucking in love with you, I will."

I don't need it; the offer alone caresses and overflows me. I cup the base of his skull and breathe, "Just kiss—" Our mouths are already colliding.

The aggression arouses each synapses of my brain. I grip his hair in between starved fingers, and his clutch tightens on my face. I break apart his lips with my tongue. Deeper, I try to draw forward, but Farrow lowers so I won't move my chest.

And he slows the kiss to a scorching, unhurried pace that pricks my fucking nerves with hazardous voltage. Our heavy, husky breaths meld. He bites my lip, and a deep groan inches its way up my throat.

Farrow mutters a rough *fuck* after I run my tongue against his tongue.

My sore muscles strain, but I only crave him closer.

Nearer.

I try to shift my dominant hand—it jerks in the sling, and I turn my head, ripping our mouths apart. Pain annihilates my whole right side. "*Fuck*." I clench my teeth.

Farrow eases his knee off the bed. Backing up slightly from me.

Not what I want.

I hunger to thrust my hips upward, for his hips to thrust down on me. Until hard cock grinds on hard cock, and a rough, wild and crushing kiss leads to wrestling. Pushing and pulling. Until we're one tangled mess of muscle and bone dying to come.

All of that feels out of reach with this injury.

I look at him. He's already studying my body. My lips sting, and I want that force to return. Thinking he's afraid to hurt me, I say, "That was my fault."

"It was," he agrees easily.

"I meant it was your fault," I backtrack as irritation nips at me.

Farrow smiles like he's already beat me and raced miles ahead. "See, I would've never touched your right hand even if you blindfolded me. And I'm a doctor. I know which parts of you are off limits. So technically, if you feel a sharp pain, it's your fault."

Everything he just said…stirs my cock. My blood rushes downward, and the *beep beep* of the heart rate monitor suddenly accelerates to *beepbeep beepbeep beepbeep*.

Fuuuck.

Farrow laughs hard.

"Shut up." I growl out my frustration and rub my face with my left hand. Alright, new plan. Focus on other shit besides sex.

I remember what Rowin said about Dr. Keene offering him a concierge job.

"You want to talk about your father?" I ask him seriously.

His laughter dies, and he shakes his head and nears me again. "There's nothing to say. He may not be an evil bastard stalking you, but he's still nothing to me. That's the truth."

I wish that Dr. Keene fought for Farrow. Not because his son is a great doctor but because that's his son. I can understand why Farrow stopped talking to him and why they have no real relationship. He only values Farrow's talent, not who he is.

Farrow towers above me, and I follow his tattooed fingers that graze my neck before retying the loose strings of my hospital gown.

"I thought you wanted me naked," I joke, but I can't mask the real disappointment in my voice.

His mouth edges upward. His cool confidence overpowers the room. Intoxicating. "Do you want me to blow you?" he asks huskily.

I open my mouth to speak, but arousal swells my dick. I stiffen and an army of rules bears on me. "We're in a hospital."

He lets out another whistle. "Again, your perception today—"

"You're not worried someone might walk in?" I try to gesture to his chest with my *bad* hand. I grimace, but thankfully, he's not coddling me.

Farrow smiles wide and rests his knee back on the bed. "I don't worry as much as you about anything."

He does worry about my safety more than me, but I don't point that out because his amusement is full-blown. "I'm not a prude," I retort.

"I didn't say you were," he says, but he's still staring at me like I'm the "purest" twenty-two-year-old human on this planet.

My left hand rubs my exposed thigh, wanting to dip under the blue fabric and touch my shaft. "*Tattooed Boyfriend Gives Maximoff Hale Hospital Blowie*—you like that fucking headline?"

He tilts his head, considering for half a second. "Eh, it could use an adjective or two. *Best, Greatest, Most Earth-Shattering Blow*—"

"Alright," I say, pent up and needing friction. I would pull him against me if I could, but I have to settle with my commanding, unflinching voice. "Suck my cock."

His chest collapses in arousal, but he ends up smiling. "You want me to suck your cock?"

I start to really harden. "Not if you keep teasing me."

Farrow rubs his bottom lip with the hoop piercing and eyes the length of my body in a hot wave. He only has three piercings in right now: his lip, a silver hoop for his nose, and an obsidian spear earring that dangles. That last one was a Christmas present from me.

"Farrow—"

"Don't sit up," he tells me. I started drawing upward in a crunch, and I lie back against the inclined bed.

He leaves my side and puts his knee next to my leg. In one swift movement, his other knee is on the mattress. I already lie above the sheets.

I tent my legs and spread them a bit more. Just so he can… "Come closer."

Farrow grips my kneecap. "Okay, Bossy, here's how this works." He plants a blazing kiss on the outside of my knee, his mouth ascending my leg, towards my exposed thigh. "You get *one* free blowjob for almost dying. But after that, you need to pull your weight."

Pull my weight. Meaning, mutual ejaculation. We always both come unless we run out of time. Then we fight to be the one to shoot a load. Usually by flipping a coin.

That won't change.

And this...

This is why I love the fuck out of him. Why he just fits with me. He's not giving me any slack or reprieves for being hurt—except for one blowjob. I like that push-and-pull and to work for that affection. Not just someone lying down and offering themselves to me.

I also love giving head. And he'd say he loves giving it more than me.

His mouth brushes my flesh, his eyes on my eyes. "You're smiling."

I feel my grin. "What can I say? Assholes turn me on. Metaphorical and literal."

"Me too." His broad hand slides down my other leg. "Only I love the tight-laced assholes. Metaphorical and literal."

Fuck me.

I lean back, my muscles contracting. The sheer idea of Farrow's mouth wrapped around me in a hospital room makes me come undone. He's my boyfriend, and there's no NDA needed, no pre-planning or precautions. No worry that he'll steal my clothes or my phone.

Public sex was never anything I could indulge in, and now...

His hand drives towards the hem of the hospital gown while his mouth works up my other thigh. His lips trace the faint scar from a four-year-old wound. A cut that he stitched.

As his eyes flit to me, I see that long-ago memory in them. Where he was twenty-four.

I was nineteen. At Harvard. Struggling. And he made my life easier, better—he was a comfort that I couldn't quite grasp until I let myself. Until he let me.

Now he's twenty-eight and on his knees for me. I know, I know, his mouth should be around my cock by now.

"Stop teasing, man," I say in a heavy breath.

Farrow lifts his head, his earring swaying, and he slowly, slowly—agonizingly slow—rolls up the thin blue fabric. Stopping short of my rock-hard erection.

I groan. "*Farrow*." I rub my thigh, trying not to give myself a hand job when his mouth is better.

Farrow nips my thigh with his teeth. Heat blisters in my veins, and high-speed mechanical beeping pitches the air.

His eyes meet mine again.

We're both highly aware that we were just in a car crash together. Where I broke my collarbone. And I'm in a sling and hooked up to a fucking machine.

But maybe that's why this is happening.

Because we need the distraction. Because being with each other, right now, feels like the calm inside a storm. Sometimes it's just nice to feel good.

And sex—it feels really damn good.

Farrow frees my dick, wrapping his tattooed hand around me, and his tongue laps up pre-cum that drips off the tip—*fuck*.

I buck towards him, and he pulls back, a smile playing at his lips.

"Easy," he tells me coolly. Like I'm too eager.

Goddamn. I root my left hand to the back of his head, my fingers lost in his dyed hair. "You're a giant cock tease," I tell him.

"And you love getting your cock teased." *Yes.*

"Maybe," I say flatly.

His pleasured eyes undress me. He squeezes my balls, and my legs spasm, my body almost shuddering.

Holy fuck. My eyes tighten as arousal amasses, aching for harder pressure.

Strands of hair fall to his lashes as he lowers his mouth again. He fists the base and sucks me in an up-and-down melodic rhythm. The friction tempts my eyes to roll backwards.

I narrow my gaze, breathing hard through my nose. *Jesus Christ.*

He takes all of me to the back of his throat. Sucking deep and hard. Electrifying sensations build up towards a shockwave.

Beepbeepbeepbeepbeepbeep.

"Kiss me," I suddenly say.

Farrow breaks his intense rhythm and stretches over my body. Careful not to touch my chest. He holds my jaw, and I kiss him roughly, our mouths crushing together. He grips my shaft with a firm hand, rubbing me with perfect force.

To deepen the kiss, I tug forward—

"Dammit," I wince, pain nailing my ribs.

Farrow looks more concerned, but he's still jerking me off. He's a keeper. I mean that seriously. "Lean back, Maximoff."

I do.

"Relax. I know you're obsessed with me, but try not to jump my bones."

I'm nearing a nerve-scalding edge. So all I can get out is a non-threatening, "Fuck you." My narrowed eyes drill into the ceiling as he sucks me off again.

"*Fuck*," I growl into a low groan. *Fuuuck.* I lose concentration between the pressure his mouth wields and his grip on my balls.

I lose thought, and my eyes roll.

My waist arches, and I release against the back of his throat. Muscles burning, I ride the peak, and he milks my climax with his tongue and hand.

My head lightens for a bit, a good kind of dizzy, and as I come down, he rolls the blue fabric back to my thighs and wipes his mouth with the sheet.

"Can you come closer?" I ask in a deep whisper. I ache to hug him. To wrap both of my arms around Farrow. For his arms to wrap around me even tighter, stronger, and none of that is possible with my fucked-up shoulder.

"Put your legs down," Farrow breathes.

I lower them flat to the hospital bed.

Farrow nears and then rests his knees beside each of my quads. Straddling my lap without lowering his weight. He leans in, gripping the top of the hospital bed.

I live my life for most of the world to see—for you to see—but there are a lot of moments just meant for him. And this is one.

We look into each other, and the toll of tonight catches up to us. How much he had to stay calm under pressure. How he's depended on by security, how I'm the rock of my family—and sometimes, *sometimes* it hurts. Emotion pours over his face, my face. His eyes reddening, mine burning, and I slide my good arm across his shoulders.

Dying to bring him against my chest. *I can't.*

I can't. I hate that I can't.

"I want to hold you," I breathe.

His forehead almost touches mine, our lips nearly skimming as he whispers, "You're holding me." His husky voice quakes, his hand clutching my jaw. "And my arms are tight around you, and your chest is against my chest."

Tears scald our eyes, and we breathe and breathe, and I whisper, "You know, my heart is in your hand."

His lips are agonizingly close. "I hope not. Because then you'd be dead." He kisses me before I react. Just one tender kiss, leaving me longing for more.

My good hand rises to the back of his neck, our breaths slowing together. I murmur, "Cicero said, *'The life of the dead is placed on the memories of the living. The love you gave in life keeps people alive beyond their time.'*"

Farrow almost smiles. "That one is just okay."

I eye him. "What's your favorite then?" I'm sure he can recall whatever he fucking *skimmed*.

He leans closer, kisses me—and I kiss back stronger, my lips swelling beneath the pressure. Until he has to pull away so I won't fuck up my shoulder.

His chest rises and falls heavily, his thumb stroking my cheekbone, and he finally tells me, "Dum spiro, spero."

I circled that phrase in my paperback. I know he took Latin in college, but I ask anyway, "You know what that means—"

"*'While I breathe,'*" he translates, "*'I hope.'*"

It overwhelms me.

Hope.

Him.

Love.

Pain.

I inch closer, but a knock sounds at the door. We both rub our wet faces, and as our bloodshot eyes meet again, I know and he knows that what we share is greater and stronger than whatever the world has to throw at us.

We won't end here.

9

MAXIMOFF HALE

Anesthesia fogs me, especially after my surgery. I can't recall how I ended up back at my townhouse. Maybe I apparated or a teleportation power kicked in. I do know that I slept most of the day.

At 7:56 p.m., I'm more coherent, but I'm sweating.

I kick down my orange comforter. A red sling braces my right arm to my chest, mostly secured by a cross-body strap and a wide band velcroed around my upper abdomen.

Noise booms from downstairs. Music mixed with tons of chatter— it echoes off the brick walls of my small attic bedroom, but I'm alone up here.

I sit up more—the room spins three-sixty-degrees. So damn lightheaded. Breathing through my nose, I move to the edge of the bed. My bare feet hit the floorboards, but I don't stand.

Dear World, you should know this is the worst pain I've ever felt. Worst Regards, a pained human.

Every muscle screams at me, sore from the crash. But sharp stabbing radiates in my shoulder.

I've broken my ribs before, and I had a minor ankle fracture when I was thirteen, sliced my palm pretty badly on a rock, and I've torn my hamstring.

None of those required a metal plate and screws. None of those immobilized me this badly. I want my shirt off, the white fabric drenched in sweat.

So I reach back and try to unwrap the sling's band. I'm struggling when the door opens.

My mouth falls. "Your hair."

Farrow subconsciously combs his inked fingers through *bleach-white* strands which contrast his brown eyebrows. He looks beyond fucking sexy. His Third Eye Blind V-neck molds his muscles and reveals his neck, throat and chest tattoos. Black pants fit snug on his legs and package.

And I'm sitting on the edge of my bed. Sweating my ass off.

But I also notice the concern that grips his eyes while he studies me.

"I just dyed it," Farrow explains, kicking the door shut and drowning out the downstairs commotion. "You're breaking a rule."

"What rule?" I ask as he nears me.

His brows ratchet up. "You're not supposed to take your sling off for four to six weeks." Off my confusion, he realizes, "You didn't hear the post-op instructions."

I want to combat him, but I'm in too much pain. "A lot is hazy. I gotta get out of this shirt," I tell my boyfriend, slowly rising to my feet. I'm unsteady—Farrow reaches me, his sturdy hand on my waist.

We're practically eye level.

"Let me," he says, his tone like rough sex.

I watch him reach behind my back and detach the band. Gently, he slips the strap off my neck. My pulse thumps, and I'm a billion times hotter.

I'm not even protesting and saying *I can do it myself.* Right now, I need him.

Farrow helps me take my arms out of my shirt and fills in the hazy pieces of my memory. "You can't pull, lift, or stretch with your right arm for about eight weeks. Stretch rehab starts after that. In three months, you can add strength exercises."

Three months.

That seems like forever without full mobility and swimming. Butterfly stroke requires total range of motion on *both* shoulders.

"Christ," I mutter, and I try to pull my shirt over my head, my gray drawstring pants low on my hips. "What else did I miss?"

He frees me of my soaked shirt. "You were groggy after you woke up from surgery, and your dad asked you how you were." Farrow tosses my shirt aside and starts carefully reattaching the band around my bruised abs.

I'm hanging on his every word, and he notices. He's irritatingly drawing this out.

"What the fuck did I say?" I have to ask.

Farrow is close to laughter. "You told your dad you're naming your son Batman."

My eyes pop out of my head. "No I didn't." He has to be fucking with me.

"Yeah, you did," Farrow smiles wide. "Your dad asked you, *what son?* And you said the one in the Batmobile."

I blink slowly. "I killed my dad. He's dead, right? Death by Batman talk." *I'm* dying right now because the one time Farrow and I have spoken about our future like marriage and kids—it was last night. When I was lying beside the wreckage. And we haven't resurfaced what Farrow told me in the rain.

Except my anesthesia-brain decided to talk about a fictional *kid* named Batman. Of all damn things.

I feel like I'm bathing in a broiler.

"Your dad is alive," Farrow says easily, "but he said your son sounds like a little prick."

I nod stiffly. "That's definitely something my dad would say about a kid named Batman."

"I think you mean *your* kid," he corrects.

"No," I shake my head. "I wouldn't name my kid Batman. Can't be mine." I attempt to retie my drawstring pants with one hand. They slip way too low on my waist. I struggle to get the job done.

My pulse is beating out of my chest in his silence.

Farrow takes the strings from me, stepping closer. "That's good because that couldn't have been mine either."

I lick my lips, a smile trying to pull my mouth. I nod stronger, and we're looking at each other more deeply. His fingers are perilously close to my dick, and he knots the strings.

Any other time, I'd ache for those fingers to go lower. But right now, I cringe at the sensation in my collarbone. Like a knife is staking me on repeat.

"What's your pain level?" Farrow asks.

"Zero," I joke. "I feel absolutely amazing. Like I body-swapped with an angel." I force a smile.

"You look like shit," he tells me and puts a hand to my damp forehead. His other hand falls to my ass.

I make a face. "Pretty sure I look gorgeous, bangable, like *hot* shit."

He rolls his eyes. "Okay, smartass. You sure you don't want Vicodin or Oxy? Because ibuprofen isn't cutting it."

"I'm alright," I say more seriously. "I can handle it." With a family history of addiction, I don't want to mess with any addictive painkillers. It's a personal choice that my dad and my uncle have made before. Though, I'm weighing my sanity because this isn't a cakewalk.

Farrow combs his hand through his hair again. "Truthfully, I hate seeing you in this much pain. You understand that's why you're sweating?"

I nod a couple times. "But it's also hot in the attic."

Farrow reluctantly pulls away from me. Just to reach the thermostat attached to the brick wall. Near my dresser.

I sink down on the bed. With my right arm imprisoned to my chest, I use my left to scoot back against the headboard. Gauze is taped to my right collarbone, and I haven't peeled it back to check the stitches yet.

I'm about to ask about my cousins and my siblings, but I hear the old stairs creaking. People are coming up here.

Farrow nears the bed. "I'm going to get a fan and an ice pack. Need anything else, wolf scout?"

He's the only one who really ever asks me that. But I can't forget how he was in the crash too. How he had to talk to a porn star at the auction, how he apparently sold his *motorcycle* for me, how he's given me so *damn* much—and he deserves every good thing.

"I'm alright," I say. "You need anything?"

Farrow smiles at me like I stole his line, but he rubs his bottom lip with his thumb and tells me, "For right now, I'm good. No one's crying, no one's dying."

Life moves on.

I nod, and he walks backwards and taps the doorframe like he'd rather stay longer. But he turns and leaves. From the stairwell, I hear Farrow say, "Walrus, you little bastard."

Not long after, a calico cat darts into the attic and leaps onto my bed. Walrus nudges my foot with his furry head, but I can't reach out to scratch him—I look up at a noise.

Charlie raps the doorframe with his crutch. Music still booms downstairs, so I'm assuming more family must be hanging out at my townhouse.

"Hey," I say, surprised to see him. But the Charlie Cobalt Disappearing Act has been dying down since the FanCon. "How's the leg?"

Charlie supports his weight on both crutches and comes closer. His entire right leg is bound in a white cast, and he rolled his sweats to his thigh.

I seriously can't remember the last time I've seen Charlie in sweatpants.

"I don't know," Charlie answers and lowers on my bed. Sitting near me, he leans his crutches on my end table. "I'm too high to feel anything." He scans my black and blue abs, sweat beaded up on my skin.

"I'm okay," I tell him.

"Swallow a Vicodin, Moffy. There is a list of weak people in our families who'd drown in a craving, and you're not one of them."

I tense at that backhanded compliment. He just called my parents weak and whoever else he's pinpointed as vulnerable to addiction. I shake my head on instinct.

Charlie arches a mocking brow. "The world will still see you as noble and gallant if you take a painkiller."

I let out a laugh. "Christ, Charlie. This isn't me being performative. I'm not trying to gain sympathy or kudos. You have no fucking clue how afraid I am..." I trail off and sit up a bit more, grimacing. Hating that my right hand is restricted.

Charlie said that I'm not on his list of *weak people*. But I don't know if I am strong enough to beat a craving. And I don't want to find out. My dad and my uncle have made the same decision as me with painkillers.

Alcoholism runs in the Hale and Meadows families. You know that. Everyone knows that.

My dad has lectured me about addiction my entire goddamn life, and I'm terrified to awaken that monster inside of me. It's been dormant for twenty-two years.

Charlie stares up at the ceiling rafters, tiny lights wound around the beams. "For almost anyone else, your choice would be a smart one. For you, it's stupid."

"Thank you," I say sharply. I'm not sure he'll ever understand me fully. I like to be in control, and that's partly why I'm so afraid of an addiction. Of this monstrous thing controlling me.

Walrus hops on his lap, and Charlie strokes the cat. "You're stupid and you're strong."

I give him a look. "Who are you?"

"I am a fractured leg," he says. "And I'm drugged." He plants a hand on the bed to keep from sliding off the edge. "I didn't come here to chat about Vicodin." Charlie lowers his voice. "I wanted to see how you were doing with the whole Xander situation."

The Xander situation.

My lungs burn, and he doesn't break eye contact from me. I don't see empathy staring back, but I know he's not asking out of some sort of sick curiosity or to stir up trouble. He wouldn't do that. Not when it's about my brother.

"Why do you care?" I just straight out ask.

He opens his mouth and then closes it, rethinking something. He shakes his head and says, "I don't understand what it's like to be so desperate for friendships that I'd give my pills away, just so people can like me."

I want to curse him out, but I'm doing this new thing with Charlie, where I let him talk. Where I wait.

After a short pause, he continues, "But I do understand what it's like to be a big brother, and your position isn't enviable." He angles his head. "If you want to talk it through…"

"Okay," I say, not hesitating.

His lips part, shocked.

I reach for my half empty water bottle next to my bedside clock. I accidentally knock over one of his crutches.

Charlie lets it clatter to the floor. "You really want my advice?" he reaffirms. "Or at the end of all of this, are you just going to tell me how I can't relate because my baby brother is only four years younger than me, and yours is seven years younger than you?"

"Charlie, I wasn't even thinking that," I tell him. I've always valued his opinion, but sometimes it comes after running through barbed wire and dodging explosives. I'm not always equipped for that kind of obstacle course.

I try to unscrew the water bottle cap with one hand.

Charlie watches me struggle and asks, "Are you going to tell your parents?"

I've thought that through about a billion times. My mom and dad know that my siblings and I keep some shit just between us. In fact, they like that we all have a close bond, but this is big. And I'm unsure if it'd be worse for Xander, if I let them know. Plus, it'd kill my dad… my mom, and I know they're strong, but maybe it's better if I just talk to my brother and get him to stop without involving them.

"I haven't decided," I admit. Then I wonder, "If it were your brother, would you tell your parents?"

"No." It's a direct and flat *no*. It leaves more questions than answers.

"That's it?" I ask. "It's that easy?" Why am I struggling with this then? There's a right and wrong path here, and I don't want to take the one that leaves more wreckage.

He sighs heavily like I'm slow to catch on. "You tell your parents, and it'll travel to my parents and then reach Aunt Daisy and Uncle Ryke's ears. You have the six of them involved, and it'll proliferate into a bigger mess for Xander." His yellow-green eyes puncture me. "It's just a conversation with him, right? He loves you. That's why he calls you every day. Talk to him. He'll listen to you. Everyone in this family does."

I hear the bite on that last comment.

He makes everything seem so easy.

Maybe it is. Maybe I'm just overthinking.

"Not everyone listens to me, by the way," I tell him.

He barely blinks. "I'd listen if you had better things to say."

I shake my head and finally unscrew the bottle cap—my hand slips and I spill water all over my bare chest and sling. "*Fuck*," I curse, picking up the bottle fast. I mop up my wet chest with the comforter. The cold water actually feels good on my hot skin.

Charlie watches for a short beat before eyeing the door. "Seeing you struggle isn't as entertaining as I thought it'd be."

"Thanks?" I chug what's left of my water. A teeny tiny sip.

Stairs creak.

Quickly, Charlie says, "I won't be heartbroken if you don't take my advice. It's there for you to stupidly ignore if you wish."

"Good talk," I tell him dryly and pat his hard cast. This wasn't a particular painful conversation. Progress?

But he also called me stupid today.

So, *slow* progress.

Walrus skips across Charlie's lap as my old door squeaks. Being pushed wider open, Beckett emerges and carries two rolled air mattresses that need inflating. My twenty-year-old cousin makes lugging hefty objects look beyond graceful.

He practically glides into my room. Black cotton pants are tied low on his waist, and arm tattoos peek out of his Carraways band tee.

"You look bad," Beckett instantly tells me.

"I feel great," I say sarcastically. "How are you doing with the auction?" I learned from Jane that another of our grandmother's socialite friends won Beckett, and even Charlie, who was bid on without being present.

Beckett drops the air mattresses. "I deal with Grandmother Calloway's crotchety friends at the ballet almost every week. I can fake nice for a night."

"I can't," Charlie admits.

Beckett passes his twin brother the fallen crutch, and Charlie hoists himself off my bed with both crutches. The mattress undulates without his weight, and a shrill pang stabs my shoulder and ribs. I shut my eyes tightly and clench my teeth. Breathing hard through my nose.

"He looks extraordinarily awful."

"The fucking worst."

Those aren't the Cobalt brothers. I open one eye to see pajama-clad Jane and Sulli. Standing at the foot of my bed, they cradle pastel beanbags, pillows, and fuzzy blankets. Charlie and Beckett flank the girls. All four staring at me. Sympathetically. Charlie, more so pityingly.

I've had every teenager, every kid in the family, make me promise that I wouldn't die on them. These four are the ones that see me less like Captain America and more like an imperfect human.

I need them in my world.

I can admit that.

"I'm alive," I say with a sharp breath.

"Sadly," Charlie quips.

"*Charlie*," they all chastise.

A pretentiously coy grin plays at his lips. "Only joking."

Jane hones in on my bruises. "No wonder Farrow was so quiet," she mutters, setting down the sleepover loot. I figure they all plan to crash in the attic. When we were kids, we'd pop out sleeping bags and air mattresses and spend the night at each other's houses.

My brows knit. "Farrow was quiet?"

"He spoke to me." Beckett plugs in an air mattress.

"Only because you were being a fucking ass," Sulli tells her best friend, and then she pats my foot consolingly, a turquoise blanket slipping from the heap she holds.

"What'd you say to Farrow?" I ask Beckett, my shoulders constrict and that *hurts* like a thousand pitchforks poking my bone. I wipe my perspiring forehead with the heel of my palm.

"I thanked him for helping Ben, Winona, Charlie, and you in the crash, and then I said if he has anymore exes that *you* should know about, you deserve full transparency."

I groan. "Beck." I'm not surprised everyone knows about Rowin Hart. He was introducing himself to our families at the hospital.

"You do need transparency, Moffy. Farrow knows everything about you—"

"I know *every* goddamn thing about Farrow that I need to know." I understand that Beckett is protective because I'm the first to be in a relationship—the first to combat these strange dynamics since we're strangely famous—but he can't keep shitting on my boyfriend. Farrow has been through enough. "I don't want the names of his other exes, Beckett. If I asked, he'd tell me. Give Farrow a fucking break."

Charlie leans against my dresser. "He said he thanked your boyfriend."

"Great," I say, "and what did Farrow say in return?"

Beckett bends down to plug in the air mattress. "He told me to get the fuck out of his relationship."

"His *boyfriend* almost fucking *died*," Sulli tells Beckett, helping him spread the air mattress out. "You're lucky he didn't deck you in the face."

Beckett fiddles with my old outlet. "I'm willing to take a punch for Moffy. And for you and the rest of our family."

Sulli slugs his arm hard, but playful.

He pushes her back, smiling.

I watch Jane tie her hair in a low pony, and she brings a tin of chocolate turtles to me. "You must be starving. You haven't eaten since yesterday."

"I'm not." I cringe, no appetite from anesthesia and now pain. Nausea roils deep, and I try to ignore the queasiness. Having my family here helps.

She carefully crawls on the bed beside me, dressed in baby blue coffee-print grannie jammies. I lean into my best friend and whisper about Xander, not able to keep this in. Not from her. She doesn't ask for more details, just nods and listens.

"Uh, cumbuckets." Sulli just banged her elbow on the dresser, trying to inflate the air mattresses. I need to text Farrow to let him know that Omega can join us up here. If they want. It's been a long, exhausting day. And we've gone through some shit together.

My phone is lost in my sheets.

Fuck.

"What are you looking for?" Jane asks, wanting to help, but a black cat hops on the dresser behind Charlie. If there's anything that can steal Jane Cobalt's attention from family—it's her cats.

Purring, Lady Macbeth collapses and rolls on her back. "She's slow and old," Charlie says to Jane. "I'd give her two more years maximum."

Jane looks murderous.

"Charlie," I snap.

"*Lady Macbeth*, come here, my love," Jane says quickly, trying to cajole the cat away from Charlie. The cat looks up at the ceiling.

"And she's deaf," Charlie notes.

"She's most definitely not. Wait and see." Jane leaves my bed to prove her point, and the stairs creak—I'm hoping to see that tatted guy breach the doorway.

Instead, my gangly little sister stumbles in. She wobbles like she's fueled on energy drinks and sleeplessness from writing fics.

"You okay?" I ask Luna, her *Metallica* T-shirt stained with paint and glitter.

"Yeahyeahyeah." She almost trips over Beckett. "Sorrysorry."

"You're fine," he says, watching as she careens towards my bed.

I sit up like I can stupidly help. Pain explodes in my chest, *fucking Christ.* I grind hard on my teeth.

Both Sulli and Jane react fast and catch my sister's hands on either side, stopping her from collapsing on the bed and bouncing the mattress.

Sulli lets go of Luna's hand as Jane twirls her in a dance move. Luna wobbles and outstretches her arms. "Whoa," my sister says.

"Are you drunk?" Charlie asks outright.

"I had a Four Loko." Green marker scribble runs down her arms and stains her cheeks. Her light brown hair is a matted mess. "The world is spinning."

I'm not used to Luna drinking beer or liquor. At all. But I've never seen her exceed one drink. Sometimes I hate that I'm so fixated on alcohol, but it's always in my face. Always brought to my attention by the media, by my family history, and I just can't ignore it.

What's even in a Four Loko? Is that a beer?

I try to crack a knuckle—realizing, I can't even do *that* without the use of my right hand. "You're not going out, are you?"

"Nopity." Luna drifts to the windowsill. "I'm home for the night. Per Farrow's request."

So my boyfriend hasn't been completely quiet. It's clear he's had some conversations with my family while I was asleep. It makes me feel like I was awake. Like someone grabbed my wheel and steered. Keeping everything upright when I couldn't move.

I feel myself start to smile.

"Maximoff and Farrow!! Sitting in a tree!" someone yells from outside my window on the Philly street. "K-I-S-S—" Giggling erupts outside.

"How many times does that happen?" Beckett asks, giving the window a *what the fuck* face.

"Every single night," I answer with indifference.

I'm trying my best not to let this fact grate on me. The public enthusiasm surrounding my relationship is a product of fame, and I don't want to be irritated that people shout at my window. But this involves Farrow, so it's harder to let go.

Beckett glances at Charlie. "Remind me to never fall in love."

He grins. "Already in my calendar for the rest of your life."

Luna sinks down on the windowsill. "So...maybe I'll fall head-over-heels and out-of-orbit for my date next week."

The air strains. Everyone is staring at my sister like she's actually flown into another fucking galaxy.

My gaze sets sternly. "By date, do you mean the auction, and by auction, do you mean that sixty-year-old man who bid on you?"

Luna burps into her fist. "Yep."

"*No*," I snap, a different kind of pain clawing my muscles.

"It's not a *date*, Luna," Jane says, the black cat cradled contently in her arms. "It's simply an obligatory function where you don't need to even speak. It can be a silent hour."

"We don't know how long it'll be," Charlie corrects. "It could last till morning."

My sister has her eyes set on me. "So if you're going three-fourths Loren Hale right now, I should expect a pretty harsh reaction from him?" Luna asks.

I'm completely rigid, my jaw sharpened. "Yeah, don't call it a date around Dad." Jesus. What am I doing with this fucked-up auction? Why am I letting Ernest Mangold control my sister's fate? It's all wrong. It's all cursed.

The porn star—*fuck that*.

Fuck this.

"Moffy." Luna stands, clutching the curtains to steady herself. "I retract my statement. Notta date. Just a meeting. Like a business thing." She tilts her head. "Better?"

"I don't know," I say. I lean back, my mind still reeling. None of this is okay. It's not, but I need time to think about the auction. Right now, my pain has taken the front seat, and I need to find my fucking phone.

10

FARROW KEENE

"Shotgun him," Donnelly suggests to me, his

ratty Van Halen shirt almost a decade old. That blue-eyed shameless motherfucker leans on the stove of the cramped kitchen.

We're in the famous one's townhouse. Oscar digs through the cupboard for snacks, listening to this conversation take a turn.

"I'm not smoking out my boyfriend." I spin a butter knife between my fingers. "*A.* weed makes him sick and *B.* he's Maximoff." I'm sitting on the counter next to melting ice packs, a thermometer, and a portable fan, waiting for a bagel to toast.

Mostly, I'm giving Maximoff alone time with his family. I'll be up there soon.

Donnelly adjusts his septum piercing. "*A.* edibles made him sick. We aren't sure about smoking. I gotta jawn in my pocket." His lilt is thick on *jawn,* a word which means just about anything in Philly, but Donnelly uses it mostly for *blunt.* "*B.* he's Maximoff in Pain with a capital P."

I chew Winterfresh, actually and truly considering Donnelly's pitch to resolve Maximoff's distress.

Oscar notices. "Boyfriend is in that much pain that you're taking advice from *Donnelly*?" he asks with wide eyes, tearing open a bag of pretzels.

I pop a bubble in my mouth. "Let's put it this way: I wouldn't be surprised if he pukes in thirty minutes."

It's killing me to see Maximoff in this kind of agonizing pain, and I don't know how to relieve it. Other than making him more comfortable and distracting him.

Neither of which can come close to easing fractured ribs, a surgical operation on his collarbone, and internal bruising. I didn't sustain any injuries, and my body is extremely fucking sore and my muscles are shot.

I feel like I've been in a boxing ring fighting and grappling for thirty days in a row. Nonstop.

Oscar digs into the pretzels. "He does have a high pain tolerance though. Ever seen that episode of *We Are Calloway* where he breaks his ankle? Maximoff walked on it for what...*five* miles? Didn't even break a sweat."

I've seen that episode. "He's breaking a sweat now," I say easily, but that fact wedges like a pit in my ribs. My bagel pops, and I grab it from the toaster.

"We hotbox the attic," Donnelly offers, tugging open the fridge.

I slowly chew my gum. "Man, that entails getting all the famous ones high."

"Bonus," Donnelly says and chucks the cream cheese container to me.

I catch. "Downside: Maximoff will go into big brother mode for the rest of the night if his little sister is high."

"He's probably already there," Donnelly tells me. "I saw her drinking Four Lokos while you were upstairs."

I roll my eyes. "I love that girl, but *fuck*." I'm pissed because Maximoff shouldn't have to worry about Luna tonight, and he will. Shit, I am right now. She buried her head in her shirt at the hospital, silently crying, and she's kept to herself since the crash. Now this.

Oscar scratches his unshaven jaw. "Donnelly, you're supposed to be making Redford feel better not worse."

"I gave him cream cheese."

I open the lid. "I'm having a night," I tell them, being honest. "I'll be fine later." I'm just not in the mood for more bad shit. If something else goes wrong in the next twenty-four hours, I'm going to lose it.

Friends make long days feel good, but it's the simple, little things that make the bad shit feel nonexistent. I just want to crawl into bed next to my boyfriend. Simple.

Easy.

"My guy doesn't know you like I know you," Donnelly says, bringing up Beckett, his client, who laid into me earlier. "Or else he wouldn't have said the things he said."

I spread cream cheese on my bagel. "I know." I've already told Donnelly not to meddle and share details about me with Beckett. I'd rather earn that trust on my own.

At this rate, it may take years.

I spit my gum on a napkin and ask Oscar, "Charlie ever tell you why he wanted Beckett to do the auction?" I don't ask Donnelly since he wouldn't share Beckett's secrets if he knew them.

Oscar hangs into the cabinet. "That requires having a relationship where Charlie actually tells me things."

"So that's a no," I say, biting into my bagel. I turn my head as Akara fills the archway. A backwards baseball cap pushes back his black hair, and like Oscar, he's in workout clothes: a muscle shirt and sweats.

"How you holding up?" Akara asks me.

I toss my head from side-to-side. "Better than my boyfriend." I take another bite. "How about you?" The Omega lead has been attached to his phone for hours. Handling the crash and the aftermath which involves lawyers and police reports. We both haven't slept since the accident.

"It's been a day." Akara watches Oscar take out a six-pack from the fridge. He doles out Coronas to everyone, but I pass.

Akara's phone buzzes.

"Sulli?" Donnelly asks.

Akara checks Caller ID, then pockets his phone. "No, some guys have been calling me about franchising the gym." He uncaps the beer bottle on the counter's edge, acting like that offer means nothing.

Ever since SFO has gained some fame, Studio 9 Boxing & MMA gym has too. Especially since Akara owns it.

"You can be excited in front of me." I lick cream cheese off my thumb.

Oscar pats Akara's shoulder. "Congratulations, bro."

Akara nods and swigs his beer. "I wish I could be excited, but franchising sounds like a headache. I'm already swimming in work." He checks an incoming message on his phone. "And there it is."

"Sulli," we all say, ribbing him together.

His brows crinkle. "*Not* Sulli."

Oscar smirks. "It was a ninety-nine percent chance, Kitsuwon."

Akara shakes his head. "Look, all the subtle Sulli shots at me can't happen anymore. I know you're fucking around, but at the FanCon, you threw out hints that I liked her as *more* than a friend in front of Maximoff, in front of her *cousins*. Sooner or later, they're gonna stop thinking that's a joke. So you all need to cut that shit. Just a friendly warning."

I don't mind backing off, but if I slip on accident, I won't mind that either.

"Aye aye, captain," I say with a bagel between my teeth while I grab the other half from the toaster.

"Sure thing, boss." Donnelly raises his beer.

Oscar shakes the pretzel bag, his curly hair falling in his eyes. "How sure are we that you don't like her as more than a friend?"

"*Oscar.*" Akara glares.

He puts a hand to his heart. "You know I wouldn't give you shit, if you weren't a *buddy*guard. It's not a good look. Ask Donnelly."

Donnelly swishes his beer. "Beckett and I look dope together."

"Exactly. That's weird," Oscar tells everyone.

Akara looks about ready to strangle Oliveira. My lips want to rise, partially-somewhat entertained. The Omega lead points at Oscar with his beer. "I've been on her detail since she was *sixteen*. Her dad will have my dick under a knife if he hears you. Do *not* push it."

I let out a low whistle at Oscar. "Keep forgetting that lube before you get fucked hard."

"Taking one for the team, Redford. You've been fucked hard enough today."

I nod a few times. That was a good one, and Oscar holds my gaze for a quiet beat and nods back, more serious.

"Who was it?" Donnelly asks Akara. "If it wasn't Sulli texting you."

"The rest of the Tri-Force." Akara names the powers-that-be in the security team that consist of the current Alpha, Omega, and Epsilon lead: Price Kepler, Akara Kitsuwon, and Banks Moretti. "Let's go in the living room. There's big news."

I lean my ass on the iron café table, but the granny-decorated living room has more seating than usual. Mismatched lawn chairs litter the floorboards, accompanying the ugly pink Victorian loveseat and the old rocking chair.

While Donnelly slumps on a lawn chair, Oscar stays in the kitchen archway, and Akara stands front-and-center blocking the brick fireplace.

It's hard to miss Thatcher.

He towers next to the adjoining townhouse door. Closer to me than I prefer. Arms crossed, he eyes Jane's cats that dart across the mint-green rug.

I'm hoping to keep the silent streak between us intact.

Jack Highland sits on the loveseat and fiddles with his Canon, but the starry-eyed jock isn't here to film *We Are Calloway*. He heard what happened after the auction, and he came here to check on Maximoff and Charlie.

"Put the phone away for a sec, Quinn," Akara tells the youngest bodyguard.

Quinn is bowed forward on the rocking chair. "How long will this meeting take?" He doesn't pocket his phone.

"I don't know," Akara snaps, not putting up with anyone's bullshit tonight. "You need to be somewhere? Leave."

Quinn glances around at us, and ends up looking to *me* for the right answer. I'm not solving anyone else's mini-dilemmas unless their name starts with Maximoff and ends with Hale.

Boyfriend privileges.

Before I can tell him off, Quinn starts explaining to me, "I matched with this *incredibly* cute girl on Tinder and her profile says she's down for hookups. She can only meet me in like five fucking minutes."

My brows hike, and Oscar tries to control his laughter. His little brother is asking for my permission to go fuck a girl.

"Man, I don't give a shit what you do," I tell Quinn.

Thatcher shoots me a glare. "That's really your advice?"

There goes that blissful silence. "Technically, it's not advice. It's an opinion."

Donnelly asks to see the girl's profile, and Quinn passes him the phone. Jack leans over to peek at the screen.

"Be thirty minutes late, little bro," Oscar tells his brother. "That way she won't smell your desperation."

Quinn gives him a weird look. "I'm not that desperate. I've gotten hundreds of messages since the Hot Santa video leak. But this girl is out of my league and she doesn't care."

In the public's eyes, Quinn Oliveira became the Casanova of Omega. *The Young Stud.* And I can see Thatcher weighing Quinn's dedication to this job. Like he does to me all the fucking time.

Thatcher catches sight of my glare, and he glares back.

My phone vibrates in my back pocket. Just as I reach for my cell, Akara tells Quinn to make a choice.

Donnelly shrugs and hands the phone to Jack. "It's just pussy, Quinnie. You can eat it later."

Jack doesn't flinch, used to blunt talk. "She's cute. You'd look good together, but I'm with Donnelly." He passes the phone back to Quinn.

I check my recent message from Maximoff.

You busy? — Maximoff

"Farrow," Akara calls me out for my phone while Quinn decides to stay put for the meeting.

"It's Maximoff," I say, typing back a reply.

I send: No. What do you need?

Akara doesn't nag, and he snaps his finger to his palm, "Okay, so here's the deal. Alpha is still the force that'll work the *night with a celebrity* a week from now. Price isn't compromising or letting Omega take the lead."

No one thought he would.

"Bigger news," Akara says, "Eliot and Tom Cobalt graduated high school. For those that don't know"—he zeroes in on Quinn—"Security Force Omega was formed when Maximoff left home. At that point, SFO became the division of security that protects the kids who turn eighteen and become legal adults. Epsilon handles all the minors. Normally, this means that we'd be welcoming Eliot and Tom's bodyguards to SFO, *but* the Tri-Force has decided on a restructure."

Oscar frowns. "A restructure?"

Akara outstretches his arms. "Omega has gained some fame. We're the only ones who get stopped for autographs, the only ones getting extra *Tinder* dates, and if we start adding more bodyguards, there's a chance they'll gain notoriety by association. It's not something the security team wants."

I understand now. There's no plan to add extra bodyguards to SFO. Which is perfectly fine by me.

Akara continues, "All of us here—we are Omega. Even if you're transferred to another client, even if you quit or get fired. We're the bodyguards on SFO until further notice."

Thatcher straightens off the door. "What about my brother?"

Akara nods. "We're still talking about adding Banks to Omega, and it's likely that's the way it'll fall." No one asks why. Banks and Thatcher are *identical* twins, and he's been recognized just as much as Thatcher on the street.

My phone buzzes.

all of SFO + jack. Were gonna chill tonight up here – Maximoff

After seeing his cousins carry pillows and air mattresses upstairs, I figured he'd invite everyone to this little "sleepover" thing.

Your text needs an apostrophe and capital letters. And you sure you want Thatcher up there? I send, and rise off the table as a swarm of texts hit me. Everyone in the living room is watching me.

"Boyfriend okay?" Oscar asks.

Maximoff texts me a middle finger emoji, along with these:

Bring snacks — Maximoff

Chocolate chip cookies in the pantry — Maximoff

Drinks, another sleeping bag, pillows — Maximoff

These are definitely requests from his cousins.

If you need help, I can come down —Maximoff

I instantly call him, phone to my ear. "Don't you dare move."

"Too late, I'm already doing cartwheels down the stairs." His voice sounds tight with pain.

I rub my mouth. "You're a terrible liar, wolf scout." My eyes latch onto Akara, and I mouth, *upstairs*. He nods, and I tell my boyfriend, "We'll be there soon."

Maximoff looks worse than when I left him.

His pallid skin gleams with sweat, dark brown hair damp like he took a shower, and he breathes measured breaths through his nose.

But he's not shaking. No chills.

Good.

I block out most of the background chatter as SFO and Jack settle into the attic room. Sleeping bags and pastel blankets cover air mattresses that line almost every inch of floor space. Bags of chips and bowls of popcorn are being passed around.

I'm already sitting next to Maximoff on his bed, and while he sticks the thermometer in his mouth, I reach over his chest. Carefully.

And I switch on the portable fan. I sense him watching my inked hands, and our muscular legs unconsciously intertwine.

I grab a limeade Ziff sports drink. Leaving the other half of a bagel on the end table. He has to be too nauseous to eat.

With Maximoff, and even me, there's a fine line between "coddling" and taking care of each other. I let him adjust his ice packs on his shoulder and chest, and when I unscrew the sports drink, I see the *don't do that for me* in his features.

The warning dies out the second I take a sizable swig.

I wipe my mouth with the back of my hand. "That's cute that you thought this was yours."

His cheeks flush. That's one way to return color to his face. With the thermometer under his tongue, he mumbles, "Fuck you."

I smile. "That was the most precious *fuck you* I've ever heard."

He groans, fighting his upturning lips, and he says with more bite and growl, "*Fuck you.*"

I suck in a breath. "Still precious."

Maximoff shoots me a middle finger and then removes the beeping thermometer with the same left hand. He reads his temperature, purposefully holding the screen away from me.

His brows knit.

"Give me." I motion to him with two fingers.

"Just what I expected," Maximoff says dryly, "I'm the Human Torch." He passes me the thermometer.

98.5 degrees Fahrenheit. He's a fucking dork. "You don't have a fever," I tell him.

He takes another measured breath before looking right at me. "Probably because I never get hot when I'm around you."

I nod a few times. Unable to break his gaze. Ensnared. "Must be why you're sweating right now," I tell him.

He grimaces, two seconds from a real smile, but his eyes snap shut abruptly. Pain slamming into him somewhere. I almost wince just watching him. I'm used to seeing people in discomfort at a hospital, but it's definitely different when it's someone close to me.

I massage the back of his neck, my fingers skating upward and threading his thick hair. I'm about to pull my leg off his, but he leans more of his weight into my side, like a physical plea for me to stay.

Maximoff.

I keep our legs laced.

His eyes slowly open with a sharp breath, and he's looking at Luna. She's looking at him, concern welled up in her amber gaze.

He tries to marbleize his features. Tries to be her strong unshakable big brother. These parts of him are so intrinsically Maximoff Hale that I wouldn't want him to change. He loves people so overwhelmingly, and he cares. Shit, he cares more than anyone, and when people need him to be their everything, he is always there.

But it only makes me want to be there for him.

Every time. Every day.

Twice as hard. Ten times as much.

"Maximoff," I breathe, capturing his focus. I lightly shake the sports drink at my boyfriend, what I planned to do from the moment I uncapped the plastic bottle. "I'll share with you." *And only you.*

His eyes fall to my mouth, and then he quickly snatches the drink. I notice how he doesn't attempt to talk.

"Moffy," Charlie calls. Our heads turn.

And I reluctantly split my attention between Maximoff and eleven other people. A few pillows prop Charlie's broken leg, and Donnelly leans over his cast, black Sharpie in hand. He's sketching the Philly cityscape, and to be honest, I'm surprised that Charlie is letting him. His cast has been blank.

"Yeah?" Maximoff asks, voice tight.

I survey the attic in one sweep, the room loud with chatter.

All eleven people lounge on sleeping bags, but since they're elevated on the air mattresses, everyone is basically eye-level with us.

The three girls sit beneath the curtained window. Sulli braids Luna's hair while Jane talks breezily and sips a beer.

Near the dresser, Beckett is telling the Oliveira brothers about New York clubs, Donnelly listening in as he draws, and next to the girls, Jack is showing Akara a photo or video on his camera. That doesn't shock me. Jack and Akara have been more civil since the FanCon.

Thatcher is the only one observing and not in a group, his back up against the door. And no, I don't care.

Charlie slips on dark sunglasses. "You look like shit, Moffy. If you'd just—"

"I'm not taking a Vicodin," Maximoff combats and then winces. An icepack slides down his shoulder—I fix it for him since the sports drink occupies his hand.

Jane says something to her brother in French, and he raises one hand in surrender. Conversations pop up around the room, and I hear the tail end of Oscar talking about the worst flavor of Doritos.

I tune everyone out and hone in on Maximoff.

He's pinching his eyes, and he readjusts himself, starting to slide back off the headboard.

Shit.

He's not upset about Charlie nagging him.

He's physically hurting. More.

And more.

He's even willing to lie flat and advertise his pain. Before the ice packs slip, I remove them from his body. His shoulders sink onto the soft mattress, and his head finds the pillow. Eyes closing.

I stroke his hair out of his face.

He shifts his head on my thigh. And he tries to roll more towards me but can't with his bandaged shoulder—his left hand quakes, distressed tears wet the corners of his eyes.

That's it.

I have to do something.

Spreading my legs, I pull Maximoff carefully between them, and I reach for the ice packs, placing one lightly on his chest, one below the red sling on his abdomen.

I already know it's not enough to extinguish his discomfort. With his head on my lap, I wipe the wet corners of his eyes with my thumb.

More conversations ignite in the attic, some about the *We Are*

Calloway docuseries and others about the auction. They're all good about not drawing attention to Maximoff.

The fact that he's this vulnerable, head on my lap, in front of them is the *clearest* sign that he's not doing well.

Maximoff drops his shaking left hand from his face. And he grips my bent knee in a vice, combating that post-op pain. His cheekbones sharpen when he clenches his teeth—and he tries to bury his face into my thigh again.

Fuck, I have to do more. I have to. And I've been hesitating on one option because I don't know how he'll react.

I love safeguarding the *good* in Maximoff while also being the one to loosen his tight laces. It sounds contradictory, but to me, *good* isn't straight-edged. Good is compassion and love for all people, for humanity. Good is a selfless kindness so unadulterated it stings your eyes.

If there's anything I know, it's that the offer I'm about to make won't hurt his morality. It will just take away his pain.

And I need him to believe this too.

I comb his hair back one more time, and then I dip my head down to whisper against his ear. "Can I shotgun you?"

MAXIMOFF HALE

Can I shotgun you?

The hammering pain inside my bones dulls as my brain processes those four words.

Can I shotgun you?

It sounds sexual in my head. Maybe it's the way Farrow said it, his voice quiet but rough but silky-smooth all at once.

Or maybe it's because I have no goddamn idea what *shotgun* entails.

I know about "calling shotgun" in terms of a passenger seat in a car. And I've seen a guy puncture a hole in a can at college and shotgun a beer. Neither of which seem that relevant right now.

So I'm lost and too inexperienced to make complete sense of his question.

I swallow a ball in my throat. "With…?" I can't even get any words out; a stabbing sensation detonates again and again. *Fucking Christ.*

Imagine a nonstop sledgehammer banging on your bones and insides—and you can't cast the sledgehammer aside.

It just slams and crushes.

Ignoring this torment—it's close to impossible.

I clutch Farrow's knee in a death-grip. *God,* I'm nearing a point where I just want to pass out.

I need this to end.

I need this to end.

"Donnelly," Farrow calls, and to distract myself, I try to focus on things that my brain loves. Like Farrow Keene's precise movements.

How he stretches his arm out and takes something from his friend.

I try to concentrate on his age.

Twenty-eight. Six years older than me. I breathe through my nose at a sharp pain. *Brain, you annoyingly love that he's older. Don't act like you're disinterested now.*

Twenty-eight. He's twenty-eight.

I shut my eyes for a longer second and open them slowly. Lying down between his legs with my head on his thigh, my view mostly consists of the ceiling rafters and Farrow.

My head is in his lap is a song that plays too softly on repeat. That track should be blaring and drowning out I_Feel_Like_I'm_Dying.mp3 and Fuck_This_Shitty_Feeling.mp3.

Farrow bends somewhat over me, blocking the rafters from view. Pieces of his white hair fall to his lashes. "This is a blunt," he explains, pinching the blunt between two inked fingers. "Shotgunning is where you take a hit from me. You don't need to hold the blunt. Okay?"

He's asking for my permission.

Because he's a good guy. He'll tell you he's not, but he is.

I think for half a second and then nod with my chin. Giving into my body's pleas. I'm not as afraid of weed like I am Vicodin or Oxy.

And it helps that I trust Farrow with my body. I'd never fucking agree to this without him.

"Okay," Farrow repeats in relief, and he collects a lighter that's thrown on my bed. I can't tell from who.

But I just watch Farrow. Every damn movement. How he puts the blunt confidently between his lips. How he cups his hand around it while he strikes the lighter.

How his eyes lock on mine.

You wouldn't even believe how much this helps. Just observing Farrow. Because for a fleeting second, I forget I'm in pain, and I'll take that second, even brief. Christ, I'll take anything.

A flame eats the paper as he inhales. Blunt now lit, he blows smoke up at the twinkling rafters. After that, he spins the blunt backwards, the burning end facing his lips.

I'm confused about how this works.

"Suck in the smoke, wolf scout," Farrow tells me. "That's all you need to do." With two fingers, he places the blunt between his teeth, burning end *in* his mouth, the other side sticks out—and he leans over me again.

Lowering his head down.

Down.

Until the paper is an inch from my lips. Our mouths are lined up like an upside-down kiss.

His large hand sheaths my jaw. Protectively. Comfortingly. His other palm rests on top of my hand that death-grips his knee.

Farrow has told me how cinematic we are together, and I realize that I didn't *fully* get it. Not until now.

Not until this blissful, out-of-body moment crawls to slow-motion and our intimacy intoxicates me. Dizzies me. Fills me to the brim. And I haven't even inhaled a thing yet.

I could freeze-frame this second for eternity. But it plays out.

With the burning embers in his mouth, Farrow exhales. Smoke billows from the unlit end, and I breathe in. A silky line of smoke trickles down my throat.

I cough. *Fuck.*

He lets go of my jaw to take the blunt out of his mouth. Assessing me, and I try to relax and adjust to the new sensation. Smoke plumes around us, the smell more pungent than cigarettes, and Farrow draws back down for another hit.

He blows out, and I suck in smoke again. Trying not to cough this time.

My muscles unbind, and with a few more inhales, my hand loosens on his knee. I'm not spinning like the edible made me feel.

Probably since *pain* is my current state. Slowly, my joints ease like oil drips into every rusted crevice, and the torment begins to dull. Pushed to the background.

"One more time," Farrow says to me, his husky voice too damn sexy. My brain starts tuning into the Farrow 69.1 radio station, volume on blast.

For once, thank you, brain.

Farrow is careful not to burn himself, like he's done this a billion times, and he lowers his head again.

Now I gain enough energy to move my hand off his knee. I clasp the back of his head, gripping his bleach-white hair between fingers.

When I inhale the smoke, I see his lips curve upward.

He plucks the blunt out of his mouth, leaning back against the headboard, and he eyes me deeply. "Did you like that?" he asks.

I breathe better. "Not more than you," I say, gritting down as I use one hand to sit up. The cool ice packs fall off my chest and thud onto the bed.

My first move is to go to grab them…with the wrong hand—*goddammit.*

Pain infiltrates, and I try to remind my subconscious that my right hand is firmly bound in a sling for a fucking reason.

In a good distraction, Farrow breaks his legs open a bit wider, and I slide back until my spine meets his chest. His arm curves around my bare waist. At nearly the same height, our broad shoulders frame, almost parallel.

Before I ask for the blunt, he's already passing me it. Knowing that I'd want to try on my own. I take a normal drag myself, and my throat burns. But I force myself not to cough.

I pass it back.

Farrow takes another drag too, and then he reaches out and hands the blunt to Donnelly.

I'm now unconscionably, totally, *colossally* aware of the eleven-person audience. Most of them pretend to be interested in Cape Cod chips or the mound of pillows on sleeping bags. But their eyes dart over to us and land on me.

I thought they'd look surprised. That I'd smoke anything. But like Farrow, they all seem *relieved.* Happy that I'm not suffering.

Blue eyes shimmering, Janie tips her beer towards me in cheers. If I didn't have Farrow, she'd be next to me. Not wrapped up in a blue blanket beneath the window.

But I'm more assured than ever that Janie wouldn't be able to fill Farrow's spot in my life. Just like he can't replace hers.

I need them both.

I want them both.

When Jane finally reached the hospital before my surgery, she broke down. My voice kept cracking, and she couldn't stop rambling about the mathematical probability of life and death. And how she should've been in the car with me.

Tears leaked out of her eyes, and then we agreed that we'd survive this. We can survive anything with a bit of luck and a whole lot of love.

In the quiet but crowded attic, I tell my best friend, "Je suis vivant, ma moitié." *I'm alive, my other half.*

She smiles into a sip of beer. "Je ne voudrais pas de toi d'une autre manière." *I wouldn't want you any other way.*

Farrow's heartbeat thuds in a calm rhythm against my back, and we both see Luna perk up from her sprawled face-planted position.

"Does this mean you'll get high with me, Moffy?" Luna asks, head propped in her hand.

Ever since the FanCon with the pot cookie debacle, I'm still forever processing the fact that my little sister has smoked weed before. My brows cinch, thinking about a situation where I'd *want* to be high while she's high. I'm fine with her smoking if she's careful, but I want to be coherent in that instance.

"Not a chance, sis," I say truthfully.

"Not even right now?" Luna taps her nose since I'm out of reach and she can't tap mine. A gesture we did as kids that kind of means *hey brother, hey sister.* Then she swings her gangly arm to Donnelly for the blunt.

"Nah." He finishes the blunt himself. "Four Lokos and weed don't mix." He blows smoke off to the side.

"Dammit," Luna mutters and says to me, "Next time."

I smile. Feeling how much she wants to stay close to me, and I know letting her move in was the right decision. Now I just have to figure out if letting her do this auction is a decision I'll regret forever.

Lights off by 2 a.m., everyone has crashed and fallen asleep in my attic bedroom. It's pretty much what happens when you endure a massive doomsday and stay up late talking.

I can't sleep.

I was conked out for so long after my surgery. Now my mind is wide-awake and playing mental catch-up: *talk to my brother* (later). *A porn star bought you* (Jesus Christ). *Protect your brother, protect your sisters, protect everyone* (always).

Don't let Farrow go (I won't).

Marry him.

Put a ring on it.

What if he's not into marriage?

What if that's why he rejected his ex's proposal?

But we talked about kids. Twice.

Jokingly?

No, it was fucking serious.

I think.

You can have kids without being married.

Don't name your son Batman.

I squeeze my eyes shut. Alright, my mind can shut the fuck up now.

I think I'm the only one awake until the clock hits 2:30 a.m. And I hear whispering. From the right side of the room.

It's not Farrow.

He's dead asleep turned towards me, barely stirring beneath the comforter. I try my best not to wake him. Farrow needs shuteye more than anyone.

His inked arm splays over my lower abs. I didn't realize how badly I'd want to lie on my side until tonight.

I crave to just turn into his hard chest.

But here I am, stuck on my back. If anything, it makes me want to speed through physical therapy that much faster.

"You can't go on Sunday anymore?" Sulli mutters more loudly than she realizes. As much as I wished for bionic hearing as a kid, I don't have that superpower.

I strain my ears to catch the reply.

"Sorry," Jack whispers, sounding really apologetic.

My mind swerves onto one track: *Jack Highland is awake while my little cousin is awake and everyone else is asleep.*

I have no clue what that means. So I prop myself on my usable elbow and peer over Farrow to see...

My brows scrunch. *Akara* is awake too. Both guys lounge on the same air mattress, leaning on the brick wall. Right in between them, Sullivan slumps on a donut-shaped pillow and twists her frayed string anklet.

"Oh hey, you don't need to fucking apologize," my cousin whispers not as softly. "It's alright." Even in the dark attic, she looks noticeably bummed.

"Rain check?" Jack whispers. "I should be free next Sunday. We can go swimming then."

"Yeah," she nods, scooting up more against the wall. "That'd work."

Akara is playing with her chocolate brown hair, and he coils a long strand over his upper lip in a fake mustache.

Sulli cracks a smile and shoves his chest.

I used to overthink their dynamic because in my personal experience with Farrow, *teasing* equals *affection*. But that can't always be the case.

Right?

Now I'm being paranoid, but for Sulli's sake, I *can't* Hulk-Smash anything that makes her happy. I won't. And her friendship with her bodyguard is pretty much centerfold.

Akara laughs lightly and whispers to Jack, "She thinks she's a mermaid. You know, no swimming for one week means her legs grow back."

"Hey, there is some fucking logic in the mermaid debate," Sulli tells Akara. "I love water. Mermaids love water. Therefore I am a fucking mermaid."

Akara ties a piece of her hair in a slipknot. "Sharks also love water."

"They do," Jack agrees. "And eels. Stingrays. Manatees."

"Salmon," Akara whispers. "Walruses—"

"Hey, maybe I'm a fucking walrus then," Sulli jokes in another loud whisper. "I could *also* be a mermaid too."

Akara loosens the knot in her hair and gives her a look. "You're not a walrus, Sul."

My elbow already aches from the crash, and being propped up this long isn't that easy. But I strain my muscles for another second.

Sulli smiles softly. "Want to go swimming this Sunday, Kits? Just at the Hale pool."

Akara winces a bit and scratches the back of his head. "I, um…" He glances at Jack.

Jack is staring at the Omega lead like they're in on something that she's not a part of. I can't help but fucking *glare*. They haven't noticed me yet. Probably not able to see me well since it's dark and Farrow conceals most of my build.

"What?" Sulli frowns, looking between them. "Cum, shit, that's your day off work, Kits. Fuck, I'm sorry. You can do whatever…"

This isn't going well, and I can tell my cousin is scrambling for the right thing to say. She does this, and then she'll just go quiet.

"It's not that," Akara says. "Well, it…kind of is, but Jack and I have this thing that day."

What thing?

Sulli nods slowly. "Like a production-security thing?"

Exactly what I'm thinking.

"No." Akara pauses. "Jack is friends with two girls from Penn that we're going out with," he whispers. "It's a double date thing."

Huh. That's good that they're finding time to date. I know it's been hard for most of security. But the more I scrutinize them, the more I can't read Sulli's expression.

Maybe because she's not sure what she's feeling.

"Oh yeah," Sulli frowns, fingers to her full lips in deep thought. "Yeah…" She shakes the cobwebs out of her head. "That sounds fucking fun. You deserve some P-in-the-V action. We can do whatever…swimming or you know, any time. And Moffy will swim with me—or not since his injury." She winces at herself and then slumps down.

"Sul," Akara whispers.

"EAT THAT ASS!!"

Greaaat.

The drunken street heckling wakes a quarter of the room. As Philly bars close, the jeers will escalate. And you know what?

It irritates the fuck out of me this time. I don't care that my family and security can hear. I care that *eat that ass* has woken up my boyfriend, who's been majorly sleep-deprived.

Farrow slips his arm off me, eyes fluttering open into a glare aimed at the window.

"LICK MAXIMOFF HALE'S WOUNDS!!"

My jaw sharpens.

Farrow combs a hand through his white hair, and I sit up more—he puts a hand on my leg. I read his gaze quickly: *don't rush outside.* And I spot the heat in his brown eyes.

"They're pissing you off?" I ask, both of our shoulders propped against the headboard.

"Yeah." His brows lift at me. "You just had surgery. You don't need this shit right now."

"Neither do you," I say strongly.

Farrow sweeps the length of my build, combing back his messy hair for the second time. He opens his mouth and—

"LICK HIS HOLE!!"

Farrow rolls his eyes.

My scowl darkens.

And Oscar is on his feet, staring hard at the curtained window.

Jane and Luna wake beneath it, and when Akara starts texting, I realize all of the room is now alert and agitated.

They look to me, to Farrow, back to me, and I tell them, "Welcome to my attic."

"MAXIMOFFFFFF!" a drunk guy slurs. "SUCK MY COCK AFTER YOU SUCK FARROW KEENE'S!!"

No.

Beckett is giving the window a bigger *what the fuck* face.

Sulli cringes. "This is fucked up."

Donnelly stands and shuffles between the air mattresses. Trying to reach the door.

"No." Akara points at him, still texting. "No one do anything yet. Don't turn on a lamp. They'll be able to see the room light up from the street."

Donnelly listens and stays put, and Thatcher towers at a stance, guarding the exit.

Oscar studies the window again. "We can tell these drunk fucks that this isn't Maximoff's room. Get Jane to call out to them—"

"No," Thatcher interjects. "Then they'll start harassing *her*."

"I can do it," Luna offers. "This can be my room." My sister starts peeking beneath the curtain—

"Luna, don't!" I yell, and before I try to slide off the bed, Janie is already pulling my sister away from the windowpanes.

Paparazzi wait on the street nightly. Camera lenses are constantly pointed at my window. And there is a 100% chance of hecklers with a shower of ridicule tonight.

I don't want that for any of my family or SFO.

Quinn adjusts the curtains, the room fully obscured from the street.

Farrow eyes me and twists his silver rings.

"FARROW! MAXIMOFF!! WHO'S THE BOTTOM?!"

I glower. Blood boiling.

Oscar quickly heads over to Jack and Akara, speaking hushed to both of them.

I'm putting *Farrow* in this fucked-up situation. If he weren't in a public relationship with me, no one would shout that on a goddamn city street.

"WHO TAKES IT IN THE ASS?!"

Are you fucking kidding me?

I'm about to stand, but Farrow draws me back on the bed.

Swiftly, he turns sideways and tents his legs over mine. Caging me. "Don't let that shit bother you," he says easily, and in his peripheral, he's watching SFO figure out a plan. "Because my natural instinct is to defend you, wolf scout, and I know yours is to defend me, but we're a target together and we have to take some of these hits." He stares deeper into me.

Some of these hits.

Not all of them.

We both have our limits. But these hecklers shouldn't be a breaking point. This is easy in comparison to what else could be thrown at Farrow.

My chest rises.

People have always tried to hurt who I love. My parents, my sisters, my brother, all of my fucking family. Attacks from online, from on the street.

And now the world knows that I love Farrow.

You know that I'm in love.

For real.

All I want is to protect him, and all he wants is to protect me. It's been our motto since the damn start. But Farrow is used to people mocking me, hating me, shitting on me. I'm not used to seeing him beneath a burning spotlight that leaves scars.

"This isn't easy," I admit.

"I know," he says like he's met this irritation, this frustration and anger time and time again while we've been together in private. When he's not allowed to bear his fists to protect me.

Just take the hit.

I tilt my head back, my sore muscles begging me to relax.

"RIDE HIS DICK!!"

Farrow raises and lowers his brows in a teasing wave.

I lick my lips, heating up in a better way. "Never happening."

He cocks his head and whispers, "It's definitely already happened."

"Has it?" I feign confusion.

He rolls his eyes into a short laugh—and then he notices the same thing as me. "Cobalt, what the hell are you doing?"

My best friend straps a sequined purse across her grannie jammies.

She has a switchblade and pepper spray in there, and we watch her quickly fit on fuzzy cat slippers.

"Janie," I call out, already figuring out why she's angry. "We can post an Instagram video. You don't need to confront them on the fucking street."

Jane ties her hair in a low pony. "There is a bold line, Moffy, and these fools have crossed it."

"They're *drunk* fools," I remind Jane. "They're here to incite one of us. This is what they fucking want." I've said all of this a million times to myself. Right before I land a fist into a heckler's jaw. Sometimes these facts feel meaningless, but we have to repeat them for each other. For ourselves.

Or else we'll all go out of our goddamn minds.

Charlie and Beckett watch their sister carefully, but they don't stand up and join Jane.

She unzips her purse and procures her pepper spray canister while marching to the door, guarded by Thatcher.

Jane reaches him and lifts her chin since he's a whole foot taller. "Excuse me, Thatcher, but there are people I need to have words with on my best friend's behalf. Move aside."

Yeah, alright, I'm smiling.

Thatcher never budges. "I can't, Jane."

"PUT YOUR DICK IN HIM!!"

Farrow suddenly reaches for the bedside drawer.

For a condom?

No.

There's absolutely no way he's grabbing a condom.

Jane clears her throat. "Mr. Moretti," she tries again, "I need to go break a few dicks. Can you please step aside?" Her angry face crinkles her nose.

"No—"

"MAXIMOFF HALE IS GONNA FUCK A PORN STAR!!"

The attic goes silent. No one is speaking.

Farrow's jaw tics. That one got to him.

I go rigid.

The auction news has probably made headlines, and I just haven't checked the internet yet. I've been unaware of how the whole world perceives my relationship with Farrow. Purposefully.

But now I think about the porn star.

I think about what people must be saying online, whether they're calling my relationship with Farrow a fucking sham or not monogamous or maybe they just think I'm cheating.

I don't know.

And now I need to know. So I can defend my boyfriend with a tweet, an Instagram video, and an airplane banner over the Pacific Ocean.

While Jack, Oscar, and Akara near the window—most likely with a plan that doesn't involve the last resort: call the cops for noise disturbance—I search for my phone under the covers.

"What are you doing?" Farrow asks.

I find my phone tangled in the sheets. "Looking at the internet—"

Farrow seizes my phone. "We'll look together. Downstairs." He climbs off the bed, standing. And as he combs his hair back for a *third* time, I realize he has something serious to tell me.

In private.

I stand, the pain in my collarbone thumping more consistently than a half hour ago. Farrow rounds the bed, careful of the air mattresses, and Oscar wrenches the window open. Jack sticks his head out with Akara.

"Maximoff isn't here!" Jack shouts. "Production is setting up for the show! You all need to leave!"

"Or we'll be calling the police for noise disturbance!" Akara threatens.

"AKARA KITSUWON!" a drunk girl shouts. "PROTECT MEEE!!"

Akara yells one more threat and then leaves the window. Annoyance lines his forehead. I can't imagine how frustrating the lack of anonymity must be for SFO.

As Jack closes the curtains, they all discuss waiting to see if the heckling worsens or dies down.

I cut in front of Farrow before he reaches the door. Just so I can tell Thatcher, "We're just going to the kitchen. I need more ice."

Thatcher nods, no argument, and let's us pass.

12

MAXIMOFF HALE

We're in the kitchen pantry. I'd say that I led us here, but I clearly trailed behind Farrow, broken collarbone and all. I'm slower, but right now, I'm not as frustrated about it and he's not teasing me since we're dealing with heavier things. Waist-deep in quicksand.

I swear we can't catch a break.

Farrow tugs the string to the ceiling light bulb. A warm glow casts on cluttered wooden shelves, stocked with cereal boxes, protein bars, candy, and crackers.

We both agreed on this spot.

The pantry is the quietest place in the townhouse. Farrow and I have fucked against these shelves more than once. Rough enough that as I pounded into him, soup cans fell to the floorboards. No one upstairs heard, and with the door locked now, our voices shouldn't echo up the staircase.

So it's climax-proof.

I hold out my left hand for my phone that's still in Farrow's grip.

He rests his elbow beside a half-opened box of Pop-Tarts, not relinquishing my phone. He tilts his head at me. "I meant it when I said let's look together."

I don't stand next to him yet. "Farrow, just let me be the one to check the tabloids."

He frowns. "You realize I've dealt with internet trolls calling *you*, my boyfriend, a sack of shit, a dumb fuck, a spoiled bastard, and much, *much* worse. I couldn't do a fucking thing, and still, I'm standing. I haven't broken down yet, so what the hell are you protecting me from, Maximoff?"

Farrow is used to internet trolls harassing me, but it's a different feeling when the unwanted opinions are about *us*.

"Street hecklers are my kryptonite," I admit, then I gesture to his chest. "Grating, unsolicited commentary about our relationship is going to be yours."

Farrow is close to shaking his head, but he stops himself and looks up at the pantry ceiling. Cringing slightly. Eyes reddening. He rubs his mouth a couple times. We've been around each other every waking minute for almost a whole year.

I know him.

I fucking *know* Farrow like he knows me. He will tell you that he has no best friends. He has two that he treats like brothers. He will say that he's an open book. But it's a book he only allows his boyfriend to open. His casualness reads to some like indifference. Yet, he lives to save people.

He's independent and self-reliant, but he seeks out companionship and love.

If he says you're "good people"—he'll surround himself around you, and you'll be glad. Because he's the kind of man who puts his whole soul into what he loves, and if he loves you, *goddamn*.

So when his eyes fall back to mine, I say, "I know you. You can barely stand Beckett prying in our relationship. You think you can stomach the entire world?"

Farrow touches his obsidian earring, contemplating for a millisecond. "You think you can stomach it?" he asks me. "It's not like you've had a public relationship before me. I'm your *first*—hopefully your last. You've never experienced this shit either."

Hopefully your last.

I hang onto those three words. Unblinking at him.

Farrow is trying to read my expression at an *alarming* rate. Is he nervous? I think…

I think he's nervous.

It makes me ten billion times more nervous.

My pulse accelerates, heart beating out of my chest, and Farrow's breath quickens like he's running the same marathon. He sets my phone on a shelf.

"Are you still high?" I ask.

"No." Farrow keeps sweeping my face for my reaction. "Not at all."

"Same." I'm completely lucid, mentally shutting out any pain, because I can't get over those three words.

Hopefully your last.

He wants to be my last, and he's not just saying this on the side of a road, thinking I'm about to die. He's saying this when we're about to face the roughest storm together.

Farrow combs both hands through his bleach-white hair, his chest elevating. "Maximoff…"

"Am I your forever guy?" I just ask.

His eyes are bloodshot, so much emotion slamming into him, then me, and he says, "I don't want to scare you off—"

"You're not scaring me," I shake my head repeatedly, my pulse on a sky-scraping ascent.

He drums a shelf with his fingertips, prolonging whatever you want to call this moment. When he does speak, each word comes out like fifty tons of brick that he's wrenching forward. "I'm afraid that if I say anything else, I'm going to fucking lose you…we can do this another day—"

"Why the fuck would you lose me?" I cut him off, brows furrowed.

He leans his weight back. "We're really doing this right now," he realizes.

"Yeah, unless you'd like me to overthink for the next millennium."

His mouth stretches. "I wouldn't take that long, wolf scout." But the fleeting smile completely disappears as he processes what he needs to say.

His gaze slowly rises to meet mine. "See, you're twenty-two and I'm only your first—and there is better than me out there. Shit, even Oscar is waiting for you to realize it, and I've dumped my fair share of guys. For the first fucking time, I'm the one terrified…" He stops himself short, eyeing me hard. "You look petrified."

I clear my throat. "This is me looking nervous," I tell him, my brows cinched and eyes a bit wide. I'm actually scared to lose *him* in this whole conversation.

Maybe that's why we prefer joking around than having serious talks. It always takes us a while to reach the center, but we usually find a way.

His smile starts widening to new profound levels. "I've seen you nervous plenty of times. That's not it."

"Not *plenty* of times," I retort. "Sometimes, a *few* times…no times. Less than you."

Farrow laughs, and then as the sound quiets, our eyes melt against each other.

"There's no one better than you," I tell him, assured about this. "And I get why you haven't brought this up before." I nod to myself a few more times, and I stop there.

Farrow waves me onwards.

I feign confusion. "Isn't it your turn? Pretty sure it's your turn."

He rolls his eyes, but they land on me as he says, "So you must know you're brick-walled when it comes to future shit, particularly *our* future."

I nod strongly. "Highly aware." I think about how to say this perfectly, but I don't think there's a perfect way. "I always thought I'd never be in a relationship….for as much as I overanalyze my life, I never let myself imagine a boyfriend, let alone something more…"

Farrow props his elbows on the shelf behind him. "I figured, but you realize you've had me for a while. Fuck, anytime I mentioned marriage, even jokingly, you looked ready to piss your pants."

I grimace. "Did I?"

"You did," he nods.

"I'm not right now." I rake my hand through my thick hair—a pained groan tangles inside my throat. *That fucking hurt*. A sharp pang stabs my bone. Even raising my good hand pulls my bad shoulder sometimes.

"Careful," Farrow whispers, concern deepening his voice.

Something swells in my chest, but I continue on. "I guess I didn't want to think about it before," I explain, "because thinking meant *overanalyzing* and for once, I just wanted to live in the present. With you."

Farrow nods slowly. Understanding in his eyes.

"But after the crash, I've been thinking a lot more about the rest of my life. Where I go from here, and now I can't stop thinking about us and it."

"Marriage," he says matter-of-factly.

"*Marriage*," I say with stubborn emphasis, not allergic to the word. "Yeah. I keep thinking…" I gesture to my head, more careful this time. "Do you even want to be married someday? Maybe you're not into it, maybe that's why you rejected your ex's proposal—"

"No," Farrow cuts me off, his foot kicked back on the shelf. He looks cool even when we're discussing life-altering, earth-changing topics. "Man, I want that commitment one day. I just didn't want it with him."

So he's into marriage…

"Maximoff." He catches my attention before I stare into space, and he's already straightened up, no longer lounging against the shelves. He nears until our legs knock together, his fingers toy with hooking my fingers.

And he asks, "What do you want, wolf scout?" He clutches my hand.

What do I want?

I can almost feel the rain from the crash site. Water kissing my face and how Farrow hovered over me. How he painted a picture of our lives together. Decades, *longer*—which, for Farrow, means an expanse of time that lasts forever.

I could've died happy inside that future, and I can't think of a greater sign than that.

So I know… "I want everything you said in the rain. All of it."

Farrow easily recalls each word, and his eyes stroke mine in hot, tender affection. "That's good because it looks like we want the same thing."

I inhale like I haven't taken a breath in eons. The one constant in my off-kilter world has been *us*—Farrow and me. Hearing him say that he wants to stand upright next to me, for the long haul—it's a goddamn dream.

The corner of his mouth rises. "You're smiling," he breathes against my lips before kissing me. One of those brief, teasing kisses that stings. Aching for more.

"I'm really happy," I whisper, but my brows cinch at a thought. "Strangely since we're in a DEFCON 1 situation."

Farrow nods and drops my hand, just so he can return to the shelves. He grabs my phone next to the Pop-Tart box. "Do you remember what I asked you?"

I try to rewind my brain, but all I remember is *hopefully your last.*

A knowing smile edges across his face. "I said that you've never experienced this shit either. You can't know how it'll affect you when you read about us." He makes a *come closer* gesture with two fingers and unlocks my phone with the passcode.

I near him, my red sling rubbing coarsely against my chest. "I've also had paparazzi and journalists ask about my love life since I was *fourteen*." Our eyes meet. "I've dealt with speculations before. Maybe not about us, but I'm better equipped for this."

Farrow waits to open a web page. "Okay, but I'm not sitting on the sidelines. I'd rather learn to deal with it than avoid it."

I nod. "I can get behind that."

He reaches for the Pop-Tart box. "That's because you love getting behind me." Farrow tears open the silver individual pastry wrapper with his teeth, his smile my fucking undoing.

My blood heats, but I also eagle-eye the phone in his other hand. "Let me prep you first."

His brows shoot up. "Prep me?"

I rest my hand on my neck, the strain in my muscle uncomfortable. "It's what I used to do when I was younger. You tell yourself what people are probably saying before you see or hear it—that way it doesn't cut as badly."

Farrow passes me the cinnamon Pop-Tart. "You would prepare. Pack your survival gear, remember your life raft—"

"Alright," I interject. I get that he's *him* and I'm *me* and we'll handle every crisis a bit differently. But I had to offer anyway. "So you don't want a raft then?" I take a large bite of the cold Pop-Tart.

I haven't eaten in forever, and Farrow knew that. He must've also known that I wouldn't be as nauseous. My uneasy stomach is instantly grateful for the food. Settling down.

"No raft," he confirms, typing on my phone. "Let's just dive in, wolf scout."

I'm the better swimmer, so in this analogy or metaphor, I can save him if the current pulls him under. I wonder if he's thinking about that.

I lean back, shelves digging in my spine, but my side is up against Farrow's, our shoulders nearly at equal height. He wraps his arm around my muscular waist and searches the internet with his other hand.

Janie's cat scratches and meows at the pantry door, slicing into the short silence.

"Try *Celebrity Crush* first," I tell him.

He types the tabloid site into the search engine, and as soon as we're on the homepage, we both read the biggest headline:

Popular Male Porn Star Buys Night with Maximoff Hale at Charity Auction.

It's pretty generic.

Something we both expected.

I swallow the last of the Pop-Tart while Farrow clicks into the article. He scrolls really goddamn fast. Skim-reading, and then he reaches the comments, slowing down...

It's all a fucking hoax. Their relationship is #FAKE

Ugh. Why would he let a porn star buy him if he's dating someone? Gross.

They have no chemistry anyway. This just confirms it.

He's only dating Maximoff to get famous.

My eyes glaze over more of the same, and I do what my parents have always told me to do.

I take a breath.

Remember that *they don't know me, they don't know us.*

Repeat it.

They don't know us.

Their opinions are just opinions, and they don't get to live inside my body and make my choices. The world watches my failures, my mistakes, and you criticize me and my relationship, but in the end, you don't have the full picture. Just whatever narrative you've created in your head.

I glance at my boyfriend. He keeps scrolling through the comments, his cool exterior not shaken, but his eyes seem to tighten. So something's troubling him.

I extend my left arm across his back and hold his shoulder. "They don't know us," I tell Farrow. "They'll never really know us."

He pauses scrolling. "I don't understand why they'd say that I'm in it for the fame. I've barely been on your social media so far."

Since I've been dealing with the auction, I haven't posted a lot in the past two weeks. The pictures on my Instagram of him are the *lovers like us* photo from my parent's vow renewal and one where he's cooking breakfast. I haven't even recorded an Instagram story with Farrow yet.

"They'll make up anything off nothing," I say, but I notice how he's fixated on another *fame whore* comment. "That's what's getting to you?"

Farrow scrolls again. "It's all eating at me differently, but people questioning my intentions with you is probably my least favorite thing." He glares at another comment on a different article. "I'm protective of you, wolf scout, and the thought of people believing I'm fucking you over..." His jaw muscle tics.

It's not sitting well with him.

Before I can reply, Farrow adds, "See, I understand how this works:

I appear on your social media more, I only strengthen their 'he's in it for the fame' bullshit, but *fuck*." He lets out a deep, aggravated breath.

There is no permanent fix.

After being around my family, he knows this too. People will always believe what they want to believe—and it'll hurt. With the rumors about my paternity, I felt like I needed to scream and *scream* for people to hear me.

I still have to talk about the truth. How my dad is Loren Hale. And I'll occasionally wear red to honor him. Like now, I consciously chose a *red* sling. But using my voice is the best thing I can do. It's why *We Are Calloway* exists.

My sore arm falls to his hip. "I was going to ask you to do an Instagram video with me, but if you'd feel better backing away from social media, I'd understand."

I'd be okay with whatever he decides since this is new for him and since my world is the thing that's drastically changing his life.

"I don't have to post pictures of us—"

"No," Farrow says, shutting off my phone. He rotates to face me, resting his forearm on the shelf, and he opens his mouth to speak, but I'm already talking.

"Joining me in videos, posting more pictures together, it won't change public perception in the way you want," I remind him.

"It'll most likely make it worse," Farrow agrees. "I'm ready for that, wolf scout." He runs his thumb over his lip piercing.

"You sure?" I ask.

Farrow notices me watching his hand, and his lips begin to lift beneath his thumb. He moves that hand to the back of my neck.

His grip feels better than good.

And his gaze plunges into me. "When I love someone," he says in a rough whisper, "I love them *proudly*, and you deserve the achingly normal, romantic shit more than anyone. Everything you've never had. All the pictures you post, all the videos you do on your own, I want to be in them—and it'd kill me not to give you that. Especially now that we're public."

The declaration overwhelms me. I swallow the ball in my throat. And I zero in on how fast that was for Farrow. "Just like that?" I ask, my brows cinching. "You didn't even think about it."

"Because I do what I feel is right, not just what I think is right." His hand ascends into my hair, and mine is on a descent to his back pocket.

Farrow listened to his instincts, and I've been ignoring mine that have screamed at me for weeks on end.

A sudden clarity washes over me.

And I say, "I'm cancelling the *night with a celebrity*." Content with this choice.

His hold on the back of my head is twice as protective, ten times as comforting. "When did you decide this?" he asks, skimming my features for signs of what I'm feeling.

"Right now." I look at him. "I've been fighting against what I feel is right. Anytime the *night with a celebrity* is brought up, it's like a parasite crawling down my body." I cringe. "I can't put you through that fucking night. I can't put my sister or my cousins through that night. I don't care if you're all willing to go through with it—something inside of me is pleading with me to just stop."

Concern narrows his eyes—Farrow looks like he wants to hug the fuck out of me. But with my broken bone, he can only draw closer. "Maximoff." He whispers my name like he's caressing each syllable. "Shit, if I'd known you were feeling like that...I thought you were just paranoid."

I was that, too. "What would've you done if you'd known?" I ask, my eyes tracing the wings and crossed swords inked on his neck.

"I would've told you that if something is so parasitic that every instinct is screaming at you to stop, then stop. Because at that point, doing it isn't benefiting what or who you love. It's hurting something or someone you love." He runs his hand through my thick hair. "And then I would've held you."

I stare at his mouth for a second, my blood hot. "Or I would've held you."

Farrow doesn't play into the banter like usual, or even say *we would've held each other*. He's focused on the crux of my choice. "You're going to lose your job for real."

If no one goes through with the *night with a celebrity*, Ernest Mangold won't give me a second chance to be reinstated as CEO of H.M.C. Philanthropies.

It doesn't knock me backwards. I inhale a stronger breath. "I think I'm okay with that."

Something inside of me has changed. I can't tell you if it's being in love or almost dying or maybe I'm just getting older—but something in me is different. And being CEO of my company doesn't feel as important anymore.

I also recognize that I'm leaving my family's wealth in the hands of a prick. But Charlie is still on the H.M.C. board, and I need to trust that he'll take care of our families.

I'm letting go.

"Are you okay with that?" I ask him.

His eyes brush my cheekbones. "You look more unburdened, and now there's no porn star run-in. This is win-win any way you turn it."

I think about Ace Steel. How he was a *straight* porn star. I don't get it. "I wonder what Ace Steel wanted—"

"You don't need to wonder," Farrow interjects.

Off my confusion, he reaches behind his back and then he guides my hand that has slowly crept towards his back pocket *into* said pocket.

The ass-grab doesn't make sense…until I feel the outline of a card. This is what Farrow must've taken from the end table earlier. Which I theorized was a condom.

Not a condom.

A business card.

"That dickhole told me what he wanted when we were at the auction," Farrow explains. "It's why I wanted to talk to you in private in the first place. The topic just kept getting derailed."

I read the card and immediately freeze at the name: *Sensual Flixxxs*. "This porn company used to call me a hundred times when I turned eighteen. I had to block their number." I look up at Farrow.

His jaw hardens. "I figured. Apparently they sent Ace on their behalf to convince you to do a scene. He said the company thought he'd be able to sell you on the idea since he's a sex worker and not a producer."

I scowl. "They really thought I'd fuck someone else even though I'm with *you*?"

"No." Farrow lets out a short, vexed laugh at the memory. "He told me—and I quote—'Sexual Flixxxs wants to film you fucking Maximoff Hale in the ass', and I said they could film me fracturing Ace's cock with a hammer."

Since Farrow is literal a lot of the time, that threat or offer seems more real than mine would've been. Though, I think I would've just punched the porn star.

My face twists as I process. "So they spent millions of dollars on me, just for a meeting? In *hopes* that we'd agree to fuck on camera, and what…they hoped to make a profit on the video? It's an insane gamble."

"They couldn't get ahold of you," Farrow says. "The auction was the only way they could even breathe on your fucking neck. If they thought they could manipulate you during the one-on-one night, it could've been worth it on their end."

If my choice to cancel the auction nights wasn't already cemented, now it's marbleized, staple-gunned and set to stone. "It's never happening." I'm about to rip up the business card, but I only have one damn hand. So I crumple it in my fist.

13

Things that royally suck with a broken

collarbone:

Wearing a seatbelt.

Buttoning my pants.

Taking a shower.

Topping in missionary—it's not easy.

Walking at a speed faster than a slow, unbearable pace. (*See on every page:* trying to keep up with Farrow Redford Keene.)

Typing on a computer—I look like a goddamn dinosaur.

Riding in a car.

That last one I'm feeling tenfold. Every small bump in the road jostles my shoulder and pain drills through my collar like a million serrated needles poking and cutting flesh.

I breathe.

I try to breathe. Whenever Farrow is behind the wheel, he avoids potholes and the badly paved streets while also driving slowly. Cautiously. More than ever. So it's not him.

The blame rests solely on my collarbone that won't heal at lightning speed like I hoped. It's why I'm practically thanking the heavens and skies when we finally reach my parent's house.

My old Basset Hound greets Farrow and me in the foyer.

"Gotham," I smile and bend down like a stiff board. Just to scratch his floppy ears.

He slobbers on me, and as he tries to anchor his paws on my shoulders, Farrow chucks a tennis ball—don't ask, I don't know where he found that—but Gotham is more interested in me. Licking my cheek.

"He loves me," I tell Farrow, patting my Basset Hound's torso and keeping his four paws on the ground.

"I'm not surprised," Farrow says as he glances at family photos hung on the foyer wall.

I stand up, rigid. "Because I'm easily lovable."

He gives me a pointed look. "Because dogs love everyone."

I blink slowly while his smile grows, and I don't have the chance to reply. Voices in the kitchen pull our attention. We leave the foyer and pass through my living room. Superhero figurines line a couple bookshelves, and *X-Men* single-issue comics are framed above a comfortable sectional couch.

Once we enter the spacious kitchen, we spot my dad and uncle. Both immediately stop what they're doing, their heads veering towards Farrow and me. Uncle Ryke has a hand on a blender, and the machine grinds to a halt.

My dad abandons a volume of *Love and Rockets* by Jaime and Gilbert Hernandez that he'd been reading at the island bar.

Silence falls, both of them sweeping me in once-overs like they're checking and establishing my mortality. It's the first time they've seen me since surgery, and they hardly pay attention to Farrow who leaves my side and tugs open the fridge.

He may as well be wearing an invisibility cloak.

I cut the tension by saying, "Two stops to death and straight on 'til morning." It's a play on a *Peter Pan* quote that I know my dad will get.

He does.

He glares at me and says, "Not even a good joke."

"Fucking terrible," Ryke agrees.

I catch a water bottle that Farrow throws to me—

"*Be easy* with him," my dad warns, voice supremely edged.

Farrow slows down his movements as he reaches back into the fridge, eyeing my dad with more uncertainty.

"Dad, I'm fine." I love that Farrow isn't treating me like a wounded puppy. *Please, God, do not let this change.* "And Farrow has an MD."

My dad is only looking for Farrow's response.

Farrow shuts the fridge door, a container of blackberries in hand, and he leans back casually. But his brows pinch. "Trust me, I'm not going to hurt your son."

My dad mulls this over for a second, and I draw his attention when I head over to Farrow. I'm unscrewing my water bottle. Not well.

Uncle Ryke is also zeroed in on my every step. Like I might break. I can barely look at my uncle.

We haven't spoken since the hospital, and I can't imagine what he thinks of me. His daughters are his life, his world, and I was supposed to look after them. Instead, Winona ended up in a car crash with me. Needing stitches on her *face*.

That fact fucking hurts as much as the short walk to the fridge. I breathe out a measured breath through my nose. Farrow looks me over in a warm wave and pops a blackberry in his mouth. His inked fingers moving meticulously.

"Farrow," my dad says, capturing our gazes. "Is Moffy pushing himself too hard? Because he looks like shit."

"I'm right here," I tell my dad.

He flashes a half-smile. "I'm talking to your boyfriend."

"Never heard of him." I look to Farrow. "You know I have a boyfriend?"

"Yeah." He watches me watch his fingers pick up another blackberry. "Because my memory is better than yours."

"Never mind, I do remember," I say and take a swig of water.

Farrow smiles wide like it's too late. I've already lost whatever lead I had. And he answers my dad's earlier question with, "He's Maximoff. Pushing himself too hard is basically his middle name."

My dad leans forward on his barstool, looking at me. "Funny because I didn't give you a middle name."

"Really?" I wipe my mouth with the back of my hand. "Could've sworn I was named Maximoff Fucking Hale."

My dad cringes at my features. "How about Maximoff Paler-Than-My-Ass Hale? Are you even taking anything?"

Uncle Ryke pulses the blender. "Toradol should fucking help, but you should talk to your doctor first." Green liquid churns in the glass.

I don't have a primary care physician, and that unsaid thing noticeably tenses Farrow beside me. He closes the blackberry container.

Toradol. "Is that a narcotic?" I ask.

"No," Ryke says and pours his shake into a to-go thermos.

"He's on some decently strong NSAIDs," Farrow answers.

"Then stop moving around," my dad snaps at me, his voice sharp and harsh. "You shouldn't even be here." He points at the door. "Bed. Rest—"

"I have things to do," I interject. Which…is a lie. I have nothing to do now that I don't have a job, but I can't just lounge.

I want to move.

To swim.

To run.

And I have an ultra marathon to train for—I *promised* Sullivan that I'd race with her in Chile. I'm not missing it for anything. Not even a broken collarbone. And that—that is the last thing I need to surface in front of my dad and uncle. They'll bombard me as soon as the word *ultra* leaves my mouth.

My dad's brows scrunch at me. "Did your mom and I not teach you the art of being a couch potato? Jesus Christ, I've truly failed as a parent."

Ryke almost laughs, but he turns more to me. This time, I don't look away. And he tells me, "You've got time to rehab. Your dad is right. With these first few fucking weeks, you need to take it easy."

I freeze even more than I already am. Ryke is offering advice like this is just another day of my life. Not the day after his daughter…I shake my head, confused.

Almost wishing he hated me. "You're not upset?" I ask.

His brows furrow. "Upset?"

Farrow wraps an arm around my side. He knows. He knows that

I'm beating myself up about this, and I can't help it. I can't stop the fucking guilt from attacking me.

"Winona was in that car with us," I tell him. "She has a gash—"

"It'll fucking heal," Ryke says, scowling hard at me. Now he's pissed.

"It'll scar—"

"Don't do this to yourself, bud," my dad interjects.

Ryke adds, "You couldn't have protected her from a car crash. That's not on you. Don't *ever* put that fucking weight on yourself."

I breathe.

Farrow watches my expression, and I think he knew I needed them. He's been urging me to see Ryke, maybe because my uncle is the only one who could come close to absolving me.

But I'll always wonder if we could've prevented the crash someway. Somehow. Stayed in the alley, waited out the storm. If Charlie or Farrow had driven from the get-go. If we pulled over sooner. Anything, *anything* different and maybe they'd be okay.

It takes a lot of energy just to leave Farrow

in the kitchen with my uncle and dad. He'd tell you he can handle the probing questions and sharp sarcasm from my dad, but I'd much rather be there to take half the heat.

Still, I have a goal today.

One that has to be done alone.

Walking down the second-floor hallway, I come to a stop at a door-less room. My fifteen-year-old rapidly growing brother is sprawled on his bed. He's already six-foot-one, and the day before the auction, he texted me a selfie of pieces of toilet paper stuck to his shaving nicks. His message: *Razor vs. Man.*

He's growing up, and he's going to fuck-up. And as his older brother, I'm trying to figure out how to minimize that damage and protect him.

I have to.

In his bedroom, Xander has on bulky headphones and flips through a thick fantasy novel.

I knock on the doorframe.

He glances up and slides his headphones to his neck. His straight brown hair is tucked behind his ears. "Hey, I didn't know you were coming over." His amber eyes light up like he's genuinely happy to see me.

My stomach twists because the conversation I'm about to have— it's not going to be pleasant. And I've been sprinting around inside my head, trying to determine the best way to phrase this stuff without it sounding accusatory.

But it is an accusation, any way I turn it. He did something wrong… he's *doing* something wrong.

Before I say anything, I walk further into his room. Distracted at the sparkling clean area. No heaps of clothes on the floor. No soda cans stuffed under his bed or empty pizza boxes littering the ground. It hasn't looked like this in *months*.

The metal of his life-sized armored knight seems polished. I look at my little brother. "Did mom cave and clean your room for you?"

Xander snorts. "No way," he says. "She said if I didn't clean it, I'd have to do inventory at Superheroes & Scones." He shuts his paperback. "I think…I really scared her last time. She's been super strict again."

Last time.

Where he locked his door and retreated to a low point that scared pretty much all of us. It's hard to touch that memory. The one where I was on tour and received the phone call from Kinney.

But I'd return to that place if he needs me to.

I roll out his desk chair near his bed and take a seat. "You wanna talk about it, Summers?" I ask him.

He considers for a long moment, and then he shakes his head. "Not really. I've already been through it about fifteen times with Dr. Kora. You know she told Mom and Dad that if she didn't see improvement, she's going to recommend me going to this inpatient treatment center for depression and anxiety."

I watch him fan the pages of his book. I didn't know about the inpatient center, but I'm not surprised that I wasn't told until now. It's not something my parents would share with me, and they'd let Xander tell whoever he wanted in his own time.

"But," he continues. "There's a zero percent chance I'm going. Check this out." He rises off his bed and sidles to the desk.

I roll my chair backwards, out of the way so he can bend down and slide open a bottom drawer.

Xander pulls out a folded poster board. "Don't laugh, it's rough."

"I'm not going to laugh," I say seriously. In all honesty, this is the most excited I've seen my brother in years. I don't know what's changed. I don't know if it'll be a blip, but I'm overwhelmed for him because I recognize how big this is, even if it's just today. An hour. A moment. It's something.

He unfolds the poster board. It's a collage of different medieval and fantasy-inspired costumes and fabrics.

"Mom and Dad helped," he explains. "I've already figured out the LARPing schedule for this summer, and Mom says that if I want to wear prosthetics to look more elf-like I can. That way, you know, less chances for being recognized."

He's getting back into Live Action Role-Playing.

It's huge.

He stopped a while ago, said he just didn't enjoy it anymore. Falling out of love with things is something he does a lot. But LARPing was *so* good for him, got him out of the house.

I smile at the costume sketches that resemble the elves and hobbits from *Lord of the Rings.* "This is awesome, man." I point out a couple drawings and fabrics, imagining my brother dressed up and out in the world. Doing something he loves. "Which one's your favorite?"

When I look back at him, he almost smiles. "This one." He rubs a glassy eye roughly with the heel of his palm, and then points to the elf sketch. "But I'm thinking of going with the red fabric. I'm not that into light blue."

While we discuss his costume and LARPing, a sinking dread starts washing over me. And by the time he stuffs the poster into the desk, pressure nearly crushes my shoulders.

How the fuck am I supposed to bring up the pills?

Xander is happy.

Really goddamn happy. And maybe you don't understand. Maybe you couldn't, but my brother is literally glowing right now. He looks like he found a bottle of hope and chugged that shit down.

I don't know how long that'll last, and I'm so conflicted on what to do. I'm afraid of bulldozing this situation and coming in swinging. I need to think about this. Because on one hand, Xander needs his pills and this other guy shouldn't be taking another person's medication. On the other hand, Xander is doing better than okay right now, and I can't rip him apart.

Tough love is easy for me, but not at this cost.

Biding my time, I reach for his *Game of Thrones* Daenerys Targaryen figurine on his desk. "What prompted this newfound love of LARPing again?" I ask.

Xander plops back onto his bed. "Nothing really. It just sounded fun again." He pauses and then adds, "I know you used to go with me, but I think maybe I should do it on my own this time. No family. Like, I love you guys, but you just make it harder sometimes to…blend." He gestures to me.

I've been front-page news lately. Going public with Farrow cranked the spotlight on me, and it sucks that I can't experience this with my brother because of the media attention but I want him to be comfortable.

I nod. "I get it."

"Not that I can *blend* that well on my own." Hair falls into his eyes and he brushes it back. "Yesterday, there was a Tumblr debate about my shampoo preferences because Mom was photographed buying men's shampoo at a salon. I was almost tempted to just shave my head." He touches his chest. "But then I thought—do I really need more teenage and preteen girls now having an opinion about my new hairstyle?"

I'm surprised that he saw any gossip. He's not supposed to search for that bullshit. "How'd you hear about that?"

"It was on my dash," he rolls eyes. "I was just searching for some Shannara gifs." He folds his headphones and zips them up into a case.

"You wanna know what else is all over my dash? Gifs of you and your boyfriend."

I haven't actively searched for those, and I have to restrain myself from asking him to surface them. I spin on the desk chair. Facing him more. "I thought you don't follow pop culture blogs."

"I don't," Xander says. "You two are popping up in the *The Fourth Degree* fandom. There's this theory that Mom's going to push the studio to cast Farrow in the next movie as Turner Clarke."

Christ. "They can't be fucking serious," I say. Turner Clarke is a tattooed comic book character who has the ability to manipulate mercury.

Xander shrugs. "They think Farrow is a wannabe actor just dating you for the connections."

I almost groan, and I rub the back of my neck, knowing this shit is what frustrates Farrow. "Don't mention this to him," I tell Xander. It's all baseless and over the top, but it won't stop the theories. Some people can't even for a second just believe he's dating me because he loves me. The truth is too boring.

"I'm never dating anyone," my little brother declares. "I have too many people up in my business as it is."

The public's frenzied reaction towards my relationship is scaring a lot of my siblings and cousins away from wanting one. And that's not what I want.

"You could change your mind," I say. "I did."

He contemplates that and then just shakes his head. "No way."

A knock sounds on the doorway, and we both turn to see my tattooed boyfriend. He leans a shoulder against the doorframe. His brows lift at me. "I just got a call from Quinn. One of Jane's cats escaped into security's townhouse and is missing. I have to go help him find the little bastard before she gets back home." He glances from Xander to me. "I'll be back to pick you up."

I rise from the chair. "I can come with you."

"You sure?" He frowns and looks between us, but then he realizes the same thing I did. His eyes dance all over the clean room. "*Damn*. Xander, your room looks great." His gaze refocuses on me like I'm the cause.

I shake my head.

"It was all Summers," I say.

"Nice job," Farrow tells my little brother.

Xander tucks the headphone case under his bed. "It's just a room."

For anyone else, maybe. For Xander, it's a big deal that he took the energy to do something as minimal as cleaning his room.

"Yeah, but now it doesn't smell and look like that trash planet your brother won't shut up about," Farrow says as I head to the door to meet him. He gives me a sharp look like *you didn't talk to him.*

He can tell.

"Saakar," Xander explains. "It's from *Thor: Ragnarok.*"

Farrow smiles casually. "That's the one." He nods to Xander. "See you later."

"See ya," Xander calls out, and I say goodbye to my brother before we make our way out of the house. It isn't until the front door closes behind us and my boots hit pavement that Farrow broaches the topic.

"What happened?" he asks, his hand resting on the hood of my Audi.

I try to cross my arms, but it's kind of fucking impossible with a sling. "He was happy," I defend. "*Really* happy. I couldn't break that."

Farrow blinks hard.

"You don't agree with me." I can tell he doesn't.

"He's not my brother, wolf scout," he replies. "You know him better than me. But the alternative is telling him during a low, and that feels like a worse move."

There's no obvious path, but I'm doing what feels right. "You tell me to go with my gut," I remind him. "And my gut is saying *not today.*"

He nods strongly. "That I can buy," he says. "But what if your brother is still happy tomorrow, next week, next month? How long?"

"I thought we were doing the whole *no planning, relying on impulse* thing?" I counter.

"If you're only doing it to avoid shit, then you're doing it wrong."

I take a deep breath and swing my head back to the house. I can't go back inside and tell him now, but I'll keep an eye on my brother. And

I come up with a new plan. "Not today," I tell Farrow. "But sometime soon, I'm going to talk to him."

That's a promise.

14

FARROW KEENE

I have a huge decision to make. And I need Maximoff's help.

But as I watch him stubbornly try to workout, I find myself delaying what I need to surface. I'm certain that my mere presence almost always distracts him, but he's definitely hooked me in today.

On gray gym mats, Maximoff tries to bite his shoelace and use his left hand to tie his Nikes. My smile is killing me. I stare at him while I easily tie my own shoes.

I already see how this is ending: me, helping him. But I let him try a little bit longer.

Mostly because it makes him feel better.

Partially because his tenacity is fucking attractive.

I usually work out at Akara's gym, but around the time that SFO gained fame, a celebrity gossip blog started posting about Studio 9. Citing how it's a hotbed of "bodyguard activity" for the famous families and how Omega can easily be spotted there.

Cut to the third week of May, and the gym has turned into a zoo. People will flock to the windows like it's Superheroes & Scones. Hoping to catch sight of Omega. Namely, Quinn.

And I'm certain that if I arrived with Maximoff, it'd incite a larger crowd.

Simple solution: skip the gym.

Maximoff has only worn a sling for six days, and he's not even allowed to stretch until the eight-week mark. I figured Studio 9's crowds would be an easy excuse to bench him.

My boyfriend's solution: find another gym.

More specifically, a home gym that belongs to his uncle.

An afternoon rain shower drips down three glass walls and blurs the view of a landscaped backyard and wooden treehouse, along with the Meadows' quaint cottage. The gym looks like a garden house from the outside, and the inside is equipped with two treadmills, gym mats, a weight bench, and a small-scale rock wall.

Since we're in the famous one's gated neighborhood and in a cul-de-sac, it's private and quiet and I'm considered off-duty. He invited his little brother to join us, and Xander turned him down. I'd say it's out of the ordinary, but Maximoff usually always tries to invite him to things, especially the gym. Xander's response is nothing new.

"Race me," Maximoff says with the shoelace between his teeth. He motions with his head to the side-by-side treadmills.

Race him.

Honestly, I thought he'd do a few one-handed push-ups and then call it a day. But I've hopped on this batshit crazy ride, and I'm not hitting the brakes. If he derails, I'll catch him.

I finish knotting my shoelaces. "How long are you planning to pretend you didn't just have surgery six days ago?"

"Tomorrow," he mumbles through the shoelace, "because then it'll be seven days."

I roll my eyes and end up shaking my head, smiling. I lean back on my palms and watch him do a halfway decent job at tying his right shoe.

Marvel stickers and Elfish words decorate his red sling. Handiwork of his brother and sisters. His right arm is still braced to his upper abdomen. We're both shirtless and in gym shorts, but he's the only one with lingering bruises.

Fuck, I've never liked seeing him bruised, and while I'm a few feet away, I skim the yellowish-green marks on his ribs…

I smell rain on metal. I glance at the windows. Rain softly pelts the glass. I almost feel wet cement beneath my hands, gravel digging into my palms.

My smile fades. I'm still on a gym mat, and I try to train my focus on Maximoff.

"Goddammit," he growls, his laces coming completely loose. On both shoes.

I push myself to a stance and tower over him. "Let me help, wolf scout."

He nods after a short pause. As he rises to his feet, his gaze scales my six-foot-three frame, fixating on my chiseled abs and chest tattoos. His carriage rises in a heady breath.

Fuck, Maximoff.

My muscles contract. I slowly lower to my knees and my carnal gaze drips down his swimmer's build on my descent.

He's watching my fingers as I tie his left Nike, and before I mention how he's obsessed with my hands, Maximoff says, "Let's place a bet on the race." His deep voice comes out raspy.

"The race," I repeat with raised brows. "You really want to place a bet on that?" I knot his lace and work on the right shoe.

"Yeah." He nods. "I can run a faster mile than you, man."

I laugh. "The fact that you think you can run a mile right now is truly something else."

Maximoff tries hard not to smile. "Maybe I can…maybe I can't, but we'll see. And if you beat me, I'll give you head."

I can't fucking tear my eyes off him. "You must really want to give me head. Because there's no chance in hell you're beating me."

"There's *a* chance," he refutes, his hand on my head while I kneel at his feet. His *fuck me* eyes and bobbing Adam's apple just about drive me nuts.

"Wolf scout," I say while I finish tying his other shoe, "we can easily skip the part where you bust your ass on a treadmill, and I'll let you suck me off."

His muscles noticeably flex. "Or I could outrun you, and then I'll drive my cock in your mouth."

Damn.

I breathe through my nose, my blood cranking to a red-hot simmer. I clutch his waist, my hand moving towards his ass. "Or we could pretend you outran me, and I'll gladly put your cock in my mouth." It's an out so he won't have to hurt himself.

"Maybe," he says without a pause.

I stand up, an inch taller, and my hand dives down his shorts. I grip his bare ass and watch his eyes devour me whole.

"Maybe?" I ask deeply.

Maximoff tilts his head back, almost bathing in mounting arousal and want. His daggered eyes are groaning *fuck me fuck me*.

I hold his jaw and close my lips over his bare neck. Sucking harder and harder—he rocks his hips against mine, our bodies tensed. Blistering veins pulsing.

Pulsing.

And then he says, "No."

I frown and instantly retract my hands.

He breathes heavily. Pent-up. Neither of us came this morning since he had an early doctor's appointment for a post-op checkup. But we were teasing the hell out of each other in bed with no release.

"What's wrong?" I ask, concerned.

"I need to run first." He tears away from me and goes to the treadmill.

I really don't understand why he's so adamant.

Sure, he's been managing the pain better. His uncle and dad have been sharing tips since they've both been in similar spots as Maximoff. But trying to run, of all things, will flare up his injury and hurt him.

I reach the other machine. "You realize running requires shoulder movement?"

"Pretty much everything under the sun requires shoulder movement. I'm aware." He climbs onto the unmoving belt.

I do the same on my treadmill, but I lean casually on the handlebar. Watching him push buttons to change his machine's settings. "What's so special about running?"

He ups the incline and the speed but doesn't press *start* yet. "I planned to train for the ultra marathon this summer, and before you say *I can't run anymore*, I'm not letting Sulli down. I have to fucking try."

Sulli and Maximoff signed up for the ultra marathon almost an entire year in advance of the August race day. Things change.

Shit happens.

Like a car crash.

But he's lost a lot recently. The H.M.C. board was furious when Maximoff decided to cancel the *night with a celebrity*. The charity sent out a scathing press release a few days ago, and Ernest nailed Maximoff's career in a coffin:

> Maximoff Hale continues to value himself above the needs of others, and his entitlement has caused this charity to suffer in recent years. He bowed out of an event and instructed his family to do so, which would've earned millions for our upcoming humanitarian projects. Due to his carelessness and irresponsibility, we are permanently severing ties with Maximoff Hale. He no longer represents H.M.C. Philanthropies.

He has no job for the first time in years. He can't swim, his greatest stress reliever gone. And he still has no license. When he drove, he had this compulsive *need* to push faster. And faster. Speeding, even on the days when he shouldn't or didn't need to.

It'd be easy for Maximoff to put all of his energy into the one thing he has left.

The ultra.

And that *need* to push and push won't be a foot on a pedal. It'll be on his body.

I hold his gaze that doesn't ask for comfort this time. "Okay, but you can't run, and as much as I love fucking with you, I take no enjoyment in telling you that there's no chance you'll be able to compete. The ultra is in Chile, Maximoff. It's rocky terrain that'll move your shoulder."

This morning, I drove at a snail's pace over a small speed bump, and he winced between his teeth.

Maximoff clicks into a Cross Training program. "I can try."

I roll my eyes, and the corner of my mouth gradually rises. Fuck, I adore this guy, even when he's so hardheaded. But no matter how far he pushes, I'll be right by his side. Ensuring he's not killing himself.

I glance at his machine's screen. He's on a speed setting that shouldn't overexert him right now.

And as our eyes lock, I tell him, "Prove it." See, I'd much rather Maximoff realize he's not healed up yet at this pace than a speed that'll just annihilate him.

Make no mistake: I'm watching his body very fucking closely in case I need to rip the emergency stop cord.

We both press *start* at the same time, same speed.

Maximoff starts walking briskly. No pain yet.

I jog. Looking over at him.

He glances at me. And then he picks up his pace, jogging—pain suddenly cinches his eyes. We're stride-for-stride for exactly two strides.

His jaw sharpens and he steps onto the stationary track, legs spread. It always hurts seeing him hurt, a rock wedging in my ribs.

He snaps his eyes shut for a longer second.

I lower my machine's speed to a walk. "What do you need?" I ask.

He blows out a measured breath, opening his eyes on me. "Your honesty."

I stay walking on the moving belt next to his powered off treadmill. "I honestly believe you're too hard on yourself and you're too afraid of disappointing Sulli."

Maximoff listens intently. He's thinking hard, and then rests his weight against the machine's handlebar and monitor. Not starting the treadmill back up.

I'm about to stop mine—

"Don't," he says. "You wanted to workout. You should."

I can do a lot of things, but I can't sprint in front of my boyfriend while he's dying to run. It's not even my workout of choice. It's one of his, and if I stay on this track, it's just being callous towards someone who's extremely kind.

I turn off my machine. "I'm doing abs on the mats."

Maximoff adjusts his sling. "You sure?"

I hang on my handlebar and careen towards him. "I'm always sure." Shit, that's not entirely true. There is something I'm unsure about…but before I retract my statement, Maximoff gestures to me.

"You know," he says, "watching you run wouldn't upset me. It'd probably just make me hornier."

My smile reaches cheek-to-cheek.

He blinks into a glare. "I take it back. You didn't hear that."

"I heard that," I say matter-of-factly, leaning over my handlebar towards his treadmill. "Watching me run does it for you. So does when I walk, talk, smile, breathe—"

"Thank you for listing my turn-offs."

"Anytime." I remember what I needed to talk about again, and my smile vanishes faster.

Maximoff notices, and questions flash in his eyes. "I'd been meaning to ask—at the appointment earlier, you didn't like my doctor, did you?"

Now I really can't stop staring at him, a surprised breath in my throat. He hit the topic almost dead center, and it'd take someone who truly understands me to put these small pieces together.

My affection for Maximoff overflows me, swelling up inside my chest. This is the overwhelming effect of spending almost every minute with each other. To the point where being with him has felt like years stacked on top of years. And my only fear is it ending.

I comb a hand through my white hair. "No, I didn't like that doctor." I step off my treadmill. "Did you?"

Maximoff follows me to the gym mats near the rock wall. "He seemed fine to me. He was polite, professional, and it's not like he's my primary care physician." Because he still doesn't have one.

"He was professional," I agree, watching Maximoff lower to the mat, his back up against the multi-colored anchors and bolts. I add, "My dislike has more to do with me than him."

His brows furrow. "What do you mean?"

Taking a seat in front of my boyfriend, I hang my arm on my bent knee. "I was jealous." It's not a small statement. It's the start of something much larger and more consequential.

His strong-willed eyes never drift off mine. Maximoff exudes quiet compassion that feels louder than thunder. "Is your jealousy from wanting to be my doctor?" he asks. "Or because you aren't practicing medicine at all?"

I tilt my head back-and-forth. "Both." I nod, certain. *Both.* "It wasn't just this morning at the doctor's office. It was when you were rushed into Philly General on a stretcher." I pause. Remembering that night, and I explain how when I finally made the choice to leave medicine four years ago, I had no reservations.

There was no longing to return.

Only a peace to let go and never look back.

"I always thought I'd go through those hospital doors and feel nostalgic. Not bitter or envious," I tell him while he listens carefully. "I was pushed aside trying to help you in the ER, and I chalked up my emotion to being protective of you and being frustrated that I couldn't do more." I pause again.

Maximoff takes my hand into his, hard calluses on his palm against similar ones on mine. "It wasn't that then?" he asks.

"It *was* that, but it was definitely something else, too." I'm conflicted. I tell him that I am, and I explain how that same night I ran into a doctor who'd been in my first-year residency. Tristan MacNair. We talked for a few minutes in the hallway, and then he was paged.

My first thought should've been, *I'm glad that's not my call.* But all I could think and feel was, *I wish that were me.* I watched him sprint away to aid a patient. Instinct told me, *follow, go help.*

And my hunger for medicine just pummeled me.

It's been eating at me on-and-off since, and then seeing the doctor this morning, that hunger returned. I stop rehashing my story and feelings here, a pit in my stomach.

My actions will affect Maximoff. More than anyone.

Even considering what I'm considering eviscerates me. Hacks up my organs and slices me in fucking two.

You selfish bastard.

I love him.

Fuck, I love him more than is comprehensible, more than anyone can possibly see, and I've always run towards what calls me.

Maximoff. He calls out to me every second of every minute of every day, and to willingly turn my back and race away from him is unfathomable. Because it'd tear me apart. I'd sooner drop to my knees and scream, and then I'd dig my way back into his arms.

If losing him is a consequence of what I choose to do next, I physically can't do it. It'd hurt less to ignore this pull than to lose him.

My eyes burn. "I need to know what you think." I tighten my hand in his. "I'm not sure what to do yet."

I expected this conversation to surprise Maximoff. But he doesn't look shocked.

He rests the back of his head on the rock wall, his eyes swimming through my eyes. "Choose the path where you're not fighting yourself, don't be afraid of change, don't live for less than what you love—those are your words, Farrow. To me, it's obvious what you need to do."

I rub my jawline. "It's not."

"You love medicine—"

"I love you," I tell Maximoff. "You are who I love, who I live for, and if I finish my residency to be a concierge doctor, it means quitting security. It means working in a hospital for *three years* before I can even be your family's physician." There's no shortcut to being board-certified; I have to complete my three-year residency.

Maximoff is quietly thinking.

I've already drawn closer to him, my legs broken apart. His are spread open too, nearer. Fit together.

Our elbows balance on my kneecap like we're about to arm wrestle, but our hands aren't closed in a fist. In the silence, he threads our fingers, unthreads them, and then traces the ink on my hand. Like the tiny blue sparrow along my thumb.

"Maybe we were wrong," Maximoff says, brows scrunched in deep contemplation. "When we thought we only worked because you were my bodyguard—maybe we were wrong. Maybe it's just what brought us together. Because I wanted you *way* before that damn day."

I watch him watch our interlacing hands. I've recalled my past with him, every moment, a hundred-and-five times and more. "I can believe that," I say, voice husky.

He licks his lips. "Because you knew I may've been somewhat-attracted to you for a while?"

"Somewhat-attracted," I repeat with a small burgeoning smile. "That's where you're shelving your sixteen-year-old fantasies of me? In the 'somewhat-attracted' category?"

"The holy-fuck-I'm-coming category was full."

I give him a look. "Of who?"

"Some guy." He's lying. It was definitely full of me. He tries to hook our fingers, but I pull back slightly, teasingly.

He glares.

"I'm just some guy," I remind him.

"No," Maximoff says, firm and final. "You're *the* guy."

It hits me hard, and I inhale.

Damn. I let him hook our fingers, and I have to tell him this… "I can believe that me being your bodyguard is just what brought us together, not why we're good together, because I wanted you before that day too."

His mouth parts, and his elbow almost slips off my knee.

I clasp his hand. "Maximoff—"

"You never said a fucking thing." He looks a little bit hurt.

My chest ignites on fire. "Because I didn't think it mattered, and I'm going to be honest here, I didn't even realize *the extent* of how much I wanted you back then until after we got together." It's only in hindsight.

Just like for him, it's in hindsight. He never let himself dream about love or what he was looking for in a relationship until he seized it for the first time. Until me.

And yeah, he had a crush on me. Because he allowed himself to fantasize about me. Sex is uncomplicated to him. Love is messy.

I didn't know these private things about him back then, not completely, but I knew that he had one-night stands. I knew that I didn't. I knew that I needed the prospect of more if I sleep with a guy.

And I always, *always* believed he'd never act on anything. Moral, good-natured Maximoff Hale would never get with a friend of the family's and definitely not his mom's bodyguard.

I look at Maximoff now and try to wrangle these thoughts.

"I don't dwell on what I can't have," I clarify, "and in my mind, I couldn't have you for the longest time. I went on with my life, but whenever I saw you, I wanted to be around you. So it's only in hindsight that I realize how fucking much I was hooked on you."

Maximoff tries his absolute worst not to smile. "You liked me."

I smile wider and tilt my head. "You going to write this in your diary tonight? Edit out all the parts about your unrequited teenage love?"

He holds my hand in a tight fist. "You've been reading someone else's diary, man. Mine just talks about fucking you."

I laugh. "Let me read it."

"Let me read yours." His tone is serious.

I nod a few times, understanding that he wants more. "In retrospect, if I could pinpoint a day that I'd say I felt an…" I suck in a breath, searching for the word "…intense chemistry, I'd say it was when I went to Harvard and sutured your leg. I couldn't stop looking at you, and I fucking craved to know you even better. If you had asked me to spend the entire day there with you, I would've said *yes*."

He dazes off.

Where'd you go, wolf scout? I snap my fingers until his focus is back on me. I'm smiling. "You can masturbate to that later," I tease.

"No thanks," he says dryly, and then he takes a breath. "I was just thinking about which day that I felt we'd be good together. In hindsight."

"What day?" I ask, curious.

He releases my hand from our stronghold and then outlines the inked letters *k.n.o.t.* on my fingers. "The day on the yacht," he says, assured. "The summer bash when I was nineteen. You threw me your shirt after I fought with Charlie, and you made one of the worst days of my life easier. Better. Just being around you…" He threads our fingers again, thinking for a short beat. "You had a boyfriend that day, didn't you?"

I nod. "Yeah. But it was close to being over by then."

I replay that memory in my head where Maximoff was frozen next to a cooler on the yacht deck. When I caught his attention, he revived. And he looked up at me.

My lips lift because I've remembered that moment before. That one part where he reawakens always floods back and breaks my face into a smile. I remember the salt in the air and how his dark brown hair blew in the wind.

And those tough forest-greens that said *I can handle everything.*

Now years later, I'm at a crossroads with him. I've been vacillating between security and finishing my residency because neither feels one-hundred percent right. If I could speed through residency and just be his doctor right now, it'd be an easier choice. But there'll be three years where I'm not around him that much.

I do believe what Maximoff said. Being his bodyguard isn't what binds us.

It never has been.

And hell, if anything feels right, it's him and me. We're better than good together. Better than perfect. Gradually, I start envisioning what'll happen if I choose medicine. "If I'm not your bodyguard," I tell him, "that means some other prick is on your detail."

"Yeah," Maximoff says. "You'll have to be okay with that."

My eyes almost roll around the world because I'm not that excited about it. Somewhat for territorial reasons. Mostly because this'll upheave his life. He hates big change, and he's been bulldozed with it recently.

I shake my head. "I can't do this to you right now. I'll wait—"

"No," he cuts me off. "I can take a lot. And a new bodyguard isn't even that hard to handle. Unless you have an annoying clone, I'll live."

I could easily make a joke back, but I contemplate something else. And then I watch him skim his palm down my palm, our hands almost the same exact size.

His fondness for my hands ropes me in. And warms me.

I lift my gaze to his. "You said that I need to do what I love, but I love security, wolf scout. That hasn't changed. So why do you think that I want medicine more?"

He sees the path that I can't see yet.

Maximoff clasps my hand tighter. "Medicine is a part of you, and unlike security, that'll *never* change. Christ, I know you hate believing that medicine is who you are, but I don't think it ever left you even when you left it."

He lists off all that I've done just while I've been on his security detail.

Including treating his sister's infected tongue piercing to setting his dislocated shoulder and triaging an entire car crash. I could do more if I were a concierge doctor.

I'd have a license to prescribe medicine. I'd be on-call for all emergencies. But I waver.

Maximoff sees. "If you're only fighting yourself on this because you love me," he says, "I'm telling you to go. It'll eat at you for the rest of your life if you don't. So I need you to go." His voice almost breaks. "Fucking Christ." He knocks his head back to the rock wall. He's conditioned himself to bottle up a certain kind of emotion.

He could marbleize his face. But he's actually wrestling to let go and be more vulnerable.

Quickly, I pull my hand out of his. Only so I can hold his face between my palms. "You don't need to pretend that it won't be hard. Not being your bodyguard will be just as hard on me." I keep swallowing a lump lodged in my throat.

His eyes redden, and he clutches the back of my neck. "You know, the hardest things are usually the right things."

I nod a couple times, my thumb stroking his cheek. "A philosopher talking to you again?"

Maximoff starts to smile, and it's drop-dead gorgeous. "If you want to call my dad and uncle philosophers, then yeah. A couple philosopher kings told me that."

I wrack my brain. *Should've known.* I've heard Lo and Ryke say that phrase before.

"Farrow." Maximoff captures my gaze. "You better choose medicine. Because if you don't, I'm going to kick your ass."

I almost let out a laugh, but I breathe deeper with him. And in the tender quiet, my fingers skate through his hair, down the angles of his cheekbone and jaw. To his neck that aches to unwind, and up again. Maximoff closes his eyes, relaxing into my touch.

I pull him closer, a breath apart, and when his eyes melt into me, he whispers, "You know what's strange? I have *zero* job options, and you suddenly have *two*."

I push back his hair, my fingers trailing down the back of his head. "Can't be that strange, wolf scout," I breathe. "I am better than you at everything."

His grip strengthens on my neck like he's hanging onto what hasn't changed. *That.* In years of time, that back-and-forth has never changed.

He breathes easier. "Tell me the plan for medicine."

I've tried to explain what I've done in terms of medicine, but it's confused him a little bit. I've graduated from medical school, and I've completed a month of my residency.

"I need to finish my three-year residency at Philadelphia General. I also need to pass my USMLE exam and boards."

He nods, confident. "You'll do it."

There's something else. I haven't thought about what returning to medicine means in terms of my family.

I didn't want it to influence my choice.

But now it slings back at me.

"And I need to talk to my father."

15

FARROW KEENE

Today marks my last week on security, but
SFO doesn't know that yet. Clock strikes 4 a.m., and quietly, I slip out
of Maximoff's bed and find a pair of my boxer-briefs in his drawer. I
search for pants.

Almost all of my shit is in his room: clothes, toiletries, a few medical
texts that I dug out recently, and my electronics. I prefer it this way. Not
only because security's townhouse contains Thatcher, and the less time
I spend around him, the better. But because Maximoff will sometimes
scrutinize all of my belongings in his room and start to unknowingly
smile.

It's cute as hell.

I pull my black pants to my waist, and Maximoff blinks awake
beneath his comforter. He extends his left arm to reach for the bedside light.

"Go back to sleep," I whisper, fishing my belt through the loops.
"It's mail day." The Omega lead schedules a specific day and time to
examine our client's mail. It's usually at 4 a.m.—when all the famous
ones should theoretically be asleep.

Maximoff collapses back and pinches his tired eyes. "Have fun with
that." His brain must start waking up because he quickly asks, "Are you
telling them tonight?"

I pull a black V-neck over my head. "Technically, it's morning."

He growls into an uncontrollable yawn. "I don't think you realize how annoying your technicalities are."

"Trust me, I do." I smile as irritation scrunches his brows. "Man, that's partially why I keep them up, just for you."

"I'm partially honored."

I grin and hook my radio on my waistband. Before I go, I return to the bed. And I hang my hand on the headboard and dip down towards him. Close enough to kiss him, and as much as I want my lips against his lips, teasing the hell out of him is too good to pass.

"I'm going to tell SFO," I confirm.

"Need help or any backup?" he asks. We've discussed Omega's possible reactions, and the only one that I can't predict is Thatcher Moretti. The rest should be fine. My friendship with Oscar and Donnelly is easy for a reason. We roll with the punches and almost never hound each other.

"I'll be okay." I linger for a second.

Maximoff is staring at my mouth.

I smile wider. "You think I'm going to kiss you?"

"Who said I wanted you to?" He's only looking at my eyes now. Trying to beat me at the whole teasing thing. It's not going to work.

I lower closer, planning on pulling away at the last second, but he clasps the crook of my neck. Our breaths meld, and our mouths meet like a fucking magnet. I rest my knee on the bed, my hand dropping to his jaw—*fuck, Maximoff*...his tongue parts my lips. Driving the kiss deeper, a coarse noise scratches my throat.

His left hand sneaks up my shirt.

Shit.

I'm almost about to climb on top of him. I tear our mouths apart. "Damn," I breathe hard and step back before I end up in bed with him.

Maximoff smiles like he won something. "Looks like you wanted to kiss me."

I walk backwards. "Never said I didn't, wolf scout."

My words and smooth tone must relax him. He oozes into the pillow, as much as he can for being in a sling and without heavy pain medication.

It's always hard to leave when I love being around him. But this'll be our regular routine when I restart my residency. And to be honest, I'm not sure how I feel about that.

Exiting the attic, I skip rapidly down the narrow staircase. Cats dart out from under the Victorian loveseat, and then I scare Walrus with my foot. He scurries beneath the iron café table.

"Stay there, you little bastard," I warn, slipping through the adjoining door. Shutting out the calico cat behind me.

As soon as I'm inside security's townhouse, I'm met with a stench that I can't pinpoint.

Let's just say it smells worse than Ben Cobalt's rank B.O.

Akara looks up from the leather couch. "I know," he says, clutching a Lucky's Diner paper coffee cup, "I can't figure out which one it is." He motions with his index finger to the mound of boxes and envelopes. Packages are scattered across the coffee table and the hardwood floors.

Wicker laundry baskets, that aren't used for laundry, line the brick wall. A name written on a travel tag is attached to each one. And a heavy-duty trash bag hangs off the fireplace mantel.

The smell stings my nose. "I'd say it's rancid, but I'm not sure that's the right word." I step over Quinn's spread of packages that pile up at the door.

"It's probably food," Quinn says, slicing through a cardboard box with a utility knife.

"Even spoiled food doesn't smell like that, little bro," Oscar replies, ripping open a manila envelope. He's seated on a leather barstool at our high-top table. Security's furniture is more comfortable and less *pastel* than everything in the neighboring townhouse.

And it's not a surprise that Oscar is in Philly. Or Donnelly, who straddles the armrest and flips through a few letters. All of SFO spent the night since Charlie and Beckett are crashing in Jane's room, and Sullivan is asleep in Luna's bedroom next door.

We all stayed out late for trivia night at Saturn Bridges. Maximoff said most of his cousins would normally pass on those invites. But Charlie showed. Beckett showed, and so did Sulli and Luna.

Whenever they all assemble together, Omega inadvertently gathers. And very fucking soon, my role with the famous ones and security will shift drastically. I don't try to predict how it'll feel.

All I know is that I've never been afraid of the great unknown, but I'm definitely cautious going forward since I'm leaving more things behind than usual.

I pluck latex gloves out of a box. Every guy already wears a pair. Mail day is a minefield of the good, the bad, and the disgusting.

Oscar unfolds a letter. "*Dear Charlie,*" he reads. "*Get Well Soon.*" He crumples the letter and free-throws it into the hanging trash bag.

"Cold," Donnelly says, reaching for a yellow mailer.

Thatcher glances up from a letter he's been reading. "Charlie doesn't want to read his fan mail?"

"The guy rarely does." Oscar balls another letter. "I've been instructed to destroy all condolences."

I snap on my gloves and tuck one-fifth of Maximoff's mail under my arm. Drumsticks lie next to a carton of to-go coffees. I frown and pick up a wooden drumstick. "What's with these?" I ask Akara.

He answers while texting. "Some teenage girl mailed them to me."

That makes little sense. "How does the public know you were on the drumline?"

To my knowledge, most personal facts about SFO haven't been unearthed. Especially since we deleted our social medias.

Then again, I haven't been actively checking social media threats or keeping in touch with tabloid shit. When my relationship went public, I relinquished that responsibility to the tech team.

Just making that choice made me realize I was already pulling away from security.

Akara looks up from his phone. "Did you know Brock Carson from high school?"

"Never talked to that debate nerd, no." I twirl the drumstick between my fingers.

"That debate nerd posted our yearbook on Reddit." Akara returns to texting. "There's a whole thread trying to find info on 'Maximoff

Hale's boyfriend' and they spotted me in the yearbook's band section."

I roll my eyes. Not thrilled that people are digging this hard into my past. I consider myself a fairly private person. Not many ever step into my business unless I let them. But I chose to be a public figure. I've known how invasive this could be.

Still, the creep factor is real.

"Let me guess," I say, walking backwards to the open barstool opposite Oscar, "my senior photo is floating around the internet." I had green hair in that picture.

"All over," Akara nods.

Predictable.

I drop the mail onto the high-top table in a heap.

"Boyfriend's going to love that photo," Oscar says to me, being serious. I hold onto that fact and almost laugh.

I lean my ass on the barstool. "He'll most likely save it as his lockscreen."

And then he'll make an excuse about how it's because I hate the picture.

Oscar cuts a box open. "No, he'll print that one out, Redford. Then he'll frame it and hang it in every house you're in for eternity."

Eternity?

My brows rise at Oscar. He stares at me right in the eye, and I doubt anyone else but Donnelly realizes how he's not joking right now. And then Oscar nods at me like he knows.

He knows that what I have with Maximoff isn't temporary. Not just on my end, but on my boyfriend's end, too. It's not something he's expressed before.

But I remember that Oscar was at the crash site. Holding an umbrella over us. He heard Maximoff and me. Saw him say his goodbyes. Saw us together, thinking it could've been the last time.

Raw emotion squeezes my throat. I nod back.

We don't need to exchange any words. I pass him an envelope addressed to Charlie that slipped beneath my stack.

"Thatch, anything good?" Donnelly asks.

"Thatcher," he reminds him, folding a letter. "And it's private." Thatcher gently places the letter in a wicker basket labeled *Jane*.

I sort through six *get well soon* cards sent to Maximoff and save them. He'll read each one, even if it takes him hours. The next envelope, I freeze on the return address and the familiar name.

"Oliveira," I say, "why is your mom sending cards to my boyfriend?" I flash the envelope at Oscar.

"I have one for you. Hold on." Oscar lifts a few boxes and grabs a letter. He chucks it at my face.

I catch it easily.

Oscar nods to me. "She didn't know if she should send you two separate invites or one together. I went through seven phone calls in one hour, Redford. Just to reassure her that two were fine."

I cock my head. "Did you tell Sônia that I wouldn't have given a shit either way?"

"Yeah, I reminded her who you are." Oscar grabs two more letters. "And then she pulled the *Farrow has no mom* on me. Look, she's fucking frazzled that the Boyfriend is a Famous Boyfriend. Additional note: you both need to RSVP separately."

"Sure." I rip open the one addressed to me and read the invitation.

PLEASE JOIN US FOR THE CONFIRMATION OF OUR DAUGHTER JOANA RAQUEL SOUSA OLIVEIRA

My brows arch. For as long as I've known Oscar, I've only met his eighteen-year-old sister once or twice.

"I know," Oscar tells me, "but it's a big deal."

I skim the details.

Location: a local Catholic church.

Date: a Sunday afternoon next month.

I frown.

Shit.

Probability that I'll be stuck in the hospital working that day = extremely high.

What's worse: years ago I couldn't attend Quinn's confirmation for the same reason. This'll be the second time that I bail on the Oliveira family, and I'm not feeling great about it.

Maximoff will definitely want to go, and I would've loved to be his date to this. *There'll be others.*

It reminds me how Maximoff has been planning our "first" formal date. In my eyes, we've been on a hundred-and-twelve dates already. In wolf scout's eyes, they were all "semi-dates" since I had to keep up the bodyguard charade. I couldn't eat dessert off his plate. Couldn't kiss him. Couldn't even hold his hand.

All restrictions are gone now, and honestly, I love how much Maximoff is treating this like it's all new, all over again. Because there are very few feelings I love more than experiencing *firsts* with him.

I slip the invite into its envelope.

Oscar holds out two more cards to the guys. "Moretti, Kitsuwon." Thatcher and Akara grab their invites.

I eye Donnelly who easily brushes off the rejection. Caring and loving parents worry about guys like Donnelly befriending their children. On paper, he reads like a bad influence.

In reality, he's not.

I recognize the greatest benefit of having a father who really only cared about medicine. I was able to invite Donnelly everywhere. And Donnelly always said yes and came along.

I unsnap a rubber band off a package. "Joana is finally going through with it?" I ask Oscar since I witnessed the Oliveira family meltdown when she refused to get confirmed two years ago. I wasn't raised in a religious household, but her decision appeared like a familial betrayal.

Quinn chimes in, "Only because our avó stopped talking to Jo." He uncovers an alien plushie from tissue paper.

Thatcher pockets his invite. "If I'd been confirmed late, my grandma would've done the same to me."

Oscar discards a *Charlie Motherfucking Cobalt* mug. "She's lucky that I'm picking up our avó from the airport next week."

I skim another *get well* card. "You volunteer for that, Oliveira, or were you selected for the slaughter?"

"My confirmation gift to my baby sister," he explains, slicing open another box. "What'd I miss when Charlie went to the bar?" He means from tonight. We all joined in trivia with the famous ones, but we were also all on-duty. Consequently, Oscar had to follow his client away from our booth.

I trash homemade chocolate chip cookies. "Just how Ben hasn't been able to drive since the crash."

Donnelly adds, "Jane said his foot keeps shaking on the pedal."

Oscar mutters a curse. "I have fifteen years of driving experience on Ben, and *I* was having issues keeping the Range Rover on all four wheels that night."

Quinn hurls an empty box at the fireplace. "Paparazzi should've backed the fuck off."

"They won't," Akara says, flipping through a handcrafted *Sullivan Meadows* scrapbook. "The best the parents can do is keep filing lawsuits."

But none have stuck yet. The Hales, Meadows, and Cobalts have also requested that the bodyguards drive for the younger kids until further notice.

Donnelly rattles his open mailer upside-down, and a lacy thong falls to the floor.

We all see it.

"Smell it, Donnelly," I say with a rising smile. "Could be the mystery scent."

He pinches the pink thong between gloved fingers and sniffs.

Quinn gags into his fist.

"Nah," Donnelly says, "just smells like pussy." He flings the panties into the trash and reads the card aloud. "*Beckett Joyce Cobalt, I came in these thinking of you.*" He smirks. "My guy has so many admirers."

Silently, Thatcher dumps a ball gag and dildo in the trash. All mailed to Jane.

Oscar swigs a Ziff sports drink and reads, "*Dear Charlie, I want to have your babies.* She left her phone number."

"Can't blame her." Donnelly reaches for a new package. "Who wouldn't want to have some Cobalt babies?"

Thatcher casts a reprimanding look but stays quiet.

I spin a knife between my fingers and then point to myself with the blade. "Me."

Donnelly grins. "That's just because you're all up in that Hale dick."

I laugh into a smile, about to dish it back—and then the unknown stench unleashes itself tenfold. We all recoil.

"It's this," Quinn chokes and coughs into his bicep. He just flipped the flaps to a cardboard box, the contents not visible. Everyone is asking what was sent to Luna.

I'm about to stand off the barstool and see for myself. But Quinn starts taping up the package. Then he rises to his feet and places the box in Luna's wicker basket—

"Whoa!" all of us basically shout some sort of expletive.

Quinn ignores us. Leaving the package in her good mail.

Thatcher glares at me, as though I caused the youngest bodyguard's "bad" behavior from my short "mentoring" days. I'm not taking the blame for this shit.

I glare back at Thatcher.

I quit.

Slinging those two words out in anger is not what I had in mind today. I bite my tongue hard.

"It's not trash," Quinn says, still choked from the smell. He coughs into his fist.

Akara digs in the wicker basket and inspects the taped package.

"What the fuck is it?" Oscar asks.

Quinn takes a seat around his mail piles. "Really shitty perfume that spilt."

My brows spike. "Sounds like trash to me."

Thatcher crosses his arms. "Farrow, you should've instructed Quinn better. Told him that liquids *need* to be thrown out."

I did.

His assumption that I didn't grates on me. I grit down to keep from spewing out, *I'm quitting, you fucking tool.* Instead I say simply, "I'll keep that in mind." While I stand, I rest my shoulders up against the brick wall.

Thatcher uncrosses his arms. He looks surprised that I'm admitting fault.

Akara carries the perfume package to the trash bag.

"Wait!" Quinn springs to his feet and extends an arm, an angered scowl crossing his face. "Just wait a fucking second. I know what I'm doing."

Akara raises his shoulders. "Quinn, we don't allow liquids—"

"Luna asked me not to," Quinn retorts. "I get that I haven't been a bodyguard as long as *any* of you, but I've been here long enough. And I fucking know if a client asks you to do something, you do it. Sometimes, even if it's illegal—"

"No," Thatcher says sternly. "Not if it's illegal. You can say *no.*" His glare drills into me again.

I'm starting to believe Quinn Oliveira wants Thatcher to murder me.

I still lean casually on the wall. And to Thatcher, I say, "I never told Quinn that he couldn't say no." That implication is not even close to who I am.

"Wait a sec," Akara interjects, box in hand. "Quinn, did Luna specifically ask you not to discard liquids?"

Quinn scratches his unshaven jaw. "No...I was trying to keep this private, but if you all *have* to know..." He motions to the box. "Luna asked me not to throw anything away that's from her boyfriend."

Boyfriend?

Voices collide together, everyone asking the same shit.

I peel off my gloves and then comb my hair back. If anyone had known about Luna Hale suddenly having a boyfriend, it would've been her older brother.

And Maximoff knows nothing.

I question whether this "boyfriend" is real. "Have you seen him?" I ask on top of the mounting questions.

"When?" Donnelly asks.

"For how long?" Akara wonders.

Quinn runs two frustrated hands through his thick, wavy hair. "MyGod," he snaps. "Shut the fuck up and I'll tell you!"

We all go quiet.

Quinn breathes out. "It's been about a week." He shifts his weight and before Akara asks, he says, "Yeah, I did a background check. The guy panned out."

Donnelly slips a pen behind his ear. "Does he live in Philly?"

"How old is he?" I ask.

"What does he do?" Oscar adds.

Quinn hangs onto the fireplace mantel. "This stays between us." He tries to send a warning look my way, but I'm not having it.

"I'll tell you upfront," I say easily. "There's absolutely a hundred percent chance that I'll share this with Maximoff."

He frowns. "Why?"

"Because he's my boyfriend. It's as simple as that."

Oscar leans forward on his stool. "Redford can leave the room. I want the fucking details."

"Same," Donnelly says, unsnapping his gloves. Just to remove his septum piercing.

Quinn expels a breath and then nods to me. "It's alright. Stay. I'm guessing Luna will tell Maximoff soon, so it shouldn't matter." He starts unleashing the news. "So the guy is named Andrew Umbers. Twenty-two. He's originally from Houston but now lives in Philly. He created some kind of start-up for a parking app. And yeah, I've seen him."

Everyone is quiet. Processing.

Thatcher straightens letters in his hands. "Did Luna tell you not to share?"

"No...I have no fucking clue what she'd think if I told everyone," Quinn admits. "And look, before you guys say anything, you should know that their dates have consisted of eating takeout at his apartment and listening to NPR. It feels like he's just using her."

I grit down. I'm not happy about anyone using these families, let alone the Hales. This is exactly why most of them have trust issues.

And I sense the real irony here: the public believes I'm using her brother for fame.

But I'm not going to apologize for loving him. And wanting to be with him.

We all talk about Luna and the intentions of her new boyfriend. Mainly ways to protect her, and I hang back and look at each guy.

This is it.

I've had some of them in my lives long before I joined security. So I'm not losing them. But I am leaving behind *Omega*. The camaraderie, the brotherhood. A protective force of men who will jump into the wildfire, no questions asked.

And I've been here before. Way back when, I believed I'd lose my job once the families and security found out I was *with* Maximoff. I was ready to accept that, but there is more peace in choosing this path now than being forced here back then.

"Redford," Oscar calls out. "What's going on?" He's been reading into my features.

"I have something to say." I comb both of my hands through my hair and step off the brick wall. My shift in demeanor causes the living room to go silent.

Akara is confused.

I didn't tell anyone in advance. Not even the Omega lead, and that's mostly because I need this to be less of an ordeal. Just quiet and easy. Not a big mess.

"This isn't about Luna," I start off. "I appreciate everything you've all done for me so I could remain my boyfriend's bodyguard." I glance briefly at Thatcher. Because back in December, he was the deciding vote that helped me keep my job.

He's scowling like I'm far from genuine.

If I didn't believe those words, I wouldn't have said them.

I swing my head to the Omega lead. "And Akara...o' captain my captain." I wouldn't call anyone else that but him. "All the times you've put your neck on the fucking line for me, I was grateful then and I'm still grateful now."

Akara nods. "You're quitting security, aren't you?"

"Yeah," I say. "I'm quitting. I need to finish my residency." And before they ask, I add, "Not for my father, but for me." I first look at Donnelly.

His lips slowly lift, unlit cigarette in his mouth. "We're getting our Meredith back." He slow-claps.

I smile. "Man, you know I'm a Christina."

"I don't get it," Quinn mutters.

"It's *Grey's Anatomy*, little bro," Oscar says, clapping with Donnelly before he walks over and pats my shoulder, bringing me in a hug. He whispers in my ear, "We're going to keep your guy safe. Don't agonize over it."

I already have been.

A hell of a lot went into this choice. And I look at ease, but he knows this is far from easy for me. Someone else will be filling the job description of *protecting Maximoff Hale*. As his boyfriend, that job should be mine.

I protect the people I love, and choosing the medical path sometimes feels at war with protecting Maximoff. But I have to remember that I haven't lost that ability. At the charity auction, I was there for him as his boyfriend in the end. Not as his bodyguard.

And the same job got done. I don't need the radio or the gun or the title.

I pat his back in thanks before we separate.

"You sure?" Akara asks me, phone frozen in his hand. He holds the power to alert the rest of the Tri-Force. To turn my choice into a reality.

I listen to my gut that says *push forward*. "I'm sure."

Akara hesitates, looking like he wants to change my mind, but after a pause and a once-over, he sees that I'm set. And he starts texting. "You'll need to stay on Maximoff's detail for one more week while we sort out a transfer." He looks up. "Sound good?"

"Perfect." I already knew the protocol. "I've packed most of my shit. I'll be out of security's townhouse before then." It'll be more official than it has been, but I'll be living with Maximoff. And I've never "officially" lived with any of my past boyfriends before, so this is just as new for me.

Thatcher should be ecstatic that I'm no longer living one floor apart from him. I'm not expecting the guy to jump for joy. But a mocking clap seems in the realm of possibility.

But as our eyes lock, he appears the farthest thing from happy.

And I'm certain.

He's going to make this difficult for me. Messy and fucking loud. "Thatcher—"

"You've had one foot in, one foot out from the start. I told you that months ago." He tears off his latex gloves. "And I've known you're committed only to yourself, but I didn't realize how fucking selfish you are until right now." His biting tone is dying to gnaw me apart.

I run my tongue over my molars. Seething inside out. At first, I want to just let him believe what he believes. My actions haven't been able to convince him anything different. Not the marathon run in the dark Poconos mountains. Not every push-up, every sit-up, every time I listened when I would've rather disobeyed.

If he wants words, not actions, then I have those too.

"Wherever I am, I'm all there," I say strongly. "I've *always* been committed to security, and the fucking millisecond that I felt drawn somewhere else, I chose to leave." That's the truth.

But Thatcher glares.

I glare, stepping further off the wall.

And he says, "That's how you plan to spin this?"

My nose flares, hot-blooded anger craving to twist my face. There is nothing more I can give him than what I feel. He's still choosing not to believe me. "I'm not warping shit," I tell him. "If you don't see it the way I see it, then fine. Leave it alone."

Akara, Quinn, Oscar, and Donnelly all stand rigid. Watching. Tensed. But not surprised that we're butting heads again.

Thatcher steps over a pile of mailers. Rolling the sleeves of his plaid flannel. Like he's boiling as hot as me. He nears me and says, "Did you even consider Maximoff when you decided to quit on him?"

I glare unblinkingly.

He's dead serious.

He truly believes that I don't give a flying shit about Maximoff. I almost let out a pained laugh. *Fuck*, I'd do anything for him.

I'd even choose security *for* Maximoff, but here's the thing: Maximoff would resent me. Every day, every minute, he'd hate me. We are so alike in that we want to give each other what we need. And he wouldn't, for a second, let me stay in security out of chivalry.

"Wow," I say flatly. "Did I even consider my boyfriend when I made a life-altering choice that would directly affect him?"

Of course I did. Of course I've struggled. Of course I've beat myself up at the terrible timing. But I'm the one who wakes up to those forest-greens that scream *don't coddle me, just love me.*

Just love me.

Not this fucker.

"Your client, your *boyfriend*, just broke his collarbone," Thatcher spits out, pointing at my chest. "He *just* had surgery and lost his job, and you chose this moment to quit on him—"

"Say that shit again and we're going to have bigger problems," I sneer.

"When one of us quits, we have to hire someone new," he growls, unable to stop spewing more. "And these families have to learn to trust a stranger to protect them *all over again.*" His glare grows hotter in a single pause. "Your client, the guy you left behind, will get someone new in his life. You should be worried about that after what's happened between you two."

I hear what he's insinuating. "You don't know what the hell you're talking about."

"I know Maximoff is impressionable." He cups a hand around his fist. Like he knows what he's about to say will set me the fuck off. "If he fell for someone like you, he'd have no problem falling for his new bodyguard—"

I explode forward to hit him; I'm going to fucking slam my fist in his fucking face—and then Oscar wrenches me back, my feet smashing boxes. And he means well by restraining me.

But the other guys don't catch Thatcher in enough time. I jerk in Oscar's grip as a reflex, seeing the pair of knuckles, and my friend lets go too late—Thatcher's fist *slams* into my cheek.

My head whips, the stinging pain familiar from all the blows I've taken in a ring.

Yells pierce the air. Oscar shoves Thatcher backwards, and Donnelly tries to jump the six-foot-seven guy. But Akara stops another fight from breaking out.

I don't move.

I'm staring at the floorboards, my self-restraint greater than my rage, and I look to the door that connects the two townhouses. And I'm confident about where I want to be and where I need to go.

Tuning out SFO, I head to the adjoining door to find Maximoff.

It opens before I even grab the knob. And my boyfriend fills the doorway. He looks at the welt on my face, and then his eyes basically murder Thatcher a hundred different ways.

Maximoff almost charges.

"Wolf scout," I say, quickly putting a hand on his waist. Guiding him into his townhouse. I kick the door closed behind me, my smile almost rising. Maximoff trying to protect me has definitely become one of my all-time favorite things.

His thick hair is disheveled like he just sprung out of bed, and his drawstring pants ride low like he just raced down the staircase. He must've heard the shouting.

He holds my hip and glowers at the door like he's cursing Thatcher for eternal damnation. He really wants to go back in there and fight on my behalf.

I can't stop staring at him. Feeling how much he cares about me, his hand rises to my cheek. Hovering over the welt.

I clutch his hand in mine and lower them to our sides.

"He fucking *hit* you," he says.

I nod a few times. "I love that you want to stick up for me. But among other things, your dominant arm is bound to your chest."

Maximoff glances at his red sling, then looks right at me. "I'm stronger than you with just one arm."

I laugh.

Shit, I can't believe I'm laughing after that shit show. But he brings me this effortless joy, and I cling onto that for dear fucking life.

"He took you quitting that badly?" he asks.

"I'll catch you up in the car." And before he asks, I tell him, "We're going to my old neighborhood. And I'm going to talk to my father."

Right now. There's not a better time than the present. Because there will never be a good time.

Maximoff doesn't question the abruptness. As soon as I start to lead him to the garage, he's pace-for-pace in step with me. Hand-in-hand.

Like a soldier prepared for love and war.

16

FARROW KEENE

Door is unlocked. I'll be in the sunroom. — **Dad**

No face-to-face verbal contact in almost four years and that was his reply. I only messaged him that I wanted to talk in person and that I was on my way to his house with Maximoff. I can't even be surprised by my father's lack of enthusiasm. It's not like I texted: *I'm returning to medicine. You're welcome.*

I'm treating this interaction like a meeting with a college professor. That's all it really is.

Maximoff knows this too.

It's why he didn't ask to change clothes to impress my father. He's shirtless, still in the same drawstring pants that hang low on his muscular waist.

His ass looks great. But he wouldn't catch me checking him out, even if I waved a hand in front of his face.

Because as soon as we enter the foyer and hallway, he soaks up our surroundings. Like he's placing my younger self everywhere.

I watch him with a growing smile. He's lost in the décor of Italian painters and overflowing vases of wildflowers. He looks up at the vaulted glass ceiling and down at the marble floors beneath his scuffed Timberlands.

Where his family home is warm and inviting, mine is a poster child for blue-blooded pretentiousness.

Maximoff glances at the dining room's table set for twelve. "Did your house look like this when you grew up here?"

I toss my head from side-to-side. "Somewhat. Less paintings. Rachel is an art collector," I remind him in case he forgot. He knows my stepmom moved in around the time when I went to college.

We turn a corner into an open living room, cigar bar, and upscale kitchen. I put a piece of gum in my mouth.

He zones in on the baby grand piano near a towering bookcase. "You can play?" he asks.

I leave his side and approach the piano. I look over my shoulder. "Can you, wolf scout?"

Maximoff gestures to me. "I asked you first, man."

He can't play. I pop a bubble in my mouth. "How badly are you hoping I'm a shit pianist because you are?" My fingers brush the keys.

"Who said I was a shit piano player?" he combats. "Maybe I'm the best there ever was, the goddamn best piano player of all piano players."

My brows rise. "You're definitely the most conceited pianist." Every time I say *pianist*, he grimaces a little bit.

He nears me while I rest my knee on the velveteen bench. He skims my hands that hover above the keys.

"So you can't play either," Maximoff concludes since I'm prolonging this and he's impatient as hell.

"And you just admitted that you can't play," I point out and sweep him in a slow-burning once-over.

He's trying fucking hard not to smile. He licks his lips, eyeing my mouth. "I didn't say that."

"I love when you pretend to have amnesia." I smile as he breathes out heavily in agitation, just wanting me to hurry this shit up. But I could bask in this moment for hours on end.

"Farrow," he starts.

I bang on the keys harshly. Shrill chords jumble and pitch the air. I watch his smile take shape like he beat me.

"You like that?" I ask huskily.

His forest-greens pour through my brown eyes with so many *yeses*, and I'm tempted to draw closer—

"Farrow."

That's not Maximoff.

With no urgency, I retract my hands from the piano, the room deadening. Maximoff rigidly faces my father, and I glance over at the old man.

He stuffs his hands into khaki slacks, sporting a warm smile. His brown hair is tied back in a small pony, graying at his temples, and his forehead is lined with age.

Part of me almost wishes I could be a resentful bastard. Rub salt in his wounds before I give him what he's wanted for so long, but I've never really enjoyed being needlessly bitter. That shit just isn't for me, and if I can help it, I try not to be.

His eyes flit to the welt on my cheekbone. The one that Thatcher gifted me. My father doesn't say anything about it, and I bet he's assuming it's from the hazards of security work.

"Let's talk on the patio," he suggests. "I'll grab a few cigars—"

"No, we aren't going to be long." I drop my boot to the ground. My father contributes a lot of money to Philadelphia General, and they'll easily let me restart my residency where I left off, so I'm not going to ask him to pull strings when my last name already will.

Nepotism. It's real.

My father glances at Maximoff and hones in on his bandaged shoulder. "How's that healing?"

"It's alright," Maximoff says, not intimidated. By anyone. He keeps eye contact until my father has to look away.

I'm about to speak, and then my father tells me, "If this is about Rowin, I hired him onto the med team because I've built trust with him. In thanks because of you—"

"Stop." I shut my eyes for a long, annoyed beat. "Don't tell me that."

"Then tell me why you're here," he says, cordial. Non-confrontational. He ambles to the kitchen bar and yanks open the fridge.

Maximoff and I follow so we won't have to shout across the huge room.

I rest my sole on the rung of a barstool. "I came by to tell you that I'm finishing my residency."

My father pours a glass of ice water for my boyfriend. Digesting my words slowly like he didn't hear me well. He scrutinizes my earpiece and mic to my radio.

"This is my last week of security. I'm going back after that," I explain. "I don't need anything from you right now, but I'm doing this because I want to be a concierge doctor—"

"You will be." His face brightens like I've given him all he needs to die a happy fucking man.

He never asks why I've had a sudden change of heart. I didn't expect the *why* to be important to him, and that's perfectly fine by me. He makes it easier to stay at a distance.

I pop another bubble. "That's it. I'll stay in touch for work." I lower my boot off the barstool.

"Good. I'll be available." He pours a glass of water for himself, and he feels the need to tell Maximoff, "First-year doctors are filled with fear and doubt, and rarely do med interns run towards codes. But my son always did."

I didn't run towards codes thinking I'd bolster the family name. I ran towards them because I was confident I could handle the pressure. And I wanted to help. That's it.

Maximoff curves his left arm around my shoulder. "You should be proud of your son," he says so entirely that I can feel *his* pride for me. For so much more than just this choice. My eyes are only on him.

"I am proud now," my father tells Maximoff. "But not these past years—"

"Of course not," I say.

He sighs. "Farrow, you don't understand. *You* are gifted. More than me, more than your grandfather. You can't waste talent like that—"

"Why don't you tell Maximoff the story about how I came out to you?" I ask to make a point that I've never made before.

My father chooses this moment to take a sip of water. He clears his throat and glances at Maximoff with the shake of his head. "There's not a lot to say."

"Because you don't remember." I stand more upright. "It's okay." I hold out a genial hand. "It's not a bad story. Shit, I actually like it." I touch my chest. "You asked me about my crush. We talked for a few minutes, and things were easy. They always were, but eventually you'd forget about that boy. You'd forget we even spoke."

"That's not fair," he says. "That was years ago."

"Name one memory that doesn't involve medicine."

He lets out a deeper sigh. "Farrow…" He's thinking. My life is entangled with medicine, but there are plenty of memories he could choose.

My first high school dance—he let me take his Bentley to pick up my date.

My mall excursion at twelve-years-old where I got my nose pierced—he signed the parental consent forms.

My second grade chorus recital—he made me blueberry pancakes as a *good luck, do well* thing.

He exists in memories that are void of medicine, but he has trouble coming up with one. He just never placed value on any of them. While he raised me, he looked through one lens and never widened the scope. I know how this ends before it even does. I tell him it's okay. Don't worry about it. We exchange a few more words about medicine.

And then I leave with Maximoff.

I'm not clairvoyant, but *that* I can predict.

"*FARROW! Boxers or briefs?!*"

Gotta love paparazzi. Asking the good questions. And by *good*, I mean *trivial*. Kind of funny if not predictable, but pretty trivial.

You should know that I'm not annoyed, but I'm more than cautious. This is one of the first times Farrow and I have walked hand-in-hand on a sidewalk in Center City together. He's used to being the silent bodyguard companion.

Not the *boyfriend* to a celebrity.

The *click, click, click* of cameras that follow our trek to dinner—this is my normal. I have almost no recollection of walking without paparazzi in Philly.

And it's all immortalized on videos they sold to tabloids. You've seen when I was a toddler, my dad threatened paparazzi who pushed too close to my mom while I was in her protective arms. Then I'd grow up and be the one holding my sister's hand. Yelling at paparazzi to *stay back, she's only a kid.*

Now I'm twenty-two, and if I could conceptualize a public first date scenario, it would've looked pretty close to this reality. Eight or nine paparazzi crowding Farrow and me. Cameras flashing in blinding succession and illuminating our features in the pitch black night.

His unwavering, assured stride that matches mine. His aviators that block the exploding light, and his hand that squeezes my hand with each incoming question. As though to tell me, *I'm okay, wolf scout.*

I don't know…it makes me smile.

Maybe because this is my life, and I've always tried to accept the crazy parts that I can't change.

"I love you!! I love you!!" a middle-aged cameraman constantly praises. Being overly complimentary is a thing paparazzi do. Others will just try to piss us off for a money-shot.

"Farrow!! Maximoff! Who hogs the blankets?!"

I steal a glance at Farrow. We're both pretty good about not hogging the comforter, and as the sweltering summer approaches, we've only been sleeping with a sheet.

A smile plays at the corner of his mouth, and he squeezes my hand before telling them, "Definitely Maximoff." He's not changing our dynamic for them, for anyone.

My lungs inflate in a bigger breath. "In an alternate universe," I tell the cameramen. "In reality, it's *definitely* Farrow. Every damn time."

I picture his eyes rolling around the fucking globe behind his aviators. My Ray Bans shield the incoming flashes that hike up a notch.

"Where's Jane?!"

Family dinner at the Cobalt Estate.

"Why isn't Jane with you?!"

My brain blares *first public date, first public date, first public fucking date!* And my stomach does this weird flutter-kick thing. Brain and body are way too excited at the prospect of tonight.

It's not like I haven't been out with Farrow before.

But in this capacity, it *feels* new.

"Farrow?! Are you on a date with Maximoff right now?!"

His brows jump, surprised that they guessed right.

"Is this a date?! What are you eating?! Who's paying the bill?!"

Farrow risks a glance at me. Seeing if I want to answer. But I'm looking at him. Trying to see the same thing. He's been selective about which media questions he'll respond to. I want him to do what feels the most comfortable and not be fucking pressured.

"Who thought of the date?!"

Me.

"Where are you headed?!"

We're nearing our destination. At the corner of the street, a red neon light spells out *Tony's Pizza*. I know, I know—our first date is insanely inventive and revolutionary.

Pizza.

It only took me a solid month of overanalyzing.

Farrow pushes back pieces of bleach-white hair that fell to his lashes. And he subconsciously touches his belt—where his radio would normally be attached.

He's only been off the security team for a couple days. We're both still adjusting. Ahead of us, my temp bodyguard for tonight marches like a brick house.

I haven't been assigned a replacement yet.

"Is this a date?!"

I let go of Farrow's hand and wrap my arm around his shoulders. *Fucking Christ.* Pain wells up, and I breathe out through my nose. My left arm is considered my "good" arm. But lifting one shoulder sometimes inadvertently moves the other.

Outwardly, I'm stoic.

Inwardly, I'm kicking my ass into another galaxy for not being more careful. My muscle throbs like a dull hammer. Just so you understand, I'm not dropping my arm.

I plan to hold my boyfriend.

So I'm fucking holding his shoulders. Sex is already challenging with the sling. I don't want to eliminate the forms of physical affection that I can finally, *finally* do in public.

As we near the pizzeria, Farrow sweeps my build a couple times. Trying to study my state of being. He must've felt my body tighten. Flashes blink on my face like strobe lights in a horror film. So there's no way he's reading the pain that I barely reveal.

"Why hasn't Loren tweeted about your relationship like Lily?!"

My sore muscles bind at the mention of my parents. Farrow's carefree stride never grows panicked or pissed.

He knows my dad isn't enthusiastic about *any* couple relationships online. Not even his own brother's. He mockingly calls my uncle and aunt *raisins*.

On the semi-flipside, my mom overcompensates and will tweet fifty times a day about us:

#Marrow for life!

This is what love looks like #Marrow

Proud mom #Marrow

Fans created our couple ship name, and it really stuck after my mom used it.

"Does Loren not approve of your relationship—"

I cut in, "He does approve." My dad is just overprotective, and I think he feels like a better dad if he gives my significant other a hard time.

"I love you!! I love you!!"

Farrow picks up his pace. Purposefully so that my arm will fall off his shoulder. When it does, he swiftly catches my hand, and I lengthen my stride. In line with him again.

I replay his smooth as fuck movement over and over and over. My blood starts pooling south. I'm agitated and unbelievably hot. Probably because I'm annoyed. *Annoyance turns me on.* Christ, that's a weird thought.

We ascend a couple cement steps to the pizzeria. A glass entrance in sight. Last-ditch questions erupt in the air. Most about my parents and Farrow.

But our heads swerve back at this one:

"Did Farrow force you to quit the auction?!"

I glower. "Are you fucking kidding me?"

All of them thirst after that topic. Too many voices jumble.

"Slow down," Farrow snaps at the paparazzi.

They let the middle-aged photographer speak. "*Celebrity Crush* published an article tonight. Maximoff would never quit a charity event, and you're the only thing that's different in his life."

"The *only* thing that's different? I got into a fucking car accident!" I yell, my neck straining. "Because *your* friends sped after my little cousin's car on a goddamn highway!"

"They weren't our friends!" They all disassociate.

Farrow rolls his eyes.

We've both seen these faces before. Paparazzi in Philly are a tight network of people who call each other when they spot someone in my family. Then they rush out and capture a money-shot.

I've always tried to empathize with them. And I get it.

This is their job.

But this is my *life*.

And they need to know... "It was *my* choice to quit the auction," I almost growl, needing to defend him. "Not Farrow's. If anyone is territorial in this relationship." I motion back and forth between his chest and mine. "It's me."

Farrow tilts his head at me, his eyes raking me up and down. And he says, "I'm just as territorial of you, wolf scout."

He's not letting me take all the heat to protect him.

We are a publicist's worst nightmare. Setting fire to our public images out of stubborn love.

Tony's Pizza smells like greasy cheese and

beer, and after a half hour, it's completely packed. Rowdy kids in soccer jerseys span a long checkered-cloth table and help drown out the paparazzi outside. So do the mounted televisions that air the Stanley Cup and NBA playoffs.

But not much can distract my stupidly in love brain from him.

"It's not that bad," I say while I pick black olives off my slice of supreme pizza and look up at Farrow, whose brows rise the longer I defend my motorcycle's capabilities.

Our table is against the wall, and behind Farrow, an orange neon sign hangs that says *true love* with a pizza between the words. I keep skimming him.

All of him.

He sits slightly sideways. His tattooed arm hangs casually over the back of his wooden chair, and he set the sole of his boot on the empty seat next to him.

Farrow Redford Keene is infuriatingly cool, and God, I can't believe he's mine.

I'll never get over it. To think that I'd be here one day. On a public date with the only guy I've ever truly needed or wanted—it's a dream.

He watches me checking him out, and then his gaze drops down my naturally rigid body in a sweltering wave.

I'm aware that I look ready for an Armageddon. I always fucking do. But I think about how Farrow is attracted to that part of me. To every part of me. I'm already comfortable in my skin, but he makes me love who I am times infinity.

I feel the start of my smile. "I can push seventy-five on it," I add, returning to the motorcycle talk.

The corner of his mouth lifts with a short laugh. "Your bike's throttle is shot. I couldn't even accelerate to thirty when I tried. If anything, *I* should be buying you a new bike for your birthday in July." He hoists his dish and holds it out to me.

I scrape my black olives, which I hate and he loves, onto his pizza. "You can't get me a bike," I say. "I only got you a pair of boots for your 28th." He's wearing those boots right now.

"Rip up the Birthday Rulebook." Farrow folds his slice of pizza. "Because if you want to start comparing the prices of our gifts to each other—I only spent five bucks on you for Christmas." He smiles before taking a large bite of pizza.

That five-buck gift is buckled on my left wrist: an olive-green wristwatch. Right beneath lies the gray paracord bracelet that he gave me out-of-the-blue.

And I loved that the watch was really cheap. He wasn't trying to replace my old one with something flashy. He gave me what fit *me*.

"Look, all I'm saying," I tell Farrow, "is that if you buy me a bike, I'm gonna buy you one. I can't even ride a motorcycle until I'm out of this damn sling. You need it more than me." I've wanted to buy him one since he sold his FZ-09 for the auction, and this whole conversation started because his residency begins *tomorrow.*

He has to drive my Audi until he can get another vehicle. I offered my bike to him, and he called it a piece of shit. And that's how this spiraled here.

I bite the thick pizza, bell peppers and sausage falling onto my plate. "Fuck," I mumble.

Farrow looks too amused. Like he has me beat at something else. He's eating his pizza without an avalanche of toppings.

Yeah, I don't fold-and-hold my pizza, and I don't know how he made that look cool.

After he takes a swig of water, he tells me, "Okay, let's do this." His eyes meet mine. "We're not gifting any bikes since we both need new ones. I can't afford a brand new MT-10, and that's the Yamaha I'd want. I'll split the cost with you, and then when you buy a new bike, we'll split the cost of that one."

I swallow my food. Thinking about this. "So we'll both own both bikes?"

His pizza hovers near his mouth. "Technically, my insurance will be on mine, but personally I'd consider them both of ours."

Both of ours.

I repeat that.

Both of ours.

"You're smiling," he points out before eating.

Yeah, it's hard to grimace. "What can I say? I like your *personalies* more than your *technicalities.*"

His rings clank on wood as he taps his chair. He swallows his food. "Technically," he starts, and I'm already groaning, "personalies don't exist. It's not a word."

I fill my mouth with pizza to free my hand—and I flip him off.

He rolls his eyes into a smile. As he eats the crust of his, I zero in on his cheek. Where Thatcher hit him. The bruise is almost gone, but Jane has helped Farrow conceal the blemish with makeup whenever we go out.

Farrow didn't want a tabloid to spin a story about *me* punching him.

I'm still majorly pissed at Thatcher. More than even Farrow at this point. I don't understand why Thatcher keeps shitting on my boyfriend, and if he does it again, I'll snap on him.

I told Jane what her bodyguard said, and immediately she told me, "I won't speak to him. I can't." Out of loyalty to us, she's been on a gigantic silent treatment with Thatcher until further notice.

I know it's hard for Janie. She likes to engage in conversation, even if it's a one-sided chat and the person rarely answers back.

In the pizzeria, my gaze falls from his cheek to his carved biceps. More distracted by his tattoos than his muscles. An inked ribbon circles a compass with the words, *go your own way*.

The media keeps speculating what my next career will be.

A recent headline:

MAXIMOFF HALE, HEIR TO THREE CORPORATIONS. WHICH ONE WILL HE CHOOSE?

You believe that I'll be hired to one of the family companies: Fizzle, Hale Co., or Halway Comics.

I can even help out at Superheroes & Scones. But I don't know where my heart is yet.

"What are you thinking?" Farrow crumples a napkin.

I retrace my brain's endless paths. "I'm thinking about life. How I left my family legacy, and tomorrow, you're returning to yours." My head turns as someone approaches.

A waiter brings over hot tea that I ordered. I thank him, the water steaming and cup too hot to touch.

As he leaves, I tell Farrow, "And how I have a gigantic load of free time and maybe I should build a house with my bare hands or go into the wild and figure out the philosophical meaning of my fragile existence. And then I think about how I'd rather go into the wild with you." I add, "And how my ass is better than your ass."

Physical, mental, and sexual—those are the routes of my mind.

He looks me up and down, his earring swaying. "I have the better ass, but I can let you believe that you do."

I picture his ass now. And I instantly imagine my cock sliding inside of him and the way his muscles contract in scalding arousal—*fuck me*. I blink a few times to avoid fantasizing.

His knowing smile spreads wider and wider.

I scowl. "Your smile is ripping your face apart."

"Anatomically impossible, but nice try." He laughs as I grimace, and then my phone vibrates. *Texts from my family.* Asking about the date. It's been constant all night.

I take out my phone just to ensure it's nothing serious.

But I'm distracted.

By you-know-who.

Not Voldemort. Someone hotter. Not that I think the villain in the *Harry Potter* books is even remotely hot—*Christ, stop thinking*.

Farrow tears apart a straw wrapper, his eyes falling to me, before rising to the television. The Philadelphia Flyers are in the Stanley Cup playoffs. We both like watching pro sports, especially if our hometown is involved.

But that's not what's getting me.

His molten eyes fall back to me again. Pricking my nerves, and then they lift to the TV. Eyes on me, then the TV, me—his lip rises, then the TV.

My cock strains against my jeans. I'm aware that within the crowded pizzeria, phones are aimed at us. Some better hidden than others. We're being recorded from inside and outside.

We're public.

I remind myself that. *We're public*, and I'm allowed to touch my boyfriend. So I stand up about the same time that he drops his boot. He gestures me over, but I'm already heading to his side of the table.

When I sit beside him—so close that my thigh is up against his thigh and his strong arm wraps around my lower back—flashes ignite outside. Glaring through the windowpanes.

My temp bodyguard sits one table away, faking interest in his phone and bowl of soup. I briefly glance at my cell, too. No *emergency* text messages. All should be well.

More flashes.

More bright light.

Paparazzi won't leave if I ask. The only way to fix this is to leave myself, and the cameramen will follow me.

But out of all nights, I don't want *this* night to be short-lived. So I drape my left arm over his shoulders and ignore the thumping in my sore muscle.

Farrow slouches a bit so my arm drops to a lower angle. Ten times less strain on my shoulder, but I'm still holding him.

His inked fingers dip beneath my jean's band, not going far. Just enough to warm the skin on my waist with his skin. We tune out the gawking and the lenses. And we watch ice hockey in public. Clearly romantically linked.

It's the most casual, ordinary thing.

You have no idea how much this means to me.

"Maximoff Hale." All of a sudden, a stocky guy in a local college sweatshirt approaches our table, and my temp bodyguard bobs up and down in his seat. Hesitating to intervene. I usually let fans near.

I motion to the bodyguard to sit.

Farrow is super-glued to the guy, even as he whispers to me, "Recognize him?"

18

MAXIMOFF HALE

"No," I whisper back to Farrow, and then I smile at the guy who raises a hand in hello. I tell him, "Hey, man. I'm kind of busy tonight—"

"I was just hoping for an autograph." He reaches over the half-eaten supreme pizza, trying to pass me a napkin and a ballpoint pen.

I have to take my arm off Farrow to grab both. To me, it's not a big deal to sign a napkin. It'll take a half a second and could make someone's day. But I notice how the guy checks over his shoulder and smiles impishly at a booth, a potted plant shrouding the other faces from view.

It puts me on edge.

But I don't falter, uncapping the pen. "I'm right-handed, so this'll be sloppy." It looks nothing like my actual signature.

"Whatever's good," he says distantly, zeroing in on Farrow. "Can I get your autograph too?"

Farrow barely blinks. "I'll pass." He's turned down autographs and pictures before, but not with this much coldness attached.

The college-aged guy almost...smiles.

This isn't a fan.

"Here." I extend the napkin and pen to the guy. "Have a good night, man." *Please leave. Please don't ruin my fucking date.*

Pocketing the autograph, the guy loiters for another half second. And stiltedly, like he's rehearsed this line with his friends, he tells me, "I didn't think Farrow was your type, Maximoff. I thought you'd end up with a rich dick, not a fame whore."

I narrow my eyes. "Are you fucking serious?"

"I said—"

"Get the fuck out," Farrow cuts in, standing up. But he can't usher him away that easily. I'm sure he wants to, but he's not a bodyguard or a bystander. He's a part of the confrontation.

The guy laughs, then looks at me. "Is your boyfriend gonna hit me?"

Farrow rolls his eyes. He's intimidating to most, but as my boyfriend, the worst of the worst kinds of humans will try to provoke him for fifteen minutes of fame.

Chair scraping back, I stand up next to Farrow. "Kids are here," I growl. "Go back to your goddamn booth."

My temp bodyguard is speaking into his radio. Hesitating.

"You seem tense, Maximoff." The guy takes a single step back. "That's what happens when you trade down—"

"*Fuck you,*" I sneer, and Farrow fists the back of my shirt—because I almost lunge. Then he holds the back of my head, protective. Comforting. Telling me not to defend him and let street hecklers get to me.

Take a breath.

"You're just like your dad." He smirks at me. "How's Ryke Meadows doing, by the way?"

My fist stays at my side. Ryke isn't my dad, but I've lost the urge or need to spit that truth. I don't move. I don't charge at him.

But I also can't speak.

Farrow raises his brows at the guy. "Your opinions are fucking ugly. And we're not here for that shit. You want a fight, go fight with the little fuckers you call friends." He points at the booth.

The guy chokes on a breath. He opens his mouth to say something else, and then shuts it. His eyes dart to the left where my temp bodyguard finally nears.

Farrow turns to him first. "Call SFA and get a couple guys over here. We'll be in the bathroom until you kick this shithead out."

"I'm not leaving," the heckler snorts.

I look to the temp bodyguard. "You have five minutes," I tell him, my voice stilted and firm. I'm just on automatic at this point. Farrow clasps my hand and quickly leads me through the packed restaurant. Towards the men's bathroom.

Everyone is looking. Filming us.

My eyes are on the bathroom door.

And then hot liquid suddenly splashes my face. "*Fuck,*" I curse, rubbing the...coffee off my burning cheek and temple. It's all so damn abrupt that I have no time to think.

People gasp and shout, while others stand up from their chairs, cell phones pointed at me.

Farrow shoves someone back and yells a threat that rings in my ears. I press the bottom of my shirt to my face that's on fucking fire. *Goddammit.*

I'm disoriented. Catching shocked expressions. Some people are weirdly smiling while they film this with their phones. I miss sight of the culprit. But all the people recording are getting great footage. Maybe they're thinking about how much money they can sell it for. How many likes and retweets it'll get.

I'm walling up.

I'm shutting down.

This is my first date.

"Maximoff," Farrow says, hand falling back into mine.

I'm not angry. Just numb, and I fall in line with Farrow. Able to open the door to the single bathroom first, and I slip inside. One out-of-order toilet stall, one urinal, and sharpie and pen is scribbled along the chipped maroon walls.

Farrow locks the door behind us. We're quiet. It's calmer here.

I touch the stinging burn, and I glance at the mirror. Skin is bright, bright red along my cheekbone, beneath my eye, and beside my temple.

He snatches paper towels out of the dispenser.

"Welcome to my world," I say dryly.

He glances back at me while he turns on the sink faucet. "I've been in your world, wolf scout." He runs the paper towels beneath cold water, then wrings them out.

"But now you're in it, *in it*," I tell him.

His brows rise, turned to me. "You know I love your fucked-up world. Because you're 'in it, in it'." He uses air-quotes and then presses the cold towel to my cheek and temple.

Our eyes caress for a second, and I breathe deeper. Better.

He shakes his head a couple times, his jaw tightening. "I should've been faster." Meaning, he wishes he jumped out in front of me.

"I'm glad you weren't." Because in that alternate universe, he'd be the one with the stinging pain.

He holds my gaze and then frowns at the burn, lifting the soaked paper towel that soothes my skin. "If your new bodyguard is as bad as that one, it's going to fucking kill me every time I leave you."

"They won't be that bad." My hand glides up his back muscles, and I replay what happened. "About what that guy said—"

"I'm okay, wolf scout." Farrow holds the wet paper towel to my face again. His perpetual confidence fortifies him and me together. Over and over and over. "You?"

"Yeah." My hand reaches his neck, about to bring his mouth to mine—a knock pounds on the bathroom door. Our heads turn.

"I need to piss, dude! Hurry up!"

On top of that hollering, Farrow's phone rings in his pocket. Without taking it out, he drops the call with one click.

And then he kisses me quickly. Like a *peck*. Not what I want, but he tells me, "Be patient."

"I don't know that word," I say sarcastically.

"Because I'm smarter than you." Farrow soaks up my irritation like a sponge.

I blink slowly. "Thank you for the bucket of lies. I needed those—" I cut myself off because his phone buzzes not once or twice. Repeatedly. Incessantly.

Notifications start pinging too.

We both frown.

Farrow digs back in his pocket and pulls out his phone. I stand beside him, and he flips the cell over.

Texts pop up, one after the other.

OMG FARROWWW — 993-555-4343

Fuck me good, baby — 876-555-2908

You and Maximoff are the cutest. Just wanted to tell you that. Xoxo — 404-555-3888

Hey asshole, Maximoff is a good guy. He deserves better. — 202-555-1010

Fuck you. He would have never cancelled the auction. You're a horrible influence. I hope you die. — 342-555-9876

That auction was for CHARITY. You're too jealous for him. He could do waaaay better. —161-555-2800

Maximoff should be with a cute soft boy that he can cuddle and love. Not you. — 675-555-4323

My stomach nosedives off a hundred-foot cliff. We exchange a cautious look, and then his phone *rings* with an unknown number.

"Don't answer that," I tell him.

"Wasn't going to." Farrow skims the screen. "Give me your phone."

I pull my cell out of my pocket. At the same time, someone calls me. Caller ID: *Oscar Oliveira*.

Farrow takes my phone, and I listen fixatedly. Ready and prepared for damage control. Another DEFCON 1, here we fucking go.

My boyfriend presses the *speakerphone* button. "Oliveira."

"It's bad, Redford," he says. "Your info has spread across the whole internet. Phone number. Childhood address. Names of your family: father, stepmom, stepsister, and ex-boyfriends."

Farrow shuts his eyes before they roll in a giant arc.

"Your seventh-grade MySpace page," Oscar continues, "the name of your pet guinea pig." *Scuttlebucket*. The only pet Farrow ever had died when he was twelve. "Email address, any old usernames on social medias, a password to your bank account—"

"Where's the security tech team?" I ask, and Farrow hands me my phone. He puts his own cell to his ear, calling the bank to freeze his accounts.

"Tech team is preventing a phone hack. But, Hale, this info is coming from other sources. Like Redford's friend-of-friend-of-friend's social media accounts spread over fucking years. Anytime he popped up in pictures or by name, people are connecting it together and finding more info about him. It's snowballing."

Farrow speaks hushed near the sink. Talking to the bank.

"He's being doxxed," I realize.

His private information is being leaked for public consumption. I've tried to prepare for this doomsday. I've told myself for *years* that it could happen to whoever I dated publicly.

And I won't let anyone, especially doxxers, make me regret our decision to go public. But fuck those people who do this to human beings for shits and giggles.

I've never had complete privacy. So I've never experienced what Farrow is going through right now. I imagine it's like you're suddenly being disrobed in front of the whole world. And you can't grab the robe back—and I hate that I can't shield him. That I have no power to protect him.

All I can do is just be here.

It doesn't feel like enough.

Oscar tells me that the security team is calling an emergency meeting. Even though Farrow doesn't have a 24/7 bodyguard and he's not one himself anymore, he's still being protected by Alpha, Omega, and Epsilon.

They're treating him like family. And I don't just mean a part of the Hales—I can't take credit for this. I think it's mostly because the security team loves him.

I hang up with Oscar.

"I need to piss!!" Knocking on the door.

"Fuck off!" I yell.

"…okay. Bye," Farrow says before hanging up his call. He slips his phone in his pocket. He's relaxed, but there's a tinge of frustration and anger reddening his eyes that I can't miss.

I just want to help.

Any way that I fucking can.

Farrow leans on the sink. "Looks like we're not going to be fighting over who pays for this date."

I near him. "They drained your money?"

"Two grand five minutes ago. Gone. The bank flagged the activity and froze all of my accounts."

As soon as I'm in arm's reach, we draw together. Instinctively, our hands roam and hold and grip. He whispers, "I don't have any cash on me."

I trace the wings on his neck. "I planned to pay anyway."

He stares into me. "And I planned to ruin your plan." His palm runs up back. Pushing me as close to his chest as possible with my sling.

I hug him tighter around the shoulders. His jaw skims against my jaw. His fingers massage the back of my head before clutching harder.

I don't let go of him.

I can feel his chest collapse. I hold stronger.

Breath deepening.

We stay in this embrace for a long moment. Our pulses thumping together, and the world seems to go calm. And quiet.

As we pull back, our eyes say the same thing:

Let's get out of here.

109k viewers and counting listen to me talk

about *boundaries* on an Instagram Live. Coffee thrown at my face, Farrow being doxxed—this is not how I saw our date going. Instead of drowning in resentment, I remind myself to look on the bright side. I went on a public date with my boyfriend.

We're here today. Breathing, living, and we have love—so much damn love. *He's okay.* We're okay.

Leaning against my bed's headboard, I angle the phone, everything below my abdomen not in frame. I already struggled out of my shirt and attached my sling to my bare chest.

Farrow helped. Kind of.

Kind of a lot.

And then he had to take a phone call from the hospital. *Paperwork shit,* his words. So while he stepped out of the attic, I decided to go live and get this off my chest.

Boundaries.

Human decency.

Don't fuck with my boyfriend.

"I get that you all will have your opinions on Farrow. But shitting on him because you love me makes *no* damn sense." Emoji hearts flutter up the screen, and the tickertape of comments speeds rapidly. Making them hard to read.

But I catch these:

sry. you could do better than him

Marrow 4 life

I love you, Maximoffffff!!

that sucks what happened with Farrow

OMG the burn on ur face, r u ok??

he's not good enough for u

we just don't want you to get hurt!

"Farrow is the *last* person in the whole universe who'd hurt me." On the live stream, my sharp features stare back at me. My forest-green eyes look greener tonight and almost pierce the screen.

he looks upset omg

are you mad?

WE LOVE YOU!

ur a dick

When's WE ARE CALLOWAY airing?????

don't be sad!!

I rest my head back. "When you fuck with Farrow, you hurt me. So if you care about me at all, don't come at him with things like *I deserve better* and *he's not good enough for me*. Farrow Keene is the only one I let in. *The only one*." I'd point at my chest if I could. "That's not by accident. It's because he's more than enough for me. He's every damn thing."

The door squeaks open.

Fuck.

I had no plan to make some *sappy* declaration. One that Farrow would love to quote for eons upon eons of time. Just to agitate the fuck out of me.

Dear World, tell me my boyfriend didn't hear me profess a colossal amount of love. Sincerely, a human in love.

Farrow kicks the door closed with a growing smile. He nears my dresser and then leans his elbows on the surface. Looking only at me.

He heard what I said.

Without a doubt.

Using my feet, I push myself higher against the headboard. Gray sheets are crumpled beneath me. Sitting straighter, I'm careful not to jostle my phone in hand. And I focus on the live stream.

"You all should know…" I pause, layering on severity. "…I'm Farrow Redford Keene, and I have a gigantic, massive crush on Maximoff Hale."

I look up, and Farrow rubs his bottom lip, giving me a long scorching once-over. He approaches, the bed undulating with his weight, and he's suddenly *right next to me*.

In the camera frame.

The comment section explodes.

OMG it's FARROW!!

he's here holy shit holy shit

I'm dying!!!

Me too.

Farrow looks at the live stream, both of us able to see ourselves in the screen. He cups the back of my head, his fingers running casually in and out of my hair. "I'm Maximoff Hale," he says to the 117k viewers. "And thirty-four seconds ago, I lost my honesty merit badge."

I try to feign confusion, but laughter rumbles in my lungs.

Farrow lifts his brows at me like *you liked that*. All comebacks and potential one-upping flits away, starving for more physical contact, for his mouth against my mouth and to connect hard body to hard body.

Before the viewers see me flash *fuck me* eyes at Farrow, I shut off the video. Tossing it aside, my phone slips off the mattress and clatters to the floorboards.

I turn into Farrow; he turns into me, and our eyes meet head-on first, pulsating with need.

And our lips collide. I break apart his mouth as I breathe into the kiss, and I taste mint against his tongue. Our hands wrestle with our clothing. He unzips me, unbuttons and wrenches my jeans to my thighs.

My cock pulses and pulses, and he eats up the arousal in my eyes like my pleasure feeds his pleasure.

I tug his pants halfway down his legs. Farrow grips the back of his black shirt, pulling the fabric off his head. Revealing his nipple piercing and the inked dagger and skull pirate across the ridges of his abs.

Fuck me. I pull off my jeans, and he throws his own pants off the bed.

Down to boxer-briefs, our mouths crush together again. And we inch off the headboard, until his head meets a pillow.

I split his muscular legs open with my knees, and while I deepen the roughest, most untamed kiss, I lower on top of Farrow, my left forearm braced on the mattress.

A tinge of pain flares up in my shoulder, but I hone in on the mounting heat that ignites us.

I grind my hips into him. His mouth-watering erection rubs against my hardening cock every single time I drive forward.

Sweat builds, and between each kiss, our heavy grunts break the quiet. Farrow digs his fingers in my back and rakes his short nails across my skin. Scratching down towards my ass.

Fuckfuck.

Our tongues tangle more languidly than the forceful thrust of my hips. His hand—his hand draws down my boxer-briefs and seizes my ass with the hottest goddamn squeeze.

I tear from his lips, a raspy groan expelling from my burning lungs. Spurring me to grind *harder. Rougher.*

His muscles strain. "*Fuck*, Maximoff," Farrow groans, his other hand clasps my jaw in the best grip. He grapples for the lead and control. About to flip me. But I bear more of my weight on his chest. Staying on top.

Our eyes attach for a nerve-pricking beat.

"You want to fuck me?" he asks, his graveled voice stroking my cock.

Goddamn. "More than you want to fuck me," I breathe heavily.

He nips my lip between his teeth, and he whispers, "Not possible."

I rock harder, fabric of boxer-briefs still separating us. My ass flexes beneath his palm. I grind and grind—he grits down, nose flaring in intense arousal.

"*Fuck*," he grunts, his lips almost splitting apart in a coarse breath.

Blood pounds in my veins, and I groan against his neck. *Fuck, Farrow.* He pushes me as hard against him as he can without causing me pain.

My bound right arm obstructs our bodies from *completely* meeting. And my arm jerks in the canvas, *wanting* and *aching* to be all over him like he's all over me.

I lift my head. "Fuck my sling," I mutter, frustrated.

Farrow pants as hard as me. "It'd be easier if you weren't on top. If you'd let me flip us—"

"I'm doing great, thanks," I say, too stubborn to lose the lead right now. Plus, once I'm on my back, I won't have enough strength to wrestle out from under him.

Farrow studies my body.

My left arm is more carved and toned than ever since it's been picking up my right arm's slack. And whatever pain exists in my collarbone has melted beneath five-hundred degree, blood-boiling desire.

I rock slower and kiss him again, lips stinging beneath the force. And he pushes my ass for a deeper grind. *Fuck.*

Me.

I need inside of him.

Soon.

I lower my mouth to his chest, trailing over the inked lines of a pirate ship. Reaching his nipple, I suck and flick my tongue over the metal barbell.

Farrow lets out a rougher breath, and he palms my cock.

I lose balance on my left hand. "*Fuck*," I curse.

He hooks his legs around me, and before I even blink, he flips us in one careful and effortless movement. Tapping into his strength and MMA skill, he tops me.

And my back *gently* meets the mattress. He's protecting my body from my aggressive self-destruction.

I like to manhandle and be manhandled. Not new news. But it's pretty difficult with a surgically repaired collarbone that's in the process of healing.

He straddles my waist, and his chest is hoisted off mine. Tattooed hands splay on either side of my shoulders on the mattress.

Our eyes create hot tracks along our faces, and I run my large hand across his rough jaw, a less-than-close shave. God, his masculinity fists me, and my carriage elevates in a blistered breath.

He turns his head slightly and kisses my palm. I rake my fingers through his bleach-white hair, and then hold his warm neck.

Farrow rubs my bicep before whispering, "I'm being as rough with you as I can be without hurting you." He wishes he could give me more.

If he had fractured a bone, I would've been the same way with him. Not hesitating or bubble-wrapping him, just highly aware of his physical limitations. And knowing that he'd want to push against them.

I nod once. "I get it, man."

Farrow starts smiling.

"What?" I ask.

"How you call me 'man' in bed," he tells me, lowering his lips to mine, a teasing breath away. He must catch my confusion because he clarifies, "It's the way you always say it with extra force. It sounds more like I'm your man. Not just any fucking man." He raises his brows at me. "It's hot."

I barely have time to react to that. Because Farrow lowers more of his weight into me, and I throb.

Fuck. I reach down and free us from our boxer-briefs. Shedding the last fabric, we kick the underwear off our ankles.

I grip his length and mine together, rubbing us in a tight fist. Pre-cum slick in my palm—I flex, breath knotted in my throat.

Farrow shoves my hand aside and sits up off me. "Don't jack us off." He reaches for the end table, his mosaic of pirate tattoos cascading down cut muscle. I watch his hands, two images inked on top: sparrows by his thumbs and skull-and-crossbones in the middle.

I crunch upward and push myself to my knees with one hand. He's knelt too, holding my gaze. Farrow shakes a black bottle and squirts lube in his palm. He strokes us, mixing lube with pre-cum, while we kiss.

More aggressively. Passionately.

He tosses the bottle aside, and our mouths break, catching our breaths.

"What position were you thinking?" Farrow asks since many have been hypothetically eliminated. My brain says most sex positions are doable.

And by *most*, I mean *all*.

"Me topping you, on our sides facing each other."

He tilts his head at me like I've flown to Mars by myself and built a colony of one. "On your side?" he repeats. He makes a point of eyeing my shoulder, the bandage gone. A thick reddened puffy scar lines the length of my left collarbone.

"Yeah." I don't concede.

"No, fuck no," he says easily and waves me on. "Keep going."

I glance at his long, hardened cock. I want that in me as much as I want mine in him.

"I spoon you." If there are proper terms for these positions, I don't know them. I have a lot of sex. But I don't research the fuck out of it on the internet.

"That's also on your side," he says. "Keep going."

I exhale a hot breath. "Doggy-style or the one where your legs are splayed to the side and I'm standing off the bed and entering you from behind. But I could bottom for that one." It's one of my favorite positions I've been in as a bottom. I think because he wrapped his hand around my neck while he pounded into me, and I was so into it, into him, and I saw how much he got off on that.

Farrow contemplates for a half a second, and then waves me on again. "Getting closer."

"With you flat on your back, missionary."

He shakes his head, motion with two fingers to *keep going*.

My brows knot. "I'm getting the feeling you just want to know which positions I like."

He smiles at me like the word *pure* is on his tongue. "That is part of the point, wolf scout." His matter-of-fact voice pumps my blood.

I growl out and then exhale roughly. "I'm picking one now. Dresser. Standing."

19

MAXIMOFF HALE

I climb off the bed buck-naked, and while he rises, equally buck-ass-naked, I gesture him to me. "Come over."

Farrow doesn't hesitate. In one blink, he's reached me. He clutches my face and kisses me hard before he tears away and seizes the edge of the dresser.

My pulse thrashes. Pent-up and fixated on that simple movement and his confidence that matches mine over and over.

With my chest up against his tattooed back, I clutch his waist—and that's when I realize that he never grabbed a condom. He lubed us without one. "No condom?" I ask him.

Farrow looks over his shoulder. "No condom," he confirms. "But if you want one, that's okay."

This is a big deal. We've both been tested; we're both clean and monogamous, but we haven't taken that next step. Until now.

To let me bareback, Farrow has to have complete trust in me that I won't cheat. *I'd never.* Same if we flip, I have to trust him.

And I do.

Completely.

"I want to," I tell him, assured. He's barebacked with a serious boyfriend before, but I haven't.

Farrow cups the back of my head, and we kiss with slow-burning intimacy that feels like descending gradually... gradually in warm... soothing... waters.

My head dizzies, and we part with ragged breath. Farrow angles forward again, his knee bent in a slight lunge, and he hangs his head, muscles relaxed.

He glances over his shoulder to tell me, "You can come in me." I catch his smile as he adds, "I know you want to."

God. "And I know you want me to," I say, too hot now. Too ready, and he doesn't deny that we're both dying for the same thing.

While I tease his hole open with two fingers, I kiss the back of his neck. He rubs himself twice, and then reaches backwards and grips my ass.

Fuckme. I clutch *his* ass before I take my erection and press the tip to his hole. Easing myself in—the pressure around me narrows my eyes into aroused pinpoints.

"Fuck," Farrow groans, the further I go in...now all the way inside. "*Ah,* fuck. *Maximoff.*" His throaty noise combines with mine, a raw sound scratching out of me.

Christ. I rock my hips, pounding against him with mind-numbing friction. My hand shoots for his waist for deeper entry, gripping him. He white-knuckles the dresser, gritting down as a tangled moan ejects. *Fuckfuckfuck...*

I run my hand up his back muscles. "*Farrow,*" I groan, and he pushes back into my cock. My head tries to loll back—*fucking fuck.* I grip him harder. Ramming, my ass flexing beneath his strong hold.

"Harder," he grunts, his forehead on his bicep. I pick up my pace and slam into him.

He moans as I hit his prostate. I know the spot. Very goddamn well.

I wrap my arm around his abdomen. Aching to bow forward where my chest melds his back, closer than close. *Fuck this sling.*

Slowing, I eek out the movement, and more sweat beads up on both our bodies. Skin slick, and hair dampening.

"Fuck," I groan. "*Fuck.*" I quicken my rhythm, and I fucking explode. *Fuckfuckfuuuuuuck.* Lights burst in my vision, nerves scorched alive. I dagger a glare on the ceiling, another gnarled noise in my throat.

Farrow moans lowly into his arm, his tendons straining in his neck. Face reddening, he cages breath, and I come inside the guy I love. With a few more pumps, I milk my climax, and I watch his grip loosen on the dresser. Glancing back at me, he absorbs my pierced *fuck me* eyes that still exist for him.

He's really hard.

Slowly, I pull out. Cum dripping off my tip, and I switch spots with him. As our paths cross, we draw together and kiss.

Not able to separate for a while.

We push-and-pull for a lead, and I bring his back to the dresser—then he spins me. My back to the wood. I hold his jaw and kiss Farrow with my whole body. My waist, torso, and chest arch into him. Reaching out for his fucking heart.

And then willingly, I turn and face the dresser. I grip the edge with my only available hand. Giving him access to push into me.

This is still new for me. But the more and more I allow myself to be vulnerable with Farrow, the more my life feels at peace. I've found someone who can ease me in this intangible, miraculous, cosmic way.

Farrow places a warm kiss to my bicep before he pulls me back some. Adjusting my stance. "Pain?" he asks, referring to my arm.

"Not that much." I must've rolled my shoulder and neck too far because the tendon sears.

"Where?" he asks, his inked fingers toying with the outside of my hole. I drown in the fucking sensation. He stops. "Maximoff."

Focus. "Closer to my neck. I'm alright; just fuck me." I glance over my shoulder, and pain hammers my collarbone.

"Maximoff. Fuck, I'm not putting my dick in you if you keep hurting yourself to look at it."

I hang my head forward. My muscles burning. "Who said I was looking at your cock?" I breathe heavily. "Maybe I was looking at the *carpet.*"

I was looking at his erection.

"Sure," Farrow says. "Let's pretend you like the carpet more."

I picture his tattooed hand wrapped around his length. I'm not at the right angle to see a thing, so my imagination has to be good enough.

Farrow slips a finger inside of me, then works another. *Fuck.*

"Relax," he breathes, one of his hands holds my waist and squeezes like *come on, wolf scout. I won't hurt you.*

I exhale a controlled breath and try not to tense. My pulse beats harder, body stirring.

He retracts his hand, and a second later, I feel greater pressure against my ass. My fingers dig into the dresser.

"You're still ridiculously tight," Farrow exhales. "Hold on." He pushes in a little bit, then out. Inching his way inside of me. My body reacts to his kindness more like teasing, and I'm getting worked up again—

Footsteps.

I hear footsteps. Racing up the staircase. To this attic.

Farrow hears. But the door should be locked…it's not.

It's not locked.

Farrow is closer, and he pulls out completely and in two strides, he reaches the destination. He flips the lock as soon as the knob jingles and knuckles rap the wood.

"Moffy!"

That's my little sister.

Farrow and I exchange a look, our eyes widened at each other. Yeah, we just dodged what would've been the most awkward moment of *both* our lives.

"Moffy!" she calls again, sounding a bit panicked.

"Just a sec!" We're in a mad dash to clean up. I throw a towel at Farrow. He wipes up the cum that drips down his leg, and I rub my hands and body with another cloth. Next, I struggle to put on underwear and new jeans.

Somehow Farrow beats me at getting clothed. His boxer-briefs and pants are on, and he even pulls a black Studio 9 shirt over his head.

"Come here," he whispers.

I relinquish my fight with my jean's button. And his fingers effortlessly fish my button through the hole.

Farrow tries to fix my disheveled hair, but I've already accepted the fact that she'll know we were fucking.

I move his hand and point out, "It smells like sex in here."

"It does," he says easily. "I'm assuming you have a plan, wolf scout."

I do. "I'm not letting her past the doorway." I'm pretty sure our lube is in plain sight, and the sheets are twisted and knotted like we've wrestle-fucked for hours.

Farrow nods. "Okay."

And just as she calls my name again, I unlock and swing the door open. I solidify. "Are you okay?" I ask immediately.

Luna doesn't look like Luna. Her light brown hair is pulled into a pin-straight pony. No marker streaks, no neon green makeup or star stickers on her cheeks. Black mascaraed lashes shade her amber eyes, and I realize she removed her earrings and tongue piercing.

She's wearing a pink sundress—Jesus, I've never seen my sister wear a *pink sundress*.

"Uh-huh," Luna nods, and I step onto the third-floor landing where she stands. It's a small space before the stairs drop.

Farrow leans his shoulder on the doorframe and cracks the door behind him. Shutting out her view of our bedroom.

Our bedroom.

Never gets old.

I'd almost-maybe smile but I'm dealing with my eighteen-year-old sister who's been body-snatched. Possibly by aliens. Maybe this is a bizarre role-playing theater thing—I don't know.

I'm concerned. In case you weren't aware.

"Hi, Farrow." Luna throws up a hand in greeting.

"Hey, Luna." Farrow skims her in a quick sweep, brows spiking. "What's with the new look?"

Luna tugs at the hem of her dress like it's uncomfortable. "Just... you know, thought I'd try something out." She shrugs; a soft smile appearing as she looks at our unkempt hair and clothes. "Sorry to disturb your date night."

Farrow smiles wide and loosely crosses his arms.

"It's okay," I tell my sister, just happy she's not in serious trouble. "What do you need?"

Luna fixes the spaghetti strap of her dress. "A condom."

I process. At a snail's pace. My brain has short-circuited.

Farrow is turned towards me, full-on entertained. Wanting to see how I'll handle this.

I prepare for a lot of situations. But I can honestly say I did not prepare for my sister to ask me for a condom. That's on me. She's living with me now, and I should've known. Because she's not a little kid anymore, and when I left home, she was only fourteen. Four years later, and *yeah*, things change.

People change.

I've been starting to realize that.

Just as I go to respond, she adds, "I know that you know that I have a boyfriend."

"You know?" My brows furrow. Farrow told me what security discussed, and I wanted to wait for Luna to tell me herself.

"Quinn felt guilty and spilled everything he said to SFO," she explains. "I didn't care that he said anything…except I *really* don't want Mom and Dad to know until me and Andrew are serious, *serious*. We're still in that middle phase, you know?"

I don't know about middle phases.

I don't know what the fuck that means.

Farrow nods. "Make sure you're on the same page with this guy. Middle phases can be tricky."

Luna smiles. "Yeah, I will."

I glance at Farrow. I'm glad he has experience in this and can help my sister when I can't. I don't know…it feels right. Like this is how life is supposed to be.

"Andrew's coming over?" I ask Luna. "Or is he already here?"

"He's coming here in a bit." She bobs her head. "So? Condom?"

I adjust my sling on my bare chest, the material cutting into my shoulder. "Didn't Mom take you to get birth control?"

"I want to be extra prepared." She looks between us. "I don't want another scare, okay?"

Farrow nods. "Fair enough." He tips his head to me. "We don't have any condoms that this guy can use." That realization dawns on me, too.

Luna scrunches her brows. "Why not?"

"JANE!" I call down the stairwell.

Farrow taps the doorframe, considering withholding the truth, but he tells her honestly, "The probability that this guy is the same size as us is low. And you're not going to want the condom to slip off."

"Aren't there just three condom sizes?" Luna asks, and as Jane ascends the stairs in a purple tutu and knit sweater, cupping a mug of coffee, my sister repeats the question, "Jane, aren't there just three condom sizes?"

Janie smiles brightly at me like I'm dealing with the most curious, intriguing familial dilemma that's occurred in the past 24 hours. We would both prefer a condom crisis over any of our siblings or cousins being emotionally or physically hurt.

"Ma soeur a besoin d'un préservatif," I say to Jane. "Le jour est venu." *My sister needs a condom. The day has come.*

Three stairs below, Jane props her hip on the wall. "Ils grandissent si vite." *They grow up so fast.*

We're the oldest of these families, and everyone just seems *young* to us. I can't change that.

Jane answers my sister in a breezy voice. "There's a great and terrible variety, but the main sizes are small, regular, and large. How can I help...?" She trails off, smile fading at Luna's odd appearance. But Jane tries not to draw attention to it.

Luna steps down a stair. "I need one."

"More than one," I tell Jane. "Her boyfriend is coming over."

"I have every size," Jane notes, sipping her coffee. "I'll give you all of them."

All of them? I know why, and my face falls. "Janie."

"Cobalt," Farrow says with the same tough concern.

This is about Nate, the Asshole With Benefits that stalked me for a while. He wanted to hurt me, and he ended up mostly hurting my best friend...and my boyfriend, who can't shake that night. And even Thatcher Moretti, whose guilt lingers.

It's ironic.

Because hurting Jane and Farrow is a direct shot to my heart. So really, that asshole got what he wanted.

Jane pries a piece of frizzy hair off her pink lips and only looks at me. "I have no use for *condoms* when there's no dick in the world, small, regular or large, that I'd trust to enter my vagina."

I shake my head. "You could, eventually—"

"These condoms will expire by then." Jane raises her mug. "So let them not go to waste, Moffy. They should be used by people who can have glorious and beautiful sex."

While I've been basking in a newfound world of sex without compromise or fear, my best friend has taken five million steps backward because of this fucking asshole. And I want her to be safe and feel loved and free.

Farrow straightens off the doorframe. "You're really planning to be celibate for the rest of your life?"

Jane lifts her blue eyes to him. "I can live fine without falling in love, so I can live just as easily without a penis."

Farrow arches his brows.

"You love sex," I tell my best friend.

"I love to masturbate." Jane sips her coffee again.

"Same," Luna nods.

I rub my face with my one hand. Not sure how I should feel. My neck is hot, and Farrow looks partially amused, partially ready to wrap this up. I didn't get him off yet, and the mood has been pretty much slaughtered. But I'll revive it.

Jane motions for Luna to descend the staircase. "Come to my bedroom, Luna. I'll teach you everything the men can't." Janie glances back at me.

I mouth, *merci.*

She taps her cheek and mouths, *feel better.* She's referring to my burn from the coffee.

I almost smile, and when I return to my bedroom with Farrow, my mind reels through the whole day. "Was everything okay with the hospital?" I ask while we draw together. He took the call while I did the Instagram Live, and I forgot to ask.

He unbuttons my jeans. "They wanted to make sure I could comply with HIPPA."

"Isn't that the thing that protects a patient's privacy?"

Farrow starts to smile. "That *thing* is a *law*. And yeah, it's there to ensure healthcare providers will keep medical records and other health information private."

I think harder. "They called because you were doxxed," I realize.

Farrow looks surprised that I figured it out, but also he looks like he loves me. Like *really* loves me, and I wrap my arm around his shoulder as he tells me, "They were afraid I wouldn't be able to maintain privacy for a patient, but I talked them down." He eyes my mouth as much as I eye his. "Everything is fine, wolf scout."

But I sense an uneasiness. "Really?"

He nods, clutches my jaw, and whispers against my lips, "I hope so."

20

MAXIMOFF HALE

"This is my thing, Moffy. You can't have it."

We're at a 1920s speakeasy-themed bar. It's nearly empty. I sit on a round leather stool, and my best friend rattles a silver cocktail shaker on the other side of the counter.

Jane's mixology instructor is an actual bartender, dressed in a fedora, bowtie and suit vest. While he slices limes next to her, I catch him scrutinizing her, then me. Not pretending that this conversation doesn't interest him.

I focus on Janie. "I'm not trying to take your thing," I say seriously. "But maybe we can try to find a passion together seeing as I am *passionless* now—"

She snatches an ice cube from a bucket and tosses it at me.

I dodge with a smile.

"You have a passion," she says. "It's just been disrupted for the time being."

I'm aware that charity exists beyond the company I built. I can still attend functions and donate money and time. But I'm not looking to head a corporation.

"I don't want charity to be a job," I tell Janie. "I'd rather not set an alarm to it."

For the longest time, I've chased responsibility, and I won't stop running towards my family—I won't slow down for anything. But with Farrow, I've experienced what it's like to just take it easy, to exist and breathe, and when it comes to work life, I want the simple enjoyment.

Not a CEO position. Not managing a hundred-some employees.

"It's official then?" Jane asks, setting down the shaker. Frilly sleeves of a shirt stick out from her Cheetah-print tee. "You won't return to H.M.C. Philanthropies?"

"It feels official," I say with a nod.

A smile pulls her freckled cheeks. "In that case, you most certainly must join me in *our* quest to find a passion—"

"No, you were right," I interject. "This is your thing." I'm not sharing in Jane's Quest for Passion because she'll be so determined to find mine, she'll forget her search. I see that in how excited she is for me—I can't do that to her.

Jane looks like I punctured her grand, elaborate plans for eternal life friendship. "Moffy."

I feign confusion. "I could've fucking sworn I'm supposed to be your super amazing, unbiased taste-tester for all the nonalcoholic drinks." I gesture to the bar. "Is my drink invisible?"

She smiles softly. "Fine. I'll be solo until you change your mind."

Last month, Jane finished her online degree and graduated from Princeton. Her deadline for finding her passion ended with the diploma. She was supposed to give up her search and become the full-time CFO of H.M.C. Philanthropies. But when I was ousted, she quit her position.

It's an upside that I don't forget. Because Janie as a CFO of any company sounds like a royal circle of hell for my best friend.

While Jane rattles the shaker again, I catch Thatcher risking a glance at her from the very end of the bar where he's been standing guard on-duty.

I've been nice to Thatcher in the past. But *Fuck Him* with capital letters blares in my head on repeat. *Fuck Him* for punching my boyfriend. *Fuck Him* for thinking I'd cheat and hookup with my new bodyguard. *Fuck Him.*

I drill a glare into his forehead, and he sees, rotating more towards the entrance. If he feels any sort of regret, I can't tell. He just looks stern to me.

I rest my hand on my tight shoulder.

"Jane." Jack Highland calls out to my cousin. The exec producer has a knee on the stool next to me. His frayed shorts and tank look more Long Beach style than Philly, and while he grips an expensive camera, he directs the lens at Jane. "Are you afraid that if your passion involves alcohol, the public might think it's insensitive? Considering both of your uncles' history of alcoholism?"

My head swerves to Jack. "Going with the hard-hitting questions there, Jack." He's filming us for *We Are Calloway*, and sometimes I forget he's recording. Until the questions start rolling in.

Jack never shifts the camera off Jane. "You don't have to answer if you don't want to," he reminds her. "But this is naturally what people will think."

Jane places a martini glass on the bar. "The public will always have an opinion," she answers to Jack. We rarely speak into the camera unless it's a sit-down interview. "So I can't let them decide what my passion should be. Even when it's easier pleasing other people, I need to try to be true to myself."

"Plus," I say to Jack and check my texts. "She loves beer."

"Oui," Jane smiles. "La brasserie est la semaine prochaine." *The brewery is next week.*

No new texts.

I was hoping for an update from Farrow. And I'm strangely all caught up on family group messages. No unread emails. No notifications.

It's almost like I have all this free time and no job.

Even my brain is making pitifully sad jokes. I'm an heir to multiple Fortune 500 companies. If I wanted to not work for the rest of my life, I could. My troubles are insignificant. You don't need to tell me.

Jack translates French on his phone app and then asks, "If you've scheduled a brewery next week, do you already think mixology will fail?"

His questions will appear on TV with closed captions. The audience is led to believe a random producer is talking. No mention of "Jack Highland" will be on screen. You don't know his name unless you search on IMDB.

The docuseries is cinéma vérité style. Where we acknowledge that we're being filmed and talk directly to the producer.

Janie copies an earlier demonstration from the bartender and pours mint-green liquid into the martini glass. "I'm just following the numbers," she says to Jack. "My success rate is zero percent. Chances are I need to have other options lined up."

Jane plops a cherry and slides the glass to me. "Okay, give it to me, Moffy."

She means *my opinion*, but the bartender interprets this differently. He makes a choked noise, then coughs to hide it.

I narrow my eyes while he wipes his hands on a dishrag.

Thatcher angles towards us again, arms crossed and out of camera shot. He glares at the bartender, who remains the only stranger in the speakeasy bar. He already signed an NDA.

All the buttoned booths and wooden tables are empty.

"That was *not* sexual," Jane says to the bartender, beating me to the words. "You thinking it was—that says more about you than me."

He fixes his fedora, cheeks reddened. "I'm sorry. I really don't believe you two are..." He cringes, and he won't even look at me.

My jaw is cut like sharp marble.

"I know it's just a rumor," he adds. That confirmation is a good indication that our FanCon tour helped.

Jane smiles more kindly than most would.

I exhale and motion to the guy. "We'll move on if you do." And I'd like to move on.

So would Jane. She wipes the wet counter around my nonalcoholic martini.

"Yeah, definitely," he nods and apologizes again to my cousin before asking her what drink she'd like to make next.

"A dirty martini," she says.

He reaches for a bottle of gin on the shelf and starts spouting off instructions.

My phone buzzes, and honest to God, my heart flutters like I'm in the fifth grade receiving a valentine from a crush.

It's my boyfriend.

One week.

It's been one week since he returned to his residency at Philadelphia General, and my brain translates a text as Farrow gifting me a piece of red construction paper shaped into a heart, glitter glued to it.

Fuck.

My.

Sappy.

Brain.

But I understand my semi-infatuation. Farrow and I haven't spoken or seen each other since he left for an excruciatingly long shift at the hospital.

He said he probably wouldn't even get time to text. Something about double shifts, low staffed. I don't get how any of it works, but it's been twenty-nine hours since I last heard from him. I'd be lying to say I haven't been counting.

Twenty-nine hours without talking.

Twenty-nine hours without touching.

And with a high sex drive, that last one has me pent-up and resorting to jerking off more than usual. I typically try to come every day or else it feels like my balls are going to explode. Even on the FanCon bus, I managed to masturbate when Farrow and I couldn't fuck.

Being horny—it's nothing new for me. Being horny and having a boyfriend who's not around all the time—*that* is new. I trust myself fully, and my hand is a decent alternative.

But I've never fantasized more about him than I have when he's gone. I've replayed the first time he topped me on loop.

I tune out the bartender's dirty martini instructions and pop open the text. Scanning the words, my spirits burst like the pop of a balloon.

Running late. Sorry, wolf scout. — **Farrow**

Before I type a reply, another text pops up.

I'm still going to make it. Save one of Jane's terrible drinks for me. — Farrow

"Est-ce que ça va, Moffy?" Jane asks while measuring gin in a shot glass. *Are you okay, Moffy?*

"It's Farrow." I set my elbow on the bar, phone in hand. I reread the text. "He's going to be late." I look up. "Jane—"

Gin overflows her shot glass. "Merde," she curses and sops up the spill with a dishrag. She flashes me a consoling look. "There's a seventy-two percent chance your drink may cheer you up, old chap."

I smile and reach for the martini. Just as another text pings.

Miss you — Farrow

My chest tightens. I quickly respond: no worries I'll save u that drink

Lately I haven't bothered typing out the correct spelling of "you" and I've stuck with just the letter. He's gotten onto me about it a couple times, and it just makes me want to do it more.

I'm about to add *"can't wait to see u"* but then I think about how it'll make him feel. Maybe concerned. Like I'm sitting here pining for him and not living my own life. I can survive without Farrow around me all the time. But I do feel his absence.

I overthink the text. Typing and deleting and typing and deleting.

I take too long because Farrow replies first.

You okay? — Farrow

Fuck. I clutch my phone harder. Thinking. I don't know how to do this. Large intense gaps of zero communication. We barely even used to text because we were with each other all the time. It's weird to think back to the day he became my bodyguard. I couldn't even imagine my childhood crush in my life 24/7, and now, not having him is a struggle.

And I'm overthinking again.

My phone rings. Great, Farrow is calling me.

But I'm selfishly glad he did. I think it would've taken me a solid millennium to type out a text.

I put my phone to my ear and reach for my mint-green drink. "I was texting you back," I say before he can speak. "I'm sorry, man. I don't want to take up your time or distract you—"

"Maximoff," he cuts me off. "If I didn't have time to call you, I wouldn't have called you."

I nod a couple times to myself. *Alright.* "How are you doing?"

"Good. Shit has finally slowed down."

"I thought you liked the high-intensity stuff."

"Not at the end of a shift." He's quick to ask, "You okay?"

"I'm alright. Just drinking this drink here…" I take a sip of the martini and as soon as the liquid hits my tongue, my cheeks pucker. *Jesus Christ, Jane.*

She notices. "Oh no. Too sour?"

"Yep." My cheeks hurt.

"I'll make you another." She swipes my martini glass out of my hand.

On the phone, Farrow tells me, "I'm glad you're having fun, wolf scout."

I wish you were here. I rub my lips together before replying. "All the fun in the damn world. It's a regular rager here," I say dryly. "I'm planning on trying shrooms next. But the non-drug kind. Like a Cremini mushroom, maybe a Portobello."

I can practically feel his eyes rolling before he laughs. And as the sound fades, the line goes quiet; the silence is like a raw, aching thread of longing.

"I miss you," I admit out loud.

"I know you do," Farrow says, like an ass.

I groan, but I'm not able to shelter a fucking smile. At least he can't see it. "I meant I don't miss you at all. I haven't been thinking about you for even half a second." It's hard to even joke. It hurts.

"That's too bad," Farrow says. "Because I've missed you." His words are tender like I can't touch them. I shouldn't. Voices muffle in the background on his side. Quickly, he tells me, "I need to go, but I should be finished here in thirty minutes. See you soon."

See you soon.

"See you."

We hang up. I refuse to look at my watch as a countdown to his arrival. I already catch myself doing it once.

And once is enough.

Luckily, a great distraction bounds through the entrance.

Sullivan arrives from the pool, wet brown hair soaking the shoulders of her jean jacket. "Fuck, sorry I'm late," she apologizes to Jane. "I didn't want to leave until I beat my morning time."

"Butterfly?" Jack asks, panning the camera to Sulli.

"Backstroke today." She claims the stool next to me, not flinching at the single camera. The FanCon tour helped ease her in. I've been on the docuseries since I was three-years-old, Jane since she was six, and for Sulli, this'll be her first time. And she's twenty.

I notice how Sulli watches Akara and Jack fist-bump into a hug in greeting, and she hangs her head and focuses on braiding her wet hair.

A few days ago in the Meadows treehouse, she told me about how Akara and Jack are becoming good friends, and she's been feeling weird.

"I'm not sure why," she explained to me, hugging a beaded pillow.

"Maybe you're into him," I speculated.

Sulli frowned. "Him, who?"

"Akara," I said.

Sulli laughed. "No fucking way…Kits is like…" She stared up at the treehouse ceiling, handcrafted paper flowers cascading off wooden beams. "…he's Kits."

The way she said that reminded me of me. *And how I couldn't make sense of my feelings for Farrow and what he meant to me, in my life. I just knew he meant a whole hell of a lot.*

"I think you're into him, Sul," I said.

"I'm fucking not." She chucked a pillow at me, and when I threw it back, she repeated strongly, "I'm not, Mof. If I thought I was, I'd fucking tell you."

I didn't expect her denial. "What about Jack then?"

She frowned more and shook her head before groaning into the pillow. I rubbed her back, and we started talking about swimming.

At the speakeasy, I think about that moment in the treehouse. Especially as her bodyguard rests against the bar, out of the camera's frame.

Akara tells Jack, "The time was Sulli's personal best."

My cousin ties the end of her braid. "It's still too fucking slow, Kits. I couldn't even qualify with that time."

"But backstroke has never been your thing, Sul," Akara reminds her. "It's a good time." He saunters around the camera and ends up standing beside Thatcher Moretti further down the bar.

And I spot my new bodyguard.

He's been at a wooden table guarding the entrance. Sky-scraping tall, bulky, bald, bearded, and the former bodyguard to Loren Hale.

My dad requested that Bruno Bandoni be transferred to my detail. He told me, "You don't need to deal with a new inexperienced bodyguard, bud. Take mine."

Thanks to my dad, it's been an easier transition. But there'll be times where I search for my bodyguard. Expecting to see that widening know-it-all smile and the cocky raise of his brows.

Instead, I meet a stringent severe face, and the wind dies in my sails.

I turn to Sulli who stretches over the bar and snatches a cherry. "Why are you swimming backstroke?" I ask since she used the word *qualify.* She's not competing anymore, so I'm confused.

"I need a goal," Sulli tells me.

I go rigid. "What?"

Jane looks between us and pops an olive in a martini glass. "Moffy—"

"You *have* a goal. The ultra," I say toughly. "It's been your goal for months, and that's not fucking changing." *It's not changing because of me.*

Sulli bites the cherry off its stem. "The course can be fucking dangerous solo. It doesn't feel like a good idea to do it alone, and my dad's bad knee can't handle the terrain—"

"*Sulli,* I'm running this marathon with you," I say, adamant. Not backing down. "I've already started training."

She coughs on a cherry. "What? You're in a sling, Mof."

Jane shakes her head at me like I'm a disaster to myself.

"I can do a lot in a sling." I've spent most of my free time in a gym. My hamstrings and quads are sore from the nonstop leg days, but I'm strengthening every muscle until I can work on my right arm and shoulder. "And I ran a mile yesterday."

Sulli looks horrified.

"Alright, it was a walk, not a run," I clarify. "A PT was there so I wouldn't kill myself." I recognize that I need another person in the room to stop me from overexerting myself.

And I'm not proud of my lack of self-restraint.

Sulli contemplates this now. "You really think you can run a 250k?"

250 kilometers in 7 days. That's 155 miles.

In Chile.

For Sulli.

"I promise I can." I nod repeatedly.

Sulli hesitates before nodding back.

Jane slides over the dirty martini. "Here, Sulli," she says. "I've named this drink You Can't Say No To A Stubborn Maximoff."

Sulli smiles. "Yeah, fucking feels that way." She tilts her head to me and holds the martini. "You know you're as hardheaded as my dad." She cringes. "Fuck, sorry, I didn't mean—" *to compare me to him.*

"It's alright," I say truthfully, and I catch Jack's warm smile behind the camera.

I know how much I'm like Ryke Meadows, and I've been reaching a place where I can be proud of the similarities. I no longer feel like who I am is a knock against my dad. And I've realized something.

My dad raised me to be like Ryke. Because he loved his brother more than he loved himself.

That's the hard truth. Because I just wish I could reach back in time and tell my dad that he'd have a son who loves him so goddamn much, and then maybe he'd realize that he's worthy of being loved too.

Sulli sips the dirty martini.

"How is it?" I ask while Jane shakes another nonalcoholic one for me.

"Strong." Sulli smacks her lips together. "But most drinks taste fucking strong to me." She goes in for another sip.

"Good sign," I tell Jane while Sulli gulps the liquor.

My best friend smiles brightly and procures a clean martini glass.

Sulli rotates slightly to Akara. "You want to drink, Kits? I can get a temp bodyguard for the night. You can go off-duty."

Akara fixes his earpiece. "Not tonight, Sul. But I appreciate the offer."

She faces the bar, lost in thought, and then she takes another sip.

Jane polishes a glass and makes a concerted effort to angle away from Thatcher. About this time, she'd be chatting to her bodyguard and tripping over her words like she normally does around him. I almost feel badly that she's lost someone to talk to, even if he doesn't say a lot back, but then I picture the welt on Farrow's face.

And my sympathy dies.

Thatcher braves another glance at Janie, and his hand slides over his hard, scruffy jaw. The longer he looks at her, the more frazzled my best friend becomes.

She fumbles with a shaker. "Thatc——" Her voices dies in a croak, and she clears her throat. "*That* drink"—she motions to the polished glass—"is…empty. But just wait, Moffy, it'll be dreadfully beautiful."

"Je n'ai aucun doute," I say. *I have no doubt.*

All I know is that Janie deserves the best, and Thatcher is one of the only names on my very short shit list. He's not the fucking best.

He's far from it.

On impulse, I glance at my wristwatch. Thirty minutes have passed, and Farrow still isn't here.

I just hope he's okay.

21

FARROW KEENE

"Farrow, look here! Look here!"

I'm not looking at these fuckers. Paparazzi try to be blood-sucking ticks, but for me, they're more like gnats. Cameras swarm me and my parked motorcycle while I pull off my helmet.

"Look here!!"

"What'd you do at the hospital?!"

"How are you, Farrow?!"

Pissed.

That I'm not on time for this mixology thing. When I say I'm going to make it, I'll make it. But shit, I don't enjoy being held up. Especially when I could've been with Maximoff.

My favorite part of the day is returning to my tight-laced, strong-willed boyfriend, and traffic had been bad. But it's not what made me an extra half hour late.

I run a hand through my messy hair and leave my new Yamaha on the curb, right outside the Philly bar.

"LOOK HERE!"

Still not looking, I make my way to the entrance of Killer Gatsby and send a quick text to Maximoff: here.

Before I push into the bar, the door starts cracking open. Maximoff wedges himself in the entrance, and the first thing I notice: his mar-bleized, impassive face.

Something happened.

My pulse spikes. And I immediately skim him, up and down, jumbled emotion slamming into me from all angles. *He's okay.*

He's okay. But something must be wrong with his family. I clutch his hand the same time he grabs for mine, and Maximoff pulls me inside.

I shut the cameras out behind us, and I frown at my surroundings. "Where is everyone?" Fringed lamps cast dim light on crystal bottles shelved behind an empty bar. All the tables are bare, but if I strain my ears, I can pick up muttering.

"In the back lounge area." He brings me in that direction.

I stare hard at Maximoff. Concerned about him. He's bottled up, but if this were a 9-1-1 severe crisis, he'd be running. He's walking, so I'm guessing he's settled this storm and I'm here for the aftermath. "Is it Jane?" I ask.

"Sulli." His body is stringent. "I need you to check on her."

"Okay." I squeeze his hand. *I'm here, wolf scout.*

His chest tries to rise.

We turn a corner near an old record player. Gold and black beads drape an archway, and once we walk through, I hone in on an extremely passed out Sullivan Meadows.

On a dark-green buttoned couch, all six-feet of her athletic frame slumps lifelessly against Akara's side. Her squared jaw starts sliding off his shoulder.

Akara pulls her closer and holds her waist to support her weight. Seriousness hardens his gaze, and he looks up at me like *she needs your help.* "She's been out for the last fifteen minutes."

"How much did she drink?" I let go of my boyfriend's hand and rest a knee on the couch. Leaning over, I put my fingers to her carotid artery. Akara brushes Sulli's thick hair off her neck for me.

"Not a lot," Maximoff answers, his left hand clutching his slinged-elbow. An attempt at crossing his arms. I'd joke about how he's inexperienced with alcohol, but time and place, and plus, he adds, "I think."

I'm about to double-check with Akara.

"I'm calculating her blood-alcohol concentration level," Jane chimes in, voice unnaturally high. *She's upset.*

I turn my head and see Jane seated on a Queen Anne velveteen chair. Right next to an unlit fireplace, she presses a pink calculator with guilt-ridden urgency. I ignore Thatcher who towers three feet away from Jane.

Jack Highland is on a chaise nearby. His camera is powered off and lens turned away from Sulli. Any footage of her passed out won't be aired.

I focus on Sulli and talk to Jane. "I don't need an exact BAC, Cobalt. Just tell me what drinks she had."

Jane speaks so quickly in her breezy-as-hell voice that I can't understand a fucking thing.

I raise my brows at Akara.

"Two shots, two cocktails," he answers. "A single shot was in each cocktail."

"Okay, that shouldn't knock out a six-foot girl who weighs…one-sixty, one-sixty-five?"

"Around there," Akara nods.

Her BAC has to be low, but she's not a regular drinker. "How much sleep has she had?" I step back since her pulse is normal. I stand next to Maximoff.

"Not much," Akara says, adjusting Sulli again.

There you go. "That's most likely why she passed out after four shots." I glance back at Jane who's stuck calculating. "She'll be fine, Cobalt. People pass out from drinking. Shit happens."

Jane raises a finger at me. Not a middle finger. A pointer finger to *shut up.*

Maximoff whispers, "It'll make her feel better." I assume that Jane was the one supplying and mixing Sulli's drinks.

And I don't need to ask why they're all tense.

From an outsider's standpoint, having a friend facedown drunk is a nuisance at best. I've lugged Donnelly's ass up a flight of stairs at 4 a.m. before, and we cracked jokes about it the next morning.

From a security standpoint, having a celebrity pass out—one who is female and has a family history of alcoholism—is a fucking PR nightmare. The moniker *Drunken Heiress* will follow Sulli around for the rest of her life.

From a friend and family standpoint, none of us want Sulli to have to deal with bad shit.

I turn to Maximoff, sweeping his sharp features again. "Who's carrying her out of here?"

"Akara already picked her up, and she looked *dead.*" He shakes his head once, neck stiff. "She can't be carried out, and there's no way outside without a camera catching us."

Not good.

Akara says what I've realized. "We're staying here until she wakes up."

Maximoff tries to crack his knuckles. The longer I stare at him, the more I know something is eating at my boyfriend, and *fuck*, I just want to be alone with him. It's the only way he'll unwind.

"Follow me, wolf scout." I take his hand and try to lead him to the men's bathroom. He ends up next to me, step-for-step, and he opens the dark wooden door.

I easily let him have that lead. Teasing him isn't a good idea right now.

The bathroom is as elaborate as the bar: gold fixtures and faucet, three obsidian sinks and urinals, two varnished wooden stalls.

Maximoff puts a hand to his neck and glares at the fringed chandelier.

"What are you thinking?" I lean casually against a sink and grip the granite counter behind me. To be honest, I want to hold him. *Badly.* But I have to wait until he'll let me. Until we talk this shit out.

And I love driving along the weaving and crisscrossing roads of his ever-turning mind. The fact that he lets me in means everything to me.

He tries to blow out a breath. "My chest is on fire."

Just watching him, my chest is burning alive too.

Before I respond, he adds, "And I almost *hit* Akara."

I quickly replay Akara and Maximoff's interactions in my mind. They seemed normal. "He didn't act like you swung at him."

"Because I stopped myself from even moving my arm." Maximoff tugs at the collar of his Philadelphia Eagles crew-neck. "I don't know what I'm supposed to feel, but all I could reach was anger when Akara said this has happened before."

I frown. "When?"

He tries to roll his taut neck. "A few weeks ago at Charlie and Beckett's apartment. Apparently Sulli thought it was some fluke happening since she only drank three beers and conked out. Not asleep, but fucking *unresponsive*." He holds my gaze in a tight vice. "And I keep thinking…*Maximoff*…" His eyes redden. "*You had a chance to keep her away from alcohol. You stupid fucker. Why'd you let her drink at all?*"

I take the strong breath that he can't take. Staying at ease when he can't be at ease. "Because despite loving to be in control, you're not a controlling fucker, Maximoff. You don't make other people's choices for them. You're just there for them." And when he needs to be reminded of that, of anything, I'll be the first to tell him every time.

He pinches his eyes.

I move off the counter. *Please let me wrap my arms around you.* I stop when he backs up for a second. "Maximoff."

He lowers his hand. "And I keep thinking about how you just spent forty-million hours working nonstop to come back to this."

I almost smile. "Thirty hours," I correct.

He scrutinizes my unruffled state of being. "I don't get how you're okay with this." He gestures from his chest to my chest. "I've taken so much away from you, and I can't stop it. I can't change the fact that my family is chaotic, messy, and bizarre-as-fuck because I love them as they fucking are, and I feel selfish wanting you to be a part of that."

I inhale. "The media took my privacy; you haven't taken a thing from me, Maximoff. You're giving me something so fucking precious: your chaotic, messy, bizarre-as-fuck family, and I also love them as they fucking are. Plus, I look forward to coming home and putting out wildfires with you. It's not that complicated."

I knew we'd need to talk this through again. It's different now that I'm finishing my residency and not working directly for his family yet. He thinks he needs to give me peace and quiet away from the chaos.

But I want everything that comes with him.

Maximoff stands still, taking deeper breaths. His gaze fastens tight to me, and love is written all over his eyes. "I was excited to see you," he admits. "Like stupidly excited."

I picture that, and the corner of my mouth rises. "Your infatuation is showing."

"I don't care."

It swells my chest, and my eyes burn. I give him a once-over before I move closer.

He steps back. "Wait."

I stop a few feet from him, and I comb my hand through my hair.

Maximoff pinches his eyes one more time, then stares upward like he's wracking his brain. When he looks down at me, he asks, "Did April call back?"

"Yeah." My older stepsister never used to dial my number, and in the past few days, April has bombarded me with phone calls and texts. "It's why I was late." I run my tongue over my molars, almost wincing.

"That bad?" he asks. Now Maximoff looks like he wants to hold me. But we wait a little bit longer to bridge the space.

"It's not good," I say. "She said she still doesn't feel safe at her house. Someone threw a bouquet of flowers over the gate."

Maximoff shakes his head. "We can hire more private security for her."

"We've already hired three around-the-clock security guards, plus installed security cameras, *plus* we had a gated fence put up." It all happened after April called me. Panicked about how people kept ringing her doorbell and asking her questions about me and Maximoff.

My stepsister's home address in Palo Alto was leaked when I was doxxed.

Maximoff nods. "Then she needs to move houses if she still doesn't feel safe. I'll pay for any costs."

"That's exactly what I told April." I raise my brows. "And she started screaming at me about how I don't have to move out of *my* house, and it's not fair since I did this to her."

His eyes flash hot. "Jesus Christ, you didn't *ask* to be doxxed. This isn't your fault."

"No shit," I say, and I catch him smile-grimacing at that. I almost laugh, and after a short pause, I tell him, "I don't feel that guilty anymore. Right now she has more protection around her house in Palo fucking Alto than your townhouse in Philly."

Maximoff nods again, and it's taking all of my energy not to walk forward and close the gap that separates us.

I feel my lip piercing beneath my tongue. "Still stupidly excited to see me?"

He smiles, his eyes welling. "You have no goddamn idea."

It overwhelms me, and I move forward.

Maximoff moves forward. Our arms find each other, and our mouths crash together, hungry and starved—I clutch the back of his head, and his arm hooks around my shoulders. Pulling me closer. And closer.

With passion that builds hot tears and spurns all types of heartbreak. I live and breathe inside this emotion. He pins me to the outside of the stall, a sink on our right. My back slams to the wood with a *thud*.

And we break apart to breathe, keeping our hands on each other. We both look at the door.

Locked.

Maximoff tries to unbuckle my belt with one hand. "We have time to kill."

I thread his hair with my fingers. "We do," I agree.

He pauses his mission and lifts his forest-greens to me, commanding *kiss me, man*. I don't yet, and he tries to come in for one.

I shift my head out of the way, and then I turn back and kiss him myself.

He groans against my mouth, "*Fuck.*"

My blood cranks to a swelter.

Maximoff palms the outside of my pants. *Fuck, that feels good.* He pulls his head back and orders, "Unzip your jacket."

Okay, Bossy. "Someone loves my fingers," I say and slowly, slowly unzip my leather bike jacket. He watches my hand, and I use my other to unbutton his jeans.

My palm dives down his pants, his boxer-briefs. I fist his gorgeous cock, and he bucks his hips into me. More than once. More than twice. *Fuck*—a deep noise is trapped in my throat. And I devour his arousal that narrows his eyes to burning points.

We kiss again, pulled into a rough, ravenous undertow. And I'm always careful of his collarbone. I even look for signs of pain, but he's so far gone in pleasure.

I drink in his expression that's pure sex, pure love. Wound hot together.

We rub each other with mind-numbing pressure, our pants low on our waists. As a rough sound escapes his lips, I ask, "Have you been fantasizing about my dick?"

"More like my dick in your ass."

My nose flares, blood pumping. "You want inside me?"

"Hard," he whispers against my mouth.

I'm roped into him. "Good." I kiss him, then I bite his lip, and he arches into me again. *Fuck, Maximoff.*

He's simultaneously melting and hardening. His erection grows in my tight grip. My fucking muscles strain, our bodies pushed up against each other.

I'm about to rotate us, but he presses a firm hand to my chest. Keeping my back to the stall. His thumb flicks over my nipple ring, which is caught underneath the fabric of my black shirt.

We stare each other down, and more and more arousal pools in my blood and bones.

I roll his boxer-briefs further down his ass and then free his large, swelling erection. *Damn.* There is no cock I'd want more inside of me than *that* one.

He does the same to me, and he hones in on my dick and spaces out like he's imagining the feeling of it inside of his mouth and ass.

I snap my fingers at his face. "You can suck me off later, Space Cadet."

"I barely spaced out," he combats. "Like not at all."

"Okay," I say with a smile, and I distract him by stroking his erection. He stares fixatedly at my inked hand that moves up and down his hardened shaft. I spit in my palm for lube and return course. That one action draws a breathy guttural noise from him.

My body tightens. His chest rises and falls heavily.

That's enough. I stop here. Not wanting him to come by my hand. "You have lube?" I ask.

Maximoff digs in the jeans bunched at his thighs. Finding his wallet in a pocket. He tosses me a travel-sized packet, and then he watches me warm it in my hands.

I rip it open with my teeth and hand it back. "Be careful with your shoulder."

He rubs the lube, glistening his length. "Thanks, I'll keep that in mind while I'm pounding inside of you."

I let out a short laugh, turning around to face the stall. "Always a precious smartass."

"Always a know-it-all asshole."

I nod. That's definitely true. I place my hand on the wood to brace myself. And I reach back with my other to hold his waist. His skin is warm beneath my palm.

Before he pushes inside, his arm curves around me and he pumps my erection—*fuck,* my neck pulls taut, breath trapped in my lungs.

"Maximoff," I groan.

That pressure disappears to carve room for a new one. I careen my head, looking over my shoulder to see his hand wrapped around his shaft.

Lubed, Maximoff sinks into me. *Fuckfuckfuck.*

Pleasure explodes my nerve endings, and he kisses me as he pushes deeper, *deeper.* The fullness dizzies me.

"*Fuck,* Maximoff," I moan a low, graveled moan that burns my insides. My nose flares again, and I turn my head forward. *Fuckfuck.* He thrusts in and out.

In and out, the hypnotic, blistering pace lights me up. My muscles tighten, his heavy breath against the back of my neck.

He kisses my deltoids with another thrust in—*fuck yes*, I seize his ass. Feeling him flex beneath my palm.

"Farrow," he grunts, rocking his hips. "*God.*"

Fuckfuckfuck.

He plants his hand on my waist. Steadying me while my palm slips on the stall. Not getting good traction, I take my hand off his ass. Both hands to the wood.

Our bodies rock together with each thrust forward, and he hits my prostate, the intensity like a sudden burst.

"Fuck," I moan, biting down.

He hits the spot again.

My mouth breaks apart.

Again. I can't breathe.

Again. I'm rock hard, my balls aching to detonate. Thoughts flit out of my mind—again, he nails my prostate. *Fucking.*

Hell.

Every muscle in my body pulls taut, ready to snap apart. He quickens his pace into me. Deep, hard thrusts that thunder my body.

It feels...*fucking incredible.*

I turn my head back, and our eyes fuck as hard as our bodies. I let go of the door to hold the back of his head. He thrusts forward—a deeper, overcome noise breaches my lips.

"*Fuck me,*" Maximoff makes a wolfish, hot-as-sin groan.

I kiss him, only once.

He pushes quicker, faster, like he *needs* that climax now.

But then he hits the spot again—and every muscle snaps, every nerve bursts. I am fucking gone.

"*Fuck,*" I groan, a climax roaring through me. I sheath the head of my erection with my hand, cum warming my palm. I pulsate in long, pleasured waves.

It takes me a second to reorient my mind. But I do. Maximoff is already pulled out, coming in his hand, and we clean up with paper towels. When he returns, we kiss strongly, and Maximoff tries to hide his smile.

But I feel his lips rise against my mouth, and I pull back. "Are you going to say it or are you just going to dream about it?" I tease.

Confidently, he says, "I made you come hands-free." It's what he's been obsessing over, and his tone says, *I'm better than you at sex.*

I don't tear from his gaze.

Shit, he's hot and cute. And I love him hard. "You realize I made you come hands-free the last five times I fucked you?"

"That's different. I'm a billion times easier to get off on prostate stimulation than you."

I can't deny that truth, and he moves away from me to use the sink, turning the gold faucet. I watch him while we get dressed, boxer-briefs and pants back on our waist.

I tuck my black shirt into my pants. He's gone eerily quiet. Almost dazed.

My pulse skips a beat. I buckle my belt and then near him after he zips up his jeans.

"Maximoff?"

He trains his faraway look onto me. "I did this wrong."

My ribs tighten, and I fish his button through the hole, helping him. "We just established that you fucked me really well."

Maximoff hangs his head.

He almost never hangs his head like this.

"Hey." I tilt my head sideways and bend a little. "Wolf scout, look at me."

His chest collapses, and bloodshot eyes rise up to me. He looks conflicted, and I try to trace the paths back to what happened. *What happened?*

I shake my head. My stomach is in knots, and I hold the back of his neck in a protective grip. "Talk to me."

He swallows hard, brows cinching in deep, anguished thought. "After thirty-hours apart, I saw you and I just really wanted to fuck your brains out. God, I didn't even ask how your day was at the hospital."

I see where this is going, and I knew we'd be here one day. But my chest hurts seeing him wrestle with this shit.

Maximoff explains more, "And I don't know if that means something's wrong with me. Or if I just love sex. Or if I'm overthinking everything because my mom is a sex addict, and even if I think I'm in control, there's a part of me that wonders, *what if I'm not?* And I can't get out of my own goddamn head." His voice actually cracks.

I cup his cheek. "You're okay." Each word is like a knife in my gut because I feel how tormented this whole thing is for him. "You're just overthinking."

"Which part?"

"All of it," I whisper and kiss him tenderly.

He's still pained.

When we first started having sex, I asked him if he was worried about being a sex addict. He said *no.* But before he was with me, he tried to control his sex life with parameters. Hookups at night. Never the same person. Never in public.

See, our *public* relationship has opened the door to *public* sex. We can come out of a bathroom together and not give a flying shit if anyone catches us.

We can also fuck at any hour, any day. Unlike the controlled one-night stands before. I figured at some point, he'd reevaluate everything and question what's normal.

I just didn't realize how much it'd pain me to see and feel.

Interlacing my other hand with his, I say, "There is no handbook, wolf scout. You're not docked stars because we decided to fuck now and talk about boring shit later. We do what feels right, when it feels right. That's it."

I need him to understand that this was my choice too.

He looks into me. "What if it's different for me because of her?" Guilt obliterates his features, even blaming his mom. "I didn't mean it like that."

"I know. And you're not a sex addict," I tell him. *You're not like your mom.*

He shuts his eyes, taking a smoother breath. "I just fucked you in a bathroom." He opens his eyes to the shake of my head.

"This might hurt you to know, but I don't give a shit right now—I have fucked other men in bathrooms," I say bluntly. "I've had sex on beaches, sports fields, bleachers, other places outside, and it was fun. Like what just happened was fun and healthy, and it's all been done before by plenty of people. You're not the first person to enjoy public sex, Maximoff."

He thinks hard, and he lets go of my hand. He rakes his fingers through his hair. "I've never questioned it like this before. Not once."

I nod.

He breathes. "I can't drive. I can't swim. I can't throw myself into work. And I love sex, but for the first time, I'm terrified that I could take it too far and I wouldn't even notice."

"I'd notice." I brush his cheekbones with my thumb. "You trust me?"

His eyes toughen, not soften. "Of course."

"If I see that you're changing to a point where it looks bad, I'm going to tell you. We're together. We fuck each other. Your doubts are always my concerns, and I'm here for you anytime, every time."

Maximoff inhales. "I must've missed that page in the Boyfriend Manual."

I look up at the ceiling in short thought, then back to him. "If manuals for this shit existed, we'd be on a much different edition by now."

"The Son of a Sex Addict Manual."

I let out a short laugh. "I was definitely thinking of a word that's stronger than 'boyfriend', but sure, we can go with Son of a Sex Addict."

The bulb burns out of a gold light fixture above us. Cutting into our banter, and then Maximoff tells me, "I need you to know that I don't regret fucking you here."

"Good." I nod. *Thank God.*

"And I don't want you to have sex with me and think in the back of your head that I'm an addict—"

"Man, that's the last thing I'll be thinking about while we're fucking." I zip up my leather jacket, and this time, his eyes are only on my eyes. "I'll be enjoying myself. Like always. Hopefully you will too."

22

MAXIMOFF HALE

Nights are the worst.

I stare up at the rafters, my mattress hard beneath my back. I can't turn onto my side. Can't curl up into a ball or shift for a better position. With my injury, I suffer on my back every damn night. If the pain ramps up, it usually takes me an hour to drift off.

Tonight, it's different.

Legs aren't intertwined with mine. My head doesn't careen onto someone else's shoulder. I don't feel the presence of another body. It's just me and my thoughts, and I can't say it's been an enjoyable experience.

Farrow is at the hospital, working a long shift, and I won't see him until the afternoon. The clock glows an annoying *3:02 a.m.,* reminding me that I've been trying to fall asleep for three excruciating hours.

I'm not used to being in bed alone, and I crave for those days on the FanCon tour bus where I could easily crawl into Farrow's bunk.

Three years.

That's how long Farrow's residency will last. Three years where I'll have nights where he's not around. And goddamn, I miss him. Talking to him. Having him annoy me until I'm a smiling idiot.

I also feel like a whiney bastard silently complaining about *some* nights where he's gone. There are people dealing with worse separation over longer time periods and distances. And I don't envy that. I don't even like stomaching this.

I pinch the bridge of my nose. Needing my brain to shut the fuck up. I reach over and grab my cell off the nightstand. No missed texts. No cousins or siblings messaged me since the last time I checked. They're probably all asleep.

Pulling myself up, I lean more against the headboard. Floorboards and brick walls creak loudly inside the old townhouse. Tonight, heavy gusts of wind beat at the window, and my gray curtains sway back-and-forth. Tiny lights that are wrapped around the ceiling rafters start flickering.

Power might go out soon.

To restrain myself from texting Farrow, I scroll through my little sister's tweets. She roasts me daily on Twitter. One time I was on a late-night talk show to promote a charity event and the host had me read Kinney's tweets out loud.

And I was happy to.

I smile at some new ones.

@KinneyGothHale: Older brother has been talking about Aristotle for 30 min at breakfast.

She included a yawning sloth gif.

@KinneyGothHale: Also Moffy's boyfriend and me are the only ones who can make fun of him. You try, you die.

I love that my youngest sister likes Farrow. But I slow down on another tweet.

@KinneyGothHale: 1st Rainbow Brigade outing in the works. What should we do?

She added a poll for fans to vote, but she included the same three options: bowling, bowling, and bowling.

Kinney already texted me, our cousin Tom Cobalt, and then Oscar and Farrow the details about the meet-up. She picked a date in June. LGBT Pride Month.

I think about how my little sister will be deathly furious if Farrow is late. And I told him, "If you can't make it, don't let Kinney scare you."

He chewed his gum with a rising smile. "Man, I'm not afraid of your thirteen-year-old sister. Especially because she thinks she can commune with dead people," he said. "I promise I'll make it."

That image of his amused smile is cemented to my cerebral cortex. *Fuck it.*

I text him. He already told me that if he's busy, he'll just ignore me. So I'm not really worried about disturbing him.

Quickly, I type and send: thinking Of u

I purposefully fuck-up the grammar to piss him off a bit. Wind wails, and power suddenly cuts, my clock goes blank. Room darkened, I instinctively reach for my end table—my right arm fights against the sling, *fuck me.*

I bite down, and I've had it with this thing.

I reach behind me and tear off the Velcro that attaches the sling to my abdomen. And I pull the strap off my head. Slowly, I free my imprisoned right arm, and I throw the red sling onto the floor.

Then I gradually lift my right arm off my thigh. The higher I go, the more pain shoots into my collarbone and batters my shoulder.

I drop my arm back and try again.

Better. Or maybe I'm just smothering the pain with determination. I don't know.

Whatever the case, I reach for the end table again with my bad arm. Purposefully this time to stretch the muscle.

I breathe a measured breath through my nose and slide the drawer open. Grabbing a flashlight. And my switchblade for extra precaution.

Leaning back, I pick up my phone.

No new text.

I breathe out and click into some articles that Uncle Ryke sent me. All for stretch rehab on my collarbone. I'm not supposed to try any of these until eight weeks post-surgery. It hasn't even been four weeks yet, but maybe one workout won't be that strenuous…

A lube ad on the sidebar distracts me, and I immediately imagine

Farrow. Buck-ass naked, pirate ships, skulls, and sparrows inked all over his six-foot-three body.

He's standing at the end of my bed. Grinning because he knows he's aggravatingly sexy.

My veins pulse, skin hot to the touch. I rest my head back. And I try to stop myself from fantasizing by unscrewing the flashlight with two hands. Dumping out the batteries and refitting them in.

These past few weeks, sex has infiltrated my mind like hot-and-bothered battalions. I've always had fantasies. Always drifted. And it's never affected my job or relationships.

But I'm more concerned that it will now that I have all this free time.

My phone pings. I desert the broken apart flashlight and click into the text.

In your thoughts, what position am I in? — Farrow

I almost rock back. Goddamn, I did not expect that response. We've sexted before, and I gauge the healthiness of it now. Seems enormously normal.

It's not disrupting my life. And he initiated it. All pros at the moment. So I type and retype a sentence before settling on this:

Under me. On top of me. All over me.

I send the text, and something *thwacks* my window. I point my cellphone's light at the window since I dismembered the real flashlight. My curtains blow softly, and I strain my ears.

No street hecklers tonight.

Huh.

There are no trees near my window. So it couldn't have been a branch. I remember that I checked the front door after Janie and Luna went to bed. It's locked. *They're safe.*

My phone buzzes.

Sounds vague. Needs more adjectives. — Farrow

I groan in frustration. Sexual and just plain annoyance. I type two words fast: Fuck me.

Sent.

My mind tries to crawl into my spank bank and pluck out images of Farrow sliding his dick between my lips—another text comes through.

Smartass. — Farrow

I don't overthink for once and just text:
You're putting your cock in my mouth. I can taste you beneath my tongue.

I send it.

He replies even faster.

We've now established that you don't know what an adjective is. — Farrow

I'm smiling and glaring as I text back: or I just don't like them.

My dick is starting to throb, especially as I picture Farrow straddling my shoulders with me lying back. His inked abs right up against my face, along with his cock. I take him between my lips, and Farrow clutches the back of my head. Gripping protectively. Tightly. I bring his length to the back of my throat—*thwack*.

What the fuck is that?

I reassemble my flashlight in two seconds. I shine the bright beam onto the gusting curtains.

If I stand up and go shift the curtains, it means I'll need to peek out the window. And to peek out the window means there's a good possibility paparazzi will snap a photo of me. Then I'll draw hecklers to the area, and it's been nice not hearing a bucket load of bullshit about me and Farrow tonight.

I listen for the noise again, but it's quiet. So I check a missed text.

Shouldn't you be asleep by now? What's keeping you up?
— Farrow

His absence.

Being alone with my own head.

My collarbone that refuses to heal at the speed of lightning.

All of the above.

Just can't sleep. I send that text. And then I think about the lube ad, and I wonder…

I send him another message: I'm going to watch porn.

If he thinks it's a bad idea, he'll tell me. Maybe porn will exhaust me, and I can't deny that ever since I started dating Farrow and he admitted to watching it, my curiosity has piqued.

Maybe I'll see porn in a new way now that I'm in a committed relationship. I don't know. My brows furrow in heavy contemplation.

I text back: never mind.

He's calling me.

I knock my head back on the headboard. *Fuck.* Either I worried him or he's pent-up now, and both options, I'm just feeling fan-fucking-tastic about.

I put the call on speakerphone. "I'm not trying to interrupt you at work—"

"You didn't. Relax, wolf scout. I'm just charting in the on-call room." Papers shuffle on his end. "You watching porn or not?"

"I don't know yet." I open an internet browser on my phone. "What's a good site?"

He pauses. "Maximoff." Somehow, his husky voice contains his forever-widening smile. "I'd love to watch it with you since it's not something you do often, and I'm not saying this because I believe you shouldn't do it alone. You can do it alone if you want, but it'd be more fun with me." He adds, "Everything usually is. Even sleep apparently."

I blink slowly. "Thank you for those unnecessary additions."

"You're welcome." His voice fades with the shuffle of papers.

I think about experiencing this with him, and it's more appealing. Maybe it's what I really wanted all along. And I click into a "news headlines" tab on my browser.

Thwack. I swing my head.

"What was that?" Farrow asks.

"A noise," I say dryly. With the constant stream of hecklers, it's been more difficult to secure the outside of the townhouse lately. Someone could be chucking something at my window from the street. But rocks and pebbles sound more like *pinging* against glass.

Whatever hits the window is heavier, but not enough to shatter through.

"Shit," Farrow curses, and I hear papers scatter.

"They make you chart on paper?" I ask. "I thought they would've moved onto some space-aged technology. Like astral projections." Looking at my phone, my brows knot at an article series, not on *Celebrity Crush* but on its more reputable parent site and online magazine called *Famous Now.*

I pause before clicking into the articles. Farrow lets out a vexed breath, his stress or maybe just frustration ekes over the line. He's great at living inside hectic situations, but whenever he calls me at the hospital, I feel this wound-up tension inside Farrow that he normally never carries around.

He won't say much about his shifts there, but sometimes I think it's worse when I press about it. So I haven't really dug in yet.

"If you need to get back, we can talk later—"

"I have time," Farrow interjects and finally answers me. "There's an old attending in internal who refuses to move onto tablets, and since half the hospital thinks he's Jesus, all Med-Peds first-years are required to chart on paper because this old fucker said so."

My face twists. This sounds like a rule that Farrow would break. He'd consider tablets more practical and efficient to do better work, and he'd disobey the paper-only requirement, even at the cost of angering the staff and damaging his reputation.

It's just who he is. Risking it all to do the *best* job he can.

"Why not just say *fuck this rule* and use a tablet?" I ask.

"I haven't thought much about it," Farrow says distantly.

Thwack. Thwack.

"Maximoff?" Concern deepens his voice.

"It's just the wind." I shine my flashlight at the creaking ceiling rafters, then down at the window. My curtains dance more madly, and I'm tempted to stand up and peer through the closed blinds.

"That's not wind," Farrow says. "Where are you?"

"Bedroom." I balance my flashlight on my thigh. Keeping the beam aimed at the curtains. And I focus back on the internet and these daily articles on *Famous Now*.

Each one compiles all the public photos of Farrow and me. Some pictures are from my Instagram like a selfie at the grocery store. I mockingly flip off Farrow who's smiling insanely wide behind me, also he's biting into a nectarine. He was eating the fruit in the store, all before we checked out.

Yeah, he still does that.

Other pictures are from my family's social media, and then there are paparazzi photos. Like one where we're on a date at a baseball game. Waiting in the ticket line. Choosing to be normal and not bypass the crowds.

Paparazzi were everywhere, but I didn't care. Neither did he.

In the photo, his hand is in my back pocket, and I'm laughing. I didn't see his smile or his expression in that moment, but I look at it now.

Farrow is staring at me with palpable, overwhelming love. Enrapt with my whole essence. Like I'm joy and his happiness.

It knocks me backward.

"Have you seen these articles of us on *Famous Now*?" I ask Farrow while I take a screenshot of that baseball photo. I like it.

A lot.

I screenshot more pics. I like this site since there's no malicious intent attached. The intro summary at the top is brief to describe us, and it doesn't bother me.

Farrow shuffles more papers, and then says, "Alphas Like Us?"

"Yeah."

That's the title of the daily series.

ALPHAS LIKE US.

Based off the summary:

> Admittedly territorial, admittedly protective, Maximoff
> Hale and his new boyfriend are the couple of the year.
> Whether you love them or hate them, they're everywhere.

"Donnelly sent me a link," Farrow says. "You should scroll and see if you can find the photo where you look infatuated with me. That's my favorite one."

He might be fucking with me, but I scroll anyway. Quickly, I realize that I look sickly in love in practically every damn one. Like I'm sixteen again with a major crush on Farrow Redford Keene, a crush that needs to be restrained.

Immediately.

But I start thinking…

I got the guy.

I'm with my crush.

My crush wants marriage. And kids.

With me.

Eventually.

I rub my face; my cheeks hurt as my grimace becomes a smile. "This must be an imaginary photo," I tell Farrow because there's no way in hell I'm admitting to the truth.

"Not imaginary," Farrow says. "It's all of them—"

Thwack, thwack, thwack, thwack. My back straightens, and I smack my flashlight that flickers.

"Maximoff? Talk to me."

"Do you have access to the security cameras outside?" I climb off the bed and leave my phone on the mattress, still on *speaker.* Then I grab my switchblade in my right hand, flashlight staying in my left.

"No. Not anymore." Long strained silence passes through the line. I know Farrow hates that he's not able to protect me, and he's stuck across the city. "I'm texting Bruno to check the cameras," he says. "Don't open the window."

My floorboards squeak beneath my weight, and I near the blowing curtains. *Thwack.*

Thwack. That can't be a rock. It's all I can think. Not a rock.

Not a brick.

Not a baseball.

"Are you scared?" Farrow asks since I'm not speaking.

"No..." My pulse pounds, but not out of fear. "I just want to know what the fuck it is." I turn off my flashlight, and I draw open the curtain. Revealing the shut blinds.

Thwack.

A hard object bangs the glass, and I hear something else from outside. *Buzzing.* But not like a phone vibration. More like whirling...

"Shit, this is killing me," Farrow says, close to pained. His unsaid words: *I wish I were there.*

I glance back at the phone on the bed, my stomach coiling. If he were here, he'd be right next to me, and he wouldn't stop me. We both would do exactly what I'm about to do. Only we'd do it together.

"I'm not opening the window," I assure him. "It's probably nothing."

"Stay on the line with me."

"I will." Wind howls, and I use the blade of my knife and lift up a blind. And then I peek out. *Thwack.* I don't flinch. The heavy, whirling object...

"It's a drone," I tell Farrow as this mechanical helicopter thing flies into the window again. *Thwack.* "It has a sign. It says..." In big bold letters, someone wrote on a piece of paper. "...*I see you.*" A chill pricks my neck.

I see you.

Farrow goes quiet.

I back away uneasily, the blind shutting. "I think there's a camera on the drone." It could belong to anyone, and I don't care which human decided it'd be fun to film me in my bedroom.

It's fucked up.

Flying drones over private property is a gray legal area, but coming onto private property to shoot footage of me is pretty much illegal.

Paparazzi always stay on the sidewalk for a reason. As long as journalists don't use telephoto lenses to look into my bedroom and don't harass or trespass, they can get away with a hell of a lot on public property.

"You okay?" Farrow asks.

"I'm going to check on Luna and Jane, and then I'll call the Tri-Force to handle it." Anything that veers into lawsuit territory, they deal with.

"Okay, but that's not what I asked," he says in that matter-of-fact voice. I miss the face that goes with it.

I stand in a darkened room with wailing wind, creaking wood, and a camera drone thwacking glass. And the only thing that frightens me is loneliness.

I wish you were here.

I can't tell him that. I can't make this harder for him than it already is. Because I know it's already destroying him that he can't be next to me. I'm not stabbing another blade into the wound.

Three years.

"Yeah," I say, "I'm fine."

"I'm going to try to come home early—"

"No," I cut him off. "You don't need to do that, man." I toss my flashlight on the mattress and pick up the phone.

The line deadens for the longest second. "Can you spend the night in Jane's room?"

If it gives him peace of mind while he's at work, then my answer is a no-brainer. "Yeah. I can do that."

"I'm being paged...I have to go," he rushes.

"See you—" I cut myself off before I say *soon*. I'm not sure when his shift will end.

"I love you, wolf scout." It's the last thing he says. Five longing words that ache greater than silence.

23

MAXIMOFF HALE

Charlie is the only one who agrees with my new plan.

That should be a red flag.

Jane and Farrow have excised themselves from the situation "on principle" while the cousin I've been feuding with for years has joined my party of one.

> I'm heading into the ER. It looks busy. Won't be able to text. I'll call when I can, but I'm going to remind you for the sixteenth time: it's a bad idea. — Farrow

I reply: Got it.

> We can talk about your unreasonable stubbornness later tonight. — Farrow

We don't see eye to eye on this issue, and it's not the first time. It won't be the last. But it does twist me up knowing the two people who should be in my corner have left it. My fingers hover over my cell, trying to think of something to say.

I land on this: OK. Love u. I text back.

> Love you, too. — Farrow

Soon after that text, another pops up.

Still a bad idea, wolf scout. — Farrow

It reminds me of his feelings about my sling. I took it off permanently one week earlier than all the doctors advised. *Bad idea, wolf scout.* We kind of had a fight about it.

A short fight, but Farrow shook his head at me and said, "Give me a second." He went into the bathroom, and I could tell he was upset. My stomach felt like it dropped out of my body, and I didn't know how to course correct.

I wanted him on my side, but I also recognized that we're two different people. And we won't always agree. As he came out, he checked my shoulder, and the quiet tension strung between us just grew and grew and grew.

And he said, "I wish I'd been here."

"You wouldn't have stopped me."

Farrow looked at me, his eyes reddened. "That's not why…" *That's not why he wanted to be with me.* He just wanted to be with me. And I heard his voice in my head: *it's as simple as that.*

Pushing out that raw memory, I take a shallow breath and lean against my parent's mailbox. Wind whistles inside the gated neighborhood, but the air is a little too hot for early June.

Last night, Farrow was working at the hospital, so I joined in on a movie night with my family. Instead of going home to an empty bed, I ended up crashing in my old room. It was supposed to be my second chance to talk to Xander.

The do-over.

He finished his LARPing costume. A fantasy elf-inspired look: a fur-lined hood, long trousers, a distressed red tunic, leather armguards, makeshift bow and a leather quiver for his arrows. He dressed up, and even let me take some pictures like a mini photo-shoot. Just thinking about that night, my eyes sting.

Because he was happy.

And I didn't say what I needed to.

I couldn't do it.

Maybe that makes me a coward, but I'm protecting the good days he has. It's all I can think about. I just want to ensure that he's okay, and I feel like if I say something, I'm pushing him in the "not okay" territory.

Farrow is right about one thing. I can't do nothing.

Which brings me to my new plan. A different plan. I don't know if it's better, but it's something.

In the distance, I spot Charlie ambling down the street, crutches underneath his armpits. He makes slow work of it, so I kick off from the mailbox and meet up with him.

"I thought you were going to take the golf cart," I say while I pull my Ray Bans to the top of my head, and he stops walking, out of breath.

"I was." He squints from the sun. "Until I learned Tom and Eliot took the golf cart on a joyride and crashed it into Aunt Daisy's porch." I knew that happened, but I thought the golf cart wasn't too fucked-up to drive.

I nod a couple times. "I heard about that."

He cringes. "Of course you did."

I try to stay calm. "Please don't make this hard today. I'm already tense. You have no idea what it's like going against Farrow and Jane's advice."

Charlie stares at me blankly. "Not Farrow, but Jane, yes. My sister has offered plenty of bad advice that I've ignored."

I glare. "Alright, let's start over." Otherwise, I'm going to throw a fist, and just the thought of hitting my cousin is making me sick to my stomach. "Which house is Easton's?"

"According to my brother, the stucco mansion two streets over." Charlie rotates and hobbles forward using his crutches.

Keeping pace with him, it's slow, but I don't run and leave him behind. Even if I'd like nothing more than to rip this off like a Band-Aid. In my head, confronting Easton Mulligan is the second-best solution to the problem. He's the neighborhood kid asking my brother for pills, and once he stops, this will all be over.

It'll be good for Easton who shouldn't be taking other people's meds and for Xander who needs them. On top of that, Xander won't have some asshole teenager coming around who he feels the need to impress.

Only problem is that Charlie's entire right leg is wrapped up in a cast, and despite being out of a sling, my right arm looks weak and lifeless. I can't lift or stretch that well.

I tell my twenty-year-old cousin, "We don't look threatening."

He stares straight ahead as we pass the Cobalt Estate. "We don't need to threaten him."

I stop abruptly on the pavement. "That was the fucking plan, Charlie."

He faces me. "That was *your* plan—"

"This is about *my* brother," I snap. My fingertips squeeze onto control of this situation because I need it. And want it. Giving Charlie the reins wasn't on my to-do list for the day. He's here as backup. Support. I'm taking lead.

My brother is in trouble. It's all I think. *My brother is in trouble.* And I have to help him, and Charlie is unpredictable. As much as I love my cousin—and I know you may think I hate him, but I love him too damn much—I can't see where his head is most of the time, and I have *no* goddamn idea what he'll do in charge. I'm not playing a chess game. I'm dealing with people.

Real people and lives—and my brother's life.

I don't want either of us to move Xander around a board like a rook on H-6.

Charlie's golden-brown hair blows in the wind. "I'm not seeing many volunteers here to accompany you on this excursion," he says. "So we do this my way."

I shake my head. It can never be easy with us. "This is bigger than the bullshit between you and me."

Charlie looks annoyed. "You think I'm here for some petty reason, but maybe consider that I'm the only one by your side because I actually understand." He steals my Ray Bans off my head and slips them on his eyes.

Those last three words cave my chest. *I actually understand.*

"What do you mean?" I ask.

Charlie shifts his crutches beneath his armpits. "Nothing." He glances at the Cobalt Estate, pink tulip trees lining a driveway that leads up to a regal fountain and ornate mansion. It's nothing like my childhood house that I just passed, which is stone and brick with a fir tree in the front yard.

"It's not nothing," I say, failing at softening my tone. I'm trying. *I'm trying.* I know I need to try harder for him. "Charlie, I want to understand."

He's quiet.

"I'm fucking sorry. Please."

He hooks my Ray Bans on the collar of his button-down, the leg of his slacks cut to make room for his cast. Charlie looks tormented, his features fracturing in emotion that I can't pick apart.

I put my hand on his shoulder. "Charlie..." Something happened.

He pinches his eyes, then he puts his weight back on his crutches. And I remember that any act of "heroism" on my part causes him pain and frustration.

And it's plunging a knife into my gut.

I drop my hand, and we don't continue our trek yet.

Charlie stays still. "I've thought about telling you before now..." He struggles to make a decision, staring up at the sky. "My brother needs more than me to care about him, and you're the logical choice because you'll care excessively to the point of stupidity."

I ignore that last insult. "Which brother?"

Charlie takes his weight off his crutches again. "My twin brother." *This is serious.* "Every night Beckett is on stage, he strives for perfection in ballet. It's an impossible goal, and he's worn his body down to the point of pain. A couple years ago, he found a fix."

A lump makes its ascent in my throat.

"Cocaine," Charlie says plainly, clearly.

I didn't know. I doubt many people in our families do. "Charlie," I breathe, so much tunneling through me. Concern for Beckett, for

Charlie, and wanting to console them both, but I don't know how in this instance. I don't know what they need.

So I wait and listen.

"He's a beautiful dancer," Charlie says, clearing his throat, almost choked. "One of the best in the world, and it won't take words from me or anyone else to convince him to stop. Not even you."

It slices me open for a second.

He winces. "And now that you know this, there's a sick part of me that loves that you'll be hurting with me." His chin almost quakes, and he drops his head, dragging his gaze across the cement.

Then he ambles forward.

"Charlie, wait." I'll hurt with him if that's what he needs. I'll share in his pain. I'll do anything for him…I know that's partly the problem. *Heroism*.

He stops. Looks up at me.

"We're doing this together?" I ask. "Don't leave me behind."

Charlie takes a breath and nods. "I understand watching your siblings make a mistake and not having the ability to shake them. And all you can do is search for a solution. Any solution."

Everything clicks. "The auction," I realize.

He slips the sunglasses back on and pulls at his hair. "I convinced Beckett to do the auction because I knew he'd have to take leave from ballet again. He missed *Swan Lake*, and he won't return until rehearsals for *Cinderella* begin. He's clean for now."

That's good. "Who knows?" I wonder.

"Me, Oscar, and Donnelly," Charlie says. "Now you, and I'm assuming Jane and Farrow won't be far behind. But don't let it go further than them."

"I won't." I'm surprised that Charlie's bodyguard knew. If I remember correctly, Farrow told me that Oscar didn't know anything. Since Farrow never lies to me, I'm assuming that Oscar lied to Farrow.

Charlie supports himself on his crutches. "So now can we do this my way?"

I fight every instinct in me that says to hold on to the figurative wheel, but I nod once and relinquish control.

We ring the doorbell on the stone stoop of a

stucco mansion, a welcome mat beneath our feet. Hanging ferns flank the wide front door, and Charlie leans most of his weight on one crutch.

We wait.

A few tense seconds pass before the wooden door swings open. I prepared to meet Easton's mom or dad or maybe even a sibling—it seemed more plausible—but the face staring back at me can't be older than sixteen.

First impressions: messy chocolate hair, long aquiline nose, pale sheet-white skin and pinpointed hazel eyes. A navy blue Dalton Academy honor society shirt hangs on his lanky frame. Definitely not built like a jock, and for some reason, I thought he'd be buffer. Older.

He just seems young to me. Really young.

I don't know what it is with me and kids around my sibling's age, but it fucking gets to me. Like there's a part of me that just wants to protect this boy. And I don't know him—but I do know he's a wrench in my brother's life and I know Xander is partly to blame—but I also see a human being in front of me.

I never forget that. I can't.

"Are you Easton Mulligan?" I ask, ready to solve this crisis with Charlie.

"Yeah…" he says slowly and looks from me to my cousin. "And you're Maximoff Hale and Charlie Cobalt." He hangs onto his door. "Um…so Xander didn't say anything about you two coming over." He hones in on Charlie's cast.

Even with a broken leg and bent on a crutch, Charlie evokes supreme confidence. His take-no-shit demeanor intimidates the kid so much that he tries to look at me for comfort.

I'm not that soft either, but I think I'm empathetic enough that his uncertain eyes linger on me.

"We'll make this quick," Charlie tells him. "We're here because you're getting pills from Xander Hale."

Easton frowns. "How do you—"

I raise my phone, already on the text that I screen-shotted from Ben's phone. "You've been bragging about it."

"Shit..." Easton curses again. His widened eyes flit between us.

"Here's what'll happen," Charlie says, sharpness to his voice. He hands me the crutch that he's not using.

Don't ask me what he's up to. I don't know. I'm on edge, holding my breath.

Charlie slips out a piece of paper and passes it to Easton. "This is a phone number to a doctor in Philadelphia. He'll prescribe whatever you want. Just give him a call, let him know who you are, and you can get your pills legally."

What the fuck.

Easton frowns and reads the paper. "I don't understand. Why are you doing this for me?"

"Because you're going to stop taking Xander's pills," Charlie says.

Easton shakes his head. "I'm not—I mean, I am, but..." He looks to me. "You do know that Xander gets refills about a month before he's even out. For me."

I don't move or flinch or react. *I didn't know.*

The boy glances back into his house, then comes forward and shuts the door behind him. Fully on the front porch. He speaks more to me than to Charlie. "My parents aren't as nice as yours...I tell my mom I'm not doing well, and she tells me it's summer allergies." He shakes his head. "Dude, I would *never* take pills Xander needed. That'd be...that's fucked up."

This...is not what I expected. I try to grasp onto the truth. Uncover it. Xander was helping this kid? I don't understand, and it's still not okay that my brother was giving someone his meds. Even if he had extra. A pressure mounts on my chest, something screaming at me: *I don't know what's right. Fuck. I don't know what's right.*

I crawl onward. "Why were you bragging about it then?"

His face crushes. "I...because Colton Ford found out I was getting into LARPing with your brother. He kept calling me a..."

"A pussy?" I'm guessing.

"Yeah..." He nods.

I had that word slung in my face in high school too many times.

"Your friend is an idiot," Charlie says bluntly.

Agreed.

Easton shifts his weight. "I panicked and I said that stupid thing, and then the next day, I told Xander and apologized. He knows." His brows knit. "And shouldn't you know this? He would've told you..." Realization floods his face. "Wait, he doesn't know you're here?"

Charlie and I stay silent, not giving information to a stranger.

In the quiet, Easton folds the paper like a treasure. Unable to look Charlie in the eyes, he tells him, "Thanks for this."

I'm uneasy, and I want to interject. But I can't figure out what to say fast enough. And I wonder if the right thing would've been having my parents talk to his parents. Let them help him. But what if his parents are assholes and it makes his life drastically worse?

"No problem," Charlie says, and I pass my cousin his crutch. He braces his weight on them.

Easton steps back to his door. "I have to go." And to me, he adds, "Xander really never mentioned me?" *Not once.*

I shake my head.

"I'm sorry," I say, my head heavy on my shoulders for too many reasons.

He nods, a little hurt, and then he slips back inside his house.

Charlie and I leave the front porch, and as he slowly descends the few steps, Charlie tells me, "Well, that was not exactly how I saw that going."

I watch him to make sure he doesn't trip, and when we walk across the long driveway, I keep shaking my head. "You know a doctor who's writing illegal prescriptions, and you just gave a sixteen-year-old their number," I say out loud.

Dumbfounded.

"And I solved the issue," Charlie tells me. "It's done."

"That doctor should be stripped of his license, and that kid could use that contact for something other than antidepressants," I counter. "If he gets hooked on opioids—"

"Not my problem." His crutches make a *thunk thunk* noise on the cement.

"Fucking Christ." I rub my mouth, distressed. Everything is wrong about today.

Charlie halts at the curb. "I'm sorry," he says. "Did I swindle you into thinking I'd choose the moral choice? People make stupid decisions, and I'm not you. I don't bear responsibility for other people's choices. How do you even live with that? How are you not dying from that?"

So many emotions slam at me.

So much has changed. So much is in flux. I don't know what's up and what's down. Right from wrong anymore. It's like I have paths and choices and I keep running down the darkest one.

I'm not even sure if what we did here today was right.

And I just want to shut down.

To go numb. Really, I want to call him. To talk to Farrow. Because when my universe feels like it's spiraling and trying to drag me under, he has this ability to make me feel lighter than air.

And then I remember his text about being unavailable.

I can't call him. I won't fucking disturb him at work.

So I just walk forward, shoulders locked. And I carry this weight.

24

Missing Jane's 23rd birthday party is par for the course by now. My schedule at Philly General doesn't allow for sick days or personal hours. Add in the overtime charting and other bullshit—and I'm sufficiently MIA more than I like.

It's not my favorite thing.

Not even close.

Working inside a hospital wields a certain kind of discomfort for me—suffocating, aggravating, choked—and I didn't forget its existence but it's amplified this time around. For too many reasons.

Like missing the quietest, purest moments. My recent 22-hour shift means that I didn't go to sleep with Maximoff. I didn't see him wake up, and I couldn't rake my fingers through his hair. Couldn't see him struggle into his jeans and glare in my direction before he flips me off.

Hell, I wasn't even there to laugh or smile or help. And there'll be other moments to make up for those. Sure. But I sense what I'm losing because I've had those powerful minutes, those unbearably beautiful seconds before.

I'm trying my best not to keep tally of what could've been with Maximoff. Because then it starts feeling like *regret*. And I can honestly say that I don't know how to deal with that emotion other than change course.

I can't change this.

I just have to remind myself that the goal isn't to work at a hospital. That's not what I'm chasing.

I'm running after the concierge position. To be a doctor to these famous families so I'm not an outlier but involved. And needed.

Unfortunately, the path to *that* ideal job is this residency at Philly General.

Three years.

Just three fucking years, and then I'm out and working for the Hales, Meadows, and Cobalts again.

I climb stairs to the rooftop of Superheroes & Scones, motorcycle helmet tucked beneath my arm.

It's still June 10th. I may've missed Jane's birthday party at the Cobalt Estate, but I'm on time to make the tail end of her birthday tradition. Typically it's just her and Maximoff (plus their bodyguards) but Jane extended an invite to me.

I swing open the metal door to the roof, and before I come face-to-face with the eccentric putt-putt course—made with milk bottles, garden gnomes, antique gas station signs—I hear a phrase that I really, *really* do not want to fucking hear.

"Is it Rowin?" Jane asks.

Rowin.

As in my ex-boyfriend. As in an official concierge doctor to the famous families.

If they called him, then someone must be injured.

Maximoff.

A pit is in my stomach, and with more urgency, I walk onto the makeshift putt-putt course, door thudding behind me.

Strung outdoor lights twinkle in the night, and Jane and Maximoff have their phones out like pistols. I assess each of them as I near.

Maximoff drapes his metal putter over his left shoulder like a baseball bat. He grips his cell in his right hand, and Jane leans her weight on a pink putter, blue eyes on me.

Both look okay.

"I've been trying to get ahold of you," Maximoff says, hurt somehow hardening his face. "Christ, I've called you like seventeen times."

Shit. I absolutely hate being inaccessible to the people I care about, and he's my number one. "I had 1% battery before I left the hospital," I say. "My phone must've died." I hook my motorcycle helmet on the arm of a six-foot red-and-black Deadpool statue. The third putt-putt hole is an overturned bucket between the statue's legs. "Why'd you call Rowin?"

His eyes dance over my features like he hasn't seen me in years. I look at him just the same, sweeping his jawline, his chest that falls and rises in time with my chest, and his stiff neck, the fresh scar peeking out of his T-shirt collar.

Before I reach Maximoff, he starts redialing a number. "Since you weren't picking up, he was the only choice. I'm trying to get ahold of him. To tell him not to come."

"Out of loyalty, we would have waited longer," Jane says to me. "But Thatcher started looking pale."

And that's when I notice six-foot-seven brooding-as-hell Thatcher Moretti. He's uncharacteristically sitting down on a lawn chair, and a plaid flannel shirt is wrapped around his hand.

Blood soaks the fabric.

His cheeks are a little pallid, and as soon as our gazes meet, he glowers. "I told them I could just go to the hospital." He braces his forearms on his knees. "I don't need to get involved in your petty drama."

Petty drama.

Wow.

See, the concierge team extends to security. It saves time and resources from a famous one having to call in a temp bodyguard for the day. But Thatcher Moretti asking to go to a hospital is a motherfucking surprise. Because that means he's choosing to break security rules just to avoid me and my "petty drama."

My brows rise. "Interesting." I dig in my pocket and cup a silver chain in my fist. "Considering you didn't care about me and my petty drama when you socked me in the face." I turn to Jane. "Happy Birthday." I drop a necklace in her palm, a cursive pendant spells: *merde.*

She's distracted a little since her bodyguard is bleeding, but her face brightens as she says, "A *shit* necklace."

"Love it?" I ask.

"Oui." She presses the necklace to her chest, and then she looks over at her bodyguard. Concerned and troubled.

This is all more complicated than I like.

"I thought I was defending a client," Thatcher suddenly tells me.

I turn and roll a yellow golf ball beneath my boot. "A client, as in *Maximoff*. So you thought you were protecting my boyfriend from me?"

Does he realize how that sounds?

Thatcher lets out a heavier breath. He's trying not to glare at me, even when I'm definitely glaring at him. "I was wrong," he confesses. "I crossed a fucking line just to set you off towards the end. It was out of anger, and I've already apologized to Maximoff tonight."

I glance at Maximoff, and he nods once to me, still dialing Rowin's number. My ex is going to have about fifty missed calls from my boyfriend.

Thatcher tightens the knot on the flannel shirt. "You want to lay into me. Go ahead, but don't fucking come at me for wanting to go to the hospital so your ex doesn't have to share a rooftop with your current boyfriend."

I kick the golf ball at a gnome. "You *really* think you're doing me a favor?"

It takes him a hot second, but he admits, "No." He curls a piece of hair behind his ears. "I think my hand is sliced open from a rusted sheet of metal. And I'd prefer not to be stitched up by the guy who hates me. Nor the guy who hates you."

Okay.

Okay. I'm here and more than capable of helping this tool, and he needs to suck up his fucking pride like I'm about to do. "I have a med kit on my bike," I tell Thatcher. "Do you really want to wait five hours in an emergency room when I could do it right now?"

"Rowin is still on his way," Jane reminds me.

"I'm better at suturing," I say. It's just a fact.

Thatcher rolls his eyes and just shakes his head. But the words out of his mouth are, "Go get it."

Thank you.

It takes me three minutes to jog back down the staircase, grab the med kit and then return to the roof. And when I arrive, Thatcher has changed seats to a picnic table bench.

Jane is on the phone, chatting to someone. Hushed and serious. She paces up and down the makeshift putt-putt course.

"What the hell is going on?" I ask Maximoff, who calls Rowin again—*that's it,* I steal his phone, and he glares.

"Farrow."

"It's fine. He's coming here. Don't worry about him, wolf scout." Once I finish my residency, I'll be working with Rowin Hart on the newly named *med team*, and I haven't been imagining what that'll be like. It'll happen when it happens. In three years time. So there's no point in obsessing.

But Maximoff—I wonder if he's been overthinking. He hasn't mentioned anything about my ex and medicine and me.

I look him up and down, more concerned. "Are you okay with him—"

"Yeah," he cuts me off, definitely knowing where this is headed. "It doesn't bother me." He drops his putter off his shoulder.

I'm not sure I believe him. "If it does—"

"It doesn't," he says, voice firm.

I let it go. It's not a talk that has to happen tonight. I return his phone to him, and he slips his cell in his back pocket.

Maximoff glances briefly at Jane and then tells me, "Your father called her back. She messaged Dr. Keene earlier asking for tips on how to treat a cut from a sheet of metal."

"Sheet of metal?" I repeat, and he points to the rusted metal shaped like a mushroom.

"That was on top of a Grinch statue," he explains. "It fell and almost hit Jane. Thatcher caught it."

Thatcher is a good bodyguard, and I wouldn't deny that just because I dislike the guy.

"Let's get this over with," I say and we head over to Moretti. Dropping the trauma bag on the picnic table, I rummage for gloves and other supplies.

Thatcher watches tentatively.

And as Maximoff leaves to go speak to Jane, I'm left alone with him. We don't talk. I rest my knee on the bench next to Thatcher, hovering slightly over him.

I snap my gloves on and take his hand. He's already removed the plaid flannel shirt. The air pulls taut every time our narrowed eyes meet, and believe me, I've thought about punching Thatcher plenty of times. But digging a needle in further while I'm treating him, just to hurt him—I would never.

That's not who I am, and since he's let me stitch him, he at least believes that.

I inspect the wound. A deep gash slices diagonally across his palm. It missed his thumb and fingers. He's lucky.

"You have all your fingers," I tell him, cleaning and disinfecting the wound.

Thatcher doesn't wince. Or blink. He looks over at Jane and Maximoff, but I can't read his gaze that well.

With a needle and syringe, I pierce his skin to numb the gash. Gentle and precise. He takes his eyes off his client and watches me work.

"I want stability for these families," Thatcher tells me. "It's why I voted to keep you as his bodyguard. Maximoff needed you to stick around. And if you planned to quit, I just wanted you to fucking do it—and I was pissed when you finally did. Because you just proved me right, and I wanted to be wrong."

I suture his cut. "Well, you are wrong." I don't look up at him while I stitch. "I'm going to be honest, I don't know a lot about you, Moretti. We don't talk about personal shit, and I'm okay with that. But for you to act like you know me inside-and-out and for you to presume all of my intentions...that's annoying."

He opens his mouth, closes it, and in his silence, I lift my gaze more. He shuts down, staring impassively at me. Expression hard like reinforced steel. I recognize that look.

This is something my boyfriend does.

I don't prod Thatcher to speak, and I finish the last suture, clean up, and bandage his hand.

"Done," I tell him.

He stands, opening and closing his hand in a fist. I straighten up and snap off my gloves, discarding them...

Something wet drips down my forehead. I touch the droplet and look at my fingers...I see blood. My pulse spikes. I blink. *No.*

It's not blood. It's clear, but I feel like it's all over me. Drenched in blood, limbs slipping against my limbs while I try to hold a body down. On floorboards. I can't get a good grip.

I blink.

I look up. I see the night sky. Not ceiling rafters. I'm on the roof. And rain starts pelting my face. I smell rain on metal. My heart speeds. I hear the violent crunch, I feel the impact against my body—I struggle for the next breath.

Fuck. I shut my eyes tightly.

Fuck.

I hear screaming in the distance.

Fuck.

Slowly, I open my eyes, and I block out everyone but him. Maximoff is in front of me. Unyielding forest-greens holding me upright. "Farrow," he calls out to me. "*Farrow.*" He grips my neck, and I'm more alert. Looking at him.

He knows.

He knows what's wrong.

My eyes burn, and I shake my head. These traumatic events have clung on, and I can't rip them off now. And I'm pissed that this is happening.

"It's the rain," I say, something thick in my throat. Each word is heavy and coarse.

I grit my teeth, breathing through my nose.

"Let's go downstairs," Maximoff says, his tough gaze cradling mine which grapples for clearer focus, and I hold his hand before we move—

The door opens abruptly. Light rain showering the rooftop as Rowin emerges, med bag slung over his shoulder.

Maximoff is about to speak, but someone else beats him to it.

"You can go," Thatcher says, nearing the entrance. He holds the door open and motions for Rowin to leave back through.

Rowin glances at his bandaged hand and then to me.

"I said you can go," Thatcher repeats, more sternly this time.

Rowin gives Thatcher a nod, and then he shoots me an annoyed look, as though I made him drive through traffic for no reason.

Right now, I'm honestly just trying not to have sensory overload from the car crash or the confrontation with the stalker.

He leaves, and as soon as I'm downstairs with Maximoff, in the empty Superheroes & Scones store, we wrap our arms around each other. Chest against chest, my pulse beats with his, and I hold the back of his head.

I breathe in his chlorine and citrus scent. He probably shouldn't have been swimming with his injury. But smelling *summer* on Maximoff makes me smile.

It grounds me to the here and now.

25

MAXIMOFF HALE

"What are the antibiotics for strep?" I quiz my boyfriend. Printed flashcards fill my hand and scatter the coffee table inside the loft of Superheroes & Scones. Three-day-old red velvet cake from Jane's birthday lies next to more study materials and energy drinks.

It's afterhours in the comics shop. Empty. The only real time I can enjoy one of my favorite places on Earth.

Farrow slouches on a yellow beanbag, his muscular legs splayed over my lap, and I reach for my mug of tea. Sitting straighter than him.

He flips a page in a comic book on his lap and answers, "Ampicillin, amoxicillin, and PCN."

Yeah, I have no clue if that's correct. Not until I flip the card over and read the answer on the back.

Farrow is grinning at the comic. "You don't have to tell me it's right, wolf scout. I know it is." His eyes finally flit to me. "Keep going."

He has a USMLE Step 3 exam tomorrow. *Tomorrow.* He said it's the test he has to pass to get licensed. And he hasn't studied a single minute for it.

So when I heard that, I printed out a tower of flash cards and bought practice materials. Here we are. Only now I'm starting to think he agreed to this study session just out of pure amusement.

That know-it-all smile stretches his face, and he raises his brows.

Like he's waiting. But he's also skimming a comic book. He grabbed one from the store downstairs.

I set my tea down and read off a notecard. "What is the most common cardiac manifestation of Lyme disease?"

"An AV conduction block or defect," he says casually. "Why does this girl talk to…wait, are those demons?" He frowns and rotates the comic to check the front cover. Like he's ensuring he grabbed an issue of *X-Men*.

He did, and I don't need to see the panel. "That's Magik. She's the sorceress supreme of Limbo."

His eyes meet mine, and he almost laughs. "Fuck, I'm just remembering how big of a dork you are."

I'd shove his legs off me, but for some damn reason, I love them across my lap. So I end up giving him a middle finger instead.

Farrow only smiles more and flips a page in the comic. "Let's go, wolf scout, show me how great you are at quizzing me."

I meant to give him something, and this is a better time than never. I straighten the deck of flashcards and put them down. I capture more of his attention when I reach for my backpack with my good arm.

I already stressed the fuck out of my shoulder muscle earlier today. I tried to lift a stack of medical texts (study prep material), and now my collarbone thumps like stereo bass is blasting inside the bone.

Anyway, I'm not as concerned about my injury. Not lately. I'm more worried about Farrow after the rooftop. I've seen him hyper-vigilant before but never unresponsive and spaced out, and I knew it was serious.

We talked about it for a long time the past few days. Inside our steaming bathroom after a shower, he was towel-drying his bleach-white hair, the roots recently dyed, and I was brushing my teeth at the sink. And he called them intrusive memories.

"It's happened before," Farrow said. "When I was five and six."

I spit in the sink and rinsed my mouth a couple times, the mirror fogged. So I looked over my shoulder multiple times, but he was relaxed, tying his towel around his waist. I listened carefully to him.

And he explained, "After my mom died, I only had one memory of her."

I remembered. "You heard her calling your name." I put my toothbrush in the mirror's cabinet, and then I turned around, my gray towel tied on my waist too. And I neared my boyfriend and scraped my wet hair back with my fingers.

Farrow nodded, looking me over with a small smile. He leaned a shoulder on the misted shower door and reached out for my hand.

I drew closer before I grabbed hold. Our pulses slowing in the fucking heat, and there was comfort passing between us. Some kind of solace in the steam, and he looked at ease. I know, I know—Farrow Keene is always at ease, but more so than he has been in recent days.

He whispered, "I'd hear my mom saying my name at random times. I wasn't thinking of the memory, but it'd surface involuntarily. It's more of a sensory thing, and my father had his colleague speak to me. I was a kid, so I was confused." Farrow held my gaze. "But he told me to focus on whether there could be a trigger. A time of day, a feeling, a sound."

"Was there one?" I asked.

"Yeah." His eyes trailed over my cheekbones. "A bed."

Farrow explained that every time he'd crawl into his single-bed as a kid and pull the covers up to his chin, he'd hear his mom say his name. And instead of avoiding the bed, he returned to it every night. "I tried to ground myself to something else. Another sound, another feeling, and after a while, the memory fell back."

It made more sense why he immediately told me, *"it's the rain,"* on the roof. He was identifying the trigger, and he wasn't panicked. He's been mostly angry that it's happening at all.

So recently, my aim is to take more stress off him. Make his days lighter and better. In any way.

Now that I have my backpack in front of me, I unzip the main section. Farrow is watching from the yellow beanbag with escalating interest.

He scrutinizes the tower of flashcards I put on the coffee table. "Quitting early isn't going to win you high marks," he tells me, ditching the comic and reaching backwards for a hacky sack from a bin.

"This is called a fucking break," I tell him.

"A break," he repeats. "That doesn't sound like the Wolf Scout way." He tosses the blue hacky sack, and I watch his fingers wrap around the crocheted ball. He stares into me. "I must've really loosened those laces…" he trails off as I pull out a gallon-sized baggie from my backpack.

Farrow crunches up to me, shoulder-level, and he takes the baggie from my hands. Inspecting the contents through the clear plastic. His brows keep rising and rising at me like *what did you do?*

"This is for the first day," I explain, my elbow on his knee and hand on his thigh. "I have another one for the second day."

Step 3 is a two-day exam. The first day is seven hours, and the second day is nine hours. Only a forty-five minute break during each day.

It's brutal—or so I've read—even if it's the easiest of all the step exams.

Each baggie contains two protein bars, crackers, mixed nuts, grapes, a whole apple, and two turkey sandwiches.

"It's important you're not hungry during the exam since it's long," I tell him. "At least that's what people say on the sdn forums."

His smile slowly expands wider and wider, overtaking the whole damn room. He's not saying anything, and I don't know. It makes me fucking nervous.

My neck heats, but I double-down on confidence and gesture to his chest. "Preparing for stuff is my thing," I tell him.

He laughs, and before I interject, he tells me, "I love your thing." His smile is a million watts of power and fucking beauty. He waves the baggie. "Thanks for these; they're perfect. And now you've successfully earned your ninety-fourth *preparedness* merit badge."

I feign confusion. "That many?"

He almost rolls his eyes and leans in, cupping my jaw. My hand slides down his thigh towards his ass, and our eyes rake each other for a boiling minute. And our mouths meet—I pull back, our lips separating before they even sting or swell.

Farrow frowns. "What's wrong?"

"I'm not distracting you before your exam, man." My broad shoulder brushes his hard chest when I reach forward and collect the flashcards.

He tips his head. "You do realize I'm going to pass this exam even if I kiss the fuck out of you? Hell, I could fuck you all night, and I'd still ace it."

I swelter, my muscles blazing with a hundred-degree desire. I try not to look at Farrow. Because if I look at my childhood crush who just said he could fuck me all night—I'm going to flash *fuck me all night* eyes.

"You can't be that sure," I retort.

"I kind of can. I know my shit, and this is shit I know."

I force a grimace. "Looks like we know who has the better vocabulary now."

"Always me, Harvard Dropout." He reclines back on the beanbag, realizing that I'm not letting up, and he watches me flip through the flashcards.

I read off another one. "What are the drugs that lead to hyper-calcemia?"

"Lithium and thiazides." He passes the hacky sack from hand to hand.

Correct. I don't tell him since he already knows. "How was your shift yesterday?" I ask while I search for another card that looks more challenging.

Farrow has been in his residency program for over a month now, and he barely ever tells me about his workday. And for someone who's a kindergartener with stress—you know: he's like rubber, stress is like glue; it bounces off him and sticks to you—working at the hospital has really stressed the hell out of him.

He just never tells me why or how.

I don't know...it's been getting to me lately. Farrow never shuts me out, and I can feel him closing that door to his work life more and more as the days pass.

Farrow chucks the hacky sack in the bin and tells me, "Nothing to rave about." He ends there, and he sits up.

And I'm determined to eliminate his stress, not bug him about it. So I don't press on about the hospital.

Farrow opens his exam day baggie. Stealing the apple, he takes a large bite, and the longer I watch him, the more he lifts his brows at me. "You're looking at me and not your notecards."

"Thank you for that update," I say and tear my gaze off his smile that's doing a number on me today. I read a card. "What do acanthocytes on a blood smear indicate? They also look like spur cells but with more rounded spurs."

I flip over the card and read the answer. My stomach sinks.

"Maximoff," he says in a silky but rough breath. He knows why I've stalled. He holds the back of my neck, his thumb stroking my skin.

The text on the card is clear.

Hypothyroidism, alcoholism, and liver disease.

My grandfather died from liver disease. It's weird how little moments that you least expect can creep up on you and make you remember people you lost. And the older I get, my feelings about my grandfather shift and alter.

"What are you thinking?" Farrow says quietly, putting the apple aside.

I flip the card back over. "I'm thinking about my grandfather." I stare faraway. "After he died, I was terrified that my dad would go out the same way." I motion to my head. "In my mind, if he even drank a tiny sip of alcohol, he'd just collapse. And that'd be it." I glance at Farrow's hand splayed on his kneecap, and I lift it up and slowly interlock our fingers.

Farrow watches.

"It was just a little kid's fear," I tell him, "but I still remember going to restaurants where my aunts and uncles would have alcohol. There'd be a beer beside my dad's water, and I'd worry all night that he'd accidentally drink out of the wrong glass."

"How'd you get over it?" Farrow asks, and he lets me slip his silver rings off his fingers and collect them in my callused palm.

"My mom," I tell him. "I told her why I was scared, and she said that my dad's liver was made of vibranium." Off his confusion, I add,

"The same indestructible steel that Captain America's shield is made of. She said that it'd take more than a single drink to destroy him."

He breaks into a smile, lightness in his eyes. "That sounds like your mom."

I nod, and I recognize that I just veered off the study track again. But while the wheels are off, I think about the hospital. His residency. One more time.

One last time.

I need to say this so I can just leave it alone. "I get that you can't tell me anything about your patients," I say to him. "HIPPA and all of that, but I'm still here if there's anything you want to share. Stuff about your coworkers or what fucking cafeteria food you had for lunch. But if you want me to drop it, I'll drop it."

"Drop it," he says, too quickly. Really goddamn quickly. And he's serious. He's not joking or fucking with me.

It hurts. God, I wish it wouldn't. "Alright," I nod, more tense, and I try to unthaw my frozen body and examine another flashcard. I close my hand around the rings I slipped off his fingers.

Farrow rubs his eyes, and then he swings his legs off my lap. Standing up, he takes his half-bitten apple and nears the mini-fridge underneath a *Thor: God of Thunder* poster.

This was the inverse of what I wanted to happen. Taking a breath, I focus on the flashcard. "What do you give a kid with chronic daily headaches?" I ask.

He squats to the mini-fridge. "A tuna sandwich."

"What?" My brows furrow.

He glances back at me. "You asked what cafeteria food I had for lunch." Our eyes dive to the bottoms of each other's gaze. "A tuna sandwich. The day before that was chicken salad, and both were extremely fucking mediocre. The food is nothing special." He takes a beat. "I'm sorry that I've been distant about work—I know that I am. Fuck, I hate that I am, but I just can't talk about it yet."

Yet.

So that wasn't all of it. I nod a few times.

His chest rises in a tight inhale. "I'm trying to protect you, wolf scout. Trust me."

I stop myself from asking, *from what?*

Because I remember that I've protected him from remorse, guilt, regret every time I withhold what he's missed. I don't rehash all the bullshit each heckler yells at the townhouse. Or how security has had trouble securing my bedroom window, even after the drone. I won't tell him how the other day I asked Bruno, my new bodyguard, *"Is something wrong?"* and he stayed quiet.

With Declan, my bodyguard before Farrow, I was used to that silent treatment and lack of info. With Farrow, he gave me everything.

Everything.

He showed me what *better* looked and felt like, and now there's this strange emptiness that Farrow once filled.

I don't tell him any of that.

Because I'm not going to hurt him, and I realize now that there must be something similar happening on his end.

He's protecting me.

I nod, more assured. "I get it."

Farrow skims my features, easing more, and he reaches into the fridge and grabs a Fizz Life.

With his silver rings still in my palm, I absentmindedly slip a few onto my fingers.

"Tricyclics," Farrow says, sitting right up against my side, on my orange beanbag. Shoulder to shoulder. He hands me the soda, and he bites into his apple. His movements distract my brain, and I shake my head. *Fuck.*

"What?" I ask.

He smiles. "Tricyclics, wolf scout."

I must look massively confused. Because I am.

"The quiz question." Farrow flicks my notecard.

Right. I glance at the answer. "Good guess," I say dryly, the air lightening. We both breathe easier, and I'm happy about that.

"Not a guess." He chews his apple, and I hone in on his upturning lips. He notices and asks, "Sure you don't want me to fuck you all night?"

Very unsure. "Positive, and you should tease the wall, the carpet, that lampshade over there." I point to the lamp across the loft. "Because it'd be more likely to give into you."

Farrow lets out a long whistle. "He wants me to flirt with inanimate objects."

I try really hard not to laugh. Christ, *focus.* I shuffle through a few more cards, and I notice the silver rings on my fingers. *His rings.*

I've worn them before today. Just like this, but it dawns on me in this second that his rings fit my fingers perfectly. We're pretty much the same size. And I've never noticed that before.

I wouldn't need to steal a ring in order to match his size. I can just buy one that fits me—and I can't believe I'm thinking about this. But it's never meant something to me the way it does right now.

This powerful moment surges through my core. Because I feel ready to do more than just dream or think about forever with him. I'm going to make it happen.

26

MAXIMOFF HALE

"Take some breaths. We're going to figure this out," my mom tells me.

I'm breathing, but I'm too aware and laser-focused on the difficulty level of what I'm about to do. And what I'm about to do is normal.

So normal. It shouldn't be this epically complicated.

Janie offers a cup of hot tea to me as a *calm down* tactic. I shake my head stiffly, and she places the cup back on the oak desk.

The three of us are huddled in my parent's home office, facing a humongous desktop computer. My gangly mom sits close to the screen, the large leather chair making her appear even smaller. Jane and I pushed up two velvet, lilac armchairs to the desk.

I control the computer's mouse. Clicking through websites and scrolling along pages of wedding bands. Nothing jumps out at me. I thought it'd be obvious when I started looking, but…nothing.

"Let's start with engraving," my mom suggests. "Yes or no?"

My pulse speeds, and I narrow my gaze at the screen. Engraving? I think he'd like that, but it'd depend on what words are engraved. "I don't know…I don't fucking know."

My mom squeezes me in a side-hug. "You don't need to worry. Farrow will love whatever you pick out because you picked it. I know he will."

It's a calming thought, mostly because it's coming from my mom. I look over at her. She's still beaming. Glowing. Her cheeks are red she's been smiling and tearing up so damn much.

Like right now, she wipes the corners of her eyes.

Jane sniffs, misty-eyed too, her retro sunglasses blocking her tears, and my heart feels fucking swollen it's so full. Thirty minutes ago, I told them both that I planned to ask Farrow to marry me.

Neither one of them thought I'd ever get married. Before I started a relationship with Farrow, I said I wouldn't even *date* someone. I've let myself be happy. Really happy, and their happiness for me just overwhelms me tenfold.

My mom asked why I didn't wait to tell her and my dad together. He wasn't in the room. It's pretty simple. My dad will spill the news to Uncle Connor and Uncle Ryke in a heartbeat, and at that point, it'll start reaching my cousins, siblings and then security, Farrow's friends.

My mom is a certified secret-keeper. One of the damn best, and I trust her and Janie not to tell a soul. Because if I want this proposal to go as planned, Farrow can't know.

The media can't know.

You can't know.

So the only people allowed in on this right now are my mom and Janie. Done and done. I'll let my dad, siblings, and the rest of my family in on it the day of the proposal. It's a well thought-out plan, but I'm not going to lie, there are a few holes.

Like this fucking ring.

"Oooh this one is nice." My mom points at the screen. It's silver.

"No silver," I declare. "He has a million silver rings. It won't be special enough."

"It'll be special because it's from you," Jane reminds me with a sappy smile.

I think it's more complicated than that. "Janie."

"Moffy," she replies. "I'm with Aunt Lily here, take a deep breath."

My mom nods vigorously. "Oxygen is good for you."

I groan and click into a new website. "Alright, say I do find the perfect ring…" I glance at my mom while she cups a *Wolverine* mug and takes small sips of coffee. "How am I going to actually get it?"

This is the part that's been stumping me.

"I don't want to order it online," I tell them. "And there's no possibility of me entering a jewelry store without the press or security finding out."

Jane perks up. "We could ask a jeweler to come to the house and bring a wide selection."

"What if the jeweler says something to the media?" I ask. "What if he breaks his NDA or what if paparazzi catch him coming into the neighborhood and they start speculating?"

Normally I wouldn't care about any of this. Normally I'd move forward without pause and be like, *this is my life.* But I want this to be secret.

Jane puts her chin to her knuckles. "Hmm."

My mom turns to me. "Would you be upset if someone else went *for* you?" she asks. I see tenderness and sympathy behind her green eyes. Because she knows in order to keep this a secret, I need to jump through extra hoops.

Jane chimes in, "And that person can pick out extra rings, so you'll be able choose which you like best."

That's starting to make the most sense. But I just don't know *who* I could send. "Janie," I start.

She shakes her head. "I'd be just as easily spotted as you. Our family is out, and sending a bodyguard is out." Anyone in security might tell Farrow. I'm not taking that risk.

"I don't trust your assistant," I tell my mom before she offers.

"That's fine," she replies, drumming her mug in thought. "Um…let me think. You scroll." She waves me back to the computer.

Jane asks about gemstones, but I don't see Farrow preferring a diamond or black sapphire. I think he'd want simple and sleek.

"I've got it." My mom whips to me. "Your Uncle Garrison. He'll easily be able to go to a jeweler's without media attention. I'll make him swear not to tell a soul. He won't. He loves you too much."

Yeah.

Yeah. That could work. You know very little about Garrison Abbey and his wife Willow Hale. They've managed to dodge the media here and there for the last two decades. No one stands outside their Philly loft unless paparazzi catch a more famous family member entering the building.

They don't have bodyguards or daily magazine spreads about them. A few times a year, they pop up in an article. Sometimes more if they're hanging with us, but no one will follow him. No one will care that he's at a jewelry store.

This could work. I'm hanging onto that hope.

27

MAXIMOFF HALE

"He's late. Membership revoked," Kinney declares. She ties her bowling shoes at our circular booth, dyed black hair cascading over her bony shoulders.

Both Oscar and Farrow asked me why Kinney is so intensely fixated on the Rainbow Brigade club. They're all used to Blasé Kinney. Not Drill Sergeant Kinney who'd put a wooden stake through your heart if you fucked with her plans.

I think my sister wants to feel more included with the older crew. Especially those of us who can go to gay bars and events. She's been left out a lot. During a Pride Festival, I went to an 18+ club and she was kind of bummed.

As her older brother, I want this first-ever Rainbow Brigade meet-up to go smoothly. That meant renting out the entire venue for the night.

The upscale boutique bowling alley has ten lanes, gourmet snacks that can be ordered at the bar, and burgundy leather booths that are more hipster than family-style. Rainbow streamers cascade from the ceiling for Pride Month, and *love is love* coasters sit underneath our drinks.

I knew Kinney would be less-than-thrilled that Farrow got held up at work. But he's only fifteen minutes late—and she's already going for the jugular.

"You can't kick him out for being late," I say seriously. "He's at the hospital." It's not like Farrow is intentionally skipping this. He wishes he could be here right now, and if she wants to give someone a hard time, I'd much rather she take out her frustration on me than him.

"Fine. Probation period," Kinney says, yanking at her shoelace with extra force.

Oscar Oliveira stacks artisanal cheese on a cracker and eats it in one bite. He licks honey off his thumb and says, "Redford will love that."

I notice the popped buttons on Oscar's navy button-down reveal a script tattoo along his collarbone. Inked on his golden-brown skin are two Latin phrases:

astra inclinant, sed non obligant and *non ducor, duco.*

I can admit that I'm not well-versed in Latin without reference help. Like the internet. I just won't admit that to Farrow.

"Did Donnelly ink those?" I ask Oscar and motion to his collar.

"*No no no,*" Oscar shakes his head. "Guy has talent, but he's not putting a needle to my flesh." Before I ask what the tattoos mean, he motions to the top line. "*The stars incline us, they do not bind us.*" Bottom line, he tells me, "The motto of São Paulo: *I am not led, I lead.*" He picks up his buzzing phone, frowns at a message and flashes me the screen.

> Ask Maximoff for updates. I'm texting him. I don't have time to text both of you. — Farrow

My boyfriend has been allergic to group chats. Pretty much ever since he's seen how many incessantly ping my phone. But that text makes me think about Farrow and his relationship with Oscar and even Donnelly. Those two guys knew Farrow when he was with some of his exes.

Like Rowin.

I'm not about to torture myself and fish for giant details about his past relationships. But I am curious about some things only Oscar can share. "Is Farrow always like that with boyfriends?"

Oscar leans back against the leather booth. Grinning and also crossing his arms, curly pieces of his brown hair sweep his forehead.

"You mean does Redford always choose the boyfriend over the friend?"

I nod, confident in this question. "Yeah."

"Depends on the boyfriend," he says, "but Hale, you've been chosen first 100% of the time, which is record-breaking."

I should be happy about that, but a nagging thought pricks me. "I've put some family before him at times."

Oscar angles forward and grabs a peppercorn cracker from a tray. "And he has to love that about you, or else he would've only chosen you 45% of the time."

I nod to him before I bend down and tie my bowling shoe. "You like him better single? Then he'd pick his friends 100% of the time."

"No, that's not how he operates when he's single. He'll go all lone wolf on us, and sometimes, he'll be harder to get ahold of. Personally, I like him in a relationship—just not with that poor bastard."

I finish knotting my shoe and look up. "Rowin?" I ask.

Oscar pours beer from a pitcher and nods. "They fought all the time. Personality clash." He wipes a trickle of beer off the pint glass. "I saw the red flags from the start. Redford, however, is a stubborn ass. But we love him."

I start to smile. Yeah, we do, but my lips fall again. Realizing he hasn't messaged in a while. Even though he told Oscar he'd text me. "I don't have any updates for you, man," I tell him.

Oscar looks just as concerned as me, taking a swig of foamy beer before he says, "He might be on his bike."

I check the weather reports. Just to ensure it's not raining. *Partly cloudy...*

"Excuse me." One of the bowling alley managers suddenly approaches. Eyes on me. Her blonde hair is tied up in a messy bun, and she seems nervous. Her gaze pings to the camera that Jack Highland holds near our lane. In order to work today, Cassie had to sign a waiver to be filmed. So she knows potentially everything she says could be on *We Are Calloway*.

She takes a tighter breath, focus returning to me. "Could you tell the member of your party that we don't allow walking on the lanes?"

Fuck.

I haven't been paying attention to Tom.

Quickly, I swing my head towards the ten empty bowling lanes. Sure enough, at Lane 1, the furthest from us, my cousin wears a pair of skull and crossbones socks (no shoes) and takes a running start before sliding down it. He skids to his knees and slams into the bowling pins. A few knock over and clatter.

Jack films it.

"Tom!" I yell. "Get over here!"

He lifts his head, longer pieces of his ash-brown hair falling into his eyes.

You know Tom Carraway Cobalt as the eighteen-year-old lead singer of *The Carraways*. Tom's band only just moved practices from the basement to concert venues, but they sell out every time. You've fallen in love with his irreverent charm, mischievousness, and the fact that he's a daredevil on and off stage.

I know him as my little cousin who will be the first to fall into chaos. Who chooses to run towards danger instead of away, and who calls me up every Saturday to talk about that guy in the back of the class he has a crush on. He means more to me than any words can describe.

Fair Warning: if you fuck with him, we will both fuck with you.

He walks casually back to our booth like he didn't just become a human bowling ball. "Don't do that again," I tell him, being a hardass. And then I add, "Bowling alley rules."

My phone pings with a text, and I glance at my cell quickly.

Still at work. Don't know how long I'll be. How mad is she?
— Farrow

He shouldn't feel badly. I text back: dont worry about her
And I update Oscar on Farrow's ETA.

Tom slumps down in the booth beside Oscar, and my cousin lets out a dramatic breath, "Some people just don't want to have fun." Mischief twinkling in his eyes, he tosses a pretzel bite in his mouth.

"Bowling is fun," I say with extra emphasis so he won't try that stunt twice and ruin Kinney's event. "*Normal* bowling." My cell pings.

How mad is she going to be if I don't make it? — Farrow

Tom dunks a pretzel in mustard. "Did you say Fire Bowling? Because yes, that's extremely fun. Dude, sign me up."

I don't even know what the fuck *fire* bowling is and I'm not going to ask. I just text Farrow back: I'll handle it.

I can't lie and say Kinney won't be upset. She's already throwing out revocations and probations.

Jack positions the camera towards Tom. "What's fire bowling?" he asks my cousin.

"Hear me out." Tom gears up, holding out two hands like he's ready to go into an intense conversation. "Douse the pins in gasoline. Light them on fire. *Fire Bowling.*"

Jack nods like he's considering this. "I'm glad I asked."

"Sounds dumb," Kinney says flatly.

"Because, Kinney," Tom refutes. "You have no imagination."

She stares at him blankly. "I'm imagining you transforming into a toad right now."

He touches his chest. "So I can find my prince charming. You shouldn't have." He messes her hair.

She sets a death-glare on him and then rolls her eyes, over the banter, and then looks at me. "Your boyfriend is now twenty-five minutes late. I'm thinking we should reconsider his probation and go straight to revocation again."

"Kinney," I say firmly. "He's trying. Give him some slack here." Like he can hear me, I get another text from Farrow.

You shouldn't have to handle anything. I'm going to try to be there, wolf scout. — Farrow

"Wait," Tom cuts in, stealing my attention. He's pointing a pretzel bite at my little sister. "You're kicking Farrow out of the Rainbow

Brigade for being late? Does that same consideration apply for your date, too?"

What? My eyes widen. "You have a date?" I ask Kinney, shocked. She never mentioned anything to me, and a deep frown replaces my surprise.

Kinney shoots Tom a look like he's spilled something.

He's laughing under his breath and springs up from the booth. Leaving for the rack of bowling balls. He does that: throw out drama-laden statements and then exits to watch everything burn.

His mom calls him a shit-stirrer.

Oscar narrows his eyes at Kinney. "This is news to me. We could bring a date to this thing?" He lifts up his pint glass.

Jack trains his camera on Oscar and the lens extends out, zooming in. "Seeing anyone?"

"Bro," Oscar says, putting his beer to his lips. "I'm not doing your show."

Jack smiles. "I say this to everyone, but I really mean it for you, Oscar: you'd look good on TV. And it's not *my* show."

Both of them are pretty eye-locked. So I just watch for a second as Oscar replies, but I'm also looking at my little sister who's ignoring me.

"Of course I would look hot on TV. Doesn't matter. I don't need the same problems that my little bro has with fame." Oscar swigs his beer. "And give yourself more credit, Highland."

Jack peeks from behind the camera, glittering charm reaching his brown eyes. "What kind of credit do you think I should give myself?"

Oscar stares at him for a long beat. "More."

Agreed. Jack is a huge part of the docuseries, and he's in a top executive position.

I try to capture my sister's attention, but she's still purposefully avoiding my eyes. "Kinney," I say.

My sister takes a trained breath, and then peers up from her bowling shoes. "Don't say it," she tells me.

"First," I start out, "I don't know why you didn't tell me about your date, but you know I'm always here to talk."

She rolls her eyes like I'm so embarrassing, but a shadow of a smile—one that she wouldn't want me to see—starts inching up her lips.

"Second, you're being a hypocrite," I tell her bluntly. "You're willing to kick out Farrow but you have a *date* who's also not here and she gets a pass?"

"Shouldn't you be happy for me?" she combats. "*You're* the one who told me to try seeing someone else after Viv left. So what do I do? I take your stupid advice and invite Holly here."

"What's wrong?" I ask her because she's made a figurative turn and is starting to take deep, spastic breaths like she's trying hard not to cry.

"Nothing is wrong," she snaps back. "She's just late like Farrow. And she'll be here…she's not standing me up, Moffy."

"She's not," I agree, layering on the confidence for her.

"We just arrived; she'll make it," Oscar adds.

"*I* know that. But you both don't know for sure," she says flatly. When she gets upset, she goes into defense mode. Attack anyone in sight, and usually it's me. She knows I can take her jabs.

Kinney swings her head to the wall clock. "How long do we have the alley for?"

"Don't worry about that," I say. "Can I have this girl's number? Let me call her—"

"Over my rotting corpse," she glares.

"I can help," I remind my sister and hold out my hand for her phone.

She considers for a long moment, then brushes me off coolly. Like none of this matters anyway, even though we all know that it does. "I'm not worried," she says and looks around at the near-empty space.

My phone vibrates again.

"Should we start without them?" she wonders as I read my text.

Almost there – Farrow

My stomach and chest immediately lighten like a huge, immeasurable weight has vanished. I glance up at Kinney. "He's going to be here soon," I tell her. "Don't give him a hard time. He already feels badly."

"We'll see," Kinney says.

The screen above the lanes illuminates with our names. As soon as I read it, Kinney and I both turn to Oscar who was in charge of giving the manager a list of the bowling players.

He's grinning into his sip of beer.

"Your membership has been revoked," Kinney declares in a deadpan.

Oscar laughs and almost chokes on his beer. He sets it down. "Hale," he starts.

"Revoked," she says and stands up. "I'll be back." She snatches up a drink menu from the table and eyes the bar.

"They're not going to serve you alcohol," I tell her, knowing she craves to be one of the "adults" but she's only thirteen.

"No duh," she replies and gives me a look like *I'm* the absurd one. "But they have a drink called the *bubbly cauldron*. I'm going to convince the bartender to make me a nonalcoholic version." She takes a deep breath and leaves us, confidence encasing her posture, despite potentially being stood up.

My eyes drift back to the names on the screen.

Redford
Filipe
Carraway
No Middle Name Hale 1
No Middle Name Hale 2

"I'm number two, right?" I ask Oscar.

"That's up to you two." He sips his beer. "I know better than to get between siblings."

The bowling alley door opens, and the noise jolts me. I immediately rise to my feet and watch my boyfriend talk to the manager beside the hostess table. He nods. She nods.

And then he turns and his gaze annihilates me.

Behind his brown eyes are disappointment and guilt wrapped into a single look.

I don't wait for him to reach us. Meeting Farrow halfway, our arms wrap around one another. We kiss briefly and then his lips find my ear. "Where is she?" he asks.

Pulling away, I tell him, "At the bar."

His brows rise.

"It's not you," I say. "She thinks she's being stood up."

On our way to the booth, I give him a brief rundown of Holly. He keeps nodding, but he has a faraway look. This time I'm not sure if it's because he missed so much already or because of what held him up at the hospital.

But I'm not going to pry for details. When he's ready to share, he'll tell me.

Still, it hurts watching something eat at him.

We both slide into the booth, and while Farrow unlaces his black boot, he spots the screen with everyone's middle names.

"The Princess of Death didn't try to curse you for that one, Oliveira?"

Oscar fills up a pint for Farrow. "Not afraid of Kinney Hale when I have a client who actually never yawns or gets tired. Alright, if anyone wants to be scared of someone they should fear Charlie. *And* he's the only one who can beat me at chess."

I cling onto the fact that Oscar isn't afraid to talk about my family in front of me. He doesn't falter or hesitate or look my way for permission.

Being treated more like a friend—it's a good feeling.

But I catch Farrow glancing skeptically at Oscar, and my boyfriend deserts his shoelaces. Leaning forward with an elbow to the table, he motions to Oscar. "I need to ask you something. Like why you lied to me?"

I curve my arm over Farrow's shoulders, the stress not too bad on my muscle. And I remember how Oscar has been telling Farrow that he doesn't have a close relationship with Charlie, his client. That Charlie tells him next-to-nothing. But if that were true, then Oscar would be in the dark about Beckett doing coke.

For me, bodyguards keeping information close to the chest is nothing new. For Farrow, one of his closest friends has been lying to him for possibly years.

Oscar checks over his shoulder. Tom is out of earshot. Five lanes down, he reorganizes the bowling balls into a rainbow pattern on the rack. Kinney is sitting at the bar. Chatting with the bartender, she tries to convince him to whip up a gothic drink.

Off Oscar's furtiveness, Jack senses that this is about to be serious and private. "I'm going to film Kinney," Jack tells us and then exits our area.

Oscar looks between me and Farrow. "You know about Beckett," he states.

"We do," Farrow nods. "And man, I didn't need to know the details from you. I understand why you wouldn't share. But I'm confused why you went through the whole charade. I wouldn't have pried if you said you couldn't tell me. Instead, you led me to believe that Charlie has *no* relationship with you. Why do that?"

His gaze swings from Farrow, to me, and then back to Farrow. Oscar slides his arm across the back of the booth. "What's the difference, Redford?" He shrugs. "He's still not gushing details. He just gives me more than he has in the past."

"Why wouldn't you just say that then?" Farrow questions, confused more than anything. "You used to boast about *progress* when Charlie told you about a flight two fucking days in advance of takeoff instead of an hour before."

Oscar drums the booth. "Because…knowing more than I should… it just makes it harder for me to brush you off."

"Okay," Farrow says easily, piling cheese on a cracker. "I'll accept that. But I do want to know your reasoning behind the charade." He pops the cracker in his mouth. "Your cunning ass owes me that at least."

I notice how Farrow leans back into my arm that's around him. Getting comfortable in my embrace. Before he catches me staring— because he's a literal heartbeat from looking over with a rising smile that says *you like that*—I focus on Oscar.

He digs into a basket of baked chips. "You know media and fans want even the smallest fact from Charlie? Like how the guy brushes his teeth, when he takes a piss. All because he's the *enigmatic* one in the press. So I position myself as a bodyguard that isn't told shit, and then people won't even ask me a single thing." He crunches on a chip. "It's not like it started that way, and Charlie is still slowly trusting me. Tomorrow, he could try to ditch my ass and fly off to Hong Kong."

Farrow nods understandingly, and he takes a swig from his pint.

I glance at my sister, checking on her briefly to see if she's okay, before I look back at Oscar. "Does Donnelly know?" I wonder.

Oscar picks up his beer. "It'd be a little difficult to keep that from him, considering."

"You're around each other all the time," I say into a nod. It makes sense since Beckett and Charlie live together. Their bodyguards would have to be close, too. And I glance at Farrow enough to ask, "Does that make you the third wheel?"

Farrow almost laughs. "I'm better than that, wolf scout." His smile stretches while he stares right into me. "Plus, I've got the guy."

Yeah, I try hard not to smile back at that. Critical failure.

Oscar slow-claps and then cranes his neck past us to glance at the bar. "What do we know about Highland?"

Farrow sets down his beer glass. "Straight."

Oscar reaches for a pretzel bite. "We sure?"

"You have a crush on him?" I ask.

Oscar chokes on his food and smacks his chest a couple times. Farrow is laughing, but I'm not sure if it's at me or Oscar.

"What'd I say?" My brows furrow.

"Crush." Oscar shoots me a look. "Bro, do I look like your thirteen-year-old sister?"

"I don't know, Oliveira," Farrow says easily. "You could pull off goth." Farrow runs his fingers up the back of my neck. It feels really good and distracts me from the fact that I'm not always great at fitting into their easy banter.

Tom drops a bowling ball a few lanes away and the clatter distracts us.

Great. I'm about to rise, but Oscar slips out of the booth first. "I'm going to go help your cousin not break a toe," he tells me. I think in part to give me some alone time with Farrow, who appears at ease, but heaviness sits behind his eyes that I'm pretty sure Oscar can see as well as I can.

After Oscar walks down the lanes, I turn to face Farrow. He tugs off his boot and puts on the bowling shoe. He looks back at me, and I know something's wrong.

"You want to talk about it?" I have to ask.

His chest falls, but he shakes his head. "Not today, wolf scout."

I nod and practice some patience.

"You." Kinney's voice pitches. "You were late." My little sister approaches with a goblet of purple liquid and a cinnamon stick.

"That looks disgusting," I tell her.

"It tastes like hell and the bottom of my soul," she says, slurping a large sip from the straw and then setting an epic glare onto Farrow.

I shoot her a warning look to go easy on him.

Farrow finishes tying his bowling shoes. "Next time I'll be the first one here, Kinney."

"There won't be a next time. Your membership has been—"

"*Kinney*," I say forcefully. "You want to be mad at someone, I'm right here."

She shifts her glare to me.

"No," Farrow says, leaning back casually. "If she wants to kick me out, let her kick me out."

Hurt flashes in her eyes and then she shakes it off by staring up at the ceiling. Like she's annoyed. She's not. She just wants this day to go better than it has.

And I really want this Holly girl's number so I can fix this.

"But Kinney," Farrow says. "If you do kick me out, I'll still show up with my boyfriend."

She slides into the booth next to him, her lips pressed in a line. As though she gives no fucks, but she's almost smiling. "Fine," she deadpans. "Membership reinstated."

My shoulders loosen a bit, and I push the basket of chips towards Kinney. Just as she goes to grab a handful, her phone rings.

"Is that Holly?" I ask.

She checks her phone. "No." But she's not frowning in disappointment. Kinney hoists the phone, preparing for FaceTime. "Hey," she greets.

"Is she there?" Audrey Cobalt asks, her whimsical voice on the line.

Kinney shakes her head. "MIA. I can't text her for a fourth time. It'd be desperate."

"I disagree," Audrey replies. "Desperation is just another word for *madly* devoted. You should try again. Fifth and sixth times are the charm, they say."

Kinney smiles and then flashes the screen to Farrow and me.

Red hair, pale freckled skin, and a smile that could charm just about anyone stares back at me. Her lavish pink room looks like it was made for a princess.

You know Audrey Virginia Cobalt as the thirteen-year-old hopeless romantic. In her spare time, she reads adult romance novels and narrates all the "blush-worthy" parts on her Instagram. You think she talks like she's been factory-made from a Jane Austen novel, and you salivate for any photo she takes with her big sister Jane. You wonder what it would be like to grow up as the youngest with five Cobalt brothers, but she rarely tells you.

I know her as my little cousin, the baby in the entire Hale, Meadows, Cobalt brood. The girl who bakes cookies for her crushes that are far out of her league. Who falls madly in love with the idea of love more than the actual reality. She's fiercely loyal to her friends and just as fierce to her family.

Fair Warning: you fuck with the baby of the family and everyone will come after you.

Over FaceTime, she waves. "Hi, Moffy. Hi, Farrow."

"Hey, Audrey," I say, watching her eyes slowly widen at the sight of Oscar several bowling lanes down.

"OhmyOhmy, KinneyKinney. Don't let him see my face." She buries herself in a pillow, and Kinney rotates the camera back to herself.

Audrey still hasn't overcome the mortification of sending apology cookies to Oscar.

Jack, who returned to our booth, asks my cousin, "Audrey, do you still have a crush on Oscar?"

We all just hear a mumbled noise from the pillows.

Kinney keeps eyeing the bowling alley entrance. I can't just sit here and hope for the best. There has to be something more I can do.

And I tell my sister, "Let me call this girl."

She looks back at me, brows pinched. "What are you going to say?"

"I'm going to ask if she needs a ride here, ask what's holding her up and tell her that I can help. That's it."

Kinney takes a giant breath, and she speaks into her phone. "I'll talk to you later, Audrey. I need to text Moffy her number..." she trails off, and all of our heads swerve as the door opens.

A blonde thirteen-year-old girl in a flower sundress nears the hostess podium.

Dear World, I'm so damn grateful for this good luck. She needed it. Best Regards, a human who's a big brother

"Holy shit," Kinney's eyes bug. "She's here." She glances at her phone. "Audrey—"

"Go fall madly in love and you must tell me everything!" Audrey hangs up first.

And before Kinney darts away from the booth, she stretches over Farrow and flings her arms around me in a short hug. "I'm sorry. I was the turd this time," she tells me. And then she looks to Farrow. "But not to you. You were late." She skips off at that, and Jack follows my sister to film Holly and Kinney greeting each other.

I'm about to apologize to Farrow, but he's laughing hard. "God, your siblings."

I love him. I love that he loves my siblings, even when they're emotional and wound up and taking jabs left and right.

And as his laughter fades, our hands intertwine, and I tell him, "You made it in enough time so I can beat you at bowling."

He smiles softly, almost sadly. It fucking hurts, and I can easily fix my sister's tiny crisis—I can try to fix anything—but I can't even attempt to fix this. And I want to be patient.

I need to be patient.

If I ask what I can do, I know he'll just say, *be here*. And I'm here. But it's been over twenty hours since we last even saw each other. Those digits are becoming normal, and I can't remember the last time his shift was under twelve hours.

"Farrow…"

I want to find the right words. To tell him it's alright if he has to be late again. To not make promises to my little sister about *next time*. Because it'll feel worse for him if he breaks it. But I'm not sure how to say anything.

And more than that, I can practically *feel* his fatigue, the heaviness that mounts on his chest and tries to drag him under. I want to take that weight off Farrow. So damn badly. I open my mouth to speak, but aching, strained words come out of him first.

"I'll be okay."

28

FARROW KEENE

I made a mistake.

It's been hitting me all week. All month. Shit, possibly even the first day I stepped into the hospital. I thought I could weather it out. What's one more day. One more week. One more year. But my boots clap along the sterile halls, and I feel my time draining away with my energy and will to keep course.

Pushing open the break room door with my shoulder, charts fill my hands, and I see the sofa. Instantly, I collapse on it lengthwise and kick my feet on the cushion.

Charts lie on my lap, but I don't have any desire to finish them. I have—I glance at the wall clock—around fifteen minutes before I'll need to check on my other patient. Unless someone codes.

It's been that kind of day.

"Can't believe he tried to shock an asystole rhythm," Dr. Shaw says, entering the break room. The third-year Med-Peds resident heads straight for the coffee pot. "Nice catch on that intern, Keene."

I stopped a first-year resident from trying to shock a flatline. Asystolic patients are non-shockable and won't respond to defibrillation. And if an attending had been present, he would've done the same thing as me.

I can't muster a response. I just click a pen.

Do your motherfucking job, Farrow.

Dr. Shaw pours coffee. "You look beat." He sweeps me from head to toe. "Rough day?"

I could explain to him how a simple diagnostic exam that'd normally take twenty minutes lasted an hour and a half.

The patient instantly recognized me and wanted pictures, wanted an autograph, wanted to Instagram Live—which I turned down. And then she called her friends, who showed up ten minutes into the exam. I had to run through the whole parade again.

It's not the same as patients gawking at my tattoos and piercings. I was used to that.

Being famous. *Not so much.*

I'm recognized every single day, sometimes minute-by-minute. I'm stopped walking down the hall. I'm stopped when I eat lunch in the cafeteria. When I'm minding my own fucking business during rounds.

If it's not the patients or their families, it's the nurses, technicians, doctors and hospital staff. They want to gossip with me about the Hales, Meadows, and Cobalts like I'm their direct outlet to secret information they'll never be allowed to have.

Every day I have to brush them off. I'm perfectly fine with a bad reputation. I don't give a flying shit if people call me cold or arrogant or an entitled bastard—but when it affects my job, when it affects my ability to be the *best* at what I do, then I fucking care.

I hate knowing that I'm not contributing enough. That I'm taking the spot of someone who could potentially do better work than what I'm doing.

I could tell Shaw about this morning.

When I had a patient who *refused* to give me a medical history. He said he didn't trust me. Not with that kind of personal information, and I tried to explain how there's clear patient-confidentiality laws, but he didn't want to hear it.

In his eyes, I have too many ties to the media and public and the things that I say aren't just a whisper in the night.

Hell, that wasn't the first time I had to hand over a patient to another intern. Or be reprimanded by the hospital board for not carrying as big of a load as the other residents in my year.

And I can't argue with them. It takes me three times as long to do a job that they can do in under ten minutes.

I thought it'd be different coming back to finish my residency, but I didn't imagine this kind of struggle. I'm not sure I could have.

I've become a "celebrity" doctor, and that's hindered my ability to help people inside Philly General. And I feel worthless here.

Three years. It's what I keep telling myself. That in three years I'll be worth more again. I'll be out of this hospital and working for the famous families. But that's three years of running at a brick wall and not being able to breathe.

I haven't been able to talk about this with Maximoff. I want to protect him from feeling at fault, or from blaming himself. Broaching the topic means that I'm reaffirming his worst fears: I've lost an immeasurable source of happiness by being with him, by being famous. And that's not how I see it.

He's my happiness, and I'm fighting for the day where I go back to him. And *fuck,* it's right there. The day is right in front of me.

Just go.

I sit up, boots dropping to the ground. I glance back at Shaw. "Just a long shift," I tell him, my mind racing.

Just go.

"Tell me about it." He downs his coffee and then disappears into the locker room.

When the door swings closed behind him, I stack the charts from my lap and place them onto the coffee table.

Quickly, I push into the locker room. "Hey, Shaw!" I shout.

"Yeah?" He sticks his head out, past a few cedar lockers. Barechested, he pulls on a Polo shirt.

"Who's on-call tonight?" I ask while I yank open my locker.

"Morris, Kim, and Bakshi." He narrows his eyes at me while I take off my scrubs and change into black pants and a plain shirt. "I thought your shift ended at ten."

In an hour. "It does." I tuck my black V-neck in my pants and buckle my belt. For me, that hour will be stretched to three depending on how many people will stop me and ask for pictures.

It's why I'm always late. To everything.

Shaw hangs on his locker door. "Is it Maximoff Hale?" he asks. "I can keep a secret if you need to talk or something."

"I'm good," I say.

"You know I'm not like those other people," Shaw continues. "I've watched Maximoff Hale on TV since I was about ten. He's practically a real person to me, not just a celebrity."

I've heard the same speech a hundred different times, a hundred different ways.

"Shaw," I say, grabbing my backpack and shutting the locker door. "*I'm good.*"

He nods, but he blisters beneath my words. "Yeah, Keene. Of course." And he coldshoulders me as he returns to his locker.

I pass him silently out the door.

Just go.

By the time I reach the parking garage, my pulse is racing. I drove the Audi to work, and I find the car where I left it. I don't slide into the driver's side. Immediately, I climb into the back, lock the car doors, and lie down on the stretch of the seat.

Resting my boot soles on the leather, I dial a number and put the phone to my ear. Staring up at the car's interior roof.

The line rings once before I hear his voice.

"I was just thinking about you," Maximoff says.

It pummels me, and my hand cements to my mouth, raw emotion surging. I can't speak yet. My eyes burn, and I know this is where I would say: *of course you were, wolf scout. You're obsessed with me.*

"Farrow?" Concern hardens his voice. "You okay?"

I shut my eyes and drop my hand to my chest. "It's sucking the life out of me," I breathe out. And I tell him everything about what's been happening.

All of it.

I knew one day I would, but I thought it'd be at the end of three years. And then I'd confess, but now it's come sooner. Because I'm done.

I'm done.

Maximoff responds with more strength of heart than anyone could ever believe. Ever know or see. "I fucking love you," he tells me, "and you should step back. Don't finish your residency. You don't need it, Farrow."

I'd been worried that he'd apologize, stuck on a turntable blaming himself for this, and thank fucking God he's not. *Thank God.*

I shift my phone to my other hand. "Maximoff…" I knew I'd end this here, and I was about to ask his feelings on that. Hell, I didn't even need to ask. He just told me. But this choice comes with a greater cost than he might realize.

See, I'm still able to be a concierge doctor. I passed my Step 3 exam, so I'm now licensed and can prescribe medication. But… "I won't be board-certified," I tell him. "It means that if any of your family has to be rushed to an ER, I can't practice medicine inside Philadelphia General." *I can't help.*

That hospital requires doctors to be in a residency program or board-certified. I will be neither.

"It'll annoy you," Maximoff tells me, "especially when you have to hand that task off. But Farrow, my family having serious medical emergencies like that—it might happen only a few times in your lifetime. It's not worth three years of being beaten down and feeling empty."

I open my eyes. The parking garage is quiet, and the Audi windows are tinted. No cameramen have found me yet. "I never imagined not being board-certified," I admit and comb a hand through my hair while I lie down. I keep my palm on my head. "It feels like halfway."

I don't usually go halfway.

I go all-in.

A bed squeaks on his end of the line. He must be sitting down. "Maybe if you only loved medicine, it'd be halfway," Maximoff says, "but I think you're going all the way and you don't even fucking realize it, man."

My eyes sear, staring unblinkingly at the interior roof. I start to smile at the thought. Medicine isn't the only thing that fulfills me. Protecting him, loving him, just being there—it's what I live for.

I look far away. "Are you implying that I love you, wolf scout?"

"Yeah," he says confidently. "I am."

I smile more. "You're not wrong."

Flashes start glaring through the car windows. The *click, click, click* too familiar, and paparazzi shout my name. But I stay on my back for another minute.

"There's a downside," I tell him. "People will have a lot of opinions about me practicing without being board-certified." Even if this isn't a measure of my worth or skill as a doctor, it definitely will be to the public.

"Fuck those people," Maximoff says.

I instantly breathe stronger. And I sit up. Phone to my ear, camera lenses pressed to the windows, I'm ready to change course. And I'm spinning his world in a new direction, but at least this one puts us together again.

29

FARROW KEENE

You want to be cremated or buried, Redford? — Oscar

He thinks he's being witty since I'm a good twenty minutes from a lunch "date" with my boyfriend's dad and two uncles. And sure, Maximoff will be at the restaurant too. But wolf scout is not the one Oscar thinks will grill me and kill me.

I was going to ask you the same thing since I keep shocking you to "death." I send the text. At Joana's confirmation—which I attended with Maximoff, no obligations in my way—Oscar admitted that he didn't believe I'd drop out of my residency a second time. And not a lot ever surprises Oliveira.

"We're all glad you didn't go after the board certification," Oscar told me. "You went full Sheryl Crow 'If It Makes You Happy' on us."

I rolled my eyes and ended up smiling. It was an old inside joke about when the shit you love makes you sad. "Oliveira, reaching into archaic history."

Oscar grinned. "I'm serving up some teenage Redford realness." Silence fell hard after that. Both of us looking at each other and feeling the void of Donnelly at the Catholic church. Whenever Oscar says "realness" to anything, Donnelly cuts in with, *because you're the realest motherfucker I've ever seen.*

Especially during the times when it doesn't make any sense. But it fit too perfectly there.

Because you're the realest motherfucker I've ever seen.

It brings me back to the present. To the Philly townhouse where the pipes groan as Maximoff takes a shower. But I'm not upstairs with him.

Eighteen minutes until a lunch "date" with my boyfriend's family, and I'm lying on the mint-green rug where the coffee table usually would be. Black pants ride low on my waist.

And Donnelly is tattooing me.

His needle pierces the right side of my lower back. Right, *right* above my ass.

A sparrow—the only bird inked without color and the largest one on my body—spans most of my back with its feathered torso in the center. The tip of each wing touches my deltoids and reaches my traps. Further down, towards my ass, its talons clutch a dagger.

The sparrow and blade leave room for more ink on the lower left and right side, above my waistband.

"Don't call Papa Hale *sir* when you see him," Donnelly says, tattoo machine in hand. "I did that after he found out I inked Luna's hip, and I'm telling you, he grew a third horn. Looked like he could've impaled me in the throat and ripped out my asshole."

I chew Doublemint slowly and glance back at Donnelly with a pointed look. "Don't talk about ripping assholes while you're so close to mine with a needle."

He smirks, not meeting my gaze as he works carefully on the design. He wears thin-framed reading glasses. "All I'm saying is that Maximoff's dad is no joke. I thought he was the funny one. Sarcastic and shit. But I almost pissed myself."

I thought Loren Hale would do worse if he found out Donnelly tattooed his eighteen-year-old daughter. "You still have your job?" I ask.

"Barely." He pauses as a calico cat jumps off the Victorian loveseat onto the rug.

I throw a toy mouse and Carpenter chases it under the iron café table.

I'm not scared of Lo. But I'm wondering what conversations he plans to start. Since the crash, we've stuck to one main topic: Maximoff rehabbing his collarbone. Easy shit.

Something tells me this lunch isn't going to be *easy*.

Donnelly resumes tattooing, the needle pricking skin. Not painful. The ink on my ribs hurts like hell, but this isn't bad. He tells me, "Cobalt parents never batted an eyelash when I inked Beckett."

Mention of Beckett reminds me about him doing cocaine to help his ballet performance. I told Donnelly that I knew about it, but we didn't talk long.

"If it's hard being on Beckett's detail," I say now, "you should see if Akara will let you transfer."

I never asked if Donnelly supplied the drugs. Some bodyguards will, but Donnelly would let another person chop off his hand before he touched cocaine.

I stay on my forearms. Not looking over my shoulder at him.

Donnelly inks me quietly. Tattoo machine buzzing, and then he says, "I can't leave him, man." He lowers his voice. "I know I can't get him to stop. I mean, fuck me, his twin brother couldn't even convince him."

I pop a bubble in my mouth. "Because Beckett thinks drugs make him a better dancer," I whisper, "and now he's started thinking that he dances like shit without them."

"I hate that," he mutters and then speaks under his breath. He tells me how he can't talk to Beckett about his teenage years. Because then Beckett would try to protect him and ask the Tri-Force to transfer Donnelly off his detail.

Donnelly doesn't explain his past to me. I already know it. When he was fourteen, his parents gave him meth for the first time, and as an adult, he prefers not to be around hard drugs. Not out of temptation. Mainly, they bring back bad memories.

"Hidey ho." Luna hops off the last stair into the living room. "Uh, I mean *hi*." She raises a hand in a hesitant wave.

Luna.

"You covered your ink?" Donnelly mimes to his forearm where lyrics to "Dreams" by The Cranberries should be. The black ink is concealed with flesh-toned makeup. Hiding her tattoos is new. The plain dress, pin-straight ponytail, and simple makeup has been happening for weeks now.

"Yeah, yeah." She comes over and sits on the loveseat.

I raise my brows at her. "Why do you keep looking less like yourself and more like everyone else?"

She shrugs. Glances at Donnelly, then back to me, and tells us, "Andrew says it's easier."

Easier *for him.*

"Luna, fuck this fucker," I say, grinding my gum beneath my molars. Maximoff has been afraid that her new boyfriend is the cause of Luna changing, and in four words, his fear has been confirmed.

"This guy wants a basic bitch. Go let him date a basic bitch," Donnelly says while he finishes my ink. "Don't turn into one."

Luna watches the tattoo machine, lost in thought. "He's not all bad. He gives okay head."

I pop another bubble. "*Okay* head sounds like *bad* head."

Donnelly wipes my skin clean. "If you're just lookin' to be eaten out, I'll eat you out—"

"*Hey,*" Maximoff cuts in on the bottom stair, eyes narrowed. His dark hair is wet from a shower, but he's already dressed: jeans and a green crew-neck. "What the fuck, Donnelly?"

He shuts off his machine. "I like eating pussy."

Maximoff looks at him like he lost his mind. "That's my *sister.*"

Luna falls supine on the loveseat in a groan.

Donnelly packs his ink. "I think you've embarrassed your sister, man."

Maximoff looks whiplashed, and I can't stop smiling. I stand up, pants unzipped and unbuttoned. My tattoo just needs bandaging.

The second he sees the new ink on my lower back, he zeroes in. Fixated. Completely forgetting about Donnelly and his sister. Now I know how to capture 100% of his attention. He even draws near me, dazed.

My smile stretches. "You're drooling."

"I'm glaring."

He's a human heart-eye emoji.

Donnelly tattooed a wolf with a pirate eye-patch, and two letters are inked on the patch.

WS

Maximoff reaches me, and I rotate to face him so his gaze lifts to mine. And he tells me, "You broke one of your only rules."

My rule: never get ink that relates to a boyfriend.

My only exception stands in front of me. Either he hasn't figured that out yet or he's still *coming* mentally to the fact. "Take it easy, wolf scout," I say. "It's not like I tattooed your name on my ass."

He makes a face. "You sure you haven't?"

I chew my gum even slower. "Damn, he wants to see my ass."

He groans, annoyed that I fucked with his humor.

I laugh hard, and his hand instinctively finds my hand. He doesn't realize he's given in that easily, and he almost pulls back. I hold tighter.

And I'm here for this. I'm not stuck in a hospital. I'm not meeting up with him later just to meet-up with his dad. Fuck, I treasure these moments so completely, but the unknown definitely lies ahead of us. I'd rather not crash and burn, but recently, crashing seems to be the name of some game I'm playing.

"Where do you see yourself in twenty years?" That's the first thing his overprotective dad says to me at this casual burger joint—and we haven't ordered food yet. I'm actually in the process of taking a seat next to Maximoff, scraping the chair back.

"We just got here," Maximoff cuts in with a glare.

"Huh, I had no idea." Lo drills his sharp-edged eyes into me. "Where do you see yourself in twenty years?"

Maximoff shoots me an apologetic look.

To be honest, I'm slightly intimidated. Mostly because I'd love to leave good impressions on them—better than I have in the past—but I can't be anyone other than me.

Connor Cobalt, Ryke Meadows, and Loren Hale have already claimed the other side of the wooden table. Three larger-than-life men. Each one had a profound impact on Maximoff, and it's always clear to me when I speak to them just how great their influence was and still is to this day.

Hell, I see them as different sides of my boyfriend:

Connor is mental. He taught Maximoff intelligence, emotional restraint and confidence.

Lo is emotional, the sarcastic, loving and empathetic pieces of him.

And then Ryke is physical, all determination and stubbornness and unshakeable strength.

I lower down in my seat. "Honestly, I'm not much of a planner."

Maximoff almost smiles. *He likes that answer.* And he extends his arm over my shoulders.

"No life plans?" Connor arches a brow.

The heat of their gazes is hotter than any camera. I tilt my head. "If by *life plans*, you mean *goals*, then sure. You can't be a doctor without setting some," I say casually.

"Are you always this vague?" Connor asks me.

"Good question, love," Lo says and motions for me to answer.

Maximoff mouths something to Ryke, and that prompts Ryke to throw a wadded napkin at Connor, who easily leans back and dodges the affront.

"Excuse the Rottweiler," Connor tells me. "Continue."

Ryke rolls his eyes and buries his attention in a menu. He mouths, *sorry, Mof.* I'm a little bit surprised that Ryke Meadows isn't going hard on me like the other two.

Then again, I helped his daughter in the car crash. And I'm not a bodyguard anymore, and that was his biggest qualm with me dating Maximoff.

"Am I always this vague?" I repeat their question, one that I've never met this directly. "With anyone who isn't in my bed, yeah. I tend to be less forthcoming."

Ryke looks up from a plastic menu. "Who else is in your fucking bed?"

"Just your nephew."

Maximoff is currently pinching his eyes like he's wishing this were one of his little alternate universes.

Lo leans forward and asks, "What is it about my son that made you want to spend time with him?"

"*Dad*," Maximoff growls, his neck flushing.

My smile is killing me.

"Let Farrow answer the question, bud," Lo says while he eagle-eyes me to death.

Just like that, my smile fades, and my eyes flit briefly to Jack Highland who films our table with another producer of *We Are Calloway*. We're in a private section of the burger joint. Photos of old rock bands hang on the green-leafed wallpaper, but I can feel the presence of a camera.

"Any portion of this can be edited out," Connor tells me, perceptive of my body language, "and none has to be aired."

I agreed to be a part of the docuseries. Anything that brings me closer to Maximoff and his family, I want to do, and plus, since my life is very fucking public, there's more to gain and less to lose with *We Are Calloway*. It's a highbrow award-winning docuseries, aired on a premium cable channel.

"Noted," I nod, and Jack flashes a charming *"you're doing great"* smile behind the camera. I shake my head, and I ball up the paper to a straw.

"Remember my question?" Lo asks me.

"Farrow remembers everything," Maximoff interjects and then groans at himself. He swings his head to me and rakes a hand through his brown hair. "I didn't mean it in a good way."

"I think you did," I tease.

He plasters on a decent scowl, and that's when a twenty-something waitress brings out a tray of ice waters. I lean back in my chair and wave her to come here.

"Can you get us a baggie of ice?" I ask since my boyfriend put more stress on his muscle earlier when he wrenched the car door open. I've noticed how he's shut his eyes in longer beats. *Wincing.*

"Of course," she says. "Anything else?"

"A coffin," Maximoff interjects. "For my immediate death."

I roll my eyes. "He's not dying, but he is dramatic."

The waitress chuckles before leaving the table, and I turn to Maximoff. He's looking really deeply into me.

My chest falls in a heavier breath, and fuck it...I kiss him. Our mouths meet, softly and tenderly, and I feel his lips rise beneath mine.

He likes that. And so do I.

When we ease back, I drop my arm to his chair. Maximoff still holds my shoulders in an assured embrace.

And Lo is waiting for me to answer.

"Dad, don't make him answer that question," Maximoff cuts in.

Lo doesn't flinch. "Are you willing to watch out for my son's well-being tonight?"

Maximoff covers his face with his hand, a second away from groaning.

"All nights," I answer, trying not to laugh at my boyfriend's distress more than anything. He's making this easier on me.

"What are you two doing tonight?" Lo asks.

"Staying in," I say easily and look to Maximoff.

He nods. "Maybe watch a movie. Farrow has never seen *Batman Returns*."

"No DC at the table," Lo snaps. "I swear to all living Marvel things, I grabbed the wrong child in the Home Goods store." His eyes almost soften when tells me, "I lost him in the toilet section carrying around a plunger in aisle four."

"I was three," Maximoff explains to me. "I thought it was a sword."

I smile picturing that, and this is one of those moments where I can feel Lo's love for his son. I didn't have that. It's just a fact. But when I have kids, I want to give them that kind of unconditional, over-whelming attention and care.

Our waitress returns to take our orders, and after she leaves, Connor tells the table, "In other news, I was offered a condom sponsorship this morning."

Ryke almost spits out his water. "You have *seven* fucking kids."

"Royal sperm," Lo quips.

"Don't fucking encourage that," Ryke says and points at Connor's billion-dollar grin with a butter knife.

With more seriousness, Ryke asks Connor, "When's the last fucking time you even used a condom?"

I don't really want this information. At all. Listening to "uncles" and "dads" talk about sex is not my forte. I'm just not used to this shit.

Sex was never a topic of discussion unless it was an academic lecture about reproduction or ejaculation.

I learned about fucking from the internet or friends growing up. I didn't have advice on lube from my uncles like Maximoff. I didn't have "the talk" from my dad. No safe sex lecture. Because the old man assumed I was smart enough to know about STDs from the medical journals that I skimmed.

I glance at Maximoff who looks absolutely unfazed. I've always loved how close he is to his family, and I only want our relationship to bring him closer to them.

"Decades," Connor answers the last time he's used a condom.

"Are you taking the sponsorship offer?" Maximoff asks while an appetizer of string fries comes out on our table.

"I wouldn't." Connor swishes his wine. "It'd have a negative impact on the children if I advertised my face or name on a condom line."

I've noticed that whenever they're just with Maximoff or Jane, they always exclude those two from "the children" category.

I unscrew the mustard bottle.

Lo focuses on me. "Are you willing to show my son the same respect that I've raised him to show you?"

Maximoff makes a face. "Where the fuck are these questions coming from?"

I watch as Lo digs into his pocket and pulls out a crumpled piece of paper. "Questions for the Overly Tattooed Boyfriend of My Perfect Son Dot Com." He gives me an iconic dry smile. "I hate tattoos."

"I know," I say with a nod. "Good thing your son loves them."

Connor and Ryke turn to Lo. Gauging his reaction. And Lo is narrowing his sharp-edged eyes at me, and very dryly, he says, "Does he?"

Maximoff pipes in, "I really fucking do."

An amused smile breaks across my face. Fuck, I can't believe he admitted that in front of me.

And Lo laughs, a real laugh, all before passing the questionnaire to his brother. Ryke reads the paper in silence.

"These are fucking terrible," Ryke says, his gaze veering as our food parades over, and while we all dig into burgers and fries, we talk about the latest *Fourth Degree* movie, the Philadelphia Eagles, and how in July all three families have planned a trip to Greece.

But instead of Greece, we keep saying *Tahiti* in case anyone overhears. It's the code name. That trip is approaching fast, and it spans over Maximoff's birthday. It's a vacation that I wasn't supposed to be attending. Because I should've still been in a residency program.

Now that I'm out, I can go.

I notice Jack Highland setting his camera down towards the end. He speaks in Tagalog on his phone to someone. I hear the name *Jesse*. His little brother.

As we're winding down eating, Connor asks me what's one thing that surprised me the most about losing my privacy. The three of them reminded me that they were in their early twenties when they became famous after a scandal, and they knew what privacy felt like.

They weren't born into fame like Maximoff.

I toss my napkin on my plate and lean back on my chair, considering his question for a half second before the answer reaches me.

I look between the three men across from me. "I consider my sexuality the fifth or sixth most interesting thing about me. Being gay isn't all of who I am, but it's definitely a big part." I take a beat. "And I'd have to come out all the time. Whenever a girl hit on me, whenever I introduced a boyfriend, I'd have to say *I'm gay* over and over again."

It wasn't uncommon for most people to assume I was straight.

That's changed.

"Being in a public relationship with Maximoff, broadcasted to the entire world, means that I don't need to come out nearly as much anymore." I start to smile with a laugh. "And that still surprises me." It still kicks me in the chest.

Maximoff shares my smile for a second, and he nods to me like *it's a good feeling, huh?* I prefer to live my truest self.

As terrifying as that can sound, there's no freer feeling than being able to be me.

"Motherfuckers," I swear behind the wheel

of the Audi.

Paparazzi bang on the car windows so we'll roll them down. The rapping fists on glass need to stop. We haven't left the restaurant's graveled parking lot yet. Maximoff's dad and uncles inch ahead of us in a Land Cruiser, and security is behind us in another SUV.

Add on these other facts: lunch ran late, the sun has fallen, and each camera flash sears like a strobe light.

"MAXIMOFF!! FARROW!!!"

I slam on the horn. "MOVE!" I shout without rolling down the window.

Maximoff yells at paparazzi, "You're going to get run over!!" He gestures them to get the fuck out, but they just crowd closer. Standing in front of the hood with hefty cameras.

It all goes to hell when the Land Cruiser finds an exit and veers onto the street. All the paparazzi that'd been crowding their vehicle suddenly rush ours.

"One of us should get out," Maximoff says.

I assess him in a quick sweep. He's been death-gripping his leg, and I know he wants to be in control in this situation. But he has no license. "Hold on. I'll be able to reach the street."

It takes a long second, but the tires meet the curb before I'm blocked in again. Hoards of cameramen put their own safety at risk. They are standing on the road. *Fuck.*

"You've got to be kidding me," Maximoff growls, squinting at the harsh glare. He yells at them through the windshield. "You're going to kill yourself!!"

Flashes burst directly through my passenger window, and my aviators aren't shielding the light. "I'm rolling down my window," I warn Maximoff.

As the window rolls, the noise level amplifies, and I scream, "Move! Get the fuck out! You're not allowed to do this!"

"FARROW!! MAXIMOFF!! Look here!!"

A cameraman puts the lens to the windshield and Maximoff almost loses it. He unsnaps his seatbelt.

"Stop." I extend my arm over his chest. "You're not fighting these bastards—"

Maximoff suddenly reaches across my body and shoves the fuck out of a camera that inched into the car. A camera that almost hit me in the face.

I roll up the window, my pulse thrashing because Maximoff is in serious pain. He stretched his right arm. Used strength on his *right arm*. Right shoulder. "Maximoff," I say tensely, lifting my aviators to my head.

"I'm alright." He shuts his eyes, breathing through his nose and leaning back against his seat. "I'm going to puke."

I reach back and find a workout towel on the floor. I toss it to him, and he throws up between his legs. Into the cloth.

The cameras go wild. Banging the glass. I keep a hand on Maximoff's back, and I check through the rear windshield. I can barely spot security's SUV through the masses.

Instinct tugs at my body to jump out of the car. Create a path. But also *keep him safe*.

Keep Maximoff safe. I need security's help. I've been in that SUV before, and sometimes paparazzi will purposefully cage bodyguards and try to jam doors. Just so they can't reach their clients.

Bruno should be widening a path for us to drive. If I could crack a guess, I'd say he's being trapped in the SUV.

I put a hand on the wheel. I'm about to drive more aggressively and whoever I lightly hit, I hit. Before I press the gas, water drips on the windshield. I hear *ping*.

Ping, ping.

I smell rain on metal, and I feel gravel…

Shit.

This is a steering wheel. A leather steering wheel. I grip harder. Fucking pissed. Out of all times this could be happening, a storm has to rip through the sky now.

"Farrow," Maximoff calls out, breathing hard through physical pain. He sees the rain cascade onto the windshield.

"Wolf scout…" I hear the crush of metal. My pulse spikes into a cutting breath. Slowly, I reach out for my boyfriend, and his hand is in mine. I bring his large palm to my face. He clutches tighter.

I breathe, trying to reorient my senses. My hand encases his jaw, smooth from a close shave. And I blink and only see his tough forest-greens.

He's searching for the intense focus in my eyes. I'm sure it's flickering in and out.

Camera flashes still shade us. A sinking realization: I can't drive Maximoff to safety.

All I want to do is drive us somewhere else, someplace else, and I'm certain Maximoff wishes he could do the same.

With another breath, I take what limitations I'm given, and I'm going to work with them. My heartbeat rides a rocky rollercoaster, rising and falling in rapid succession. "Here's what's going to happen," I whisper to Maximoff. "I'm going to climb in the backseat—"

"I'm coming with you."

I almost smile. "That is the plan." I unbuckle my seatbelt. "You'll need to call security. Tell Bruno he has to drive."

"I will."

Before I go anywhere, I hone in on his pain. I pull at the collar of his crew-neck to check his traps. The muscle is inflamed and swollen. *He needs ice.*

Maximoff's hand descends to my neck, and while he dials security, he continues to search my eyes.

30

FARROW KEENE

"There's no way to swing this in your favor," our publicist says over the phone. Speaker on, I listen to her talk to Maximoff. "It looks bad. It will continue to look bad. You should have thought about the repercussions before you took a midnight flight to a private villa in Mykonos."

I comb a hand through my dyed white hair, and Maximoff exchanges an irked look with me. Kendra isn't one of my favorite people, and as much as we're on a final straw with her, she's definitely on the last one with us. In most instances, we've chosen to take the media backlash, every hit, rather than sideslip away from it.

And the mud slung at me stings a little bit this time.

FARROW KEENE QUIT HIS RESIDENCY TO VACATION WITH THE HALE FAMILY IN TAHITI

The trending headline is not even close to the truth.

Shaded underneath pergolas, Maximoff sits rigidly on the wicker barstool, cool wind whipping his dark-brown hair. I slice a pineapple on the bar counter behind him. Our views from the villa are endless blues, the Aegean Sea serene and breathtaking, contrasting the paparazzi shit storm we left behind in the States.

Maximoff raises his phone to his lips. "Kendra," he says. "You don't need to come up with a manifestation on the meaning of the universe. Just send out a press release and explain that Farrow had to quit because he was a distraction in the hospital. That's it."

"It won't help," Kendra says. "But I'll do it." She hangs up abruptly.

"That was rude." I bite into a sickly sweet pineapple slice. "On her part, not yours." I lick my thumb.

Maximoff eyes my smooth movements. "I can't blame her." He places his phone on the bar. "This is the third press release in less than two weeks."

"It's her job," I point out, and I skim his taut muscles. "Regretting this trip?" I don't want him to wish we stayed back. I'd love nothing more than for Maximoff to take pleasure in every moment of this vacation.

No one else is in our private villa. We arrived five days earlier than the rest of his family, and the plan is to meet up with them later on their yacht, cruising around the Med.

Fancy shit doesn't compare to being with Maximoff. Just here. Now, and I want to give him the most romantic getaway that he's never had before. For five days, no kids running around, no siblings to worry about, and no meltdowns he needs to clean up.

All of that mayhem, which we both love to face head-on together, will come later.

"No, no regret," Maximoff says strongly, standing up and swinging his right arm slowly like a pendulum. He's allowed to stretch now, and he'll do this fifty-five times a day.

As long as he's not doubled-over in pain or puking, I'm in his camp.

He asks me, "Do you?"

I stare up at the baby blue sky, tilting my head from side-to-side. "Never." I eat another slice of pineapple and twirl the knife between my fingers, staking the blade in the cutting board. I almost start laughing at how much he's staring at my movements. "You're too easy."

"You're easier than me," he counters. "I saw you checking me out."

I smile into an actual laugh. Since we've been in Greece, only for five hours so far, I've made no effort to hide my attraction to Maximoff. Even if Wolf Scout's ego could be brought down a couple pegs. "You are my boyfriend."

My love.

He tries hard not to smile, and his brows bunch. "I could just be a figment of your imagination. Maybe I'm not even real. Maybe you're not real."

My brows spike with a barbell piercing. "He wants us to be imaginary together." I smile wider off his grimace, and I give him a hot once-over.

His form-fitting sunset-orange swim briefs display the cut and carve of lean muscles and mold his assets. But it's his tough-as-hell confidence that magnifies his beauty, and there are times where I catch him shutting his eyes and soaking up the sun.

When he's at peace, the entire world seems to still.

I come around the bar, and his gaze glides down the ink along my muscles. My black trunks are above-the-knee length, the fabric looser than his bathing suit.

Swiftly, I cup his face with both hands, and his chest elevates in a heady breath. "You feel very real to me, wolf scout."

His hands ascend my abs, and he glances at the crystal clear pool behind us. Looking back to me, he says, "No paparazzi. No one knows we're in Greece. It's all private."

I drink in the way he's staring at me. As though I'm the only man on Earth, the only person he'd ever choose in the beginning and the end. And I toss his words around in my mind, figuring out what he's leading me towards. "You want to walk around naked outside?"

"Kind of," he says.

"Kind of?" I repeat.

"Maybe."

"Getting clearer."

He smiles. "Yeah, I want to."

I love a good surprise, and Maximoff wanting to experience this uninhibited act is a surprise to me. I drop my hands off him, and I finger the waistband of my swim trunks.

Maximoff tries to beat me at this, drawing down his orange briefs quickly. He steps out of them in under a second. Buck-naked outdoors. With so much confidence you'd think he does this every Monday.

"This is your first time doing this?" I ask to be sure, pulling off my trunks.

Maximoff watches me. "Yeah. First time."

And he chose me to be here for it. Time and time again. He could've picked anyone in the entire world, and he wanted me. My chest rises. That feeling never gets old.

Maximoff suddenly sprints to the pool and dives in a perfect gorgeous arc. But he tucks his right arm to his chest. I'm right behind him, diving into the cool water.

When I breach the surface, we find each other. Our legs lacing, wet beads rolling down our faces—

Chiming.

That noise abruptly cuts into the moment. Must be text messages. I set my phone to *silent* when we reached the villa, so it's not mine.

"Answering those?" I ask him.

"No. It's just family group chats." He guides us towards the corner of the pool. "They're probably talking about that article." He leans in to kiss me—

Chiming. Again.

And again.

Maximoff rolls his head back in aggravation, and then glowers at the phone that vibrates next to the plate of pineapple. "Ignore it," he tells me, water lapping around us as we move.

"I am," I say. "A lot better than you are." My shoulder blades hit the stone edge, this end of the pool about eight-feet deep, and I cup his ass while he's up against my chest.

He rakes his hand through his wet hair. "Pretty sure I'm not even thinking about it anymore."

More chimes.

Now pings.

He's forcing himself to keep eye contact and not glance at his phone. My smile stretches. "Want the gold star now or later?"

"Never."

That was a firm *never*. As much as I like stoking his irritation, I'd rather train his concentration off the relentless chimes and pings, and also several beeps. The disturbance is really grating Maximoff and not in a good way.

At the corner of the pool, I hoist myself out of the water and take a seat on the stone edge. While I lean back on my hands, his mouth parts.

I'm exposed, beads of water dripping down my inked body and hot sun beating on my skin.

And I ask him, "What's your favorite tattoo of mine? And if you say *none*, then I'll just think you're copping out."

Maximoff is staring off into space.

I kick water at him.

He wipes his face and shoots me a middle finger. "I'm thinking, asshole. Give me a century."

I laugh. About to banter back, but he distracts me by swimming closer.

Maximoff fits his body between my spread legs. And he clutches both my tattooed knees, and then his hands run up my thighs. Resting his forearms on them, he braces his weight on me, using my body as a support so he won't have to tread water.

Our gazes cement.

Fuck, Maximoff. My nerves prick hot. "Need me to repeat the question, wolf scout?" I ask, voice husky.

"No. I heard you." He devours me whole. "Your newest one is my favorite."

I love that he loves the pirate wolf. "Before I got that one, what was your favorite?"

Maximoff already has the contextual meaning and significance to my tattoos. He asked me about them, back when we first started dating. It's not a long story or some heart-aching thing.

As a kid, I was obsessed with pirates the same way that a child who grows up in a butterfly-decorated room loves butterflies. Only I didn't have a themed bedroom.

On my desk, I had a framed photograph from Halloween where I wore a pirate costume. I was two-years-old. And my mom was holding me in her arms.

Inked on my fingers, *k.n.o.t t.a.m.e* is a just a play on sailing knots and also being untamed. It's not that deep. And all the skulls, pirates, daggers, sparrows, compasses, and ships are just things I loved from childhood to teenage adolescence to adulthood.

I watch his gaze roam my body with affectionate, wanting strokes. His breath shallows, and my muscles contract. I take a hand off the wet stone and glide my fingers through his brown hair, pushing the wet strands back.

He says, "I figure my favorites have to be the ones I think about the most." His mouth is hot against the inside of my thigh, lips trailing over the outline of an inked treasure chest.

My blood cranks. "Which one do you always think about?"

Chimes sound loudly, the noise hasn't ended, but for some reason, this one pulls his gaze.

I take my hand off his head and rub my rousing dick—that captures his attention. He's back on me, his breath shallow, and he pries my hand off.

He *puts* my hand on the back of his head. And he also takes my shaft in his fist. My muscles contract. *Fuck.*

Fuck. His aggression stirs the blood in my veins. I'm not surprised that Maximoff knows what he wants.

I push his hair back again. "Answer me before you blow me."

He tugs at my length. "Who said I'm about to suck you off?"

"Your eyes," I quip, my breath knotted in my lungs. I cup the back of his head tighter. "Maximoff—"

"The wings on your neck," he answers. "The swords on your throat. The red sparrows on your collar that fly between the masts of the ships. And the skull pirate on your ribs. Those ones I think about, all the damn time." He lowers his mouth to my hardening cock. Taking me between his lips—*fuck yes.*

Pressure squeezes around me, and my muscles ignite on fucking fire. Skin blazing from more than the sun. His head bobs with the up-and-down movement of his mouth.

"Fuck," I grunt. My feet flex in the pool water.

I could look at the breathtaking landscape. I could look at the blue horizon and the clearest sky and the majestic views, but I can't look away from him. From his forest-greens that tunnel into me with love and sex and soul-deep need and desire.

"*Maximoff*," I groan.

His biceps flex as he readjusts his support on my thighs. I sit up more, staring down at him—which he's not the biggest fan of. He glares and tightens his hand around the base of my shaft. *Fuck*. He pushes my chest.

I lean back, my elbow on wet stone. My veins throb, and with my hand on his head, I feel him go up and down, up and down—the friction feels fucking incredible.

I grit down, arousal skyrocketing. I apply pressure on the back of his head, pushing his mouth further down. My cock hits the back of his throat—*fuckingfuuuck*.

I pulse and just come. Hard.

A groan scrapes my throat, lips closed as I clench my teeth. *Fuck*. My head almost lolls back, my heartbeat shoved in my esophagus.

Maximoff swallows my cum, and stroking me two last times with his hand, he pulls himself out of the water with absolute ease. And he stands over me, feet on either side of my thighs.

I look up. Water drips down his sculpted swimmer's build, and his cock is in line with my mouth. *Damn*. My chest caves in a ragged breath.

I clutch his ass before he tries to put my hand there.

"No teasing," he commands. "Just take me in your mouth."

I roll my eyes. He's bossy as hell, but he's being bossier than usual. I figure out why in a split-second. His muscles bind, and he glances over at his chiming phone.

The outside interruptions are annoying him.

"You can put it on silent," I suggest.

He leaves me, and he says, "I'm turning off my phone."

My brows jump. He rarely powers off his phone. Because it means he's handing off familial responsibility to another cousin, another sibling, someone else in reach other than him. "You sure, wolf scout?"

He's at the bar, and the chiming suddenly ends. "Positive."

"You sure we should do this?" Maximoff

asks me while I massage his deltoids with lotion, our legs tangled with soft sheets. I'm careful of his healing injury, but he's not referring to my hands.

We're on our villa's king-sized bed. Sheer white drapes billow off the canopy around us, and hot wind gusts through the ajar door that leads to the private pool and patio. The front door is locked.

Maximoff is referring to the laptop he just opened with no fucking hesitation. He already typed in a porn site.

Now all of a sudden, he's slammed to a halt. "What are your reservations?" I ask, gently kneading his back muscle.

He spins around to face me, causing my hands to fall off him. Something is eating at him, and I want to call it *fear*—but it looks more like distress. It drives a knife in my gut.

I reach out and hold his hand.

"I keep thinking about the past three days here…" He gestures to his head. "I think about how I've *loved* every damn second. I love how we've just lounged in the sun, swam, fucked, eaten, and slept, but then I think, is it bad that I love that? I should want to leave the villa."

Maximoff.

I try not to smile. "But you don't want to," I say matter-of-factly.

"Yeah." He scrutinizes my rising lips, and it must be contagious because he begins to smile. "What?"

I lift my brows at him in a wave. "Man, I didn't plan anything romantic for you outside of the villa, and you didn't plan anything for me for a reason. And it has nothing to do with paparazzi. This isn't a five-day unhealthy hideout from the world. It's a five-day vacation before we link-up with your family."

He listens closely.

"And you're allowed to turn off your phone. It doesn't mean you're blocking everyone out to drown in a vice—there is no vice here." I'm guessing this is the origin of his perpetual thoughts. He's kept his phone off for three days. It's not something he does, and there is guilt in the act, especially if he's having a good time.

And we've had a lot of sex at the villa, but it's been healthy. Not compulsive, not used to squash anxiety. See, I've read up on sex addiction for him. On everything I could find.

His small smile has been fading.

He needs more; I can give him more. "You don't relax easily, but you've been extremely fucking relaxed the past three days." I let go of his hand and squeeze two fingers together. "You have a big thing for ordinary shit, and I have a bigger thing for doing the ordinary shit with you."

Breakfast in bed, massages, watching movies, laying out, swimming, showering together, these could fill his endless days. And I'd want them to fill mine too.

His eyes almost redden. "Repeat that."

My pulse beats hard. "Which part?"

"All of it."

I say it all again for him.

Maximoff smiles a gorgeous fucking smile when I've finished. "Alright. I want to do this." He leans back on the birch headboard, taking the laptop with him. I follow suit, shoulder-to-shoulder, our ankles hooking.

"You pick the video," Maximoff tells me, scrolling on a familiar gay porn site.

"How about you pick?" I'm definitely curious about what he'd gravitate towards, and I'm sure he feels the same about me.

"No thanks." He eyes my lip piercing.

I smile. "Looks like we're at a standstill." *And you want to kiss me.*

He's so impatient that he ends up scrolling and clicking into an amateur video. I skim the title: Two Passionate Guys Make Love!

"Shut up," he tells me.

"Didn't say anything." But my smile touches my cheeks, and I do say something now. "There's nothing wrong with wanting to make love, wolf scout, and being honest here, I'd say it's a preference of yours."

He turns his head, brows furrowed at me. Confused.

It stings my heart a little bit. "We've made love before." *All of the time.*

"Yeah?" He shuts the laptop. Sets it aside. "Remind me, Farrow."

I stroke his hair back, my hand running down his jaw, and our mouths crash together, nerves lighting to five-hundred degrees.

We shed our boxer-briefs, and wrestle in the twisted sheets, kissing the hell out of each other. We draw closer together when we turn on our sides, his weight on his good shoulder.

"*Fuck*," Maximoff groans after I nip his neck with my teeth. I suck harder, and then I kiss his jaw, his lips again, and his skillful tongue slides over mine.

Blood simmering, he bucks into me for harder friction while our mouths meld together. Grinding his pelvis against mine, my cock hardens.

I break our mouths and pat the mattress. Finding a bottle of lube. My chest presses firmly to his chest while we're on our sides.

Our eyes collide, and I lather my length. Huskily, I tell him, "I'm going to come inside of you, wolf scout."

He rocks his hips into me, squeezing my ass, and groans against the crook of my neck. "Fuck me now, man." He strokes his own cock.

Fuck. I tuck him more to my chest, and I lift his leg over my waist. Keeping my arm underneath his knee so he'll stay hoisted. "Look at me," I whisper.

He pulls his head back, his eyes melting into mine. He looks overcome and at the peak of arousal, and I haven't even pushed into him yet.

I tease his hole open with two fingers. His muscles flex, his breath catching. He's giving himself to me with so much trust and love and care. It amplifies an already visceral, primal feeling that connects him to me. That douses me with kerosene and lights me on fucking fire.

Sweat built on our skin, I move my fingers, and I ease my erection into him. Slowly. "Breathe," I tell Maximoff, our eyes locked.

"*Oh fuck*," he grunts. The pressure wells around my cock, his tightness overwhelming me, and I use more lube before I push deeper.

"*Fuck, Maximoff.*" My muscles pull taut, and I'm all...the way... inside of him. I rock my hips, and I hold the back of his head in the most protective, secure grip. Not letting go, our mouths a breath away, and we stare unblinkingly. Feeling every fucking thing and seeing it well in the other's eyes.

"*Oh fuck,*" he groans, his lips broken open with throaty noises.

My hand shifts to his jaw, encasing his face, holding as fucking tight as him. His eyes almost roll, almost gone.

"Farrow*Farrow.*" He death-clutches my shoulders like he's falling off a mountain and I'm his harness.

I grit down, a coarse noise tangled in my lungs. My pulse hammers in the hollow of my throat. "*Fuck,*" I groan. "*Wolf scout.*"

Water slips from the corners of his daggered eyes.

Mine burn and well.

We kiss in this final stretch. Our lips push each other's mouth open in burning aggression and desire, and my searing lungs beg for more breath.

I rock and rock.

And he pulsates around my erection—I come, my mind spinning, and our bodies tighten. Grunts and groans and curses pitch the air, and slowly, gradually, I milk my climax inside of him. Pumping a few more times, and my abs glisten from him.

I let go of his face and stroke his cock to finish him off, cum slick on my palm.

His head lolls backwards, basking in the fucking pleasure.

I smile. And I still can't stop staring, not for a moment. He's the iron-willed guy I saw at Harvard who needed all of me, and I had to wait years before I could give him everything.

31

MAXIMOFF HALE

I'm going to propose here. This five-day vacation with Farrow—*God,* it's hands-down the most romantic of my life. I have the ring. I just need to wait for the perfect moment.

Early morning, we lounge on the sunbathing cushion in boxer-briefs, a shaded pergola shielding the rising sun. A photo-worthy Greek breakfast is spread on a wooden slab: eggs baked in tomato, onion, feta, spinach, along with sesame-coated koulouri bread and two glasses of orange juice.

We talked for hours last night and fell asleep under the stars. I never used to think a lot about romance, but being with him, I think about these things. All the damn time.

"She put a *Team Marrow* bumper sticker on her car before we left," Farrow says, scooping eggs onto his fork. I catch sight of his amused smile.

How we started talking about my mom and Team Marrow bumper stickers and her unconditional love of our relationship, I have no idea.

But it turns my mind. "What do you think about our ship name?" I ask him seriously, picking up a glass of orange juice.

Farrow lies more relaxed on his side. I'm sitting upright, but every now and then, he'll reach out and rub my back or skate his fingers through my hair—and I can't hide my fucking smile.

He swallows his food and tells me, "I love 'Marrow' because you're obsessed with it."

I pause before I swig my orange juice, brows furrowing. "Why do you think I'm obsessed with it?" I'm not my mom. I haven't put bumper stickers on my car, bought *Marrow* T-shirts, or sent out a billion tweets professing my undying love. So I wonder why he drew that conclusion.

And that conclusion—it's not wrong.

Farrow glances at the orange rising sun, then to me. "Whenever anyone mentions the name, you stare faraway for a bit, then you start smiling. I figured it meant something to you..." He looks me over like he'd love to know what went on inside my brain in those moments.

I nod. "It does mean something to me." I sip orange juice, cool citrus sliding down my throat. "Have you skimmed Thoreau's 'Walden'?"

"Skimmed?" he repeats with the roll of his eyes. His lips quirk. "No, smartass. I haven't skimmed that one."

I cup the cold glass in my hand, and I hold his gaze while I quote, "'*I wanted to live deep and suck out all the marrow of life, to live so sturdily and Spartan-like as to put to rout all that was not life.*' I think about that whole passage every time someone says Marrow."

Farrow looks enamored. "Go on."

I try to explain in my own words, and I gesture to his chest. "It's in your bones; it's what keeps you alive. The foundation of your body. To suck out all the marrow of life...I think about how Thoreau went into the woods and stripped life to the barest necessities. To learn what life is really made of, the feeling of water slipping between fingers, the chilled glass in my hand, the wind that rustles your damn hair. And I think about how I feel these barest things every day with you. To live life at its most essential level so as to fully live."

Farrow has his hand to his mouth, overwhelmed, his eyes unable to shift off my eyes.

I add, "And Marrow starts with the letter of my name."

Hand dropping, he smiles unbearably wide. "That's what you have to tell yourself since my name occupies five of the six letters."

I flip him off, but I can't fucking grimace if I tried. I smile into another swig of orange juice—and I think, *this is it*. I can go to my suitcase inside the villa, go grab the ring.

And then the doorbell buzzes.

Our heads turn, but we can't see the front entrance from the private patio. We look back at each other, and I say, "It could be the villa's owner." But we're both aware that the owner said she wouldn't contact us during our stay.

Farrow places his fork back on the wooden slab, and he sits up. "I'll call the owner and see if it's her."

I find his phone beneath a light blue decorative pillow. The screen is lit up with text notifications, and I catch the name before I toss it to him. "Who's Jordan?"

He shuts his eyes in a bout of annoyance, contempt for *Jordan* raiding his features. "Fuck this guy." He exhales an edged breath before telling me, "He was a second-year resident and hated everything about me. He must've gotten my number from Shaw."

"Was this the first time you worked at the hospital or the second?" I ask while he opens the texts.

"Second time." His nose flares as he skims the texts. This Jordan guy knew where to jab Farrow because it's a direct hit. He grinds his teeth and combs his hand through his hair. Multiple times. "He sent me screenshots of tweets."

I wrap my arm across his shoulders, muscles stiffened. Ready for survival. But my stomach is knotting. Before I ask to see, he holds the phone out and shows me the screenshots.

#FarrowKeene you're a shit doctor.

#FarrowKeene is not board-certified. Can't even practice in a hospital. I don't understand why the Hales would still hire him...oh wait...

Come on, people! #FarrowKeene is probably a great doctor. But I still can't believe the Hales, Meadows, and Cobalts would choose someone who's not board-certified. It's not like them. #TheyAreBetterThanThat

Not buying this whole "he was a distraction in the hospital" excuse. #FarrowKeene

#FarrowKeene just admit that you'd rather only help famous people in a lush job than do what every other doctor has to do and go through the grueling process of residency. You either couldn't hack it or didn't want to. Just say that and be done.

My eyes narrow at the phone screen. "Fuck them," I say. Farrow isn't the only doctor who practices without being board-certified. There are plenty doing good work at clinics, private practices, and the hospitals that don't require it.

Farrow deletes the messages and blocks the number. "I'm not as angered by the tweets as I am by the fucking prick who took the time to text them to me..." he trails off, the doorbell ringing a second time. Followed by knocking.

We forget about the texts and focus on this issue. More urgently, Farrow dials the owner's number, phone to his ear.

I stand off the sunbathing cushion and head into the airy bedroom. Natural light streaming inside. For hanging here all day, all night, the villa is pretty clean. Bed made, clothes in drawers, and wet towels drying on hooks.

I rake back my windswept hair and put on gray sweatpants.

My weatherproof duffle-suitcase lies unpacked next to a birch dresser. I can almost picture the square black ring box in the front pocket—and then the doorbell buzzes.

Again.

Almost incessantly.

That's not the owner. My head swerves as Farrow rushes into the bedroom.

"The owner isn't here," he says quickly, putting on black joggers, elastic band to his waist, and my brain is reeling.

I'm pretty sure there's a natural disaster on the other side of that door, and I think, *my family*. My family.

My family.

My goddamn family. I'm rigid, wading deep in crisis mode, and I grab my charged phone off the dresser. I power it on. "My family would've called you if they couldn't get ahold of me?" I ask him.

Farrow lifts his brows at me. "A hundred percent. It's not them, wolf scout."

Knocking returns, more impatient sounding this time.

I get that my family was instructed not to come here, but there's always an asterisk that says, *unless there's a dire emergency*. If they were in trouble and needed me, I'd welcome them to interrupt everything. Like a birthday, a honeymoon, a fucking rocket takeoff to Mars.

I don't have time to comb through the hundreds of missed group chat messages. Because the doorbell jingles again.

Farrow leans on the dresser. "I'm going to call security." His jaw tics, irritated without a radio, which would be faster.

"Maybe the media knows we're not in Tahiti and our location leaked." I already know it's unlikely before Farrow tells me.

"It'd be all over the news."

And it's not.

After the umpteenth doorbell ring and urgent knock, I start walking down the narrow hall. Towards a sky-blue door with a chalkboard sign that says *welcome* in Greek.

Farrow jogs to catch me, his inked fingers in my waistband. Pulling me back. "Wait, wolf scout." He gives me a hard look that says *we're not doing this shit again*.

Again.

Nate.

My stalker.

It's why he's overly cautious. Why he hasn't bombarded the front door himself. And I can see it eating at him, having to grip onto a cell instead of a gun.

I stand like I'm ready for whatever hell exists on the other side. A war, a hurricane, I can handle it. "Bruno is at least fifteen minutes away. If that is my family, I need to answer it *now*."

Farrow speaks into the phone while staring right at me. His gaze says, *I'm with you; don't go alone.* "We're fine. Someone's at the door," he tells security. "We'd just like a couple guys out here. Yeah, thanks." He hangs up and then nods to the door. "I'm going first."

He's already passing me, his stride long and fast.

I'm right by his side.

"Stay behind me," Farrow instructs.

I don't remind him that he's not my bodyguard. He still has the experience from training and being on-duty for years. But putting Farrow in danger—it's never been as easy as putting myself in harm's way. He'd say the exact same.

So I don't slip behind him. I stay by his side. He has no time to call me stubborn, another fist raps the door.

Farrow puts his hand on the knob. "Who is it?!" he yells, his voice commanding and threatening all at once. My pulse pounds hard.

Silence ekes out the other end, and that…yeah, that sends my blood cold.

Farrow hisses at me, "Back up. I'm not messing around anymore."

I glower. "You don't even have a canister of pepper spray." I reach for my knife on my ankle—I don't have a fucking tactical knife on me. Or a switchblade. I feel more unprepared. And I'm not even positive what I'm supposed to be preparing for.

Farrow extends his arm over my chest. Keeping me a foot or two behind him. "I don't need a weapon," he whispers lowly. "You're safe; I'll be safe. Just stay back. Or this door stays closed until Bruno gets here. And I know neither of us will like that."

I hang onto the part where he says he'll be safe.

Alright.

Alright.

I don't push forward. As he cracks the door open, Farrow has the view. I only see the sky-blue painted wood, which blocks the person from my sight.

I watch my boyfriend's expression change from territorial protectiveness to outright anger. He tries to swing the door closed on them.

That person sticks their foot in the crevice. A nice leather loafer jams the door open.

"Move your motherfucking foot," Farrow sneers. "Or I will break it."

"I have photos!"

What.

Blood drains out of my head. And I don't recognize that urgent male voice. Farrow must though, and he's one second from shoving his weight into the door and breaking that guy's foot.

"Nude photos!" the guy shouts. "Of both of you!"

Bullshit.

There's no way.

There's no way, I think over and over again. I start layering my demeanor, my features, with brick and brick, mortaring down for the storm to come. "Farrow," I say, voice strict. I have to see this guy. I can't be in the dark anymore.

Farrow knows.

It's why he doesn't argue. He just yanks the door wider to allow me a better view. But he fills the doorway with his six-foot-three frame and muscular MMA build. Whoever is on the other side would have to barrel through Farrow to reach me.

Five people.

Five people stand outside our villa, cypress trees landscaping the private front yard and pebbled parking spot. The ratio blares in my brain: five to two.

We're outnumbered.

Two heftier men in the back carry bulky cameras, and two taller guys have black duffel bags slung across their chests. Lighting equipment of some kind.

But the late-twenty-something guy out in front, wearing a baby blue suit and yellow pocket square, steals most of my attention. I zero in on his ashy-brown hair, a quarterback build and gunmetal eyes.

Familiarity creeps into me, but I can't quite place him. The picture is lost in the cobwebs of my brain.

Who are you?

My boyfriend white-knuckles the doorframe, one second from slamming it shut. "You're full of shit," Farrow sneers. "Get your camera crew off our front steps. This is private property."

The gunmetal-eyed guy ignores him. "Maximoff," he says quickly. "We weren't properly introduced. I'm Ace Steel—"

"*What*," I snap heatedly. *Fucking Christ.*

This is the porn star. I wonder how much the company is paying him to be here. To try to convince me to work for them.

He starts again, "I—"

"No," I cut in. "Whatever you want from me, *no*." Anger gnaws at me, clawing to take hold and destroy before I'm destroyed. I breathe and turn to my boyfriend. "Farrow." I want him to shut the door. His earlier instincts were spot on. Get this fucking guy out of here.

"I'll leak the nudes!" Ace yells before Farrow can do anything.

He's not serious.

I charge and Farrow actually blocks me from bombarding the door, his arm across my chest.

"You're blackmailing me?" I growl. "To my face?!"

"It's not blackmail." Ace glances cautiously to the four men around him, then back to me, "I just want to talk. Give me five minutes. Do you understand what I had to go through to get a face-to-face with you?"

Yeah…he had to bid two million dollars on me at an auction, and he still couldn't get that time with me. I don't even want to know what he did to track us down here.

I don't want to know.

I don't want to feel even more violated than I do right now.

"You don't have nudes," I say like it's a real fact. It has to be. Anything else feels wrong.

Farrow has reached back and wrapped an arm around my waist, all while facing forward and keeping his focus on Ace. He's trying to protect me, but I want to raise our armies for him. I want to tear this guy to fucking pieces.

"I do have them." Ace stares unblinkingly at me.

He's bluffing. "Do you even understand the legal ramifications of you admitting that right now?" I ask, dumbfounded. "I'll bury you."

The Hales have dug graves for weaker transgressions than what he's confessing. My dad, my grandfather, have ruined countless men.

I can ruin him.

But I'm not sure that'd erase this slithering feeling that tries to worm its way inside of me.

"I didn't take the photos myself," Ace clarifies. "A drone did."

A drone. I didn't see one in the air. Neither did Farrow, who's vigilant about these things. We missed it, and we're usually careful. We think of everything, but the one time where we both wanted to feel free…

It was a risk.

I think we both knew it was.

Ace unbuttons his suit jacket, hot and uncomfortable. "But I have the photos."

"Then show us them," Farrow says coldly.

Ace takes out his phone and pops up a picture.

I see Farrow kissing me on the sundeck, his ass completely exposed, but I'm covered, pressed against his body. Ace swipes up. The next photo is just of me. Walking towards the pool.

It's full frontal.

Farrow decks Ace in the face with skilled, enraged force, a massive amount of power going into that single blow. And I hear a sickening *crack* in his cheekbone, and the porn star hits the stone porch.

My pulse jackhammers—I was about to swing at Ace, but Farrow beat me to it and now that it's done, all I want to do is get this goddamn camera crew out of here.

"Leave," I growl at them while Ace stays on the ground, moaning in pain.

A hipster-looking guy with a handlebar mustache holds out his hand. "Wait, we only want to leak a couple of these photos with your permission. We can even pick the tame ones for you."

"What?" I breathe hard, confused as fuck.

Farrow grips the edge of the door. Seconds from smashing it in their face.

"You both get to be in the press," he explains. "It'll increase your social media following, and in exchange, you'll drop some hints on an Instagram Live or two about Sensual Flixxxs. How it's your favorite website. It's good marketing and a win-win for all of us."

What the hell…

"*Get the fuck out,*" Farrow says through gritted teeth, "or you'll join your friend on the fucking ground—"

"We could film a chaste kissing scene," he adds quickly, taking a step back. Afraid of Farrow. "No sex or penetration. We've got the crew here. We could do it right now. We'll pay you twenty million." His gaze swerves to Farrow at the talk of money. Like he knows that'd be his incentive.

Fuck him.

Fuck this.

Farrow lets go of the door, about to throw another knockout punch. But I put a hand on his shoulder, stopping him from starting a drag-out fight with five men. Doing what he'd do for me.

And then an SUV slams to a stop onto the pebbled path. We both go still.

"It's not a bad offer," the hipster tells us, but we're looking behind him. "Other celebrities would have taken it."

"Redford!" Oscar yells from the car. His curly hair blows in the wind. He's the only guy here from SFO. Bruno and the rest from SFA file in and close around the camera crew.

"Confiscate their phones," Farrow tells security before the words leave my mouth, and I watch six bodyguards all descend upon the trespassers to protect us.

"We're leaving," Ace chokes out, picking himself up. His hand to his face. "We're leaving."

"You're not leaving," Farrow sneers. "I already gave you that chance. Now you're going to stay until we've—*they've* combed through your equipment."

"And then we're pressing charges," I say, my voice stilted.

I don't know what I feel. Grateful that the full frontal is of me and not him. I know I feel that.

Farrow kicks the door closed, and it shuts with a loud *thud*. I back up a few feet, and as soon as he turns towards me, we latch onto one another. Our arms slide around each other's shoulders.

Chest to chest, we tighten the embrace, and his heavy pulse thumps against mine. *We're okay.*

His hand warms my neck. "Maximoff," he breathes.

He stops there.

Because he knows.

Like I do.

There's such a small chance that those photos won't be leaked. I don't know who else has them, and if they were smart, they would have already sent the pictures to their bosses. Once a photo is taken, the line between a leak and privacy is so damn thin.

I can only hope that my lawyers will be fast enough to file cease and desists. That they'll obtain the photos before it snowballs out of control.

And the last thing I think, *I can't propose today.* Somehow, that hurts the most.

32

MAXIMOFF HALE

Being with family should have taken the edge off what happened at the villa, but last night we boarded the mega yacht in the Med; and with twenty-seven family members on the ship, I'm feeling the heat of almost everyone's whispers and silent sympathy.

It's heavy.

And not what I wanted to bring onto a family vacation. On the main deck, sleek white cushions and couches cluster around a five-foot deep pool. Cooling off in the waters, I perch my elbows out of the pool on a towel.

My thumb marks the place in a paperback: *Aristotle's Nicomachean Ethics*, but I train my eyes straight ahead. Where an overhang shades a circular table with fourteen plush chairs, and right behind that seating area, sliding glass doors lead to the main saloon.

SFO had a debate on the pronunciation of *saloon*, but Oscar shut it down quickly and let everyone know it's pronounced "*salon*."

I have a good view inside that saloon, and I see Farrow side-by-side with Dr. Rowin Hart. Both treat severe sunburns. Red fiery blisters are puckered on Winona's shoulders and arms. Ben looks worse, fire-engine red legs swollen like logs. Both of them used some kind of knockoff organic sunscreen, and it didn't do its job.

Rowin cleans a popped blister, and Farrow has been trying to keep Ben's fever down. I watch as Rowin says something to my boyfriend.

But I'm out of earshot. I notice Farrow rolling his eyes and replying back. He snaps off his gloves.

You don't know how much I dislike Rowin Hart. I wouldn't put him in the Voldemort category, but my aversion towards Farrow's ex-boyfriend has been a rising tide. Especially now that Farrow is officially on the med team *with* Rowin.

These feelings I feel—it's not jealousy.

It's fear.

Rowin isn't pining after my boyfriend. It's clear that he despises Farrow, and I see that raw, emotional pain flare up in Rowin's eyes every time he converses with him. It puts me on edge. On guard.

After all the shit Farrow and I have gone through, I can't let his ex hurt him. Physically, verbally, all of the fucking above.

"Happy Birthday, Moffy." My uncle's smooth voice tears my glare away from Rowin.

Connor towers above me in navy swim trunks, his poise and stature god-like. My dad jokes about how Uncle Connor is immortal since he only looks better with age.

"Thanks," I say to him.

Today is July 13th, and I'm now twenty-three-years-old. If I contemplate that too hard, I'll fall into some sort of philosophical stupor. So I try not to.

And I think there must be something else my uncle wants. Connor could've just yelled *happy birthday* across the yacht deck like half my family already did. Which has been a good distraction. Seriously. Every time I start thinking about all the outside bullshit, someone else howls *happy birthday, Moffy!* and tears me back to real life. To right here. Right now.

Connor squats so we're more eye-level. "The lawyers just called me," he says. "They've stopped most of the pictures from leaking. All that exists is the one photo, and that'll be it." His deep blue eyes soften with soothing powers. "I'm so sorry."

The one photo.

It was my full frontal. But in the one that's been circulating, my crotch was blurred, and as far as I know, no one has been able to find the uncensored image.

I should be happy that the world hasn't seen my dick. But really, I hate that a money-hungry company has tarnished one of the best weeks of my life.

So no, I'm not really happy.

But I also recognize I'm talking to a man that had *much* worse happen to him. "Thanks for the help," I tell my uncle. "I guess I should be glad it wasn't worse."

"A violation of privacy is a violation," Uncle Connor says. "It doesn't matter the severity. It's okay to be upset, even in front of me."

When he was in his twenties, sex videos of him and his soon-to-be wife were illegally recorded and released. And Christ, I just can't imagine that type of invasion. If Farrow and I had been filmed and that leaked, I'd be *devastated*. It's why our families are uneasy around porn companies.

"I'm not upset, I'm pissed," I tell Connor. "Like really goddamn pissed." I run a hand through my wet hair. "But I don't want to talk about it. I just…want to forget it."

Uncle Connor nods, understanding. "If you ever change your mind"—he rises to stand—"I'm always here."

I thank him again, and he walks off towards the saloon. Eighteen-year-old Tom and Eliot jump out from behind the mini bar, trying to scare him, and their dad just blinks at them. Unfazed.

I try to spot Farrow through the glass doors. But I don't see him.

Suddenly, water splashes behind me. Wetting my paperback.

I feel his hands on my waist and his chin on my shoulder. His chest presses up against my back, and I try to restrain a smile.

But I fail as soon as he places a kiss on the side of my neck. "You're tense, wolf scout," he breathes, kneading my muscles with the heel of his palm. *Goddamn.*

My waist knocks into the pool wall, my blood hot. Craning my head over my shoulder, I catch the amusement in his eyes. His bleach-white hair looks darker wet, and beads of water roll down the light stubble on his jaw and inked wings on his neck.

His barbell piercing rises at me with his brown brows. But his smile fades fast. "What's wrong?" he asks.

"You and Rowin."

He cringes, but he doesn't drop his hands. "Not my favorite phrase. Let's actually remove it from your lexicon."

"You work together," I remind him. "You're going to be around him, and my trust level with strangers has about plummeted to negative-infinity."

He nods slowly, and his hands work their magic on my traps, gentle on my bad shoulder. Whatever he's doing feels too damn good.

I add, "You shouldn't be around someone who's made it clear they literally hate you. Not only is that a toxic work environment, but Christ, he could fucking hurt you." I have more to say. So I abandon my paperback.

And I turn around completely. Facing him now, his hands fall off my back and clutch my waist beneath the water.

"I don't trust him," I continue while Farrow never breaks eye contact. "I know if I go to my parents and ask for him to be fired, it's going to seem like I'm a jealous boyfriend. But after the villa, after you've been *doxxed*, I can't watch you share space with that guy."

Farrow waits for me to finish, still nonchalant. Like I just announced today's forecast. "Done?"

I add one final thing, "But if you're utterly against it, I'll try not to do anything." It'll be hard.

"Okay, working with Rowin is irritating at most," Farrow says. "He's not going to murder me and throw me overboard. Plus, I'm stronger than him."

"Great," I say dryly.

He smiles. "But if this is something you need to do, I'm behind you. Always."

That feels good.

I nod a few times. "After this trip, I'll make it happen." Getting Rowin fired while he's on a free vacation in Greece seems callous for some reason.

My voice fades as one of my younger cousins races across the deck, darting past us and yelling, "Happy Birthday, Moffy!"

It brings me back to this morning. When Farrow gave me my birthday present. He bent down in front of me and rolled up the hem of my drawstring pants. Revealing the holster strapped to my ankle.

And Farrow pulled out my tactical knife.

When he stood up, he said, "Your present is on your ankle."

I didn't understand until I reached for my ankle and I realized he slipped a new knife in the holster. One that he bought in Mykonos. The wooden hilt is carved in intricate patterns.

He knew I loved it. And I didn't conceal the fact that I did. I just kissed the fuck out of my boyfriend. And the delivery of the present got to me as much as the actual knife. No wrapping paper or bag.

Farrow Redford Keene's movements were all over that birthday gift. My brain *loves* that to death. I replay the way he bent down and smiled up at me on repeat.

"Maximoff." Farrow splashes water at my chest.

I wake up from a slight daydream, but he's not teasing me about it. I follow his ultra-focused gaze across the main deck.

Fucking Christ *no*.

Gray hair pulled into a bun, string of pearls around a wrinkled neck, and a strawberry daiquiri in hand—nothing good can come from talking to my Grandmother Calloway.

She plays favorites with her four daughters. And that hierarchy directly affects me and my siblings and my cousins. I'll give you the breakdown.

1. Rose Calloway – Jane's mom
2. Poppy Calloway
3. Daisy Calloway – Sullivan's mom
4. Lily Calloway – my mom is dead last. Always.

Before I make eye contact with Grandmother Calloway, I come up with a kindergarten idea. But if you knew my grandmother like I know her, you'd do the same.

I tell Farrow, "Under. Now. Hold your breath." Quickly, I dip beneath the water, avoiding someone who should be avoided. At all costs.

It takes me a solid second to realize that Farrow isn't coming down with me.

33

Yeah, I'm not hiding from his grandmother.
She's the definition of a crotchety old bat, and whatever she wants to say, she can say to my face.

Grandmother Calloway approaches and halts a few feet from the pool's edge. Careful not to wet her bejeweled sandals. Her bony fingers skim the pearls at her neck. "Have you seen my grandson?" she asks me.

"He's around here somewhere," I say casually. Maximoff might be a swimmer, but he won't be able to hold his breath forever.

She purses her lips, scrutinizing my tattoos and my brow, lip, nose, and nipple piercings, all with visible judgment. Nothing that I haven't met before.

"Do you need something?" I ask in an easygoing tone. "Maybe I can help."

Her fingers pause on her neckline, and she meets my gaze. "I think you've done enough."

I let out a short laugh. For fuck's sake. *Should've expected that.* But I'm a little shocked she had the nerve to say it directly to my face. "Honestly, I don't know what you're referring to."

Maximoff is tugging my bathing suit trunks underneath the water. Wanting me to dive down. I have to hold onto the waistband so he doesn't pull them off. And fuck, I'm smiling.

Grandmother Calloway instantly sees my amusement as an affront. She bristles, her lips more compressed together than before. "My grandson had a bright philanthropic career ahead of him, and then you came along. His life would've been better-served with a…"

She falters at the sight of my cutting glare.

"…with someone else," she finishes.

"No, he wouldn't have," I say plainly. "There is no one better for Maximoff than me."

Maximoff suddenly breaches the water, wiping water off his face.

His grandmother startles backwards. Shock parting her lips, and accusations lace her eyes. That's when it dawns on me. Grandmother Calloway thinks that Maximoff was just blowing me in the pool.

I'm near laughter. Can't make this shit up. Donnelly is going to be rolling on the floor when he hears.

"I should've known." She's trying to bite her tongue, but she spits out at Maximoff, "You're just like your mother."

My smile fades. I instinctively hold the back of his head. He's stunned cold.

"Maximoff," I whisper, wanting to draw him away from his grandmother.

He's marble. Immovable. Cemented in place. "What'd you say?" Shock is seizing every part of him.

My hand falls to his left shoulder.

His grandmother shakes her head. "I'm sorry, sweetie. You know I told her I'd raise you in my home. It would've been better. She's admitted she has a problem, and that problem has obviously affected you—"

"You can't say that to him," I cut in, coldness frosting each word.

"He's my grandson—"

"That's his mother," I retort. I love Lily Calloway, and she's one of the closest things that I've had to a mom. So no, I won't let this fucking old bat try to drag Lily or Lily's son down.

She fumes and looks to her grandson. "Max?"

I roll my eyes. "Max" is the only socially-acceptable name to this blue-blooded aristocrat.

Maximoff unfreezes enough to speak. "I know you've had issues with my mom in the past. But I thought you two buried that a while ago."

My chest caves. He's more upset that what she said could potentially fracture his mom's relationship with his grandmother. I squeeze his shoulder.

Grandmother Calloway stiffens like she's never taken a shit in her life. "We're at a good place, but there's room for everyone to hear advice. Especially your mother. If she can't hear it from family, how will she grow?"

Loren Hale exits the saloon, passing the eating area, and once he leaves the shaded part of the deck and enters the sun, I see that his target is his mother-in-law. I'm glad he's intervening.

Lo sends her a seething glare. "I don't know what you're saying, Samantha, but unless you're here to wish my son a happy birthday, you need to move along."

She prickles. "I *was* here to wish my grandson a happy birthday, Loren. But come to find out he's been underwater doing things that your wife used to do when she had problems."

"Can you *please* stop talking about her like that?" Maximoff says like his heart is breaking into a million pieces, and at the same time, like he's constructing iron walls around his world.

I cup his neck, and before Lo asks, I say the truth, "He was just under the water." Shit, I'm twenty-eight; I never thought I'd need to defend something like this. We're part of the older crew here. We're not the teenagers.

Grandmother Calloway scoffs at me, like I just lied under oath. But believe me, if Maximoff had actually blown me under the water, she would've fucking known.

Lo makes a face at me. "It doesn't matter what you were doing or not doing. You're fine." He narrows in on the grandmother. "What did you say to my son?"

"I told him the truth," she says irritably. "I offered to raise him in my home while Lily recovered from sex addiction, and you both rejected that offer. He can't be blamed for how he's turned out—"

"Jesus Christ, you're going to break her goddamn heart," Lo says, shaking his head in disbelief with the same shocked disappointment that struck Maximoff.

"Like I told Max—" she starts.

"You're off the damn boat," Lo snaps. "This family has no room for your hate or judgment. I've told you that before. Go straight down to the rib: it's the smaller boat that'll take you to the city. I'll have a stewardess pack your bags." He's about to leave but then he stops and turns back. "If you try to talk to Lily before you go, I will make sure your tombstone reads *here lies Samantha Calloway, the worst goddamn mother in all of the century.* And don't fucking kid yourself, I will do it."

Her neck flushes red. "My daughters will be more upset that you're throwing me out like garbage."

Lo flashes a bitter smile. "Decades later, and you still don't know your own daughters."

She scowls before strutting away to the saloon.

Maximoff watches her leave, and I draw circles on his neck with my thumb. He leans some of his weight against my hand.

"Thanks, Dad," he says.

Lo searches his son for signs of breakage. Right now, he's one-hundred percent stoic, jaw set sharp and eyes carrying little to no emotion. But I know Maximoff will only show more in front of me.

His dad opens his mouth, but Maximoff beats him to speak. "Can you just go be with Mom?" he asks.

Lo nods. "Yeah," he sighs. "I'm sorry, bud." He focuses on me. "Whatever Samantha said to you, her opinions are light-years away from ours." I'm positive "ours" encompasses all the families.

"I know," I say.

After another short goodbye, Lo leaves. And Maximoff and I turn to each other, water lapping around us, especially with the yacht cruising through the sea.

I sheath his cheek with my hand, his emotion fighting to break through. Fuck, I just want to hold him. Love him. Be there for him when his aristocratic grandmother turns heel.

"What are you thinking?" I breathe.

He pulls my chest closer to his chest in the pool. His buff arms around my shoulders, hands riding up my neck. His forest-greens start to stroke my eyes. Like hot caresses flooded with comfort and warmth. "It feels like every time I try to come up for air, someone else shits on you or me or us, and the only time I can breathe is when I'm looking at you."

My chest swells, feeling his words before my lips slowly rise. "If that were true, wolf scout, you would've died from asphyxiation every time I left the room."

He groans out his irritation, but then he breaks into deep laughter.

"I made him laugh," I say matter-of-factly, and fuck, that sound is gorgeous. He looks surprised that the noise left his lips. That unannounced visit at the villa is still raw for me too. And I don't regret stripping our clothes outside.

I don't regret one thing we did.

I always take risks. I always live by my actions, not other people's fucked-up ones. And out of everything, it just fucking rips me apart that the full frontal was of him and not me. So easily, it could've been me, and I would've done absolutely anything to change that, to protect him, to save him.

And I know I fell short this time.

34

MAXIMOFF HALE

"You what?" I still can't believe what Farrow just said.

We're on one of the sleek couches that surround the glowing pool. Stars shine in the pitch black night, lanterns on the main deck illuminating the yacht. My siblings and cousins are spread out: some reading on chairs, others soaking in the hot tub. Upstairs in the sky lounge, all of our parents are having a "meeting" to discuss Grandmother Calloway's abrupt departure.

Out of all my siblings and cousins, I have the least contact with our grandmother. That's my mom's doing. I understand why, and I love her for protecting me. But I wish I could protect her from hurt. From that pain.

My dad would tell me that it's not my job. Still, I want the superpower to erase everything my grandmother said. Banish the words from fucking existence.

Maybe that should've been my birthday wish. Guess I still have time since it's not midnight.

July 13th isn't over yet.

Despite some bad parts, there is so much good here. And I hang onto every damn piece. Especially the small moments in between.

Like now.

Farrow is slouched against me on the couch, most of his weight anchored off my chest. He's mindful of my injury but not to the point where it'd frustrate me. His amusement fucking mushrooms. Like he just beat me at some sort of listening competition.

"I heard you," I refute while I try to raise my right arm vertically. In a stretch. But I still can't reach all the way up without intense stress on the muscle. "I just need you to say it again so it can sink in."

He slowly chews mint gum. "I wrote him a letter, wolf scout. You know: paper, pen. The Cobalt way."

"I got that," I say. "But *why?*"

The second we sank down onto the couch together, Farrow admitted that he gave Beckett a letter, but I have no fucking idea the reasons or the contents.

Farrow sits up straighter. Turning more towards me, his inked hand slides along my thigh.

Christ, I like that.

He smiles knowingly. "Because Beckett is the family member who keeps questioning my intentions with you, and normally I'd just say *fuck him* and move on. But our relationship should bring you closer to your family, not farther away. So I gently explained some things in a manner I thought a Cobalt would appreciate."

Wow.

He did that.

I breathe in, my chest expanding with something powerful. "Thank you," I say seriously, lifting my arm at a forty-five degree angle. I glance at his mouth.

His know-it-all smile has returned. "You want me to kiss you?"

"Or maybe I just want to fuck you," I combat.

He shifts, his gaze falling down me. "If you want to fuck me, you can fuck me later."

My blood heats. Goddamn. I can never tell if I love or hate flirting. The impatient parts of my brain loathe it, but the rest of me would gladly do this for millenniums with him.

"I said *maybe*," I retort.

"I said *if*," he says. "Man, your listening skills are worsening."

I give him a middle finger while my arm ascends to a sixty-degree angle. "Where's your copy of this fucking letter?"

Now he's really laughing. "You think I made a copy for you to read?"

"Not for me. Just in general," I lie.

Yeah, okay, I thought he would've made an extra one for me.

Farrow lifts his foot to the couch, balancing his arm on his bent knee. We've dried off from a night swim earlier, but he's still in black bathing suit trunks, and my form-fitting green suit is a boxer-brief cut.

He smiles at me and says, "There's only one. If you want to read it, you're going to have to get it from Beckett."

Janie bounds over to us in a peach tankini, wavy hair knotted in a high bun. "Are we talking about the letter?" she asks, overhearing the end of our conversation. She cups a steaming mug and gracefully plops down on the ottoman, ankles crossed. "Moffy, it was truly beautiful."

I frown. "You've read it?"

"Oui," she says like it's nothing.

My desire to find this letter has now escalated to a million.

A buzzing phone slices into our conversation. Farrow finds his vibrating cell on the cushion. I catch the Caller ID on the illuminated screen: *Oscar Oliveira*.

Farrow clutches the phone without answering. For a long moment. Wavering on picking up the call.

Security is on a separate smaller yacht that cruises in line with ours. And not all of our bodyguards are there. Some stayed back on land in Mykonos. Others take care of our properties in Philly.

But all of SFO are on that yacht, and it's one short boat ride on the rib to board it.

Farrow hasn't gone over there once. It's different now that he's a concierge doctor and not at Philly General all day. He's confronted face-to-face with his old life on security a hundred times more.

And he has no radio for that quick hotline into SFO, and he'll tell you that he didn't lose anything that really mattered because he has me.

But in reality, he's lost that part of his life, and I'm not sure he'll ever get it back.

It hurts thinking about it, and luckily, his ringing phone breaks apart my thoughts.

"You going to answer that?" I ask.

He keeps his forearm on his knee and flips his phone in his hand a few times. "He's most likely just inviting me to security's boat." He makes a choice though and presses *speaker*. Answering the call.

Music blasts in the background. "Redford!" Oscar yells. "Get your ass over here! Bring the Boyfriend!"

The Boyfriend. I've heard Oscar call me that a billion times, and I'm not gonna lie, it still fucking gets to me. In a good way. *I'm someone's boyfriend.*

Maybe, in time, that title can be something more. The ring box is in my yacht cabin, but I don't want to propose on my birthday.

I'm still waiting for *the* moment.

"You're on speaker, and I'm relaxing, Oliveira," Farrow says. "You're killing my mood."

Oscar laughs. "Come on. Donnelly and Kitsuwon miss your face, and my little bro is acting like he lost his favorite Golden Retriever."

"Eh, no," Farrow says like that's that.

Maybe he doesn't want to confront what he lost by being on security's boat. "You guys can come over here," I tell Oscar. "Bring SFO."

Farrow tilts his head at me, but a smile plays at the corners of his mouth.

"The parents awake?" Oscar asks. "Most of us have been drinking. We're off-duty tonight, but five-sixths of us care about making bad impressions."

"Who's the one-sixth?" Jane asks curiously, knuckles to her chin as she leans closer to the cell.

"Donnelly," Farrow tells her.

"They're not on the main deck," I tell Oscar. "They're probably not even going to be out here for the rest of the night."

"Good enough for all of us," Oscar says. "See you in fifteen."

I stand off the couch, swinging my right arm in another stretch.

Farrow tosses aside his phone and watches me.

My feet are close to the pool. "You know I'm better than you at back-flipping," I banter.

He pops a bubble in his mouth. "Marginally."

"Colossally," I rebut.

He's about to respond, but the sliding glass doors push open. My little brother storms barefoot onto the main deck in sweatpants and an old *New Mutants* tee.

I solidify.

Some of Xander's favorite vacations are on the yacht. No pressure to leave the boat, no strangers hounding him, and for the most part, he's been in good spirits.

The way he approaches me with a darkening scowl—I'm aware that something is vitally wrong.

Out of the corner of my eye, I see Janie setting down her coffee and standing off the ottoman. Farrow also rises to his feet.

I turn towards my brother. "You okay, Summers?"

"You tell me," Xander snaps loudly, his phone gripped in a fist, knuckles whitened.

The chatty girl squad in the hot tub suddenly falls silent. On another set of couches, Eliot, Luna, and Tom are smoking—and their heads turn. Charlie, Beckett, and Sullivan look up from their game of Catan at an outdoor table. And Ben Cobalt stops reading his book on nature conservatories, only two lounge chairs away.

You tell me.

I shake my head once, confused. It's not like Xander to draw attention to himself, but I'm witnessing so much hurt twisting up his face. And I step forward. "Xander?"

His chest rises and falls heavily. "So you didn't knock on Easton Mulligan's door and accuse him of taking my meds?"

Christ. "Xander—"

"Fuck you," he says. And that rips me open, but he can't see. Tears gather in his reddened eyes while I build barriers between me and my emotions.

I want to protect him, but I've never been in a situation where I've needed to protect him from something I did. From my choice, his mistake.

Our mistakes—*I'm sorry. I'm so fucking sorry.*

"You're my *brother*," Xander says like that word means life itself. He pushes the longer strands of his hair back, and I step one more foot closer.

He grew another inch this summer. We're the same height now, but I look at him and I just see my fragile little brother. And this is not what I wanted for him.

This is not how I saw things going.

I don't have a chance to speak yet; he's still getting it out.

"How could you even…?" His chin quakes. "…why wouldn't you…" His face is beet-red, and Jane nears us like she's about to put her arms around him.

Xander points his phone at her, the one in his death-grip. "*Don't.*"

She skids to a stop. A couple feet from me.

"I don't need you two doing that thing you do," he says in short breaths, "where you act like you're the big siblings who want to protect us."

"What you did was wrong," I say, my throat swollen. "And I am trying to protect you. I can't change that."

"I know what I did was wrong!" Xander screams and chokes on his words. "And I hate myself for it. And what are you even trying to protect me from?" He inhales sharply. "Myself? You can't protect me from myself. It's up here." He points to his head. "It's in here." He jabs his cell to his chest. "It's bigger than you or me. And you should have just…" His voice cracks. "…you should have come to me *first*. Not a kid down the street. Fucking…" He puts his hands on his head and glares at the night sky.

"I'm so sorry, Summers," I say, my hand outstretched to him. He's fighting tears that threaten to fall, and it hurts to watch. Hurts to speak, but I control everything for him. He doesn't need me to scream and sob. "I should have confronted you. *I should've*, but it's a heavy accusation. And I was fucking afraid. If you were supplying kids with drugs—"

"I stopped," Xander says, pained. "That's *over*." But he suddenly frowns, head hanging in a weighted thought. "You're going to tell Dad." It's not a question.

"No," I say. "You said it's over. I believe you."

"But what if I don't believe you," he says and walks backwards towards the saloon. He grinds down on his teeth and rubs his forearm to his watery eye.

I try to follow.

"*No*. I can't—I don't want to be around you," he cries. *He's crying.*

I nod stiffly. "Alright." I almost sway back, and Farrow nears me— and I shake my head at him. If he touches me, I will burst open and probably scream or cry or both. He's the only one that can make me come undone, and I'm not unraveling in front of all the teenagers.

Luna jogs across the deck to reach Xander. Her light brown hair whipping behind her, and she's still doing the plain outfit thing, no thanks to her asshole boyfriend. But Luna didn't invite Andrew on the trip. You should know that our dad hates him just as much as me, and he hasn't even met Andrew yet. Or seen how pushy and under-cutting he is.

I met him once and I almost punched him after he told my sister, "You're so much prettier when you don't swing your arms when you walk." Even though she doesn't see him as much, Luna said that I wasn't allowed to hang with them anymore. So there's that fallout. I'm just doing great with my siblings lately.

Perfect big brother.

The best, let me tell you.

I watch Luna hug Xander, and his body shudders against her gangly frame. And then Kinney climbs out of the hot tub in a black one-piece swimsuit. My youngest sister joins Luna and Xander, and they all leave into the main saloon. Glass doors sliding closed behind them.

I blink. Those are my three siblings.

All the Hales.

And I'm left here. *I hurt him. I hurt him.* I crack my taut neck, pressure on my chest.

"Maximoff," Farrow breathes.

I turn to face my boyfriend, chatter starting back up around the main deck. "You told me this would happen," I whisper, rubbing my knuckles. I see how he wants to take my hand in his hand. I see how he wants to bring me to his chest. It hurts even more to not draw closer, to not let him touch me, but I also can't—not here.

He inhales. "I said it was a bad idea. I didn't say *this* would happen."

I rest my hand on the back of my neck. "I'm okay."

"You're not okay," he says with another inhale, and his phone starts ringing. Oscar again.

Before he rejects the call for me, I tell him, "I'm going to find the letter you wrote Beckett."

He studies my expression, and I try to breathe better, stronger. Seeing that, he nods. "I'll take this, and we'll meet back up?"

"Yeah," I agree.

I think it's killing him not to kiss me in a short goodbye. He wavers. "I'm sorry—"

He cuts me off, "No, don't be. You're giving me more than enough, wolf scout. I'm here for what you need, and you need privacy." He lifts his brows. "Later?"

I nod. "Later." And I exhale even bigger.

Farrow has to redial Oscar since the call rung out, and while he returns to the couch, I pop my knuckles and head to Beckett, Charlie, and Sulli's table. Game pieces spread out, colorful cards in hand.

A gold dragon-headed cane is propped against the table. Eliot has been swapping out Charlie's canes every so often with new ones. And whenever I see my cousin, his newest cane looks more ostentatious and bizarre.

Beckett leans back on his chair, cigarette between his lips. I've been so goddamn concerned about Beckett, but since he's not using right now, the most I can do is check in with Charlie. Which is difficult since Charlie ignores me more than half the time. But until Beckett returns to ballet, it has to be enough.

"Hey, Beck," I say. "Where's the letter Farrow gave you? I want to read it." Can't think of a better pick-me-up.

"Oh yeah, it's a good fucking letter," Sulli says with a strong nod, rolling dice.

Jesus. Has everyone really read this letter but me?

"It's in my cabin. Top dresser." Beckett taps ash into an ashtray, and very meticulously, he wipes the rim. Charlie watches his twin brother more fixatedly than usual.

"Thanks."

"I like him, by the way," Beckett tells me honestly. "Farrow, he's really good for you."

My eyes almost grow. *Is this letter magical or something?*

Charlie says to the table, "Does anyone have any sheep they'd trade for brick?"

"Fuck, you can take all my sheep for wood or wheat," Sulli says.

I walk away and tune out Charlie's response. My bare feet pad along the deck, and I slip through the sliding glass doors. Entering the main saloon, this living room area is quiet and dimly lit. I thought I'd find my brother and sisters here, but all three are gone.

I ascend winding steps to the second-floor where there's a stretch of cabins. In the hall, I slow down at a door, muffled voices filtering through.

"Love you too, Luna," Xander says, his breath caught short again. A giant part of me wants to go inside that cabin and fix this. But he made it clear that he wanted space, and I think I should give him that.

I pass their door, and then another one at the end of the hall swings open.

Rowin emerges from his cabin.

He's really the last person I want to run into right now, but I try to be casual; in my head I'm taking solace in the fact that these next few days will be his last with my family.

"Hey, Rowin," I say, still on course to Beckett's cabin.

"Hi, Maximoff."

And I feel his blue eyes travel all over my body: my bare chest, my abs, my arms and legs, my dick. It's making me more aware that

I'm barely covered in a skin-tight bathing suit. And I'm used to eyes pressing on my body. Ogling and gawking, all normal for me. But not from my man's ex-boyfriend.

I glare. "Can you not do that?" Not only am I fucking uncomfortable, but I can feel just how badly this would pain and enrage Farrow.

Needing to move forward, I don't wait for Rowin to respond. I just rotate to the door on my right, and I grip the knob to Beckett's cabin. I turn—it's locked.

Great.

I suddenly marbleize...

I sense his presence encroaching my space. But my brain shrieks, *there's no way, there's no damn way this is happening.* My brows knit, and I slowly check behind my shoulder.

Rowin slinks up on me, seemingly so rapidly because my reflexes lurch in shock. His intrusive gaze is tearing off my swimsuit, his hands dangerously close. I whip around at the same time that his hands sink on either side of the door.

Trapping me for a tense beat while his mouth tries to near mine—I shove his chest with all my goddamn strength.

His back thumps into the wall, disbelief widening his eyes.

"What the fuck are you doing?" I glower, winded and pained like I'm currently running the ultra-marathon on the roughest fucking terrain.

"Come on," Rowin says like I'm oblivious, and he tucks a piece of his deep auburn hair behind his ear.

My eyes scald, probably bloodshot, and ten tons of brick compound on my chest. "Stay the fuck away from me." How I'm not slamming my fist in his jaw, I don't know. Rage is my go-to feeling, but I think...I think I'm in a lot of shock.

His face contorts in indignation. "I like you, and you're into me—"

"No, I fucking hate you," I spit out, my skin crawling. I'm about to tell him that his ass is going to be flung off this yacht, but he takes a step forward and I raise a warning hand. "You come near me, and I'll break both your kneecaps."

I'm yelling internally, my ribs concaving around my lungs and shrinking my fucking breath.

Farrow—*he's not here.* I love him so damn much that I can already feel the pain he'll feel from this moment. But for some reason, I only wish he were right by my side. Maybe because I know he can carry the weight with me. I know he can bear it.

"Come on," Rowin repeats. "You and me would fit more than you and him. You're kind, considerate and sweet, and he's..." Our heads swerve as a cabin door cracks open.

No.

No.

"Moffy?" Luna peeks her head out, concern and fear wobbling her voice. I'm not sure how much my siblings heard, but I have one mission now: shield them from this doomsday.

"I'm okay. Go back inside." I move towards her, stoic and unbending. Rowin—I feel him lingering in the hall, closer to me than I fucking like.

But I reach my sister's cabin, and I notice Kinney and Xander right behind Luna, their eyes huge like saucers. Uncertain of what to do and scared.

"I'm okay," I say strongly. My eyes have to be bloodshot because they stare at them like it's the only evidence that I'm not. "I'm okay. You're all safe, and I'm going to shut this door—"

"No, Moffy!" all three shout like I'm exiting a bomb shelter to face certain death. The intensity of their reaction startles me a bit, and I try to think back on what they could've heard:

Can you not do that?

What the fuck are you doing?

Come on.

Stay the fuck away from me.

I like you and you're into me.

No, I fucking hate you. You come near me, and I'll break both your kneecaps.

Come on.

Fucking Christ. That's it, that's all they could know.

Luna grabs my hand, looking from me to Rowin. He's in my peripheral, and I don't acknowledge him or curse him out. Because I'm trying not to frighten my siblings.

I guide her further into the small cabin, a nautical comforter on two single beds. Luna drifts backwards with Xander and Kinney, and I slip further inside, shutting and locking the door behind me.

"I'm not in any danger," I tell them. "You don't need to panic. Alright, Kinney. *Kinney.*" I force out her name; my thirteen-year-old sister has buried her face in her hands. "*I'm okay.*"

My harsh tone pops up her head, and she scrutinizes me.

"I'm okay," I repeat.

"Then stay," Kinney snaps at me, her voice cracking in a brief sob.

I can't. I need to get Rowin off this fucking yacht. She can tell that I'm planning to go back out, and she wails at me like I'm being reckless with my life and throws a pillow at my face.

"Kinney." I smack the pillow away. "I'll be back."

She gears up to chuck another pillow.

"*Stop*, Kinney," Xander cuts in, his cheeks blotchy and tear-streaked. His face is flooding with remorse and pain. "Moffy has been beaten down enough tonight from me, you don't need to do that too—"

"Summers," I say with the shake of my head. "You could tell me to rot in hell, and I'd still overwhelming, unconditionally be there for you and love you—there is nothing you can do to push me down. Alright?"

Xander rakes his hand over his face, hot tears pouring out. "I'm sorry. I'm fucking sorry. I didn't mean what I said earlier. I love you, you know I love you, right?"

I didn't think I needed to hear that, but maybe some part of me did. I breathe more, and I nod. "Yeah," I say. "In every universe."

I wrap my arms around my brother's shoulders. Same height, he hooks an arm around mine, his head hung while he rubs his eyes.

He murmurs, "I can't live without you…"

My eyes try to well, and I whisper, "I love you." I open my stance for Kinney and Luna. "All three of you." And our sisters join the hug. My arms envelope my younger siblings, and I can feel them cling onto me.

I breathe and breathe. Knowing they're safe calms me, and when we all pull back, I glance at the locked door.

Luna tries to hide her face in her white shirt. "Where's Farrow?"

"I'm about to go get him," I say. "You three stay here. I'll be back later."

They're not as uneasy. My confidence in this situation helps—the *I can handle anything* mantra pouring out of me—and they nod me forward.

I exit the cabin and shut the door.

The hall is empty. No Rowin.

New mission: find Farrow and then push Rowin off this yacht.

35

FARROW KEENE

Light rain patters the mega yacht, and an overhang shields half of the main deck from the drizzle. I'm dry, sitting behind the fully stocked bar. Mostly so none of Maximoff's cousins can see me daze the hell out.

I can't rid the nauseous scent of rain on metal.

Reaching into the bar's cabinet, I grab a bottle of Grey Goose. I try to untwist, and I hear *ping ping ping.*

I stare off into nothingness.

Listening.

And someone rips the bottle out of my hands.

Sensory overload, I'm not going to be able to discern who just stole my vodka. At least not right away.

Seeing as how six protective motherfuckers have been towering above me, I'll take an educated guess and say it's someone from SFO.

I blink, and I see Banks Moretti crouching and opening the Grey Goose. Brown hair curled behind his ears, eyes the color of a coffee bean, unshaven jaw—he looks absolutely identical to his twin brother in almost every way.

He's officially an Omega bodyguard, but I wasn't there for that security meeting. Obviously I couldn't be.

And thankfully these guys know that I wasn't planning on drinking the vodka. Banks does what I was about to do and holds the bottle beneath my nose.

"Smell that, Redford?" Oscar asks me.

I hang my forearms on my bent knees. "Not even a little bit."

"Shoulda brought the pizza from our boat," Donnelly says. "Pizza smells better than vodka." True.

My fingers press into the ground, about to rise to my feet, but I suddenly feel gravel digging into my palms. It's not real…

There's no gravel on the boat.

"Hold up, don't stand," Akara tells me, an ace at leadership, even when I'm not a part of the team anymore.

Thatcher hands a bottle of water to Banks to give me, and when he does, I unscrew the cap with more focus. I see my surroundings clearly. My other senses are a little out of whack from the intrusive memories. *Maximoff.*

I don't see him. He's not back yet, but he most likely ran into his siblings inside. Xander has a hard time staying angry at his older brother, so I imagine they're patching-up their fight.

Akara sets his beer aside. "Is it just the rain?"

"Yeah, it's been a hotspot." I comb my hair back and eye the beer bottle. "Don't stop drinking on my account, Kitsuwon."

Quinn swigs his beer at that, and Oscar gives his baby brother a look like he shouldn't be listening to me.

I almost smile, my pulse gradually beginning to even out. And I take a gulp of water.

"Should you go inside the saloon?" Akara asks.

"No, if I avoid it, it's just going to persist." This kind of PTSD isn't new to me, and I'm fairly certain I have the tools to move past this. It's just a process that takes patience, but the bad timing is frustrating as hell.

Rain on metal. It's suddenly three times as pungent. "An orange?" I ask vaguely.

"In the galley," Akara tells Quinn, and Quinn leaves to return quickly with the fruit.

I concentrate on peeling the rind. Citrus overpowers my nose. *There we go.* My pulse is slowing, and Donnelly starts rehashing a story about how Quinn slipped off the rib.

And I rise to my feet. More at ease, I lean on the sleek bar, and the glass doors slide open in front of us. I set down the partially peeled orange. Donnelly goes quiet, and we all look at who walks on deck.

"Farrow."

It's Rowin.

Fucking hell.

My ex glances cautiously at SFO while he closes the saloon doors. "I need to talk to you," he tells me. This entire yacht trip, he's been passive aggressive and petulant towards me, but as he approaches me now, he's neither of those things.

He's acting cagey as fuck.

"Go ahead." I wave him onward.

"In private," Rowin clarifies.

I narrow my gaze. "No. I don't give a shit if SFO hears."

But he does. He runs a hand down his tense face, staying about three arm's lengths away from me. "I just wanted to clear the air with you."

"You want to clear the air with me?" I repeat like his screw has come loose. "Today of all days?" It's my boyfriend's birthday.

"It only just came up." Rowin glances out at the starry night. Lanterns light up the wet deck.

And the rain has stopped.

I watch him shift his weight. I don't like this.

Something's not right. My gut is screaming, and I straighten off the bar.

Rowin jabs a thumb behind his shoulder, pointing at the saloon. "I ran into Maximoff inside. And I misread a few signals. It shouldn't be a big deal; he said he wasn't interested."

My pulse spikes as I try to decipher this shit. "Are you...?" My face twists in agonized thought. "Are you saying that you came onto my boyfriend?"

There's no way in hell that can be right.

Rowin avoids my gaze. "Like I said, I misread the signals."

I explode forward. "What the fuck is wrong with you?!" I yell between my teeth.

SFO yells over one another, trying to separate me from Rowin before we even collide. My ex stumbles back and holds up a hand in surrender.

"You're a piece of shit," I sneer and shrug off my friends that try to restrain me, and I glare at Donnelly. "*Let go.*"

He does.

They all do.

Claws may as well be shredding my entire body and heart and skull. I don't know what Rowin did exactly, if he threw out a pickup line or…I can't imagine…

I rub my mouth and take a deeper breath. I center my emotion on something productive. Bile burns the back of my throat, and everything inside of me is *screaming* to find Maximoff. Adrenaline ramped, pulse beating in my eardrums.

Find him.

I push past SFO and hawk-eye the sliding glass door, about to go inside. Four steps there, I change course. Instinct propels me, and I swerve onto Rowin. In one swift move, I twist his shirt in two white-knuckled fists and slam his back up against the glass.

"If I find out you touched him, I will kill you," I threaten.

Rowin is only looking at SFO behind me. He's waiting for the six guys to come to his aid. But not a single one moves. None of them save him. None of them want to.

Because they're not his friends.

They're mine.

And they know he's a piece of fucking shit. I release my grip because I see a figure through the glass. Inside the saloon, Maximoff just steps off the winding staircase.

"Akara," I say, but he immediately detains Rowin before I ask. Pulling him far, far away from the entrance to the saloon.

I waste no more time.

I go inside.

"Maximoff," I call out, quickly sliding the door shut. He's in almost no clothing. A skin-tight swimsuit cut like boxer-briefs—*if Rowin touched him…*

My nose flares, and I realize that Maximoff is on a fucking mission. Storming past the interior cocktail bar with stoicism and purpose, he gestures behind me and asks, "Is Rowin out there?"

I rapidly sweep his sharpened features. "What happened?" I don't move away from this door because wolf scout is coming in hot. He has one sole focus. And it's not on me right now.

"We need to get Rowin off this yacht. We can toss his suitcase in the sea for all I fucking care, but he needs out of here." He fixates on the door.

"SFO have him—" I cut myself off and sidestep before Maximoff passes me. I block him with my build.

"Farrow." His Adam's apple bobs.

"Look at me, *look at me*," I breathe, our chests an inch apart, and as soon as I capture his attention, I say, "You need to tell me what happened, Maximoff."

He blinks, eyes completely bloodshot. "Rowin trapped me against a door, but he didn't put his hands on me. I shoved him off. That's it."

I almost rock back, like I've been sucker-punched. "He trapped you…against a door?" I picture it, and my chest just collapses. I reach out to hold Maximoff. To touch him, but I wait for the confirmation.

He nods repeatedly.

Over and over.

We draw together. Chest to chest. His arms weave across my back, his rigid body not slackening. And I feel his pulse racing.

I whisper against his ear, "You're safe, wolf scout." I kiss his jaw, and he grips my neck with a shuddered breath.

"Fuck," Maximoff growls, pinching his eyes. He buries his face in the crook of my neck. And he screams. An angered, tormented noise barrels out of him. All this caged emotion is muffled against my shoulder and neck—and I hold him. Fuck, I'm not letting go.

I clutch him more securely. So he feels like nothing and no one will breach this embrace.

My pulse thumps hard, and his hot involuntary tears soak my skin. I whisper in his ear. Until he eases, and his breath matches my breath. It takes minutes. Not seconds, but actual *minutes*. I would've stood here like this for hours if he needed me to.

And when he raises his head, rubbing the corners of his reddened eyes—he sees the wet deck through the glass.

His face drops. "Did it rain?"

Maximoff.

I tell him I wasn't alone. I tell him that I love him. I tell him not to worry because I'm not worried about it, and he lets me hold more of his weight.

Earlier today when Maximoff said that he didn't like Rowin being onboard—because he feared for my safety—I should've taken that into account more. I just brushed it off because I thought Rowin would only antagonize me. Not him.

Never him.

As soon as Maximoff shared his unease, I should've had Rowin's ass on land.

I won't make that mistake again.

36

MAXIMOFF HALE

Our cabin almost seems to sway with the rocking boat. Waves crash against the window, and despite all the bad that's happened today, this right here is peaceful.

Farrow and I are intertwined together on the full-sized bed, and I can't tell you if I'm holding him or if he's holding me. We've been like this for an hour. Softly talking. Sometimes just staring. Letting the night slow with our breaths.

When we're both at a better place, I lean over his chest and reach for the letter on the nightstand, using my left arm. Someone, probably Beckett, shoved it under the crack of our door about five minutes ago. And I've been craving to read it ever since.

"Do you want me to read it out loud?" I ask Farrow. He runs a hand under my T-shirt and rubs my back, his palm warm against my skin.

His lips lift. "I wrote it, wolf scout. I know what it says."

"Thanks, I retract my offer." I fall back onto my spine, the mattress bouncing. Our limbs have been wrestling with the navy sheets; we're all entwined in them. I stuff another pillow under my head. More supported but still lying down.

In a swift, seamless movement, Farrow rolls on his side and props his head with his hand. Elbow to the pillow. Facing me, he asks, "Would you like me to leave the room?" His smile widens. "Give you some private time."

"What kind of letter is this, man?"

"According to your cousins," he says. "A really fucking great one."

I eye him for a second, dipping into my churning thoughts. "Do you care that almost everyone in my family has already read it?" Maybe this isn't something he wanted to be passed around.

His lips press to mine, a brief, loving kiss, before he whispers, "I knew when I gave it to Beckett that I'd be giving it to your whole family. I'm good with that."

I stare at the folded piece of paper. You need to know that despite all the doomsdays and all the apocalypses—excitement still bursts in my chest.

Right now.

Because of him.

I didn't think I'd feel this tonight, not after everything, but here I am. Pretty damn close to smiling, and I haven't even read the letter.

Farrow hooks his leg with mine, growing quiet while he watches me unfold the paper. About to read his words.

His handwriting is long and fluid, as casual as he is.

Dear Beckett,

You once asked if I had something to hide. And in so little words, I replied by telling you to stay out of my relationship. Looking back, I should have said something different.

I should have told you that I'm a private person. That the idea of anyone digging into my relationship was both foreign and uncomfortable. When it came to my past boyfriends, my father asked the bare minimum. Being confronted by you was a lesson in love — a different kind that I'd never known.

I should have told you that <u>I'm in love with him.</u> An indescribable kind of love. And I realize now, loving Maximoff entirely means letting his family in. Because the day that I'm the reason there's tension between him and you is the day I've failed him.

I should have told you that my mother isn't going to be here for my future. For a wedding or kids. I've known that since I was four. But what I also know is that every day that goes by, I live to make her proud. And the only way I know how to do that is to live for love and to ensure that wherever I go, whatever I do, I am fulfilled.

I should have told you that without him, my life would be empty.

I should have told you that I'm prideful, and I would never admit that I had things to learn. But I did. And still do. He's already taught me more than enough about goodness, morality, and unconditional love. But I still hope for a future where that doesn't end. Where he's still teaching me things that I'll tell you I'd already known.

I should have told you that I care about what you think. And I want you to trust me with him. One day, I hope you can.

Sincerely,

Farrow Redford Keene

My breath deepens, eyes burning. People talk about grand gestures, but this one feels monumental and immeasurably gigantic. And I know this letter was for Beckett and my family, but I think he knew it would be for me, too.

I fold the letter back, creasing the seams. He runs his fingers through the thicker pieces of my hair.

Words. So many damn words are jumbled in my head but none feel right. So I just blurt out, "You underlined *I'm in love with him*." My voice is choked.

"Yeah, I did that," he nods, his gaze roping me in. Like I'm being tugged beneath serene water, swimming. Swimming. Alive.

I lean over, hand to his cheek, and my mouth crushes against his mouth with deep, *deep* emotion that pools hot inside of me. Deepening the kiss, I push my body into him, and a noise catches in his throat.

He rolls on top of me, our breaths and bodies colliding together.

Next morning, the sun hasn't risen yet. But
I'm awake and semi-ready for a pre-planned training session with Sulli off the yacht. I'm not bailing on the ultra-marathon next month.

Which means I need to move my ass and run.

I say *semi*-ready because I'm kind of, sort of, exhausted from my tornado of a birthday. I've never had a hangover. But this has to be close to the feeling.

I breathe easier knowing Rowin is gone and fired. SFO kicked him off the boat last night, and I heard he took a flight back to Philly. Thankfully Farrow has a high immunity against regret and remorse, and I'm so damn happy that he's not eaten up with blame for Rowin's actions. For most shit storms, he maintains a *not happening again* attitude and moves forward with me.

The two of us—we're fueling a lot of family drama and gossip these days. And by gossip, I mean they're all just whispering the truth.

"What the ever loving fuck?" Sulli gawks back at me. "Is snot running out of your nose?"

I rub my sweaty, snot-running face with the bottom of my green muscle shirt and then spit a wad of phlegm. Drop-dead-gorgeous, *me*. Clearly marriage quality, *me*.

Struggling to run up all 588 steps of the Karavolades Stairs in the Cyclades Islands, *me again*.

As the sun begins to crest the Aegean Sea, warm light bathes the winding, cobbled stairs that stretch up a rocky cliffside. Starting at the seaport, Sullivan, Akara, Farrow, Jack, my bodyguard, and I have been ascending the weaving steps towards the town Fira, the capital of Santorini.

My endurance is up to par. What's really kicking my ass is the cobbled ground. The hard, uneven terrain beneath my soles sends shockwaves up my body. Rattling my shoulders and my slowly healing collarbone in this imperceptible, painful way.

"I'm not dying," I say confidently to Sulli, who has braked three stairs ahead of me. Her Camp Calloway baseball cap shades her green eyes from the growing light. She uses the pitstop to stretch her muscular arm across her chest.

My cousin is not even winded.

Whereas Akara and Farrow are panting, both drenched in sweat and catching their breaths. Jack is also beat, but he has the added weight of a light steadicam contraption attached to his chest.

All four stare down at me like *Stubborn Fool* is written in bold letters across my forehead. Farrow, in particular, has been eyeing me with a bucket load of concern but also amusement.

"I'm keeping up," I add. "Go, don't stop." I start back up into a jog.

And they follow suit before I can even pass them.

If this were a race, I wouldn't be in last. My bodyguard has fallen way behind. Bruno is in really good shape for fifty-two, but he's bulkier than us, his muscle mass weighing him down.

Each pounding step is a razor blade. And a jolt of pain.

For Christ's sake, my stomach churns. And the switchbacks, the constant curving of the steps, don't help defeat nausea.

Keep up with Farrow. I repeat that mantra. Focusing on that, I start closing the gap. He runs at Akara's brisk pace, Sulli outracing them by two stairs.

I try harder. Sweat dripping down my temples.

I go faster. Breath blazing in my burning lungs.

But no matter how far I strain my muscles, how much I push, how much pain I endure, it's not good enough. It's not where I need to be for Sulli.

Push harder.

I do.

And my rubber sole slips on wet cobblestone. Fuck.

Fuck.

I almost go down—I reach out, grabbing the back of Farrow's white tee. My boyfriend instantly extends his tattooed arm backwards, catching my forearm. And then he pulls me up to his side. All the while we're still moving.

My pulse skips a beat. The effortless affection striking me hot.

Farrow is smiling at me, knowingly, but it fades fast. And he calls out to the others, "Stop!"

I'm on my knees in a flash. Puking off the side of these old steps. Farrow crouches and puts a hand on my back.

"Moffy." Sulli skips down the stairs to me. "Oh fuck."

I spit off the cliffside, my head whirling. "I'm alright." The amount of times Farrow has seen me upchuck is startling.

"Drink this." Farrow hands me a 32 oz. blue water bottle.

"Thanks," I say seriously. I unscrew the wide cap, and I glance back at the camera pointed at me. "Possibility that tourists will take pictures next to my puke spot?" I try to lighten the mood that I've sunk.

"High," Jack says, adjusting his camera settings. "It happened to someone in a boy band."

Akara wipes sweat off his forehead. "I heard about that." He looks at Jack. "Fans sold his puke on eBay too?"

"Yep. Double whammy," Jack says, unsnapping a buckle or something to the steadicam and giving his shoulders a breather from the weight.

"Chile is fucking rougher than this," Sulli tells me while I swig my water.

"I know." I rise to my feet, Farrow's hand hovering by my waist in case I go down. I'm up.

I'm stable.

I can run.

Pain thumps in my collar, swelling like a balloon that expands inside a space too cramped, too small. I clear a knot in my throat. Take another swig of water.

"I'm alright to run," I tell my cousin.

Her grit and willpower is even greater and stronger than mine. Reverse our positions where she's the one injured, and I'm pretty sure she'd be pushing beyond the limit. And maybe that's why she's not able to stop me.

It reminds me of yesterday. I don't know why. But I think about the moment where we were on the stern's swim deck.

Sullivan was flexing, showing off her carved bicep. She kissed it.

Luna stuck out her tongue, no piercing, but she must've eaten something blue. Janie tossed her arms in the air. And Farrow and I—we were mid-teasing, our arms wrapped around each other.

My mom, out in the sea on an inner tube, snapped that picture. And when Luna saw the photo, she said, "Alpha chicks and dudes."

"Total-fucking-ly," Sulli smiled.

Jane beamed. "Oui."

The media has latched onto Farrow and me as alphas. Not always as a compliment. And hearing my sister and cousins use that word to describe themselves made me love it more.

I blink out of a short stupor. Only to see Sulli and Akara facing one another. One stair above me. Seriousness tensing their postures and faces—I must've missed the start of some sort of talk.

"You have lots of friends, Sul," Akara says.

"Who?" Sulli says wide-eyed like he's not living in the same universe as her right now.

My scowl deepens, and I slowly twist the cap back on my water.

"Dean." Akara takes off his backwards hat, pushing back his black hair. "He's your friend."

"No, he's just a swim buddy at the club," Sulli says.

"A buddy is a friend." His smile peeks.

Sulli sets her hands on her head, distraught. "It's not the fucking same when I have to censor myself with them, Kits. And I already suck at talking to people. My little sister would hate it if I said anything about her and someone spilled it online."

Saying a private thing to the wrong person—it can be frightening for us. The consequence could hurt the people we love.

"Hey," Akara says, "with that criteria you still have *lots* of friends."

"Who?" she asks, breathing harder than she has been running up this damn cliff.

"Your family," he says strongly. "*Family* can be *friends*, Sulli." He emphasizes both words. "Not all family is as close as yours, and you made those bonds. You did that."

She touches her lips, contemplating.

"And I'm your friend. And…" Akara motions to his left. "Jack is your friend."

Farrow and I look over, and Jack Highland smiles a charming smile to Sulli while he reattaches his steadicam.

Sulli shakes her head repeatedly.

"Sullivan, right in the heart," Jack says playfully, not really hurt.

"Oh hey, I know we're friends, and I was excited about that because I can trust you, but it's different…" She hangs her head, hand to her eyes.

I'm about to go comfort my cousin.

But Akara steps forward. "Sulli."

She holds out her hand to stop him from edging near. "I just feel like you stole him from me. Like Jack was supposed to be the perfect fucking friend, the guy I could hang with, the one I could talk to about anything without fear—and now you two are best friends and where am I?" She pauses. "Not that…I mean, I wouldn't *claim* a friend like that…I just…" Her cheeks roast bright red.

I walk up one step, her embarrassment eking into the air.

"Sulli," Akara starts, worried.

She looks left and right for a quick exit; she whips around and sprints. Up the hundreds of stairs. Fleeing.

Goddammit. I bolt after Sulli, and before Akara chases after her, I tell him to give us a second. Farrow and Akara are following us, but at a distance.

"Sullivan!" I shout, pain stabbing my collarbone. Water in my tight grip. I shift the bottle to my left hand since it adds weight.

She slows on the curve of a switchback. Sun growing hotter with the morning light. I breathe through my nose and wipe my temples with my bicep.

"OhmyfuckingGod," she squats, face in her hands. "What did I say, Moffy? Why'd I fucking say that?"

I crouch in front of my cousin. "Because that's what you felt. It's okay, Sulli."

"I sounded like a fucking brat," she mumbles against her palms and groans. "Nothing is going right." She's referring to more than this moment.

On the yacht, she confessed to Ryke, her dad, about passing out twice after drinking. Uncle Ryke is pretty much a pushover when it comes to his two daughters. But not on serious issues, and at the news, he looked *fucking horrified.*

Now Sulli only wants to drink if it's at home, not in a public place. I think it's a good idea. But I also think her dad's reaction scared her more than actually passing out.

"You just sounded like you were expressing yourself," I tell my cousin.

She takes a bigger breath and glances down the stairs to where Akara, Jack, and Farrow climb up. "I'm going to be replaying this moment in my head for eternity. Fuck my life."

"Don't stress about it, Sul. Really." I nod towards the stairs, knowing that there's only one thing that will take her mind off this. "Race you?"

She gives me a wide-eyed look, but I don't wait for her to say it's a bad "fucking" idea.

I just go.

And she runs with a skilled, untiring stride. Soon, she's passing me, and the three other guys catch up to my pace.

I'm not slowing. Not stopping.

I want something to go right for Sulli.

And I push and push and push. Temperature escalating, humid and hot, the harsh drumming in my bones roils my stomach to the umpteenth degree. Around the 400th cobbled step, my body revolts against my persistence.

Lightheaded, clammy, nauseous—I stop dead in place. My hamstrings spasms, and every muscle feels like it's cramping at the same time.

How I'm standing—I don't know.

Farrow skids to a halt next to me. He's slowed down the last ten minutes for me. I hate that he has, but he has and he holds my neck while I try to rub my hamstrings.

I look up at him deeply, and there's no amusement in his features anymore. I've reached the threshold of what Farrow is willing to take.

He endures more than anyone else could or would with me. Because I can't live life feeling restrained or imprisoned.

And he makes me feel so goddamn weightless. But if I don't respect my body's limits, he's going to—and my chest rises because I know this is it.

This is the end of my fight. Of all the physical pain that I've withstood in fear of disappointing her and myself.

"You're human," Farrow says toughly, clutching my face with so much love and care. "You're *human*. Step back, wolf scout."

Step back.

Maybe if I had more time. Maybe if I didn't need surgery. So many maybes could've changed this, but *maybe* this is what I really needed all along. The hardest things are usually the right things, and pushing my body to extremes is too easy for me.

I hang onto Farrow's shoulder for support. "Sulli!" I shout.

She races down the steps. "Moffy, what happened?" Once she stops on the step above mine, I let it out.

"I can't do it." My eyes sear. "I can't do the ultra."

She expels a giant breath, hands on her thighs hunched forward. "Thank fucking God."

I've known that she's been afraid I'd hurt myself, but I thought if I could do it for her—it'd mean something in the end.

I was wrong. I think quitting meant more.

37

FARROW KEENE

Beach parties with the Hales, Meadows, and Cobalts consist of one massive sandcastle competition, and since I'm with Maximoff, I've been recruited onto Team Hale.

And if I look at the water's edge—which I try not to do all that much—SFO are on-duty and placing bets on this contest.

"Wait, I'm confused," Xander says. "How do we make the towers pointed?"

"Just pack it in," Lily replies. "Pack that sand in." She pats at the base of the structure. Being brutally honest here: it looks like nothing.

We've been at this shit for ten minutes, and the furthest we've reached is a huge mound of sand that's supposed to be the mountain beneath the castle. Maximoff shaves the "sculpture" flat with a shovel, and I lean back on my hands. More or less watching.

His movements are tensed like his entire body is sore. Muscles shot. The source: the stair climb from this morning. It's hard to believe he's even out here and not resting.

But that's classic Maximoff Hale. At least he listened to his doctor and soaked in an ice bath before the beach party.

I'm his doctor, by the way.

I catch myself unconsciously smiling before I focus back on my boyfriend.

Maximoff takes a quick glance at the competition, then turns back to the mound of sand. "You know," he tells us, "we still have time to build something other than Hogwarts."

My smile widens as Xander, Kinney, Luna, and their parents look at Maximoff like he's spoken blasphemy.

"Because I love you," his dad says, "I'm going to forget you said that, bud."

Maximoff wipes sand off his hands and onto his bathing suit trunks. He's eagle-eyeing the two other sandcastles-in-the-making.

"Someone's competitive," I tease him.

He fixates on my upturning lips and my piercing. "I'm compensating for your slacking," he rebuts.

"That's cute." I just stop there.

His neck almost flushes, and he's trying to stay on course. But I'm definitely distracting him. When he gets a better look at the competition, he says, "Christ."

"What?" Lily pops up. "Are we losing?"

"We're definitely losing," I answer, not needing to look. Bodyguard Facts: if you're looking to *win* a wager, you don't bet on the Hales. I was the only one who ever did. And right about now, the radio in my ear would be full of nonsensical shit.

I almost roll my eyes at myself. Fuck, I really, *really* don't want to reflect on that. Because at the end of the day, I would never trade being a concierge doctor for security. Medicine is a part of me, and I can't shake that need and that hunger. Being able to help these families with my medical skillset, it's invaluable to me. And my father would say, *I told you so.*

But at least he never gave me a hard time when I quit my residency and decided not to be board-certified. He was just proud I'm still working as a doctor. Because using my talent matters more to him than any prestige. On top of that, he texted me this morning.

I'm sorry about Rowin. We should have enough hands on the med team with you and me, and Trip may end his sabbatical. I wanted to let you know there's no plan to hire. We're keeping it in the family. — Dad

I sleep easy knowing that I chose the Keene legacy the second time around, and my father never forced my hand.

Back on the beach, Loren Hale scours the competition like his son just did. "You've got to be kidding me," Lo says.

I turn my head and try to peer around all the famous ones and distinguish the sand structures. The Cobalts are going the traditional route and building a huge castle. Complete with four turrets and the structure has motherfucking windows.

"Is that a moat?" Luna asks.

Sure enough, Eliot and Tom dig a hole towards the ocean, and Team Hale watches as the water fills up the tunnel that surrounds the Cobalt's castle.

"We're screwed," Kinney deadpans.

Next to Team Cobalt, the Meadows family compacts sand in the shape of a mermaid. Since they only have four team members, they were given a head start. Winona uses a twig to draw scales on the tail, and Sulli places seaweed as a bikini top. Their parents, Ryke and Daisy, make the mermaid's hair with seashells.

All the Hales look back at our sandcastle. The mound of sand resembles a mound of sand.

"I kinda like our sand thingie," Luna muses.

Xander nods. "It's more like the mountain of Hogwarts without the castle."

"Hogwarts Mountain," Kinney says flatly.

Maximoff pats the sand mound. "Better than their muggle castle." He looks over at me like he knows a word that I don't know.

He's always such a fucking dork. And I actually skimmed a few *Harry Potter* books after his mom gave them to me when I was on her security detail.

I'm about to tell him that he doesn't know more than me, but his gaze suddenly shifts towards his dad. Lo just stood up, and his attention is cemented onto me.

"Farrow, walk with me." Lo brushes sand off his hands. "The rest of Team Hale can build Hogwarts Mountain."

I look to my boyfriend, and Maximoff shakes his head like he's unsure of what this is about. I roll onto my knees, and seamlessly rise to my feet.

Maximoff is about to stand, but his dad quickly tells his son, "I'll bring him back in one piece. Sit. Relax. Eat a sandwich, you look pale."

He's not pale at all.

"Thanks, Dad," Maximoff says, sarcasm thick, and his brows scrunch at me like, *see you later, and you'll tell me every damn thing?*

I will.

But let's be honest, he's going to be agonizing over every second when I'm gone. Wondering what the hell his dad is talking to me about.

And truthfully, I don't have a good guess.

I follow Lo, step-for-step with him, and I rub my palms together, trying to scrape off the wet sand. We pass Team Cobalt, and their ridiculously large castle. Nine people are building this thing.

Lo edges closer and purposefully steps on one of the turrets. Demolishing it flat to the ground.

"Cheater!" most of the Cobalts boo and yell.

"Loren!" Rose yells above her seven kids. "You've reached a new level of low. Ruining the children's sandcastle."

"So now they're children?!" he yells back. "Because for two decades, I thought you've been calling them *gremlins*." She does call her kids gremlins.

It's widely known.

Rose curses at him, and he walks off, smiling.

At first glance it might look like Rose and Lo hate each other, but they've teamed up for most of the yacht trip. They raided the teenagers' cabins for cigarettes, and they're planning to toss all that shit into the beach bonfire tonight.

As we pass the sand mermaid, Ryke gives Lo a hard stare. "Don't even fucking think about it," Ryke warns his brother.

Lo touches his chest, and we move beyond the mermaid completely. He ends up walking backwards to add, "I'd never." He flashes a half-smile.

Ryke flips him off with two hands.

Based on Lo's current mood, I'd say he's most likely not delivering shit news to me. And if he is, he's being strangely coy.

We veer towards the water. He keeps walking, and I follow step-for-step beside him. I sink on the damper sand, and water rushes over the inked nautical wheels on my feet.

I glance back at Lo.

He's quiet. And the more we walk casually along the beach, the more distance we put between the sandcastles and ourselves. Lo's bodyguard follows us, but he's too far back to eavesdrop.

As the water rushes forward, I lightly splash with my foot. I'm trying to wrack my mind for any possible topic.

Nate, Maximoff's stalker—but that was so long ago.

The photo leak.

Maximoff's physical therapy.

Rowin, which happened just yesterday. Fuck, if it's about him...

I comb my hand through my hair. "Is this about Rowin?" I just go ahead and ask. "Because the guy I'd known would've never done that to Maximoff. If I had any idea..." I trail off, because I'm still pissed and upset about it. It's fresh, and my throat tries to swell closed.

Truth is, I would never be with a guy who was capable of what Rowin did.

Never.

Not for a day. Definitely not for two fucking years. Yet, I was with him for that long, and it disgusts the fuck out of me.

Lo looks at me with this soul-cutting empathy, his care and understanding usually reserved for family or the broken, fragile people he meets. "This isn't about Rowin, but how are you?" he asks genuinely. "I know that couldn't have been easy for you."

I frown, taken aback. This is a side of Lo that I haven't seen in a while. At least not towards me. "I'm pissed," I say, being honest. I shake my head a few times, and I run my tongue over my molars.

"I hope you're not blaming yourself," Lo tells me. "It's not your fault."

I nod strongly. I didn't need to hear those words to believe them, but for Lo to even say them to me—when his son is the one who was in the crossfire—it sits with me for a while. It stings my eyes.

Warm water laps over our feet. I almost smile at a sudden thought. "Maximoff says I have an immunity against remorse."

Lo snorts. "Jesus. He's so much like Lily…and my brother." He laughs lightly, but the sound fades when he looks back at me. "You're one of those people who say they have no regrets? I hate those people."

Shit, I can't help but smile. "Yeah, I'm one of those people. Or…" I tilt my head from side to side. "I try to be."

Lo contemplates this silently, and then he slows to a stop, an abandoned umbrella and beach chair nearby. And behind us, everyone is a speck in the distance, the sandcastles shapeless.

He faces me, and I see what most people do. Sharpness. From his defined cheekbones to the sentiments wielded in his amber eyes. Fuck, he's not a soft man. I imagine it'd feel more comfortable to stare down the pointed end of a sword.

"What I wanted to ask…" Lo glares up at the sky, piecing together his words before saying, "How are you and your dad?"

I let out a short breath. Not excited about where this could potentially be headed. Lo sees the kindness in my father, and I see it too. But… "We're on speaking terms, but there's not much there, Lo. It's not like you and Maximoff. It's never going to be like that."

His brows cinch. "Maybe in time, you and him—you'll patch things up." A swell of water gushes against our ankles. "Things could get better. I know your father, and he's a good man."

I smile wearily. "Lo…" I take a breath. "Good men can be bad fathers." It's what I've always known. What I've always felt.

There's nothing to salvage or recreate. It's nonexistent. And I don't yearn for it. I don't have it. I don't want it. And that's okay.

His face almost twists, letting this sink in. He looks pained for me. "I'm sorry. I wish it weren't like that."

"Can't say the same," I say easily. "And look, I don't wish my old man ill will. It is what it is."

He looks out at the blue sea before turning back to me. "I wanted to ask you something, Farrow."

It hits me that he didn't bring me out here to talk about my father. "Okay…" I could lie and say that I'm not nervous, but this is Maximoff Hale's dad. A huge cog in his entire world. And this uncertainty isn't that much fun.

And then he asks, "Would you like your job back on security?"

My pulse shoots to my throat. I must've heard him wrong. I shake my head. "I don't follow."

"Your old job," he reiterates. "Do you want it back?"

I let out a short laugh. "Okay, right." I don't even let myself get roped into the idea. But I find myself glancing back towards the three families and security. If I strain my ears, I can basically hear Donnelly rooting on the Cobalt Empire.

"I get that I'm a sarcastic bastard," Lo says, pulling my attention back. "But I'm serious."

I comb another hand through my hair, shaking my head only once. "I love being a concierge doctor to your family. I don't want that to change."

"You can do both," he says those words and it's like someone has offered me something that makes no sense. Like golden eggs and fairytale bullshit.

"I can't do both," I say slowly. "That's…" *Impossible.* It's fucking impossible. But he's looking at me like I'm the one who's wrong.

"Your Uncle Trip called me an hour ago," Lo says, blocking sunlight with his palm. "He's returning from his sabbatical. We'll have more hands. You'll always be on-call for the med team, and when there isn't an emergency, you can be on Maximoff's detail. Another bodyguard on SFO will fill in for you when you're pulled away." He tilts his head. "So there's still the question if you want to be on security at all. You can say *no.*"

What the hell…?

I'm processing…slowly. Security has been the missing piece. The gaping hole. And I didn't want to ask for it back because I didn't think

I could. There's no scenario in my head where anyone would allow me to split time between security and medicine.

I accepted what I could not fucking change, and now he's telling me I can have both.

He's giving me both?

I shake my head, overwhelmed. I turn my gaze away, my eyes welling. Choked up. *He's giving me both.*

"Why?" I ask him. "Why offer me this?"

I don't understand.

Lo stares up at the sky again, and when his sharp-edged gaze falls to me, he says, "Because I was raised by a bad man who was also a bad father." He pauses. "And despite whatever feelings I have about it, my son thinks I'm *good*, and every day I try to prove him right." He stares into me like he's reaching into the bottom of a pool. "You want this. I think you do. And I want to give it to you."

I rub my mouth, trying to collect myself. "So I'll be…"

"You'll be his bodyguard again."

Truth. I never thought I'd hear those words. Because to me, it's more than just a job. It's so much more.

"Thank you," I say, my eyes glassing.

His do, too. "Take care of my son," he tells me.

I make that promise.

And then he adds, "My son will take care of you."

I rub my eyes and nod. Feeling those words well up inside of me.

38

There'll never be a perfect moment to propose.

It's what I've been thinking about. How today I could face a family emergency, a media fallout, the most bizarre random happening and doomsday—Christ, the man on the moon could come down and try to fuck this up for all I know. But that's okay if he does.

Because this doesn't need to be perfect.

Farrow Redford Keene fell in love with the imperfect me. The human me. And whatever happens today, before or after, it'll probably, most likely be imperfectly human.

At the island of Kythira, we sightsee in the quaint village Mylopotamos, and Farrow and I separate from the family to hike one of the most stunning trails.

Lush plane trees shade a path littered with stone ruins of old watermills. Passing blue-green waterfall after blue-green waterfall, the rushing sound calms the air.

Farrow ducks beneath a branch in his way, not in mine. My durable backpack is strapped to his back, his Yale V-neck suctioning to his chest in the summer heat. And me—I'm carrying a whole lot of nothing. Giving my shoulders a break for once.

I catch Farrow swiveling the knob to a radio on his waistband and I ask, "Turning the volume down on them already?"

His lips rise. "They're being particularly annoying right now."

"Who's *they*?" I ask for specific names from SFO.

He nearly laughs. "All of them." He looks deep into me, his eyes smiling with airy light—and I don't need to ask if he's happy about rejoining security. There's nothing more obvious.

Farrow reaches out, and our hands seem to draw together on instinct. It's the most natural, simple thing: his hand in my hand while we hike a trail. But it means something to me.

Coming up to a lagoon, we slow to a stop. I've seen a lot of breathtaking views in my life, but what we reach is fucking majestic. An azure waterfall plunges into a crystal clear, bottomless pool. Mossy stones isolate the oasis, and light dances between the leaves of a sweeping plane tree overhead. Glittering the swimming pond.

"Wow," Farrow says first, and he pulls off the backpack, setting it on the ground.

Water mists the air and sprays my cheeks. Refreshingly cool. And that deep pond has to be cold, but I'd still swim in it with Farrow.

Near the edge of the green-blue water, I squat down and untie my hiking boot. I'm trying not to overthink here. Just feel what I feel, and it'll come to me.

And honest to God, as Farrow crouches only a foot in front of me and unzips the backpack, a dragonfly flutters past his shoulders, and then zips past his face.

He's only watching me. His smile stretching from cheek-to-cheek like he's fully aware that I'm in love with this place, this damn moment, *him*.

I lick my lips, not breaking our gazes while I unknot my boot. "I think we've made it to Neverland."

"Neverland," Farrow repeats, looking me up and down with amusement. His hand descends into the backpack. "Don't *lost boys* stay young forever there?"

"Yeah." I loosen my lace, his eyes swimming against my eyes.

"That's too bad then," Farrow says matter-of-factly. "Because I want to grow old with you."

The strong promise inside those words floods my whole body. *I want to grow old with you.* It floods my eyes.

I want to grow old with you.

Staying crouched, I'm about to speak, but words catch in my throat as his tattooed hand leaves the backpack. He's holding a small wooden box.

Farrow lowers his knee to the mossy stone.

Is he...?

Before I say anything, he cups one side of my face with a protective, affectionate hand, and he tilts his head towards my other cheek, his jaw gliding along my jaw.

Until his lips brush softly against my ear.

And very deeply, he whispers, "You've been my forever guy. You are my forever guy, wolf scout." His breath warms my skin, and I curve my bicep around his shoulders, staying close. Hanging on.

Listening to every intimate word as he continues, "And you said you wanted an in-your-face, overjoyed kind of love that knocks you backwards." He takes a beat. "But our love is that and better. Our love is headstrong. It never yields, never dies. And when it knocks you backwards, it pulls you upright again."

I pinch my burning eyes, and his hand tightens on my cheek.

I feel his smile rise against my ear, his voice gravel tied in silk as he says, "I promise to give you everything you need and nothing less. Never less. Maximoff..." He draws his head back, just enough for us to look at each other.

My hand falls off my eyes and onto his bent knee. We're eye-level since I'm crouching, my boot half untied. I don't know why the fuck I think about that.

His hand runs up through my thick hair, our reddened, welled-up eyes excavating each other.

I'm smiling. For real. I can't restrain it. I don't want to. Not now.

He sees, and his own smile stretches wider and wider. He nods a few times, and he whispers, "You want to marry the fuck out of me?"

I nod just as assured, just as overcome. "Yeah." I reach into my back pocket and pull out a black ring box. "I want to."

Farrow laughs in surprise, a tear escapes the corner of his eye. Really overwhelmed.

"You had no idea I planned to do this today," I realize. I thought maybe he got word this morning since I told everyone about the proposal plan at breakfast, including my dad. My mom and Jane kept the secret, so pretty much everyone found out hours ago.

"None." He wipes his eyes. "But I'm not shocked that I beat you to it."

"Because I overthink."

Farrow laughs once, eyeing my smile. "Because you can't be first at everything, wolf scout."

It hits me that I'll hear him tell me that for the rest of our lives. And then it washes over me. Fills me to the brim.

And we rise to our feet together.

Both of us standing close, I hold the back of his neck, and our heads dip towards each other. "Since you beat me to it, does this mean I can't ask—"

"Ask me," Farrow says strongly, and I hear the unsaid words: *there are no rules, Maximoff.*

I blink, and a couple tears slide down my face. And I just say, "There's no one else, Farrow. You're it. You're *the* one, *the only* one."

His chest rises against my chest, and he nods, knowing.

Feeling.

And I ask him, "Marry me?"

"Yeah," he says like it's the easiest thing in the world. "I'll marry you, wolf scout."

Our mouths meet with emotion swelling up inside, water misting around us and light streaming through treetops.

I've never been happier and more in love.

After a long swelling moment, we pull back. And I look between the ring boxes that we both still clutch.

"Let's do this," Farrow says like he's about to share a plan. But he just pops open the wooden box. He plucks out the wedding band that he bought me, and he pinches the ring between two fingers. Showing me the simple gray band, grooved like a tree. "It's not sterling silver. It's titanium and didn't cost a lot."

He knows that makes me love it even more. And now I'm trying hard not to smile, but it's a losing battle.

Farrow slips my titanium wedding band on his own ring finger. Off my confusion, he explains, "I'll wear yours and you'll wear mine as engagement rings. And then on our wedding day, I'll take the ring off and finally put it on your finger."

Alright, my brain is obsessed with this plan. Like way too damn much. "Did you just think of this on the spot?"

"I'd love to say I did, but no." He waves me on to open the black box. "It's something I thought about when I realized we were the same ring size."

Before I open the box, I ask him, "How'd you get the ring without the media knowing?"

He pulls out his comms earpiece, as though remembering the radio connection. Even if it's muted. And he answers, "Oscar and Donnelly."

"Your best friends," I define.

Farrow surprises me by just raising his brows in a teasing wave. Not denying how close those two guys are to him. And his gaze falls to my hands.

I open the box and pull out a sleek black tungsten band. "You should know, man. It took me a solid millisecond to pick this out."

He grins like I'm full of shit, and he's about to say something— probably, *sure* or *okay*—but he notices the engraving on the inside of the band. His smile softens as he takes the ring from me. Just for a closer look.

"*Dum spiro, spero,*" he reads the Cicero quote. His eyes well up again.

On a day that rocked us both, he said he loved that quote. It was a quiet moment inside a storm. The memory is as tranquil as the quote itself.

While I breathe, I hope.

Farrow nods a few times, tears rising. "Here." He places the black band in my palm, not wanting to slip a ring on my finger yet. "It's perfect, wolf scout." And with another growing smile, he adds, "Especially since you took forever to pick it out."

I grimace. "You can't know that one-hundred percent," I contend and slip the black band on my ring finger.

"I do know that one-hundred percent," Farrow says. "Because I know you one-hundred percent."

Our last day in Greece has snuck up on us,

and Farrow and I have left the yacht to spend the night in Corfu. Alone, together, both of us soaking in the peaceful quiet before we return to a media frenzy in Philly.

We're not hiding our engagement.

So when we're back home, whatever paparazzi presence existed before may be infinitely larger, more aggressive, invasive—we don't know. Because I'm the first to be engaged out of my siblings and cousins.

I'm paving the way.

But not even the media can deter my brain from replaying the proposal. It's on loop. And I remember how my whole family and SFO joined us at the lagoon. Farrow asked them to hike the same trail about thirty minutes after us, and I had no clue.

Janie, my best friend, ma moitié—when she saw me, she had her hand to her heart like she could feel mine swelling.

Having all of them there was everything.

Warm water rains down on me in a stone shower, made to look outdoors with a fogged skylight, but I'm inside our hotel bathroom. Private. As safe as it can be, and I'm not scared.

My muscles slacken with the warmth and gathering steam. I stand right beneath the downpour, my bare skin flush from the heat. I rub soap on my abs, picturing Farrow coming in behind me, my number one fantasy.

I go lower with the washcloth, hot breath ejecting from me. And hanging up the cloth on a hook, I rest my left hand on the stone slab wall. Whatever I planned to do suddenly flits away. Because the black ring on that hand is staring back at me.

I'm wearing his ring.

My eyes burn.

And then I hear the shower door swing open. In my peripheral, I see that it's him. So I don't turn back around. I wait, and his six-foot-three build pushes warmly up against me—*God, this is real.* His arm curves around my abs, chest melded firmly to my back.

I stare straight ahead. I feel Farrow, his left arm extending across the top of my arm. And he interlaces our fingers on the stone slab wall. His hand sheathing my hand, our rings on our fingers are in perfect sight together.

Farrow presses a burning kiss to my shoulder blade. And as his other hand descends to a place of need and want, his mouth travels to my ear. In my fantasy, I never hear what he whispers. He knows this is what I wouldn't let myself dream of.

And as he kisses the nape of my neck, the line of my jaw, I wait and wait, and softly, so damn softly and huskily, Farrow whispers, "I love you."

Light bursts in me, and I spin on him, our hands instantly grip each other in starved yearning. We kiss like we haven't kissed in eons. Heat blistered and raw, we wrestle in the shower for the lead.

And goddamn, we're both smiling.

39

MAXIMOFF HALE

News of our engagement has spread like a tornado ripping through flatlands. No houses destroyed yet, but damage control mode is still alive. Just as a precaution.

Too many tabloids, magazines, entertainment sites have contacted our reps. Inquiring about front-page spreads, interviews, photo ops. Everyone is seeking the first exclusive pictures, videos, *anything*.

And they've all received the same automatic reply from our publicist:

Maximoff & Farrow are enjoying their engagement and would like to remain private at this time. Thank you for understanding.

I'm currently focused on rebuilding strength in my right shoulder. All without overexerting, without pushing too far and tearing my body to fucking pieces.

Hence, working out with my childhood crush, my bodyguard, my doctor, my fiancé—all Farrow Redford Keene.

He has strike pads on both of his hands, hoisting them up to me. I jab the pad with my left fist, protected by a red boxing glove.

Sun shines through the full-length glass windows in Uncle Ryke's gym. Heating the space. It's pretty much why I'm sweating. Because there's no way my slow pace alone could warrant me soaking through my shirt.

"How did that feel?" Farrow asks me as I gear up to do a right cross.

"Fine." I think I can try harder without killing my muscle. I go for a right cross with my right arm…and I end up lightly tapping the pad.

Listening to my body. The stretch alone pulls my tendons taut.

"Sore?" he asks.

"Not at all," I say, sarcasm thick. "I could without a doubt take you in a boxing ring. Let's go, right now."

"That's an adorable fantasy," Farrow says.

I growl into a groan.

Farrow smiles, too amused. "How about we come back to reality?" He motions me to ready myself. "Put your gloves up to your chin."

I follow the instruction, and Farrow spreads out the strike pads for me to do a hook combination. Before I even swing, the glass door opens.

I drop my arms, and we both turn to see my little brother. Xander is in gym shorts and a T-shirt that says *Winter is Coming.* Shock coils in me—surprised he's here.

"Hey," Xander says, hair hanging in his eyes. "I got your text."

He almost never works out with me. But every time I'm at the gym, I try to always invite him along. He usually brushes it off. Him, putting in this effort, whether it's for me or himself, I don't care. He's here.

That's all that matters.

"You're here to work out?" I ask him.

"I mean...yeah," he says. His eyes dance across the equipment. "What do you suggest?"

"You should start on the bag," Farrow tells him, nodding to the boxing bag that my uncle hung up a couple weeks ago. "Here..." Farrow takes off his pads and grabs a pair of black cloth wraps that hang on the wall. "I'll wrap your hands."

Xander follows Farrow's instructions to hold out his hands. Palms down, and Farrow crisscrosses the wrap, weaving the cloth between his fingers.

I swing my right arm in a pendulum stretch while I wait.

My little brother glances from Farrow to me. "So have you guys decided on when you're having the wedding?"

Farrow eyes lift to me and then his brows rise. "We have."

"We're doing a long engagement," I tell Xander.

We discussed it at length, and it seems like the best idea to wait for the public and media attention to die down before we have a wedding. There will still be chaos, but I figure if we give it some time, there's a greater chance someone else in my family will take the spotlight for a little while. I just would really love a wedding that isn't crashed by helicopters and drones.

"I figured," Xander replies.

Farrow finishes with his hand wraps and then tosses a pair of boxing gloves to him. "We'll start with an easy combination."

I watch as my future husband teaches my little brother how to box. He keeps glancing at me, a smile inching across his mouth. He knows how much I love him. How much I love this. And I think about what Farrow once told me.

It's the little things.

It really is.

40

FARROW KEENE

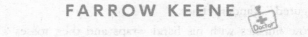

The We Are Calloway wrap party is held at an artsy studio in Center City, and I've been to one of these before on Lily's security detail. Never as Maximoff's bodyguard. And definitely not as a face featured in the docuseries. This is new for me, and I keep catching myself taking in this different vantage point.

"Few month's time, Redford, and we're all going to watch your smug ass on TV," Oscar tells me, all of SFO congregating around a few wooden high-top tables we shoved together. Plates of finger-food and nonalcoholic drinks cover the surface.

We're all on-duty.

I wondered how being a bodyguard again would work. How the guys would handle me coming back after I willingly quit. That same day in Greece, during the sandcastle contest, the news was announced.

And then all of SFO pushed me in the motherfucking sea.

In jest.

Akara knew what was happening way before. Apparently, the Tri-Force had talked to Lo in advance, and he would've never offered me the spot if they said *no*. Akara told me they were unanimous in favor of bringing me back.

I didn't need to know why the security team would want me. I just figure it's easier to have me on the team than a new hire. It's what Thatcher said a while back. Trust is invaluable with these families, and they trust me a hell of a lot.

Enough to let me marry into American royalty.

I prop my boot on the rung of a stool that Donnelly sits on. Most of us are standing, and I tell Oscar, "You can watch my smug ass in real life."

"Already accomplished." Oscar dips a fry in ketchup. A long, *long* buffet table spans an entire brick wall. Invite-only guests amble around the open space, mixed drinks and beers in hand.

The food isn't the main attraction. Cameras and lighting equipment point at a white backdrop. See, these wrap parties are always half-cocktail-hour and half-photo-shoot. The famous ones have to take promotional shots for the premium cable-network's digital apps.

"You don't want us to watch your episodes?" Akara asks, giving me a weird look.

"Eh…" I waver my hand. Being honest, I don't give a shit.

"Did you embarrass yourself?" Oscar asks. "Bro, I told you not to talk about serious shit with the parents on camera."

"It happened," I say truthfully, picking up a whole apple off my plate. "Connor was offered a condom sponsorship." I let that out, trusting these guys, and also that footage with Connor is going to be aired.

Banks laughs hard.

"Cobalt Condoms." Donnelly flips a page in a gossip magazine. "Magnum-size only."

"For the wealthy man," Oscar chimes in.

"Nah, I'd wanna buy some," Donnelly notes.

I whistle. "These are definitely fictional condoms when Donnelly thinks he can fit into a magnum."

Everyone laughs.

Donnelly blows me a middle-finger kiss. And I won't tell anyone but Maximoff, at least not to the full degree—but I missed these guys. Shit, like I *really* missed them. In ways that I didn't think I would or even could.

I glance at Donnelly who dog-ears the magazine. "We should make a drinking game out of the docuseries," he says, his Philly lilt thick. "Every time you roll your eyes, we take a shot."

Akara shakes his head, a water bottle to his lips. "Too many shots."

"How about you all just not watch the show," I say casually.

Donnelly laughs like that's an absurd idea.

Thatcher says, "That was the plan."

"See, listen to Thatcher," I tell everyone and bite into my red apple.

He sends me a narrowed look. Not understanding why I'm agreeing with him. Let's make this clear: he agreed with me first.

I watch his gaze drift to the camera set-up. Right now, a photographer takes various shots of Maximoff and Jane together. She rests her freckled cheek on his shoulder, and he has a protective arm around her waist.

Their relationship intact means a ton to me. And the fact that I didn't destroy that *good* thing and I still got the man, the love, and everything in between—there are no words for what I feel. Because "happy" doesn't seem powerful enough.

Donnelly hunches forward on the stool and clears his throat. Reading from the magazine he's holding, "'With a wedding on the horizon, you can expect interest in Maximoff & Farrow's relationship to escalate in the coming months.'"

I hone in on how they called me *Farrow* and not just Maximoff's fiancé or Maximoff's boyfriend. And the Alphas Like Us articles stopped referring to me as the "new boyfriend," and they've started printing my name too.

Either this means that the world sees me as a human being or as someone worthy enough to be attached to Maximoff by name. Possibly both.

And I'll definitely take both.

Donnelly rotates the tabloid sideways and reads on, "'They're the current *it-couple* and it's going to take somethin' huge to change that.'" He looks at me with seriousness. "Want me to do somethin' huge?"

"No, fuck no."

SFO may have a modicum of fame, but the spotlight on me is much brighter and blinding. Being with Maximoff, I've learned to not let that shit get to me.

Don't fear it. Don't run away from it. Don't fight it. Instead I hang onto the bright side and just live every day with him.

Standing beside Donnelly, Quinn peers at the tabloid and points at a page. "Damn. Jane's on the worst dressed list again."

Thatcher pulls the magazine out of Donnelly' grip and tosses it in the nearby trash. "No one should be reading that here." He retrains his attention onto the photo shoot.

Donnelly mouths to me, *grumpy.*

That's one word for it. I bite into my apple.

Oscar eats a fry and nods to me. "Fiancé is looking at you."

Fiancé. That word rushes into me. I've always wanted to be married one day, and each morning I wake up next to him, I'm still overcome with a simple fact. I'm going to marry Maximoff Hale—the love of my life.

I chew slowly, my lips upturning. "I know," I say. "He still does that." Gradually, I turn around and pool all my attention onto Maximoff.

He's alone. Standing in front of the white backdrop, dressed in jeans and a gray crew-neck. He's waiting for the photographer to fix his camera settings, maybe even for a few other cousins to appear. I'm not sure who's up next in the photo lineup.

And despite all the hell we've been through, Maximoff looks and stands like an unshakable force of nature. Ready to weather any squall because he's as powerful as the storm.

Fuck, I can't take my eyes off him, and I smile into my next bite of apple. Watching his forest-greens try not to melt over me.

The photographer shouts, "Can we get Loren and Ryke in here?"

Lo and Ryke leave their high-top table where they'd been chatting with their wives. And both men easily and assuredly join Maximoff.

Lo is on his right. Ryke on his left. And the three look straight into the camera. Severity in their gazes. Because the paternity issues surrounding the three of them aren't amusing or lighthearted. And for the most part, *We Are Calloway* hits serious tones all the way through.

The studio seems to quiet, more people compelled to look at them. Not because of the paternity rumors. Everyone invited here knows that's bullshit.

It's how striking and domineering they are side-by-side-by-side. And Maximoff doesn't look confrontational or angry. He looks proud to be standing between his dad and his uncle.

And Maximoff—pure, wholehearted Maximoff—can't even see how Lo and Ryke look even prouder to be next to him.

"Incoming," Banks says, and our heads turn as Sullivan Meadows weaves around a few tables, dark hair splayed over the shoulders of her jean jacket. She's aiming for SFO. For this table.

For Akara.

We can all tell. Even if she doesn't realize it.

"She's hesitating," Quinn narrates as Sulli pauses, turns slightly. Fingers to her lips.

Akara sets down his water bottle, brows furrowing. The two of them have been doing this concern-worried-for-each-other dance since their "fight" at the stair climb. It's a little intense, even for buddyguards.

"And she's exiting," Banks says, just as Sulli swerves around and rushes away from SFO.

"I'll be a sec." Akara detaches from our spot and chases after Sulli. And when he's well out of earshot, we all turn back to the table and look at each other.

Oscar says, "Either Kitsuwon is in denial about his feelings for that girl or he's playing all of us."

"Denial," most of us say because Akara is adamant that they're just friends. Not in the excessive way to cover a lie. In a peeved, fuck-off way.

"She's back," Donnelly says off the appearance of Luna Hale. Only he's referring to the green marker on her cheeks, the blue-painted eyebrows and graphic tee. She makes a Spock symbol at the camera, and she looks genuinely lighter, happier. She dumped Andrew last week, and she told her big brother that her and this guy just "wanted different things."

I smile into my next bite of apple. *Good for you, Luna.*

"Anyone read the story she posted online yesterday?" Oscar asks the table. A few days ago she gave SFO her secret username so we could read her fics. Honestly, I haven't had time to delve into that rabbit hole yet.

Donnelly bites into a potato skin. "The one with the blue alien goddess and the glittery king of stars?" He licks sour cream off his finger.

Oscar nods heartily. "I give it a C+. Too many tentacles."

Donnelly shrugs. "I thought it was pretty good."

I'm not even going to ask or open that Pandora's Box. The photographer bobs up from the camera and searches the studio for someone.

And then his eyes land on me.

"Farrow!" The photographer waves me over, and he's already called Maximoff back to the plain white backdrop. I place my bitten apple back on the plate.

Donnelly says, "Go get 'em."

"Make us proud." Oscar pats my back.

I spin and walk backwards, just to say, "Take notes, boys."

They slow-clap, and I let out a short laugh. Heading over to my fiancé who stands alone on a white backdrop. And I've been craving to be by his side. Even when he's facing a camera.

I reach the set, my black boots thudding on the hard floor. Our eyes never shift off each other, never deter, and no one tells me to unhook my radio or remove my gun.

I'm where I want to be, need to be, and should be, and there's nothing that could possibly feel more comfortable, more perfect, than that.

Maximoff and I draw together. Instinctively. Longingly. His chest presses to my chest, and his hand warms my neck. My palm ascends to the back of his head, threading his thick hair between inked fingers. And if I thought the studio quieted when he was with his dad and uncle, then it falls to silence for us.

Maximoff isn't cautious or worried. His lips inch upward. "You're in my world." He's excited about that.

I nod a few times. "It's a good thing I love your world, wolf scout. And that your world is mine." That gets to us both.

Instantly, we bring our mouths together in a scorching, slow-burning kiss. In our embrace, there is no fear or uncertainty. There is only peace and overwhelming pride, and we bask in this second, this simple moment of our beautiful lives.

Epilogue

MAXIMOFF HALE

The smell of chlorine overpowers the indoor
pool. Three-year-old and four-year-old kids with inflatable wings on
their arms are blowing bubbles in the water.

I wade in the shallow pool. "Go, go," I encourage. "Hannah, you're
doing amazing. Really good, everyone." A metal whistle hangs around
my neck, and I take a quick glance at the wall clock.

I blow my whistle. "Alright, that's it for today," I tell them. "Everyone
did awesome. You all look like Olympians." I high-five the kids, and
Farah slaps my hand three times with a giddy smile.

The kids paddle to the edge of the pool, and I help a straggler onto
the cement. Parents start pouring out from the upstairs viewing room.
When all the kids are collected, I pull myself out of the pool, water
dripping down.

Banks Moretti chills out on a plastic chair beside the door, earpiece
in and radio on his waistband. He gives me a nod in greeting, and I
wave back. After the Greece trip, he requested to be on my detail. The
Moretti brothers have been in contact less ever since Thatcher became
Jane's bodyguard. And with this switch-up, Banks and Thatcher will see
each other more. Because I'm around Janie all the time.

I start collecting the inflatables and water wings that the kids left behind. Tossing them into a plastic bin.

When I asked the local aquatic center if I could teach the beginner classes, I expected to be denied. This job—it's achingly normal. Not something meant for a guy like me.

But they said *yes*.

So I became certified, and I'm already on my second week here, and I can see another week. Another month. I can see a future where I'm teaching little kids how to swim and build some kind of courage. Face their fears. Jump in and paddle.

Take a breath and float.

I learned how to swim around their age, and I like to think about how a few of these kids could grow up and fall in love with the sport.

Everything about it feels right.

The heavy pool door opens, and the outdoor sunlight illuminates the dimmed space. Farrow slips inside, and the *clunk* of the closing door echoes inside the aquatic center. Before Farrow sees me, Banks stands up and greets him.

I pull out a chemical kit from the closet, and when I return, Banks is gone.

Farrow attaches his radio to his belt, clips his mic to his V-neck, and fits his earpiece in. He was called in to check up on my little sister. I don't ask him for details, patient-confidentiality and all that. But Kinney already texted me that she's bedbound with the flu.

"Back on Maximoff Hale duty," I tell him. "Your favorite."

Farrow steps over an orange swim noodle. "You are going to be my husband, wolf scout. Let's hope you're my favorite."

His husband.

His lips lift, knowing what that fucking does to me. Yeah, I'm never going to get over Farrow. And I don't have to.

In two more strides, we close the distance, and our arms curve around each other. Farrow looks deep into me, and he asks, "What are you thinking, wolf scout?"

I smile.

Dear World, thanks for listening. Love, Maximoff Hale

Hell's Kitchen — Moving In

FARROW KEENE

"When's the last time you've cleaned this room?" I lean against the doorway and land my question on Donnelly. He's holding a heavy-duty garbage bag and tossing empty beer cans inside.

Ask anyone on the security team, from Alpha to Omega to Epsilon, and they'll say the Hell's Kitchen apartment is one of the best housing accommodations for a bodyguard.

I'd have to agree.

Spacious rooms big enough for queen-sized beds, oversized windows with perfect views of NYC, and the ceilings are vaulted. The luxury apartment complex is high-end and ritzy, but the place isn't too fucking stuffy or too modern. Dark wood floors and furniture adds warmth, and the dim lighting makes the space feel like a home.

But security's guest room looks like a fucking garbage dump. I smell a faint odor of stale beer and an even stronger scent of weed. Gray sheets are stained and rumpled, and the curtains are dirty as fuck with more mystery stains.

I take a short glance at the open closet, piles of worn sneakers tumbling out. Ripped jackets and miscellaneous articles of clothing are stacked in heaps inside the walk-in.

For years, this room has been empty and dubbed "Lost and Found" by the security team. It's the crash pad that other bodyguards use when they need to sleep in the city. And also the room that Donnelly hot boxes every few weeks.

See, when Charlie and Beckett Cobalt left the nest and moved out of the Cobalt Estate, Donnelly and Oscar had to leave the gated neighborhood, too. Following their clients, they packed up and now permanently reside in Hell's Kitchen. Unless they're transferred or their clients move again, that's where they'll stay.

And the lucky fuckers landed this four-bedroom, two-bath apartment in NYC. Hellishly expensive for the area, but with the Cobalts' banks account, it's basically loose change. Charlie and Beckett live across the hallway in an identical apartment.

Things are changing.

Cobalts are getting older.

People are leaving cities. Going to new ones.

And when our clients start shifting around, security shifts too. Now that Tom and Eliot are finished with high school, they've decided to move in with their older brothers in Hell's Kitchen. Which means that Oscar and Donnelly are about to have two new roommates as well.

Two bodyguards from Security Force *Epsilon*.

Donnelly considers my earlier question—*when's the last time you've cleaned this room*—with a head tilt and shrug. "I dunno. A year ago?"

Seems about right.

Static suddenly cracks in my earpiece and his, and our hands fly to our mics.

"It's not me," Donnelly winces and adjusts his earpiece. He sweeps his chestnut hair back with one hand and fixes the mic on the collar of his old Blondie shirt.

I pull my earpiece out and hang the cord over my shoulder. "There must be bad reception." I mess with the volume on my radio attached to my belt, my black V-neck tucked in my black pants.

Donnelly trashes another beer can.

Once the static dies down, I go to the bed and start stripping the sheets.

I catch myself glancing at the shut door. I'm not expecting Maximoff to barge in here, but I am a little bit surprised he hasn't, at the very least, sent a smartass text yet.

I wonder if he's restraining himself. Maximoff has been across the hall helping his cousins move in, along with most of the Cobalt family. All of them have been in and out of the apartment to lend a hand for Tom and Eliot, and the one time I passed Maximoff in the hall, he said to me, "Look what the wind threw up."

I replied easily, "Your fiancé."

And he was lost for words. Literally. Next moment, he pretended to ignore my presence while I tried not to laugh and he carried a fifty-pound box in arm like it was his rucksack at boot camp.

He's had that run-in to dwell on for the past five hours.

And so have I.

By the way, the only Cobalt who is MIA is *Beckett*. Ever since the Greece trip, we've been in a better spot, and I would've liked to see the guy around, but I understand why he's not here. He ditched the move-in day to hang out with Sullivan Meadows in Philly.

No one really blames him.

The apartment across the hall is a fucking disaster, and with Beckett's OCD, he chose to skip out on this one. Donnelly has been slow moving all morning, not too pumped to be on "cleaning" duty when he could be in Philly with his client. But Beckett has a temp body-guard today.

I yank the last sheet off the bed and walk over to my friend, about to throw these away. I'm holding them in the few spotless places. There are too many discolored marks on the fabric to count.

Donnelly sees me coming and pulls the garbage bag away. "Those are good sheets."

I lift my brows at him. "They have foreign stains on them. Not all from you, need I fucking remind you."

"Where?"

"Everywhere, and man, I don't want to hold them for this long." I gesture with my head for him to open the garbage bag.

Donnelly can clearly see the yellowish stains. He's staring right at them, but he's considering keeping this disgusting shit.

"Donnelly," I say, "who the fuck knows which bodyguards slept in this bed and what ass they brought back. Shit, you really want to roll around in SFE's cum and other bodily fluids?"

"Bleach and wash," Donnelly tells me. "Works every time, man."

My brows rise even higher. I almost never see Donnelly work a laundry machine, but instead of ribbing him, I just tell him pointedly, "These are past bleach." I grab onto the trash bag, pulling it wide enough to shove the sheets in.

He relinquishes without a care.

"Donnelly, Redford..." A knock sounds on the edge of the doorframe, the door already silently opened.

Our heads turn and we both notice Oscar, his curly hair falling over a rolled blue bandana around his forehead.

He has a grave expression and slowly unwraps a peanut butter protein bar. "We have a problem."

Donnelly lifts the trash bag. "Yeah, Farrow is throwin' away perfectly good sheets."

"Shit-stained sheets aren't good sheets," I say matter-of-factly, taking a seat on the mattress.

Oscar bites the protein bar. "Those smelled like booze and piss too."

Donnelly ties off the full trash bag. "I've smelled worse."

Oscar points his protein bar at him. "That's not an achievement, Donnelly."

Donnelly smirks.

"Oliveira, what's the problem?" I ask about the issue he was about to surface.

Oscar glances over at me. "Wreath is pitching a fit in the kitchen. He's refusing to move into this room."

"Which Wreath?" I ask.

"Ian."

I shake my head a couple times.

Ian Wreath is Tom Cobalt's bodyguard. It's not a surprise that he's moving into security's apartment today and gaining Oscar and Donnelly as roommates. However, two days ago a transfer went through so Heidi Smith could stay in Philly, which means that Eliot Cobalt has a new bodyguard.

Look, I'm not too excited that Ian Wreath's little brother is the replacement. He's green. And not in a Quinn Oliveira way. The youngest Oliveira brother at least has a boxing background.

Vance Wreath is green like a fucking forest.

He has no real MMA training or military experience. He has a Biology degree from Penn State and a high school soccer championship.

Apparently a raving recommendation from his older brother Ian and three thirty-minute MMA classes make him a "terrific" candidate.

Truth, I wonder if Price is pissing himself after SFO gained a decent amount of fame. Akara mentioned that hiring has been more difficult. And some of the guys think Price is trying to fill slots without accidentally signing on a wannabe fame whore.

Can't be easy, but I would've chosen someone other than Ian's little brother.

I don't hate Ian, but I don't like him either. He's not always vigilant or aware of his client. In the recent past, he let his guard down and a friend stole Tom Cobalt's phone and prank called Maximoff.

That fuck-up was on Ian.

"Nothing's wrong with this room," Donnelly says. "It's got a bed and a walk-in closet."

I frown.

Oscar chokes down his protein bar. "Don't say that too loudly."

"Unless you want to live here," I add, hoping Donnelly replies with a *fuck no*.

He shrugs.

For fuck's sake.

Oscar gives me a look like *stop this*.

Fine. I stand up off the bed and grab a yardstick—don't ask—from the far wall and scoop up a dirty pair of boxers that belongs to fuck-knows-who. Donnelly watches me fling them in a new trash bag that Oscar holds out, and I tell him, "You're not sleeping in the Lost and Found."

He rubs his jaw, light stubble coming in, and he looks between me and Oscar. "I'm just sayin' it's not that big a deal to me. I'll be the bigger man here—"

"Bro," Oscar snaps, dropping the trash bag. "Don't be the bigger man. Be the man who doesn't sleep in the piss and booze bed." He crumples up his empty wrapper.

"It won't be the piss and booze bed once the sheets are bleached."

"The sheets are in the trash," I remind him.

Donnelly extends his arms wide. "And they can be removed from the trash."

Oscar gives him a hard look. "Standards, bro. Find them. Keep them."

"Fuck them," Donnelly adds.

My lip quirks.

Oscar shakes his head. "Not on the list."

"Should be, could be," Donnelly grins.

I lean a shoulder against the closet doorframe and swing the yardstick in my hand. "If you won't do it for yourself, do it for *us*." I motion between Oscar and me with the yardstick. "I'd rather not have to see Ian walk around all fucking smug like he won something."

"Agreed," Oscar says. "And the new Wreath should be the one in here."

I nod. "Let Ian put his brother in the shit room."

Donnelly nods back, not thinking about it for long. "Then you two better be helping me clean this." He motions to the room.

I tilt my head and lift my brows again. "What does it look like I've been doing?"

"Throwing good sheets away. Playing with a yardstick—"

"You can stop there," I tell him casually.

Donnelly laughs, and Oscar grins before he throws out his protein wrapper.

Another knock raps the opened door. We all turn to look.

I'm not too surprised to see the six-foot-three, sandy-brown haired Cobalt. Mostly because Charlie rarely stays in the same place for long, and if I clocked his presence at his apartment—cramped with people going in and out—it's hitting five-hours now.

Charlie saunters across the room without a single word and effortlessly hops up on the dark wood dresser, his legs hanging off.

I stay near the closet, relaxed on my heels, and I take note of the newness of everything. Because things have changed between Charlie and Maximoff.

They're starting to rebuild a tiny fraction of a relationship. Something close to what they had. I realize that it's going to change my relationship with Charlie. Before, I knew my place was to stay out of their rift as long as I could. Let them fight it out. Yell it out. Whatever they do. Now...*now* I'm going to marry Maximoff.

I'm going to be a part of his family.

I can't just ignore Charlie or silently take Maximoff's side like they're still in this huge fucking feud when they're not even in one. It leaves me in a strange position, but I won't be the reason for more animosity between them.

I have to find a way to treat Charlie like I would Jane.

Like a friend.

It won't be as easy, but even if there were playbooks for this shit, I wouldn't read it.

One problem: I may know Charlie better than the public ever will, but he's still the kind of person who creates walls and leaves when you need him to stay. Hell, I'm not looking to have a heart-to-heart with the guy, but on the tour bus, he rarely hung around long enough to shoot the shit.

Before anyone asks why Charlie is here, he tells us, "I need five minutes."

Oscar nods, understanding.

Charlie pulls at his sandy-brown hair. The strands stick up. He turns his head and arches a single brow at me. "By the way, your fiancé is doing an excellent job moving furniture in the other apartment. I thought you'd be over there acquiring some visuals for your spank bank."

His words sound a little bit bitter, but other than that, harmless. I let out a laugh, actually happy to take this bait. "That's not how it works. But speaking of getting laid," I tell Charlie and then look to Donnelly. He's scratching his initials in the closet door with a knife. "Donnelly, when's the last time you got laid?"

"Last week," Donnelly says. "Back of an Uber."

"Didn't ask for details," I tell him, letting go of my yardstick and searching my pocket for a pack of gum.

Donnelly grins and looks to our friend. "Oscar?"

"Three weeks," he says. "Not that bad."

There've been months where most of the security team—at least the single guys—were jerking off nonstop and abstaining hard. When sleep is difficult to come by as a bodyguard, finding time for sex is a talent.

I slip a piece of gum in my mouth. "You?" I ask Charlie.

"Last night," he says without missing a beat.

I choose not to be surprised because with Charlie, it's just easier to expect the unexpected. He does what he wants. When he wants. Tomorrow, if I asked the same question, it's likely I would have been met with silence or a brush off. That's just the way it works.

But there's one thing I do know—it's not a lie. Like his twin brother, Charlie prides himself on honesty.

Oscar is nodding.

Charlie's yellow-green eyes drift to each of us. "Is this what the three of you do all day?" he asks, his voice smooth. "Stand around and compare dick size?"

Oscar laughs under his breath.

"Not all day," Donnelly says.

I roll my eyes and pop a bubble in my mouth. I squat and organize some of the sneakers. "We're cleaning this room for Ian," I tell Charlie.

"About Ian," Charlie says, slipping sunglasses on his eyes. "Moffy told me what happened on the FanCon tour. How someone stole my brother's phone and used it to prank call him."

Maximoff already told me he was going to give that information to Charlie. A step in repairing their relationship is letting Charlie know shit. Like stuff that goes down with his brothers.

"Yeah, that happened," I say, putting the sneakers into a donation pile. "I told Akara about it and Ian was slapped on the wrist."

Donnelly helps me with the closet. "It's not a fireable offense unless the same thing happens," he explains to Charlie. "It's just little shit."

Charlie jumps off the dresser. "With Eliot and Tom in the city there's more room for *little shit* to happen. If any of you are around, just look out for them."

Oscar nods, "It's what we're here for."

"Yeah, man," Donnelly says.

Before I can voice my agreement, Charlie hooks his sunglasses on the collar of his button-down and rotates to me with a bomb. "We're about to have an issue."

Letting go of an old Nike, I slowly stand back up and cock my head. *What the hell?* "You and me?"

"Moffy and me."

Fuck.

I rub the corner of my mouth, my thumb brushing over my silver lip piercing. "About to have an issue," I repeat his words. "Let's avoid it then."

"I'm trying to," Charlie says. "You're aware that Luna is best friends with my little brothers."

I am.

Tom, Eliot, and Luna are usually glued to the hip. But there's been some real-life things that have pulled them apart these past months. The FanCon tour. Luna moving into Maximoff's place...

Luna moving into Maximoff's place.

Fucking hell.

"She doesn't want to move in with you and your brothers," I say like that can't even be a consideration. She basically *just* started living at the Philly townhouse, and as far as I know, she likes it there. She's been having a good time.

Charlie tosses his cell between his hands like he's thinking, but he says, "My brothers can be persuasive, especially when they're offering to bunk-up and give her the extra bedroom. Beckett doesn't mind. I couldn't care less, but a couple things are stopping her."

Donnelly rises to his feet next to me, his brows just as furrowed as mine. We're all listening in on Cobalt drama, but this is turning into Hale/Cobalt drama which isn't my favorite phrase.

Oscar digs in his coat pocket for another snack.

"Maximoff," I say, knowing that Luna wouldn't want to hurt him. Leaving the townhouse for Charlie's apartment—it'll hurt, possibly even break his heart. Any way you toss it.

Charlie nods.

Oscar shakes his head. "Would her parents even let her live in New York?" he asks. "I know she's eighteen, but she's Luna Hale."

"Can't see them letting her," Donnelly agrees.

Charlie sighs. "Her parents are fine if she's living with Beckett and me, and I've already talked to them."

He's already talked to them.

Shit. This is beyond just the initial "idea" stage. To lose Luna won't just hurt Maximoff. It'll kill Jane, who's taken Luna under her wing since Maximoff's little sister moved into the townhouse. And fuck, Charlie should've talked to *both* of them before he even went to her parents.

Charlie hones in on me, as though he can feel the heat off my glare. "It's not set in stone," he says rapidly, almost worried. "Don't fucking twist that when you retell everything to Moffy."

"I'm not twisting anything," I refute. "But maybe if you want things crystal clear, you should be telling this to Maximoff yourself."

"Fine."

My brows spike, and to my surprise, Charlie aims for the exit and disappears out the door.

Oscar opens a small pack of gummy bears. I swear, Oliveira will be a great dad with the amount of fucking snacks he carries around.

Oscar says, "Can you even imagine Luna living up here with the Cobalt brothers?"

I'm trying not to.

She'd get into a shit load of trouble.

We all know it.

Donnelly thinks about this for half a second, squinting his eyes and wincing a little bit. "Nah. It's all fuzzy. Like she's meant for Philly."

I don't ask what that means.

"You'd see Quinn more often," I remind Oliveira.

He gives me a look. "That's not an upside, Redford. We do better with space."

That, I know. "It was on my con list," I tell him.

"Keep it there."

"All cons," Donnelly muses. "Except me. Being around me is a straight up gift."

"Still all cons," Oscar proclaims, tossing gummy bears in his own mouth.

I laugh.

Donnelly blows him a middle-finger kiss.

Soft voices sound in the hallway and two bodies enter the room this time.

Damn.

My gaze drips down Maximoff, his green shirt half-soaked with sweat from lifting boxes and moving furniture. The fabric suctions to the hard carve of his muscles. I don't smile up at him because I notice how his lips are drawn in a line.

He wears a look that says *I've been told enough.*

I nod, assuming Charlie filled him in on the cliff-notes in the hall.

Maximoff sidles next to me and purposefully slings his left arm around me, wetting my black V-neck with his sweat. He smells fucking good, and I wouldn't say that about all men after a workout.

I don't even flinch, much to his distress, and I smile wide and chew my gum, my expression saying, *you're in love with me.*

He scowls, trying not to smile back. "Shut up."

I don't. "Can't stay away from me, wolf scout?" I give him another once-over.

He licks his lips, his gaze falling to my cut biceps. "I'm not even touching you," he whispers back, and I feel him start to remove his arm off me.

I easily wrap mine around his waist, and he decides to stay put. Our eyes caress for a heady second, and then my fingers slide beneath his shirt.

He leans into me to whisper again, "Don't let me hit him." He sounds extremely worried that he will, but I doubt it'll reach that point. Months ago, I would've said differently, but he's kept his short-fuse in check, especially where his cousin is concerned.

Charlie hops back on the dresser. "He's here. Now we can be *crystal clear.*"

"Good," I say.

Maximoff nods. "Luna can decide for herself. If she wants to live with you, she can live with you and your brothers. And if I'm the only thing stopping her, then…Christ. She *should* definitely be living with you." His muscles tense more at that last part, and he takes his arm off my shoulder just to cross his arms. Rigid. He won't show how much this pains him, but I know it does.

I chew my gum slowly and run my hand up his back until I reach his deltoid. I hang my arm over his shoulder, not putting too much weight on his collar, and I fit my crackling earpiece back in my ear.

Maximoff breaks apart his crossed arms, taking a bigger breath.

"That's it?" Charlie asks, disbelieving and uncertain. "You don't want to put up a fight? Luna is eighteen living in New York City, the firstborn girl in the Hale family, and you have no feelings?"

"I'm not her dad."

Charlie opens his mouth, but he's cut off by the sound of a throat being cleared. Everyone's attention veers to the door where Jane Cobalt stands confidently in pastel purple jeans and a zebra-print top.

"I just spoke to our dear Luna," Jane says.

I can only crack a guess that on Maximoff's way here, he also told Jane what's happening. She must've gone straight to his sister.

"What'd she say?" Maximoff asks.

"She wants to live at the townhouse." Jane starts to smile brightly, her freckled cheeks rosy. "She said that while she loves my brothers, there aren't any girls to talk to here."

Maximoff instantly smiles. Because it means that Luna is staying for Jane, and to be honest, that's a better reason than any.

Charlie wears a shadow of a smile too and says something in French on his way out. I don't care to ask until Maximoff groans, irritated.

Jane slips further into the room. "Pay him no mind, Moffy."

"What'd he say?" I ask Maximoff, but Oscar is the one to answer.

"He said it's better this way. You don't put a squirrel in a lion's den."

WANT MORE BONUS SCENES LIKE
HELL'S KITCHEN - MOVING IN?

Join Krista & Becca's Patreon at www.patreon.com/kbritchie

Joining Krista & Becca's Patreon will give you access to all previously posted bonus scenes. Plus new content and extras release every month! Patreon is a great place for readers who love behind-the-scenes posts and all the extra goodies.

CONNECT WITH KRISTA & BECCA
www.kbritchie.com
www.facebook.com/KBRitchie
www.instagram.com/kbmritchie

ACKNOWLEDGMENTS

Writing this book was no easy feat. We knew it'd be emotional, but we didn't expect to be so spent by the end. It's been a rollercoaster. From the start to the finish. There are feelings of longing, and we haven't even really said goodbye to these characters yet. There's feeling of joy, for knowing we gave the best story we could. We're so incredibly in love with Maximoff & Farrow's journey, and it holds this special place in our hearts that we know nothing will ever replace.

This book in particular couldn't exist without the support and encouragement of so many people. Thank you to our mom for always coming through in the clutch. You knew this deadline would be tight, and you were there with not only your editing powers but your constant reaffirmations. You're the best cheerleader, and we're lucky to have you in our corner.

To our incredible agent, Kimberly, thank you for always championing our work and for getting this baby into audio. We're so happy readers have the chance to listen to Maximoff & Farrow.

Marie, you are an incredible person inside and out. Thank you for translating our French and for all the kind words you shower us with. We're beyond thankful to have your touch on this book.

Alex, our big brother who broke his collarbone twice, thank you for answering all of our questions and providing the "dinosaur hands" bit. Your encouragement means everything to us.

The four superhero admins of the Fizzle Force Facebook Group—Lanie, Jenn, Jae, and Siiri—thank you for your endless, unwavering support and for going above and beyond to help promote and get the word out. We're forever grateful.

Thank you to the Fizzle Force. You lovelies put constant smiles on our faces, can turn a blue day into a sunny one, and if magic did exist, we know it'd be located within all of you. We know that no matter how stressful a release can get, there are always people there to lift us up.

You may not understand how big that is for us. But it's huge. Thank you.

To the readers, reviewers, and weirdos, we love you. Thank you for making it to Book 3. It means you liked something from these books enough to continue reading. And it's your continued support that is fueling our dream. We're fifteen books in, and yet, we're still in awe that people want to read our words. It's surreal. And lovely. And so very magical. Thank you from the bottom of our hearts for taking a chance on us and *Alphas Like Us*.

All the love,
xoxo Krista & Becca

Printed in the USA
CPSIA information can be obtained
at www.ICGtesting.com
LVHW032138210823
755898LV00046B/1514

9 781950 165490